W hen a Stanford post-doctoral molecular biologist plummets to his death over Devil's Slide at Half Moon Bay, Jon Hunt, his surviving roommate, doubts the official suicide story, recalling his roommate's radical personality changes after returning from a trip to England. Suspecting mind control and things darker, Jon journeys to the Negev, London, Cambridge, and New Forest, England, where he starts to see a terrible pattern. A cabal of scientific Mandarins, backed by a hidden elite, have been using breakthrough recombinant DNA technology to bring back into existence an ancient race of giants known as Nephilim. Jon learns that his deceased roommate provided the critical breakthrough for this to happen. Jon teams up with others from Stanford, Cambridge, and a local underground in New Forest, soon encountering realities and mysteries for which the present world could in no way prepare them.

Robert T. Brooke has authored nine books under other pen names and his work has been recognized in Marquis Who's Who in the World, Who's Who in America, Contemporary Authors (Vol. 93-96), and The International Who's Who of Authors. A graduate of the University of Virginia and Princeton, he has spoken at Cambridge, Oxford, Princeton, and other top Universities. He commutes between residences in Mill Valley, California, Coromandel, New Zealand and Escazu, Costa Rica

Return of the Giants

A Dark Tale of the Nephilim

By Robert T. Brooke

ISBN: 978-1-61750-529-4

Acknowledgements

I would like to thank Professor Phillip Johnson—few get into Harvard at 15 or clerk under a Chief Justice of the Supreme Court—for enthusiasm and insight upon reading several drafts of this book and seeing dimensions that those at the gateway of publishing either did not see, or saw and didn't want the public to see (the formidable power of the publishing monopoly).

I would like to acknowledge technical and literary advice from my close friend George Byron Koch, who appears in this novel and who indeed is a member of the Triple Nine Society, 4-Sigma and Prometheus ultra-high-IQ societies.

I would also like to thank George August Koch for his elegant gift of language in the copy editing of this book.

I would also like to thank Kevin Langdon, my occasional lunch companion and neighbor down the street, who appears in this novel and who is the founder of 4-Sigma as well as a member of the world's-highest-IQ society, the Mega Society, for editorial feedback.

Chapter 1

Spenser was desperately fighting to pull free from the terrible power overshadowing his mind and body. He was now bordering on a complete trance lockdown.

In the blink of an eye, he was blipped inside his sports car.

Now he was watching his arms clutching the wheel as the car sped off into the night, guided by a will of its own.

But wasn't he in England just seconds ago? Which part of this was real?

He'd just seen the terrifying creature towering over the facility in the English forest. It had been looking down at him with its powerful gaze, the most horrifying thing he'd ever seen. He was speeding away from it. Then, suddenly, he was here.

He'd just been in daylight. Now it was pitch-black.

Going in and out, Spenser fought for clarity.

He tried to control the steering wheel as something gripped it through his arms with incredible strength. He could do nothing.

He looked on helplessly, his eyes darting about for clues.

I have very little time.

His foot was pressing the accelerator almost to the floor. He tried desperately to slow the speeding car. Nothing. He couldn't lift his foot away from the pedal by even a hair.

He tried to move a finger. Nothing.

His body was completely under the control of another power, directing him—where?

Now things were starting to look familiar.

Spenser gritted his teeth, fighting to break the trance as the immediacy of the night took hold. This was real.

A recent memory got through, flashing into his mind in force. He recalled his sheer desperation to escape. It was the last thing he remembered. Was it that very night?

RETURN OF THE GIANTS

It came back. He *had* been driving this car, but in the opposite direction, along a carefully planned route from Palo Alto to the California border and beyond.

The map and notebook on the passenger's seat looked the same. His meager bag was still on the floor, his jacket next to it. The cell phone lay on the seat beside him where it was before. *But now it was open. A* new dread entered him. He'd left it closed for a definite reason.

A certain phrase now hovered on the edge of his mind in a familiar voice: *The truly gifted are able to walk on rainbows. Now take Exit One.*

He knew the voice. It explained everything. Cold sweat ran down his face.

A split second later, a terrifying sight came into view—Devil's Slide. It stood hundreds of feet above the Pacific Ocean, the deadliest stretch of coastal cliffs along California's entire Pacific Highway. Spenser's car was speeding toward the rock barrier straight ahead, where the inland road met the coastal highway.

He fought with all that he had to regain control of the car.

Suddenly his foot responded. He jammed down on the brakes. The sound of screaming tires was followed by a roar as he skidded, then tore, through the wide opening in the barrier. *Too late.*

The car sailed out over the ocean, and then went into a freefall to the rocks and water below.

The image of the giant's face melted away, and Spenser almost felt relieved as the dark Pacific Ocean came rushing at him, its blackness exploding all around him.

* * *

"I think Spenser's dead," Jon's roommate Glen yelled through the door. "It sounds like his car went over Pacific Highway. It's on the news."

Jon Hunt dashed out of his Palo Alto condominium, jumped into his car and raced off toward the coastal highway.

As he drove in the pre-dawn blackness, he listened to news reports of a car that sounded like his roommate's going over the cliffs. His mind was spinning. Odd things had been happening to Spenser lately.

At the cliffside barrier of Half Moon Bay, Jon made a controlled slide up to the barrier and jumped out of his car, leaving the engine running.

RETURN OF THE GIANTS

He stood on the roadside cliffs overlooking the dark waters of the Pacific Ocean churning below. In his peripheral vision he spotted flashlight beams resembling glowworms moving in the black mist far below.

A patrol car sat maybe 30 yards away. A CHP officer nearby was looking over the barrier and speaking into a walkie-talkie. Other patrol cars and emergency vehicles were one bend away. Jon spotted what looked like a news crew standing near an oversized tow truck with a winch, its cables disappearing into the abyss below.

Jon checked his watch. It was fifteen minutes before dawn. His car remained in fast idle near the barrier. His heart was still racing. The latest news drifted in and out from the car radio. Jon overheard nothing new: "A Mazda Miata was discovered at the bottom of the cliffs of Half Moon Bay at Devil's Slide 40 minutes ago. ... Authorities are now on the scene, trying to recover the vehicle. The occupant is believed to be dead."

Jon saw a faintly visible shape in the light of the vanishing moon. Flashlights far below highlighted parts of it.

Jon thought of the classic optical-illusion of the woman in the vanity mirror who disappears and is replaced by a skull. He feared the same thing would happen with the image below.

The black Pacific was shifting to dark blue as the sun's rays quickly grew in intensity. The visage below became clearer in the growing light. The skull was beginning to appear.

A Mazda Miata was lying far below, caught in a rocky bank between boulders, the ocean waters retreating with the tide.

He saw the signature metallic purple and custom racing-stripes that gave the car away. It was Spenser's car. *He's dead*, Jon realized. *It's the Christmas present from hell.*

Emergency workers wearing helmets prepped the smashed car to be hoisted up. Jon shuddered as he glimpsed what looked like a rubbery appendage, an arm, dangling from an opening in the wreckage.

He dreaded facing the whole macabre scene—the mangled car inevitably rising up like an elevator from the abyss, edging up the cliff face, carrying a corpse that only yesterday was a vital friend and roommate.

Jon overheard the patrol officer nearby say, "We have a Jaws of Life. We'll bring the vehicle up and remove the body here. Okay, stand by."

The winch whirred and scraped.

The patrol officer looked at Jon quizzically.

"Officer, I'm afraid that could be my roommate's car below."

"Let's hope you're wrong."

The officer told headquarters, "We have someone who might be able to identify the body."

Jon asked the officer, "Any idea when it happened?"

"Between 1 and 2:30 a.m. is what we've been told."

The officer then offered, "There's a reason they call this stretch of Route 1 'Devil's Slide.' It's notorious for such accidents—mostly suicides. The drop is close to 300 feet, and there's almost no chance anyone could survive that."

Jon saw a partial stone wall nearby that separated the coastal highway from the steep cliff. But it wasn't enough to keep a car from going over. He walked over stood where the car had plummeted. No skid marks. Disturbing. Very disturbing.

This wasn't a suicide, Jon whispered to himself as he stood near the cliff's edge.

Jon could hear the winch screaming and grinding.

He moved closer to the tow truck and watched grimly as the Mazda was slowly hauled up and pulled over the cliff's edge.

The mangled car was dragged toward the center of the road to apply the Jaws of Life.

Jon looked on in numb silence as the body was removed like a clam being ripped out of a shell. Jon felt a combination of horror, anguish and anger.

It was his roommate, Spenser, dead.

The patrol officer glanced at Jon, now barely able to speak. He nodded to the officer. Fighting back tears, Jon managed to blurt out, "Yes, that's him."

The retrieved driver's license soon confirmed the identity.

But the face haunted him—blanched, swollen, unearthly.

Suddenly the academic marathon Jon had been running for years at an exhausting pace seemed trivial. He'd wanted to step out of the paper chase anyway—the specially tailored graduate program Stanford had put together for its one-time undergraduate superstar. The leave of absence was a certainty.

When police procedures completed at 10 a.m., Jon hurried back to his Palo Alto condo. He sensed a narrowing window of time to access his former roommate's computer before officials appeared to take it as evidence or to reclaim it as the property of *the Project*—something so secretive it could be broached only in whispers. The evidence on the computer could be critical.

One small file, a bizarre memo written in the last day or so, caught Jon's attention. It sucked the air out of his lungs as he read, *"Must escape* **their** *presence. not sure how much longer I can hold on..."* Beyond the desperation in the tone, what could be a vital clue surfaced as something called the "Nephil Project" on the Negev Desert was mentioned.

By noon, when media reports saturating the Stanford community had fanned out to the greater San Francisco Bay Area, Jon had made a Super-DVD copy of his roommate's hard drive. He secure-erased most of the files once he performed the backup. If the Project reclaimed the computer—it was their property—he wanted to leave them nothing.

Jon made copies of the DVD, then left the condo for a quick bite.

After lunch, Jon phoned his graduate advisors about taking a leave of absence. The first one simply said, "Do it. This is way overdue, and you need it."

The second advisor was in the parking lot of the Biological Sciences building when Jon drove up. He looked tired and disheveled as he got out of his car. Spotting Jon, the advisor said, "Jon, that's the most terrible news. Spenser was one of the most gifted scholars ever to grace Stanford. It really makes no sense."

Then he paused. "How are you doing? You all right?"

Jon gave him a painful nod.

He looked into Jon's eyes. "It's about the leave of absence, isn't it?"

"Yes."

"I think it's time you took it. As far as I'm concerned, take as much time as you need."

"Thanks, I wanted your okay," Jon said, and then asked, "Everything okay on your end? You're looking like you need a vacation as well."

"I'm getting a divorce," His advisor flatly replied. "Just found out two days ago. So now you know what's been preoccupying me." He waved and trudged toward the Biological Sciences building, muttering something about Stanford being toxic to marriages.

* * *

Now Jon needed to deal with Glen.

At 6:30 that evening, Jon met Glen Poulet, the surviving roommate, in front of the Mandarin restaurant off University Avenue in Palo Alto.

They hadn't talked since Glen awoke Jon with the news well before dawn.

Glen, who practically lived in the physics lab, was taking a rare night out. He had scampered off to the lab the moment Jon raced to the highway. Courage and human interaction were not Glen's strong points.

News sources were sitting on the name, so Glen wanted confirmation. "Was that him?"

Jon nodded back. "I confirmed it to the CHP. Spenser's dead."

Jon knew two things right now. One, he needed to severely lecture Glen so he didn't wind up like their roommate. Two, the death was not a suicide or an accident. Something very strange had happened.

They were quickly seated inside at a corner table by a window.

As Glen nervously bit into an egg roll, Jon began, "Glen, I've decided to take the leave of absence. I got the okay this afternoon from both advisors. I've gotta do it and as soon as possible."

Glen tried to force a smile. "Congratulations. I guess the place will really be empty, eh?"

Ignoring the self-pity gambit, Jon began the admonishment: "Glen, something bad has been going on. If people come asking questions while I'm gone—and they will—apologetically confess that you know nothing and that you've been an oblivious roommate preoccupied with your own world of academics. That you now feel very bad about it all. Don't mention hearing his nightmares, the screams and midnight showers; don't mention his gradual character changes; don't mention anything. Not if you want to live. Do you understand?"

Glen nodded.

Jon continued, "I think what happened last night was made to look like an accident. I believe Spenser strayed where he shouldn't have. That's what my gut has been telling me for over a month now. He wasn't the guy we once knew. If the Project is behind it, you don't want to be on their radar. Understand?"

Glen's Adam's apple did a quick dunk as he nervously wiped his glasses and assured Jon, "Don't worry, I'll keep a low profile. I won't say anything. Remember how I used to play dumb as a kid?"

Jon informed Glen, "I plan to leave in a few days. I can't say how long I'll be gone. Just lay low and hold the fort."

Glen nodded as he attempted to hide a trace of envy, recalling how Jon had grown up traveling Europe and England in an enviably wealthy and close family that actually loved one another.

"Are you headed overseas?" Glen innocently asked.

Jon nodded but didn't give any more details. *Don't give Glen anything; he might be snuffed out like a canary.* "I'll stay in touch through the usual secure e-mail," Jon replied instead. "You know the codes we worked out, right?"

Glen nodded. Jon gave him a piece of paper. "Hide this in your wallet. These are the new encryption codes. I don't know about you, but I don't want my private messages being intercepted by the Project or the NSA or anything else, do you?"

Glen shook his head. "No."

"Remember, Glen," Jon coached, "the following are the reasons for my leave of absence if anyone asks. One, it has been a long-planned leave for me to resolve the relentless pressure of a double graduate program. I can't keep up the pace. I've got to make a choice. Add to that our roommate's death and that's the final straw. Got it?"

"Will do," Glen assured him. "And I promise to hold the fort while you're gone."

But in truth, Jon knew, Glen would bury himself even more deeply in his studies. He'd virtually live at the physics lab. Jon was among the few in whom Glen confided his tortured past. Academics had been Glen's escape hatch ever since he was a boy living in a lower-class neighborhood and trying to avoid school bullies, neighborhood ruffians and arguing parents ever teetering on divorce as they drank and screamed at one another. Glen felt like an outsider all his life. Stanford had been like a doorway to heaven.

Jon, on the other hand, Glen saw as what he had always wanted to be himself—popular, athletic and handsome. Throw in Jon's intelligence and wealth, and it was the total package.

One recent winter, when Jon took Glen on a ski trip to Lake Tahoe, Glen watched from the shadows, observing Jon's appeal to women. For Jon, meeting them was as effortless as sipping beer. Attractive women constantly sidled up, looking to be noticed. Glen also knew Jon had stepped back in an attempt to head off what was becoming a sex-addiction problem. Glen couldn't imagine what that was like or how it would ever be a problem.

* * *

Jon threw his bags into the back of the airport limo, having tied things up in two days. He was leaving before Spenser's mourning relatives arrived in force. He was also avoiding the authorities and men in black. *Time to blow Dodge.*

As he left, he told Glen, "I'm sure everything will be fine. Please keep me updated on what happens here. I'll send an e-mail when I know more. Now, remember, lay low."

Glen nodded awkwardly, still looking scared, bewildered and a bit envious as the limo pulled away. Jon knew he had to keep Glen in the dark concerning the real purpose of the trip.

A few hours later, Jon was sitting in a window seat of a British Airways flight to London Heathrow Airport.

Once out of the San Francisco Bay Area, Jon felt an unspeakable sadness come over him, the breaking dam of emotions held in check during the long adrenaline rush of getting things done as days compacted together. The reality of the catastrophe and extent of the loss was huge, and he needed time to process the whole thing.

Soon the plane was over Lake Tahoe, Jon's old playground. He reflected on those times he first detected key changes in Spenser's character. Jon pondered one milestone in particular. After the gifted molecular biologist's return from a lengthy trip overseas, he began to suffer cold sweats and screaming nightmares. Jon and Glen repeatedly stood in the hallway by Spenser's door, awakened by the eerie wail of some recurring nightmare. When the night terrors wouldn't go away, Spenser became afraid to sleep.

Jon had watched Spenser return to the same psychiatrist he initially visited for final clearance into the Project—"They need stable and dependable people who won't crack." But the recent sessions didn't seem to help at all. If anything, matters grew worse, as his signals for help became more intense.

Jon thought back to the early days of their graduate careers when Spenser was cheerful and friendly, someone from unpretentious beginnings. Then Jon recalled how Spenser went through the predictable manic glee and battles with grandiosity after being accepted into the most prestigious program there was for postdoctoral molecular biologists. But slowly Spenser's moods of self-satisfaction were replaced by guarded fear, paranoia and quiet desperation. Something was very wrong with the picture.

Over the past months of his life, it was as though Spenser was trying to evade some invisible eye watching his every move, like a cryptic chess-game of consciousness.

Some of his bizarre signals reminded Jon of someone trapped inside a body, trying to make contact with the outside world as a breaking point quickly approached. *Mind control? Monsters?*

Exhaustion overtook Jon and he fell asleep in mid-thought.

Chapter 2

As Jon's plane left London for Tel Aviv at 9:50 a.m. London time, it was 1:50 in the morning back at Stanford. It was now several weeks since Jon left on the trip.

Vikram Rabindranath, a hacker prodigy at Stanford, had just left a late-night meeting of the key leaders of the Stanford-Berkeley computer-hacker groups. The closed meeting took place in a Victorian house in Palo Alto. The only thing on the agenda was that it was just a few weeks since a Mazda Miata driven by a Stanford postdoctoral student had plunged off the local coastal highway. The hackers smelled foul play.

There were some serious unanswered questions in the wake of this and several similar tragedies around the Stanford campus—all involving doctoral or postdoctoral students of molecular biology. Members of the hacker group knew two of the earlier victims but not the most recent one.

The campus rumor-mill had been very busy. Apparently the most recent death involved a postdoctoral student in an elite program.

In announcements to the media, faculty peers grieved the loss of so great a talent. But several Internet sites didn't buy the party line and speculated the death was connected to a top-secret project.

One of the Stanford hackers volunteered, "We are fairly certain that he was seeing a shrink."

"Which could be a key source of info if we can find out who the shrink was," another one added. "Let's get the dead student's address. I think it's unlisted."

"I have the address," Vikram interjected. Doron and I are ahead of you. We plan a second visit. His surviving roommate is in the graduate physics program, and he was leaving as we got there. We only managed to have a few minutes with him."

By the end of the meeting, the core leaders asked Vikram, the most gifted hacker present, "Can you try and flesh out this thing called *'the Project'* so that we can separate rumor from reality?"

"I plan to get right on it right now, as a matter of fact," Vikram responded.

As Vikram sped off on his bike, he thought of someone even more gifted than he—Doron Swift, his best friend and the other key leader of the Stanford hacker group. Doron was now at his mother's Sonoma cabin on a three-day weekend to find and penetrate High Gate. Vikram didn't want to admit it, but he was racing Doron to see who could get through first.

He entered the Stanford Computer complex at 2 a.m. He was a regular, so his appearance was nothing out of the ordinary. Fortunately, the place was empty.

Vikram sensed that the real power behind "the Project" was the rumored *Deep Earth Lab*.

None of the top hackers had yet penetrated it, and only one of these had even claimed to find High Gate, the sentry rumored to guard Deep Earth Lab. This same hacker offered that passing High Gate would be a challenge that surpassed an 11-year-old hacking into NORAD—which meant that Vikram and Doron were game.

Vikram was nervously aware that the present venture could end his career at Stanford—a school he had set his sights on from his early youth in India. Top universities and black technology had long maintained deep connections. Stanford was among the top of the list, and its own fiber network gave Vikram unique access.

Vikram was soon flashing past the cyber-sentries guarding various elite academic sites from illegal entry, especially the stealth projects. Breaking encryption codes and passwords was a sort of ballet of the mind to Vikram, and he had an extraordinary gift in this area. His ability with computers and general science were enough to get Vikram admitted into Stanford at 15, no less.

He suddenly detected a hidden gateway beyond the Stanford academic loop. He chased down what he called a "cyber-wormhole."

In a flash Vikram saw a multicolored ocean of patterns filling his giant display. A unique 3-D cyber-sentry suddenly appeared, an ancient Indo-Tibetan god with a revolving Earth in the background. The animated cyber-sentry probed for the password, the lips moving as it asked: "Where is the footprint of Vishnu?"

Vikram's mind went blank. It was now after 3 a.m.

He realized—almost feeling ashamed—that, although his own Indian heritage should enable him to answer the riddle, the fact remained that, like many expatriate Indian intellectuals, he was an agnostic, finding his future in Western science.

When he left his homeland at age 15, the last images in his mind were temples with rising stupas of intertwined gods, crumbling temples, and the broken promises of invisible gods that never seemed to alleviate the oceans of poverty and suffering. Vikram had fled it all. Ironically, the key to this cyber-sentry's query was connected to the ancient culture he had left behind.

Vikram crashed the computer before things went any farther. He left the Stanford Computer complex under a moonless black sky of winter, the campus now magically silent.

He biked home, pondering how he would ask his uncle in Hyderabad the question of the cyber-sentry. Uncle Mohan, ever immersed in Hindu religious traditions, undoubtedly knew the answer.

Ironically, Uncle Mohan's brother, Ravindra—Vikram's favorite uncle—lived close by in Silicon Valley. He was the first Hindu agnostic in the family and had become something of a family hero. A science whiz, Ravindra was now one of the Indian elite of Silicon Valley multimillionaires whose company, HyperTech, had not only survived but multiplied through the "dot-bomb," earning him a lengthy mention in the *San Francisco Chronicle*.

The two uncles could not be farther apart, yet each might play a role in breaking this mystery.

Vikram worried that e-mailing his uncle in India could wake up one of the Internet Watchers, using the latest hotphrase-recognition programs, simply by using the phrase "the footprint of Vishnu." Vikram pictured unmarked vans outside his apartment.

Then it came to him. He would e-mail Uncle Mohan in their native language of Telugu. This should elude the Watchers, programmed to intercept English, Arabic and European syntax and fonts.

Vikram stopped outside his apartment and looked at the night sky. He pictured the fierce-looking cyber-sentry, wondering what lay beyond it.

Chapter 3

Jon arrived in Israel after resting and visiting old childhood haunts in England. He found the much warmer weather a pleasant change from the moist cold of London.

The Negev Desert was warming up in the early February sun as noon approached. Archaeological digs in Israel were almost constant. This one was unusually shrouded and under very tight security. Armed guards stood watch outside the compound as earth-moving equipment went in and out under a constant roar of engines in the background. One sound was particularly deep—like the huge burrowing machines for subway tunnels in Manhattan.

The workers going in and out were busy, suspicious, even hostile. None seemed remotely approachable, much less for a friendly exchange.

From where Jon stood, he could see very little of what was going on. Sixty-foot-high prefab pyramidal walls of drab-green fiber had been erected around the compound. Like a traveling carnival, it could all be gone tomorrow if they decided to move on, but they would restore all the earth they'd removed, thus covering their tracks. They had already done so around the Dead Sea, the last dig. Jon picked this much up at a local eatery after countless queries. It had been very frustrating. Jon was sure some of them thought he was a spy. He was beginning to feel like one.

In truth, Jon was discovering that the dig was based on breakthroughs in ultra-transportable, earth-moving machinery. It was a mobile dig that could be set up in a few days, then move on, taking up stakes and tents like the old Barnum & Bailey Circus. Few seemed to know what the project was really doing, Jon gathered. The crew was told to surrender all skeletal remains to two supervisors. But apparently nothing in the Dead Sea area was what they wanted.

Part of the frustration was the vast expanse of land that could be considered fair game. Who wanted to spend their lives like mechanical beavers, going up and down Israel, digging and covering up vast holes to look for what—skeletal evidence of something? To some of the disgruntled crew, the military looked a more attractive option than *this*.

Jon watched the goings-on from a safe distance. He already suspected, after nosing around, that this was a combined effort of unnamed foreign interests working in tandem with an Israeli government project. He gathered this was one of at least five digs presently underway—all of which part of the same project. Some of the digs were outside of Israel, and were even more hush-hush. Jon figured they were undertaken by joint international teams who could operate more easily in neighboring countries.

Most local sources were absolutely closed-mouth. Jon had managed to learn the most from Uri, a cynical grad student from Tel Aviv University and a temporary member of the dig. As Jon bought rounds of coffee and food at a local café, Uri confessed he was little more than a "go-for," doing trivial errands—a key source of his frustration. He did not have any sort of big picture, which added to the futility and meaninglessness of his efforts.

Uri confirmed that it was called the "Nephil Project" by those on the inside. It involved digging much deeper than they normally would for most ancient artifacts. And no, Uri emphasized, they were not looking for dinosaur bones or extinct animals or fossils. "This is not *Jurassic Park*," he exclaimed. "They are looking for extinct humans." Part of the frustration of all those on the project was that they were an offshoot of something much larger, and they didn't even know what it was. They were simply providing a component, if they could even find it. They were being funded for retrieval of artifacts, and that was about it.

When he got all he could at his limited level of reconnaissance, Jon quietly left the locale of the dig and headed back to Tel Aviv.

Before going to the dig at the Negev, Jon had exchanged e-mail with Glen. He was now very curious to hear back.

Glen had previously written about two fellow Stanford grad students who recently visited their condo, suspicious about "the accident." They even asked questions about "the Project." This tweaked Jon's antenna. He wondered what they might know. He e-mailed Glen: "Track down the two guys, Doron and Vikram. Gotta hunch they may be on to something important. Get their email addresses, phone numbers as well. See if you can find out what program they are in. I may contact them on the road. Thanks—Jon."

Now back in Tel Aviv, Jon was eagerly at his notebook computer at a verandah table of a popular cybercafé with Wi-Fi access. Jon was in full security mode. Glen's encrypted reply was mostly emailese—lowercase lazy-grammar:

"Doron & Vikram in accelerated Ph.D. programs—both in computing, both whiz-kids. did undergrad. in only a few years. started stanford at 15 and 16. Vikram, is at: varushanam@yahoo.com. see unlisted number. vikrams uncle is founder/owner of successful Silicon Valley company, HyperTech—listed in SF Chronicles honorable mention of companies. also appears in special feature article. will try for more info. no Doron info yet. hope trip is going well, take care, Glen."

As Jon started to reply, he overheard someone at the café announce in a Jersey accent, "Looks like the circus just came to town."

He looked up as a long line of luxury buses with American and Israeli flags blasted down the street with various slogans painted on the sides: "Christian Zionists for a Free Israel," "They get the World after we get the Rapture," and so on. The Calvary Contenders deposited what Jon called "mall-waddlers" in garish outfits at food stalls down the street. He hoped they'd just stay down there.

This was maybe the third tour he'd seen in two weeks. Jon lamented that Americans overseas, especially the spiritual tourists, were a danger to themselves, shamelessly glorying in their own mediocrity before the world, their girth ever expanded by their self-importance.

Were these tourists not such rabid allies of Israel, Jon had no doubt the locals—barely able to conceal their contempt—would turn on them with scorn.

One could always spot newly arrived tourists who acted as though they had just landed in heaven as they squinted dimly at Hebrew lettering or at various rabbis passing by.

The worst Jon had seen so far was an American televangelist named "Jehovah Bob," who ran about raving and gesticulating in some custom Rapture suit. His haircut resembled doves' wings extending from both sides of his head. He had descended on Tel Aviv two weeks earlier and was followed by a huge throng as he barked revelations at them in guttural slang. Truly the goyim had arrived.

Jehovah Bob on Armageddon, no doubt ghostwritten, was shooting up the *New York Times* Best-Seller list. Jon skimmed a copy at a local store. The message repeated like a mantra: "If America abandons Israel in its hour of need, it too shall perish." Jon wondered how such vast sums of money came so easily to such seedy characters posing as fanatic allies of Israel.

Jon, an agnostic, thought of his aunt and uncle, who had been quiet heroes of integrity to him since his childhood. These aging missionaries, of Dutch Reformed tradition, were unimpressed with the latest "American pop-prophets." His aunt and uncle had noted how few church tours from America to Israel were willing to undergo the embarrassment of visiting, or even acknowledging, Palestinian Christians—legitimately their fellow believers—who were often impoverished, broken, and for some reason less than enthusiastic about their overlords. The uncle wished, in Mark Twain fashion, these pop prophecy groupies could somehow be turned into Palestinian Christians and consigned to camps in Gaza. Then maybe someone could interview them in a few years, if they lasted that long, to see if they still gushed with praise.

As he rounded out his trip in Jerusalem, Jon was starting to feel he was there on borrowed time. He sensed he was being tolerated at best. Maybe it was the sandy hair. Jon felt like a misfit and wanted to continue on with his journey.

He now knew he had gotten all the information on Project Nephil that he was likely to get. Apart from a direct, gratuitous, full confession from a top member of the project, this was it. Besides, there were other routes to classified information.

Jon could never quite escape the feeling he was under constant observation. Apart from feeling watched in the streets, he even wondered whether the mirrors in his hotel rooms were two-way—the standard Mossad ploy.

When in Tel Aviv he had been approached by several prostitutes a little too aggressively, as though someone had pushed them directly into his path. Up close, beneath the allure in their eyes, was desperation. He'd heard numerous reports and rumors of white slavery being part of the underbelly of Tel Aviv—peasant girls smuggled in from Russia.

Now in the Arab quarter of Old Jerusalem, Jon joined a Belgian journalist for lunch at a large open eating area bordered by falafel and shawarma stands and fruit and sweets vendors. He'd seen the Belgian a few times in the hotel lobby and ran into him late-morning while walking the shopping stalls and souks. It was the end of Jon's visit, and he looked forward to moving on.

As they ate, they noticed Israeli guards with machine guns standing watch nearby. Then, some distance away, a man Jon assumed to be a Palestinian was aggressively surrounded and questioned. He pleaded but was led away in handcuffs. Such scenes were common. "It's a conflict that will never end," the Belgian said.

A church group passed by, muttering, "Thank God the Israelis were able to spot the terrorist just now. He could have blown all of us up." Another was overheard saying, "Isn't it amazing, the Israelis have turned the desert into rich farmland. Truly God has ordained this."

Jon and the journalist, overhearing this, discussed the dilemma and what it would be like to live as a Palestinian. "I have been where the Palestinians live," the Belgian said. "It's risky business even being there. These people are stripped of everything and consigned to live in a fenced-in ghetto, second-class citizens, under a police state." He continued, "Did you know these people can spend an entire lifetime in what was once their homeland and never once glimpse the ocean!"

He let that sink in, though Jon knew this already. "They are barred from access to anything but inland scrub, often desert, and cordoned off into destitute towns of concrete. They're like rats in a cage." Jon nodded, looking around for anyone overhearing them. People in Arab headdress were not always Arabs.

The Belgian went on, "Farmland that had been theirs for centuries was confiscated in the 1948 takeover when, in their view, they were colonized and put under alien rule. For centuries their kin could wander Palestine and never encounter a single barrier. They could live in houses and not have them bulldozed; their children were free to roam without the threat of being shot and left for dead." Jon quietly concurred, well aware of the European complaint of overwhelming American pro-Israeli bias.

More than once Jon had glimpsed Palestinian children with stones facing off armed troops and military vehicles with enough power to blow up a neighborhood. The Belgian complained, "When journalists take photos of these kinds of confrontations, for some reason the pictures never make it into print, and the public never sees them." Meddling journalists who ventured into the wrong place at the wrong time often wound up as collateral damage and went home in body bags. It was a clear message.

When they got to the subject of the impenetrable wall dividing the land like the Berlin Wall, Jon mentioned the common explanation, "Okay, but you've to go realize it's a final resort to ward off suicide bombers. When they're entering and blowing up people at bus stands…"

Playing devil's advocate, the journalist admitted, "Sure, there are suicide bombers among the Palestinians. … But maybe when someone is completely backed up against the wall and left with nothing, not even hope; after his family has been killed by a helicopter gunship and the house bulldozed into rubble to make room for an Israeli settlement, he's willing to die. His life is not really worth living anyway, so he shares the agony. Unless you've seen it up close, you will never know."

"People in the States don't have a clue what this kind of desperation is like," Jon admitted.

He and the journalist agreed that if Israel—in some media experiment—were suddenly given another name by the press, its abuses attributed to another nation, Americans would rise up as one collective voice of shocked outrage, vehemently protesting conditions and chanting, "Apartheid, apartheid…"

The Belgian then amended, "But once they realized that it was not an African colonial nation after all, but Israel, these American protesters would cover their mouths in horror." Jon added, "And retreat into the expected politically correct silence."

Jon had begun to grieve for the Palestinian predicament, though he realized he might be called a number of unflattering names for having such views.

Either way, it was definitely time to move on. He exchanged contact information with the Belgian and bade him good luck for an unenviable job. Jon rushed back to the Jerusalem Hilton, got his bags, sent Doron and Vikram a brief e-mail about heading to London (by now they had also talked a number of times via secure-phone), and left for the airport to catch his return flight to London.

Under heavy security, Jon passed through the checkpoints at Tel Aviv International Airport after being extensively searched, leaving him feeling like a criminal suspect or a spy. Once on board, Jon was relieved to be returning to the West. He exhaled with relief once the airplane took off.

He leaned back, pondering the mystery behind the Nephil Project as he pictured millions of tons of soil being removed, sifted, and returned by vast machines constantly tunneling into the earth. He thought of bleached bones, passing millennia, and then, in the middle of it all, drifted off to sleep once the plane passed over Cyprus in the early hours of the morning.

Chapter 4

Vikram struggled to wake up over a late morning cappuccino at a nearby café in Palo Alto. He was feeling the effects of a fitful sleep from going to bed at 3:30 a.m.

Though the weather was not as warm as in his native South India, he was grateful to be living on the Peninsula, where you could sit outside at a café in early February and where sunny days could pass for spring in most parts of the country.

It was 65 degrees, while the East Coast was still ankle-deep in snow. Vikram was pondering the "footprint of Vishnu" query. The answer *had* to be the password for High Gate.

He saw a girl pass by across the street. Her hairstyle was reminiscent of a rare Amazonian bird, carefully sprayed with a range of colors and fashioned into a sky-cup. No one else noticed. Vikram bet that a suicide bomber in a headdress and dynamite-wrapped body would likely earn no more than a 60% head-turn rating. Only Berkeley could trump Palo Alto in street anomalies—typical of college towns of the high-SAT variety.

After coffee, Vikram headed to the Stanford library to research Hindu epics and tales of the gods. Normally, if a query was mathematically based, Vikram could come up with code-breaking keys right off the top of his head. But by early afternoon, he was back at the same outdoor café, awaiting Doron's arrival and brooding over another cup. He'd come up empty and was forced to ask his Uncle Mohan the riddle. No way out of this—unless, of course, Doron had gotten through.

Since their freshman year, when they were roommates, Vikram had joined Doron on these weekend retreats countless times—but almost always when the house was empty. To call Doron's family dysfunctional would be an understatement, and it made Vikram supremely grateful to have been brought up in an affectionate, close, trusting Indian family.

Vikram opened his laptop computer to check e-mail before writing his uncle.

After loading the Telugu fonts, Vikram slowly began to compose a letter to his uncle in Hyderabad. The first attempt felt awkward and hollow. Vikram scrapped it and tried again, hoping to come up with a credible-sounding excuse to ask the riddle. He hoped to be done by Doron's arrival.

* * *

When Doron left for Palo Alto, he was utterly spent. He'd been trying to hack through the secret gateway of this mysterious project over a long weekend of sustained effort.

He decided to take his favorite stretch of the scenic Route 1 that extended the entire length of California's coast. Further up he would connect with the more inland, parallel Highway 101. He never tired of the scenery. Every weather-beaten fish house by some rickety pier, every café near a jetty that he passed, reminded him of oversized driftwood bric-a-brac in some Americana museum in *The Twilight Zone*.

Sometimes the winding, two-lane road along the Sonoma and Marin County side of Route 1, passed dense, towering redwoods; other times it hugged the rocky shore overlooking the Pacific. The coastal drive was a perfect balm for Doron when he was burnt-out, frustrated or depressed.

He wondered if his quest had been impeded by the "vibe" of his mother's cabin—the countless reminders of family dysfunction that seemed to fill it. Most of the time he enjoyed the place. But sometimes—and this was one of those times—he felt as though he'd been raised by the forces of chaos charading as parents.

No doubt the weekend started on the wrong foot when he chance encountered his mom on the road, heading in the other direction. She was speeding off to another four- or five-day convention and gave a gushingly silly wave as they passed on the road 40 miles from home near Sebastopol. Wearing oversized sunglasses with a strange lilac tint, she looked like a haggard adolescent.

Doron reflected after passing her that his parents, like most of the Who's Who of radicals from the Sixties, had pressed the outer edges of human experience in an endless quest for fulfillment and self-actualization. And what did they have now to show for it? Scary question.

When Doron entered the cabin and saw the usual wall pictures of the glory days, he reflected in irony that their reward for this self-indulgence quest was to resemble aging rag-dolls or hollowed-out gourds, wizened before their time. That same burned-out pallor you see at organic vegetarian health-food stores.

His mom, Linda, now divorced, got to keep the large rambling cabin. Aesthetically hip, it lay on the outskirts of the small town of Monte Rio, where the Russian River entered the Pacific beyond Bodega Bay.

Monte Rio also was infamous because it was adjacent to a landmark known as Bohemian Grove—a source of endless public fascination because the rich and powerful of the world came for a lavish, two-week bash every summer within a redwood compound that was guarded like Area 51. Doron had memories of this as well.

A wandering organic garden surrounded his mom's cabin. Doron often pictured his mom trying to subsidize her income through organic gardening, but only after the long overworked pump of subsidies from her parents went down to a trickle. Inevitably, the next crisis forced their consciences to give to her yet again.

Doron was momentarily jarred out of his reverie when he passed Mill Valley and saw a sign to the side of Highway 101 announcing, "You are entering a drug-free zone."

"Really?" Doron responded out loud. "This whole region is among the most drug-infested places on Earth."

His reverie resumed. *Where did she get the money to go to a convention at a prime five-star Nevada resort?* The brochure had been left on the side table—five-star all the way.

"Co-dependence." His aging grandparents had been saddled with a daughter who had less of a handle on the laws of cause and effect than a chicken clucking around a barnyard. They were still supporting this adult child. They had read all the books on guilt manipulation by "adult children" and were fighting being guilt-ridden, brow-beaten "enablers" as they entered the final stretches of their lives. They wanted peace and time to themselves, away from the tyranny of their daughter's boundless cravings and needs.

As Doron approached the entrance to the Golden Gate Bridge, he passed a commercial billboard on the side of the 101, proudly announcing, "Wed in Gay San Francisco—The Capital of Same-Sex Marriages." A mayor was gesturing smilingly to a just-married couple—two of the sweetest peas to ever fill a pod, grinning ear to ear and holding hands. This was the new moneymaker now rivaling Vegas—but the weddings were all on the left-hand side of the aisle.

As weekend traffic slowed to a crawl on the Golden Gate Bridge, the billboard's theme triggered a childhood memory.

Doron was then about eight years old and spotted an odd poster around Guerneville, the town near Monte Rio. The poster announced an upcoming "hardware convention" with "unique innovations in the use of tools." A man's face, somewhat resembling Freddie Mercury of Queen, headlined the ad. His shaved, tattooed head was turned slightly sideways. He stared out provocatively, one eyebrow raised, with a large brass-ring piercing. Behind him, a range of tools lay on a table. Clearly there was something different about this hardware convention to the young Doron.

Doron's folks, who went to Guerneville once or twice a week to shop and hang out, were on the deck of their favorite café when the "hardware convention" rolled into town—on custom Harleys. Doron's dad clapped and whistled appreciatively; his mom grinned broadly.

The man on the poster led the procession down Main Street on a large Harley-Davidson. Stud rivets ran through his cheeks, a large nail ran through his nose, large rings pierced his eyebrows, and a hemisphere of nails were "probably glued" to his shaved head so that he resembled Pinhead in Clive Barker's *Hellraiser*. His motorcycle seat appeared to be made from a fine bed of nails. Interestingly, the rear of his leather pants had been cut out. Doron noticed the hardware was clamped, sewn or pierced through the bodies, clothing and motorcycles of the riders.

"Now, *that's* hardware put to good use," his mom chortled loudly.

The young Doron asked innocently, "Why not just go to San Quentin and ask to be rendered a prisoner?"

His Dad liked that, then commented to his mom, "Betcha they could liven up a construction crew in Alabama, showing 'em how to *really* use tools." Grinning beneath a handlebar mustache and squinting at the sun, his eyes were bleary from the local grass.

Once they were on the road back to Monte Rio, his mom began singing Peter, Paul and Mary's "If I Had a Hammer." Then it mutated into "If I Had a Hamster."

Eight-year-old Doron was bored and couldn't wait to return to his computer. Like a trusted friend, his computer usually gave him a more meaningful response than his parents.

Doron had started on computers at age two. He had been accepted at Stanford even earlier than Vikram, but decided to hang back till he was 16. Doron was a prodigy.

One reason for his delay in going to Stanford was to join his parents for their touted "Atlantis Road Tour of America." His dad had talked him into joining them.

When the Atlantis tour ended and they returned, his folks soon divorced, and Doron couldn't wait to begin Stanford. By then his mom was following her inner bliss, hanging out with a guy who resembled an aging carrot with a vulgar smile. His dad, ever hungry to travel and have freedom from all entanglements, hit the road again, looking for adventure.

Doron's reverie abruptly ended as the sign for Palo Alto flashed into view. He was grateful to be brought back into the real world and made the exit just in time.

* * *

As Vikram sent a carefully worded e-mail to Uncle Mohan in Telugu, Doron was speeding through the Stanford campus. He parked off University Avenue, then quietly approached Vikram's table from behind.

Once in range, Doron threw a Sonoma sunflower from his mom's organic garden over Vikram's head. The twirling flower barely missed Vikram's coffee, landing on the table right in front of him.

Vikram turned with a broad grin, happy to see his closest friend, whose light-blonde hair was silhouetted in the California sunlight like a halo.

"Any luck finding High Gate?"

"Maybe." Doron responded. "And you—anything at all?"

Vikram answered in a low voice, "I got as far as this fierce looking Indo-Tibetan sentry that had a revolving Earth behind it."

"...asking about the footprint of Vishnu, right?", Doron anticipated.

Vikram nodded, impressed. "Right!"

Doron then added, "I wonder if the answer to the riddle parallels some kind of DNA sequencing?" Vikram shrugged. "I finally sent Uncle Mohan the query a few minutes ago." Doron cocked his head as Vikram assured, "Don't worry; it was in the South Indian language of Telugu, peculiar to Andhra Pradesh."

Doron switched to a matter high on their list for the afternoon. "Let's try to see this guy Glen again. I hope we can get more info from him this time." They drove to Juniper Terrace, less than half a mile from campus. They hoped Glen would be there.

It was a two-storied condominium with a private upstairs balcony walkway. The small attractive building with three units was part of a series of condos, surrounded by elegant trees, open land and plenty of parking.

They rang the bell.

Glen opened the door awkwardly, looking paranoid. Seeing it was Vikram and Doron, he relaxed.

"Hope you don't mind, just a few more follow-up questions."

Glen nodded. "You caught me on a rare break from the lab."

"Would it be okay if you could show us some of his stuff?"

Glen responded, "There's not much left. After the memorial service Spenser's parents and a brother claimed most of his belongings, so the room is fairly stripped."

"And didn't you mention before that there's another roommate?" Doron probed.

"Yes, Jon. He's taking a long planned leave of absence." Glen quoted Jon's explanation. "He's seeking direction and processing the death of our roommate." The two nodded.

Glen mentioned, "I did e-mail him that you'd come by earlier and that you were both hackers and grad students, so he may send you an e-mail."

"That would be good. We hope we can be of help," Doron replied.

As Vikram and Doron looked at the room, little seemed out of the ordinary. They would have loved to scour the post-doc's computer, but it was long gone. Apparently Glen and Jon had come home and noticed it missing soon after the "accident."

Spenser's family allowed the officials to take it as they packed some of his stuff—planning to get the rest later. DVDs and other property had been taken by the men in black. This elevated Vikram and Doron's suspicion of foul play.

The few books left behind were unremarkable, mostly academic stuff, a few fiction titles, trivia books about Stanford, an old illustrated kids'

book—something about the "land of giants," and a small David and Goliath in a frame. Family, friends and departmental colleagues had removed any number of books, claiming they had been borrowed. Even
an outdated department access badge was gone.

The only thing Glen would tell them—and social interaction was
clearly not his thing—was of a growing "hauntedness" in his former
roommate. "He would never tell us what it was."

Glen finally mentioned, seeing no harm in it, "We would hear a kind
of scream or wail late at night, at which point lights would go on and
Spenser would head off to take a shower, sometimes at 3 a.m.—a nightmare, I guess."

Vikram probed, "I hear he was seeing a psychiatrist." Glen paused,
then sheepishly nodded. "The shrink had labeled this 'free-floating anxiety.'"

"Would you know who he is?" Glen shook his head. "Spenser kept
it to himself."

After more probing, it seemed Spenser had virtually no social life by
the end. He avoided people. His work *was* his life—endemic to Stanford.

Glen volunteered, "He had already broken up with some girlfriend
from back home in the Midwest before he got into this program." Doron
and Vikram nodded. "Know her name?"

Glen shook his head. "Never saw her."

The unwritten rule at Stanford was that too many competing distractions only got in the way of success. Those who wanted to get ahead
were absent partners in relationships. Predictably, divorce rates were
sky-high. Contenders in the success game hid or waylaid the emptiness
of their lives by working harder, a backdoor approach to self-esteem.

Glen knew the game well, feeling empty most of the time. But it sure
beat the darker world of his childhood. At least he wasn't getting at-
tacked and beat up when he left the condo.

Doron and Vikram then learned something interesting. The supposed accident near Half Moon Bay clearly made no sense to Glen: "He
never went on Route 1—was afraid of the high cliffs, that I know. He told
me this emphatically. He didn't like to drive at night. He was a very careful driver, so I don't see him speeding or swerving over the road, above
all, those cliffs. If he had to go to San Francisco or anywhere else, he
took the main highways, the 101 or the 280, or he took BART, not the
coastal highway. I definitely can't see him driving to Route 1 at night to

commit suicide. He wasn't the type. And if he were to try suicide, it would be something painless like insulin, which he could get at the lab. But never over those cliffs, no way."

"What about where he worked. Ever go there or see the place?" Doron probed.

"I never saw where he worked. Don't think Jon's been there either, though Jon was closer to him."

Prodded more, Glen continued, "I know that it was some kind of top-secret program, or project, and that apparently only the most privileged scholars are even candidates." Glen gave a useless shrug, apologetic for what little substance he could offer.

Doron and Vikram thanked Glen and left.

Chapter 5

As Jon arrived at Heathrow Airport on the outskirts of London early Friday morning, back from Tel Aviv, it was Thursday night California time, and Deep Earth Lab was being penetrated. It was now early March.

Doron and Vikram had not only found High Gate—guarded by the fierce cyber-sentry they had encountered previously—but were passing through it. Vikram called the moment "supreme ballet of the mind."

Uncle Mohan had, indeed, provided a critical clue. The password for bypassing the fierce cyber-sentry turned out to be an anagram of the Vedic query and a particular bit of DNA trivia harkening back to the era of Watson and Crick, all forming a kind of pun. It often came down to a clever pun—vanity among the elite.

But there was another critical contributor to this code-breaking effort—Jon. Vikram and Doron both confessed later that they could not have passed through High Gate had not Jon supplied them with critical information retrieved from his roommate's computer.

Once in London on his initial visit, Jon had found time to safely examine the DVD. He spotted what turned out to be a hot clue, which he e-mailed Doron and Vikram right before leaving Israel amidst their growing dialogue.

Jon's respect and trust for Doron and Vikram, whom he had yet to meet, grew with every exchange, and vice versa. All of them sensed that they were on the brink of finding some dark, sacrosanct, scientific mystery.

Jon had told the two over an encrypted call, "The lesson of the A-bomb from the Manhattan Project was precisely this: When you have sole control of a super-weapon, as America briefly did, who is going to take you on? World War II on the Asian front came to an abrupt halt once the A-bomb was 'demonstrated' over two Japanese cities. That ended the discussion. Hiroshima was an object lesson in case others doubted." They agreed.

The moment Vikram and Doron passed through High Gate, the sentry of Deep Earth Lab announced, "Welcome to the Land of the Giants." The children's book found in the room came to mind immediately as a clue they had overlooked.

They immediately faced another mystery, making the whole effort an anticlimax. The next thing they saw on the monitor made no sense, stumping them yet again. They were gazing at an ocean of—what?—chains of molecules, maybe nucleotides, DNA?

It was a boundless ocean of rapidly changing patterns. Sadly, if it was DNA, they were gazing at another field of knowledge that was far removed from their specialty.

The conundrum of specialized knowledge in any field since the '50s meant that you had to grab one field and run all the way with it. Doron and Vikram, though acknowledged computer geniuses—and probably among the most gifted that Stanford would ever see—both felt out of their depth when faced with cutting-edge molecular biology.

This was another reason Doron and Vikram looked forward to Jon's return. Apart from a growing friendship and a shared sense of mission, one of Jon's specialties was DNA analysis. (Another discipline of Jon's was artificial intelligence, but he was burning out on the double program at Stanford—the reason for his long-planned sabbatical.) Until Jon returned, Vikram and Doron would glean all they could.

The three of them had vowed to keep the whole thing a secret. That meant Doron and Vikram could not go announcing to the Berkeley-Stanford hacker group that they had penetrated High Gate. That kind of celebrity status they did not need. The wrong leak, and in no time their adversaries might know. Deep Earth Lab would track them down. This was not an option. Till Jon returned, they had other things to do, and High Gate had already taken too much of their time.

One lead was another Stanford molecular-biology grad student who had dropped out of the program very suddenly, leaving Palo Alto for his native San Diego in a single day. This was only a few months before Jon's roommate died. This fellow's remaining roommate, still at Stanford, had not a clue why he so suddenly dropped out and fled town. He figured a "breakdown" under stress was the cause.

Vikram and Doron had reason to conjecture that this fellow may have been courted by Deep Earth Lab at one point, but perhaps something had happened during the process of evaluation. The two tried to imagine what tripped this guy up. Maybe, as Doron theorized, he was being shown around and "just peeked into the wrong room and his mind popped, so he tiptoed away very quietly and quite permanently." Mind control? Being confronted with a horror?

Recent communiqués from their fellow hackers at Cambridge University speculated a dark stealth project. One e-mail said, "Go rent the DVD entitled *O Lucky Man!* starring Malcolm McDowell, who was in *Clockwork Orange*."

They watched it Friday night. It was a long, rambling film, but in one scene McDowell stumbles into a wing of a hidden scientific complex engaged in underground biological experiments. He enters a room with a man's head grafted to the body of a pig. The man-pig is wailing in terror. There is a lingering sense in this '70s film that such experiments have been afoot.

Vikram noted to Doron after the film, "Science, unhampered by morality or conscience will break any boundaries for knowledge and power. Taboos are walked over effortlessly."

Doron nodded. "They are issues that the man on the street would never understand and, if he did, he would be repulsed and horrified."

It was Saturday morning in Palo Alto, and they were still faced with an open weekend.

Doron and Vikram had initially planned to go to Monte Rio for the weekend, but Doron's mom had a last-minute change of plans and decided to stay. Meanwhile, their entry into High Gate was already accomplished, and they felt stalemated at the moment.

They decided that now would be a good time to track down the Stanford dropout. They'd try to contact Jon, now in England, when they got back.

They hoped to get to San Diego by late afternoon. They had talked to the dropout once before over the phone. They told him that they were Stanford students, which put his paranoia to rest somewhat. The fellow also knew the deceased roommate, Spenser, and was concerned enough to open up slightly. The surprise trip made perfect sense.

The drive to San Diego was always a high point for Vikram. His arm hung out the front window as miles of California coast came into view and flew by. The contrast of this clean and vital land compared to the tiredness and heat of South India was beyond words. California was still truly the Golden State, and the Pacific was breathtaking in scope, a perpetually moving artist's work of complex hues and shifting pastels.

Going through Monterey and Carmel to Big Sur on the old coastal Route 1 was worthy of a *National Geographic* photo spread. On the other side of Big Sur, Route 1 seemed to traverse into the past as it passed small California towns with cafés, small bars with Harleys propped along the front, fruit sellers and old, bleached-wood restaurants.

Vikram's mind wandered in the Pacific breeze as he fantasized building a custom cliffside mansion overlooking the ocean. With state-of-the-art technology, it would be a place of creativity under a cathedral of natural beauty. It would have a grand master bedroom—and the girl of his dreams—Vikram caught himself in mid-reverie, engaging in "Bollywood." He smiled to himself.

Like a high percentage of the super-gifted, Vikram was not the skinny-nerd-with-glasses stereotype so often misapplied, but athletic and handsome—most would say arrestingly handsome. Growing up in India, Vikram was often compared to Amitabh Bachchan, one of India's matinee idols. Vikram was certainly considered a prize catch. Attractive Indian beauties had already written him innocent notes of admiration, including photos. He had to admit many were breathtakingly gorgeous. But he still had his eye on one girl in particular.

On the outskirts of Santa Barbara, the temperature now in the mid-70s and palm trees bordering the highway, they opted for a fish snack on the Santa Barbara pier, which jutted out into the ocean over a hundred yards. In twenty minutes they were back on the road.

To Vikram, the changing landscape paralleled America's changing culture, all fascinating.

Near Ventura they passed the bizarre town of Carpenteria. Two giant inflated spooks on the side of the highway towered over passing traffic, evidently to draw attention to a roadside stall. One of the 50 foot blow-up imps sported a top hat and was smoking a cigar.

"What an obscenity," Doron remarked. "This town was among the many stops my folks and I took during Dad's famed 'Atlantis Tour of America.' Sadly, the tour was even uglier than the blow-up demons we just passed."

Vikram wondered if the rubber giants were a dark omen of things ahead, the views now becoming rapidly more dystopian as they approached the outskirts of Los Angeles.

Smog, dense housing and bumper-to-bumper traffic invaded the landscape. Downtown Los Angeles freeways reminded Vikram of Bombay.

In the approaching sunset of the afternoon, several hours beyond L.A., San Diego's white sandy shores came into view.

Vikram was trying to reach the fellow on his cell phone. The number rang and rang. There was no answer and no message machine.

Either way, the two of them looked forward to a refreshing late afternoon swim at the La Jolla beach. As they headed toward the surf, Vikram pledged, "He's not going to get away. If we have to, we'll drive to his place and lean on the doorbell."

Chapter 6

Vikram and Doron waited at a table in the inner courtyard of the rambling Hamburguesa restaurant in the Bazaar Del Mundo section of Old Town San Diego. They were not sure Walter, the Stanford dropout, would even show. He had been as skittish as Jack the Rabbit over the phone. But at least the restaurant had the best hamburgers, guacamole and nachos around and a great Sunday brunch.

Like charming Old Town surrounding it, the Hamburguesa was the right place for a discreet meeting. The inner courtyard where they sat was bordered by stucco walls covered with vines and flowers under an open sky. It could be almost anywhere in Central America. They could talk inconspicuously and not be overheard; the round tables with sun umbrellas were separated by ample distance. In the pleasant warmth of the sun, a breeze carried the scent of flowers.

Just as they decided to hail a waitress to order, Walter appeared in an entrance to the courtyard, looking slightly sheepish. Thin and pale, he nervously approached the table, apologetic for being ten minutes late.

With introductions soon out of the way, he sat down and ordered a king-sized margarita, for which the restaurant was famous. Doron and Vikram were thinking that he should be opening up fairly soon by the time a second margarita was on the way. Then came generous platters of food.

Walter did, in fact, resemble the classic nerd with glasses. By the time he downed half of his second margarita, Doron and Vikram learned that Walter, once the local hero who had won a Stanford scholarship and the one-time great hope of the family, was quickly falling from grace.

After a number of months of his floundering at home in the poorer Chula Vista section of San Diego near the Tijuana border, his folks were no longer subtle. They told him they did not have the means to support an adult child and were also less than convinced by his reasons for dropping out of a world-class program that could have set him up for life.

Of course, Walter could never tell them the real reasons he had fled the program, partly because he didn't fully know himself. He had memory gaps.

"They've given me two weeks to find an apartment or a room. The atmosphere at home has become intolerable," he lamented.

Vikram asked the obvious: "Well, your parents have a point. Why leave so bright a future—an opportunity people would die to have?"

Doron followed it with, "What could possibly have turned you away from a Stanford Ph.D. scholarship, virtually guaranteeing unlimited career openings?" They were intentionally amplifying the frustrated echoes of his parents to push Walter over the top. It cried out for a credible answer, not lame-sounding BS.

Walter looked constipated on both ends, mouth scrunched up, hunched forward awkwardly and now clearly battling something inside. They waited to see a muscle twitch or a quick plunge of the Adam's apple. Not yet.

Doron heaped it on again: "Come on, Walter, did the head of the department spring out of a trapdoor wearing a leather mask, zip it open at the mouth, then proposition you? Something isn't clicking here. I mean, you didn't leave Stanford without a reason. Because your present options really don't sound very good."

The next move was in order. Vikram and Doron graphically went into the death of Jon and Glen's roommate, Spenser, a fellow Walter had been acquainted with, even a friend. The brain clamp had been applied. "Okay, Walter, what's going on? Why did you really leave?"

Clearly, the guy was carrying a huge weight, and at least some kind of confession would help.

Falteringly, Walter confessed that he had been friends with Spenser, as well as with one other grad student in the same program who was also killed in an accident. Doron and Vikram were aware that this fellow had died perhaps five months before Spenser sailed over Devil's Slide.

"I'm not a paranoid seeing random patterns," Walter assured them.

Walter's friend was among Stanford's army of joggers crossing the campus. "He'd been running on the side path along El Camino Real. He'd entered the crosswalk of a side street and had clear right of way, when out of nowhere a pickup truck driven by an illegal alien hit him and took off. He died en route to the hospital." Doron and Vikram were aware of this part of the story, having scoured news sources.

Naturally, the case had been waiting to be heard in court. A witness had already told the police he had seen the same pickup truck cruise up and down El Camino Real before the accident during early rush hour and things were congested.

Walter said, "I did some prying and found out that the Mexican driver, two weeks before the accident, had bought a brand-new car with cash and had made a down payment on a more expensive house. All this with no tangible change in his income situation. He had mainly done odd jobs, using his pickup truck for hauling and gardening in the region, mostly nearby Menlo Park and Mountain View. That was it."

"I did see some profound changes in him not long before the jogging accident," he admitted.

Doron and Vikram mentioned what Glen and Jon had seen. "Spenser had screaming nightmares, midnight showers, and general angst." Walter nodded, "Same kind of stuff."

"Go back to your involvement in the program. Did you see anything strange or suspicious?" Doron probed.

Walter threw out a peanut. "The initial feeling I had that things were going on under the surface hit me at one of those biotech conferences. Often companies are mining for freebies from fresh, creative minds. They pretend to be engaging you in deep discussions. A Berkeley grad student, fed good snacks and enough drinks after such a conference—that's when the real interviews take place—was thrown a hypothetical question by a biotech firm where he wanted to work after grad school. He solved it in seven seconds flat off the top of his head. It was really a million-dollar answer that solved the impasse of the biotech company. That kind of vamping is common—and I…"

Walter was wandering. Doron wanted to steer him back. "You mentioned you were approached. So we don't lose our thread here…"

Walter tensed and briefly went silent, perhaps weighing the cost. "I will mention the really big event which was by invitation only. It is the most coveted event there is. When I was invited I was sure someone had confused me with someone else. I got a platinum gilded invitation that had been hand-delivered to my apartment by a corporate courier. Right out of the movies. It was entitled the *Millennium of the Genome*." Vikram and Doron knew that they had just hit pay dirt.

Walter noted, "It took place in the grand penthouse suite on the entire top floor of the Fairmont Hotel which goes for $10,000 a night."

Vikram, who knew his history, recalled that the Nob Hill Hotel was where delegates from 40 countries met in the Garden Room "to draft the Charter for the United Nations in 1945." Walter nodded.

"I had never seen anything like it in my life," Walter continued. "The massive suite not only had large meeting halls, a circular, two-story rotunda library with an observatory ceiling window, but endless antechambers, sitting rooms, a dining room, right down to a master bedroom overlooking the Golden Gate Bridge. I learned the suite has acted as the San Francisco residence for every U.S. president since William Howard Taft." Doron and Vikram nodded, prodding him on.

"It was a Who's Who gathering with maybe 30 select doctoral students in the field of molecular biology from around the world. It was a black-tie affair all the way and included my being chauffeured to and from the hotel in a private limousine. The biggest names in the field spoke briefly, including the former head of the Human Genome Project, as well as three of the inventors of gene-sequencing technology."

Walter paused. No question, this was Walter's big moment. The kid from Chula Vista had hit the stratosphere.

"I sensed something going on behind the scenes—perhaps the event was being used for screening purposes. I found out later that a whole segment broke away and regrouped at one of the large estates in Mountain View. I wasn't invited."

He described how the two now-deceased Stanford scholars in his program were singled out. "They stayed on after I left. I saw them being given the fraternal handshake earlier by the host and introduced to a few of the heavies. I noticed that they disappeared soon after that. I assumed they were invited to one of the more exclusive rooms to be interviewed."

Walter admitted, "Twenty minutes after it was over, I started to feel out of place and uncomfortable as the crowd was thinning out. So I left before midnight."

"Your early departure may have also saved your life," Doron responded.

"I suspect that the two others from our Stanford group were among those invited to the second gathering. When I saw them a day or two later, they still looked like they'd seen God or were given the secrets of life. The event at the Fairmont was over two years ago," Walter said, looking off distractedly toward a cloud formation. "I guess a lot has happened since."

Vikram unknowingly dropped a bombshell. "You would certainly think that such an event would have had at least a few members from Deep Earth Lab present."

Walter froze, looking stunned. The pronouncement seemed to take him by surprise. "We've done our homework," Doron added, barely nodding, then asked, "What do you know about Deep Earth Lab?" His eyes were boring in on Walter.

Walter suddenly got a faraway look in his eyes and went completely silent as something in him seemed to shift.

He then quietly got up from his chair, edged away from the table, mumbled something in a monotone, and walked straight out of the restaurant as though something was guiding him. It was very odd.

Sensing Walter's fragility, they let him walk away. Both knew that "Deep Earth Lab" had been the trigger.

During the drive back, Vikram and Doron were increasingly concerned that Walter was not aware of what it was he was running from. Most likely he was still in danger. "He's running blind," Doron observed grimly.

They zeroed in on another anomaly. Walter mentioned that when the Palo Alto police apprehended what turned out to be a Mexican driver of the pickup truck a half-hour later and told him he had plowed into a Stanford student jogging across the street, killing him, the man looked shocked, scared and confused. He had no recollection of the accident or where he had been during the previous 40 minutes. He sat in the police station in a cold sweat, pleading and weeping.

When they got back to Palo Alto, Doron and Vikram called Walter.

He was polite and glad to hear from them, but didn't remember leaving the table in the manner they described. Walter remembered all of them getting up from the table together and leaving after shaking hands.

"Whether it is missing time or memory replacement, no question that the Project is doing strange things to their heads," Doron remarked.

"I think it is very powerful mind control," Vikram conjectured. "Great effort is going into hiding something."

Chapter 7

Jon's e-mail, sent after they had left, awaited Doron and Vikram when they returned from San Diego Sunday night:

"I'm at Cambridge. Possible hot lead—I met a grad student who knew Spenser. Also hoping to meet with the hacker group. Did you email them I might be coming? Let me know. Don't know how long this will take. Hope the file I sent helped. More soon. —Jon"

It was a brisk Friday afternoon in early March. Having come straight from Heathrow to Cambridge via the train from Kings Cross, Jon sat waiting to meet his contact at Trinity College on the steps of the fountain in Nevilles Court. It was where the footrace in *Chariots of Fire* took place, and Jon's imagination was working overtime.

As he scanned the college, so elegantly designed by Christopher Wren, Jon felt like an earthbound soul looking on at the Kingdom of God from a great distance. After the waterless Negev and beyond, Cambridge was like a bounteous spring. It was regal, beautiful and spoke of a golden age of optimism and hope, a world with strong pillars the old order could stand upon. It was a world that still believed in God, in goodness and all the classic virtues. Its very foundation was revealed in the names of the colleges themselves—Trinity College, St. John's, Christ's College, Corpus Christi, Magdalene, Emmanuel, Jesus College. Jon wished at times he could visit that more innocent world of bygone days.

Jon had almost gone to Cambridge for graduate studies, and he adored the place. He was feeling its rich history. If Harvard College boasted of dating back to the 1600s, then Cambridge University—John Harvard's alma mater—went back to the 1200s. Stanford was barely out of the woods by comparison.

Jeremy Saint John—the one Jon was waiting to meet—approached Jon from behind and quietly sat behind him on the steps, mimicking in mock awe Jon's absorption with the architecture. Jon turned, and they both laughed and extended hands. "I am glad to see you," Jon said with a note of relief.

"How about some tea up the street?" Jeremy asked. They headed to the Little Tea Room across from St. John's College, finding a discreet table in the corner of the near-empty room.

Jon recalled how Spenser had ecstatically shown him the gilded platinum invitation, boarded a chauffeured limousine to San Francisco for the Fairmont Hotel gathering. "If I remember, several days later he was showing you around the Stanford campus. That's when you and I briefly met."

Jeremy nodded. "Yes, I remember meeting you. I think we planned to go off and play tennis or something, but I could never quite get away from your roommate, the ultimate tour guide."

"Well, I suppose you know he's dead."

Jeremy turned ashen. "What—you're kidding. What happened?"

"Spenser went over the cliffs of Half Moon Bay. I heard the radio report, drove there. And did not want to see what I knew lay below—his mangled car. I saw his body after the car was hauled up. I suppose that's when the whole awful thing hit me full force. I'm not sure I've been the same since."

"So what are they saying? Accident? Suicide?" Jeremy queried, looking deeply bothered.

"Either of the above, but not a breath about the third option—murder."

"I definitely don't see him committing suicide," Jeremy confided, somewhat shaken. "I, too, was sent the same gilded invitation, an airplane ticket and lavish expense money, perhaps as an enticement. They even gave me a room for the night at the Fairmont. I knew I had to go."

He confessed, "I suppose I knew when to leave the big event, partly due to exhaustion from jet lag and partly because of a strong intuition—call it a survival sense. I watched carefully, by the way, as Spenser was given the old-boys'-club handshake. So, when it was officially over, I slipped out the back stairs to my hotel room before the clock struck midnight and all of us were turned to mice!"

Sensing the conversation needed privacy, Jon and Jeremy signaled one another, paid the bill, crossed the street and walked to a lone bench along the backs of St. John's.

Jon then continued the conversation, "Did you pick anything up while you were at the Fairmont?"

"I sensed a certain strange quality in those running the show. It's the same dark trait I've picked up at similar top-drawer gatherings I've been to over here. It's as though something else is really going on behind the window dressing—as though people are being seduced at some level and don't know it."

Jeremy then asked, "If you don't mind, let me ask you what signs you saw in Spenser before his death? Did you sense that something out of the ordinary was going on?"

"Absolutely," Jon answered. "He started to have horrible nightmares, cold sweats, took midnight showers, and later he visited a psychiatrist, which did not help. It may have made things worse. … It was also very unlike him to kill himself by driving his treasured new car over the cliffs of Half Moon Bay in the dead of night. That would be the last thing he would do."

Taking the conversation another direction, Jeremy said, "For some time I've sensed something very big, very clandestine going on. Whether it's the biological equivalent of the Manhattan Project, I can't tell. But if it's as big as I'm beginning to suspect, then those involved who are unable to keep a secret will be taken out. Naturally, it will be made to look like an accident. The level of secrecy and security are a strong indicator of what is at stake."

The two realized they were divulging things they had each kept bottled up for some time. And it was a great relief. A deepening bond of trust between them was quickly forming.

Jeremy pointed off to the distance, and they got up and headed along the backs of the colleges toward King's College Chapel. Along the way, Jon described the Nephil Project and how he'd first learned about it from scouring his roommate's computer upon returning from the scene of the crash. Jeremy became very interested.

DNA sequencing was Jeremy's specialty—and probably the reason he'd been invited to the black-tie affair at the Fairmont. He looked concerned as he started mentally processing something. Both he and Jon knew that genetic material could be extracted from almost anything left by a living creature—intervening centuries were no obstacle—the theme of *Jurassic Park*.

Jeremy probed, "So one of them at the dig told you that they weren't playing *Jurassic Park* and looking for dino DNA?"

"Right. They were digging for ancient human-like remains within certain geological parameters, possibly extending into Africa." Jeremy let it sink in.

King's College Chapel now towered above them. They entered the grand sanctuary for a brief look before moving on. The refrains of a boys' choir rehearsing an ancient Latin hymn was hauntingly beautiful. Jon found himself acknowledging a sense of the transcendent. Then the reverse of it came in a brief thought from nowhere: *If man is the measure of all things, alone in the universe, then that is cause for unceasing despair.*

Jeremy wanted to show Jon something at the university's Department of Molecular Biology, where he was working on an important project. As Jon soon learned, Jeremy had radically original ideas that had excited the department heads. No doubt word of Jeremy's innovations had spread to their colleagues across the Atlantic. En route to the lab, Jeremy reminded Jon of the entrance of Stanford's Genome Center. Both of them had stood there, where a marble plaque stated the original challenge. In 1972, researchers at UC San Francisco and Stanford University produced the first recombinant DNA molecule.

In 1973 the Human Genome Project sought to:
- Identify all the approximately 30,000 genes in human DNA,
- Determine the sequences of the 3 billion chemical base pairs that make up human DNA,
- Store this information in databases,
- Improve tools for data analysis,
- Transfer related technologies to the private sector, and
- Address the ethical, legal and social issues (ELSI) that may arise from the project.

It had been a heady undertaking that they managed to complete ahead of time, courtesy of Craig Venter and his Celera Corporation. But this was only the beginning. The more the molecular biologists found under the hood, the more they toyed with the vast engines of life itself.

It was now 4:30 p.m. In a locked, high-security lab, Jeremy turned on his powerful computer—a custom, super-high-speed model with a huge LCD color display the size of a picture window. He worked through a cyber-sentry, something about the footprint of Vishnu, then showed Jon something that resembled a cascading river of billions of bits of DNA. It churned with frenzied activity in the act of live sequencing. Jon did not know this was the same screen Vikram and Doron glimpsed when they got beyond High Gate. Nor did anybody else, for that matter.

"This is what I used to call ManEater," Jeremy explained. "This is mostly my work. It sequences DNA at vast multiples of what all prior sequencers were able to do, thousands of times faster than Craig Venter's best efforts. It theoretically has the power to document not just the DNA of a single individual, but work through the genetic history of the human race."

He paused.

"My interest—my obsession if you will—is to be able to find genetic echoes, the faint imprints of the far past, or carryovers of genetic material long since removed from our direct genetic steam."

He paused again.

"I am now wondering whether I might have opened up a Pandora's box, creating something that could be horribly misused. I have not told a soul all that it can do. But, for that reason, I am considering shutting down the whole thing."

Jon was absolutely stunned at Jeremy's brilliance.

They left Cavendish Lab under a darkening sky and headed back to Trinity College. Jon learned he was Jeremy's honored dinner guest. Jeremy had called ahead.

Jeremy now absolutely insisted "and I won't take 'no' for an answer"—that Jon stay in the spare room of his suite. Jon had left his bags with the porter at the gate of Trinity for safekeeping so he could taxi with them to a hotel after the meeting. Jeremy retrieved them before dinner. Jon felt deep gratitude and was very glad he had come to Cambridge that day.

Under the same majestic high ceiling of Trinity's dining hall where some of history's giants down the centuries had dined, Jeremy and Jon seated themselves at an end table before candlelight and wine. The Master's table was slightly raised in the front and seated with older, robed lecturers and professors busily conversing. On the evening menu was duck, new potatoes, shallots and greens. Dessert was apple crumble with rich custard, followed by a glass of port.

In reflective silence after dinner, the two walked King's Parade to Silver Street and back in the other direction beyond Trinity. A sobering moment was upon them, though they did not fully appreciate all the reasons why. Theirs had been a fortuitous meeting.

Chapter 8

On Saturday morning Jon and Jeremy decided it was a good time to make contact with the Cambridge hacker group—known by insiders as the Cyber gang—using the e-mail link Doron and Vikram sent Jon before leaving Israel.

Once on their Web page a cyber-sentry appeared. It resembled the quiz-show host of the popular British brainteaser *Mastermind*. Jon entered the password. Next a flexing, excited cartoon face on tiny legs began jumping up and down, cheering with a message for them: "Hello friend of Doron and Vikram, any friend of theirs is a friend of mine." A map replaced the face, showing the meeting place and time that night, accompanied by a loud bass-guitar riff, followed by a loud refrain of Sting's "Roxanne."

They had just finished having espresso in Jeremy's comfortable suite, sitting off a corner stairwell and away from the undergraduate rooms. Jeremy enjoyed the privacy of his graduate suite, which had once housed a number of great names, including Alfred Lord Tennyson, who attended Trinity in 1827.

Jeremy learned of Vikram and Doron when he and Jon were discussing the Nephil Project. Jon hadn't met them either, but already felt a strong bond.

Not being true hackers themselves, what neither Jon nor Jeremy knew was that among the Cambridge hacker group, Vikram's and Doron's reputations were at the top of the scale. It was well-known that both had penetrated top Defense Department computers when they were around 11 years old—an important benchmark in the world of hackers. Each had performed numerous cyber-feats, some less than legal.

The Cambridge hackers meeting was scheduled for 9:00 that night at the large Anchor Pub on the banks of the River Cam at Silver Street Bridge, so it also meant they had some time to kill, indeed, a whole afternoon.

Jeremy enjoyed the role of tour guide and took Jon for a leisurely country drive around Cambridgeshire, briefly stopping at the Orchard Tea Garden in nearby Grantchester. "It's a bit of history and great tea," Jeremy announced. He told Jon it was the "in" place that celebrated Fabian intelligentsia of an earlier era came to for tea and discussion—doubtless planning their versions of utopia.

The two sat outdoors in the large orchard garden among a motley of weather-beaten tables and chairs and random sun-umbrellas. Jon reflected on what an ideal getaway it was to sit back and think. Beyond that, the tea and crumpets were delicious.

Rupert Brooke, England's dashing young poet who attended King's College and lived near the famed tea spot in Grantchester, had written a brief verse about The Orchard, now reprinted on cards given out to visitors. In "The Old Vicarage, Grantchester," the famous final lines immortalized afternoon tea at The Orchard:

Stands the Church clock at ten to three?
And is there honey still for tea?

The same visitor's card listed British Fabians who had frequented the Orchard. Sometimes called the "Grantchester Group," they included Rupert Brooke, Bertrand Russell, E.M. Forster, John Maynard Keynes, Ludwig Wittgenstein, Virginia Woolf and Augustus John, to name a few. Woolf's code word for them was "the Neo-Pagans."

"They were certainly the vanguard of their day," Jon observed as he lay down the card and grabbed another crumpet.

"What a vastly different era that had been," Jeremy noted. "The Grantchester Group weren't simply interested in liberating themselves from Edwardian morality, but they constantly pushed the envelope of Bohemianism. ... Right here at the Orchard Tea Garden, their ideas leapt up like genies let out of a bottle into the world. They were the radical chic thinkers of their day."

Let the tattooed and nose-ringed minions of the present day bow and pay homage, Jon thought to himself, then observed, "But they seemed to destroy the very world that offered them so much." Jeremy nodded. Jon again thought silently, *They may have paved the way for the kind of scientific anti-morality that killed my roommate.*

Jon then reflected aloud, "What boggles the mind, Jeremy—and I have read some of them—is that they lived elegant, privileged lives in an era that may well have been, from a human standpoint, the most desirable time to live in history. In the midst of enviable privilege, eating their tea and crumpets, these very bright minds in the Orchard Tea Garden had begun bringing down the very pillars that had stood the long centuries, providing the kind of world in which they flourished. They wanted for nothing."

"Perhaps when vanity and boredom intersect in the late afternoon, something happens," Jeremy poetically responded.

"...Unfortunately, at great expense," Jon continued. "What they did ultimately to the social order would be like a hacker bringing an airport to a standstill, partly from boredom, partly to see if it could be done. Our era is certainly a footnote to the ideas they set in motion."

Tea at The Orchard had been an eye-opener for Jon in ways he would not have suspected.

Jeremy drove Jon along country roads absolutely plush with green. They passed estates, old manor houses, went through small towns and rural villages. They drove by dense woods and wide-open fields, which in harvest season would turn brilliant chrome yellow from mustard flowers. Flashing by these bright yellow fields was a classic vista from the train between London and Cambridge.

Tolkien doubtless took his imagery of hobbits from the English countryside of his day. There really had been a kind of innocence when he taught at Oxford in the early part of the 20th century.

Jon had loved England ever since his childhood period in London, several key formative years, and many subsequent visits. The entire region had what Stanford and most of America's West Coast sorely lacked—a rich and layered history that stretched back centuries; charm and beauty in old winding roads and small farms. Jon could feel Rupert Brooke's love of England through his poetic stanzas. The last lines Brooke wrote—as he unknowingly approached death as a soldier in Gallipoli—had been quoted by Jeremy before they left the Orchard Tea Garden:

If I should die, think only this of me;
That there's some corner of a foreign field
That is for ever England.

Jon and Jeremy returned to Cambridge just as it had gotten dark. They decided to eat at a decent local restaurant called The Varsity. Not feeling up to the propriety and decorum the Trinity College dining hall would require, they wanted to sit back and just talk freely, unobserved.

At 8:45 on Saturday night, they walked briskly along King's Parade, by King's College on the right, toward nearby Silver Street. They took a right and walked the short distance toward the Silver Street Bridge that spanned the Cam River. It was an attractive, two-lane stone bridge that people loved to just stand on to watch the river flowing by. The pub entrance was on the bridge.

To Jon's delight, The Anchor was where he had been once before some years back. It was a grand old pub with wandering lounges and loads of character. The lowest level let out on a landing by the side of the river, where rental boats were available for punting along the backs of some of the older Cambridge colleges. The upstairs section was more for academics and the social set, and had a great view of the Cam; the downstairs was much less formal, often filled with students. There was a lower level still, for those wanting privacy. That was where the hackers met.

Jon and Jeremy entered the sprawling downstairs lounge overlooking the river from the side bank. The Cambridge Cyber gang had essentially taken over the entire lounge. There were at least 50 of them, most drinking beer, hard cider or scrumpy. A full moon was gradually moving into view through the wide bay window. Jon's first impression was that he was gazing on the very faces so often seen at Stanford, brilliant rebels sojourning through their years at Cambridge as passing strangers in the night. Most were straight-looking scholars with an occasional Goth or punk mixed in. Doubtless there were aristocrats in this group, but their attire would not always give them away.

"Want a pinta bitter?" one of them asked Jon.

"If you don't mind, I'll have an Amstel Light," Jon replied. Jeremy went for the local cider, which was potent stuff.

Any standoffishness soon melted into sobered interest once Jon told them, "Vikram and Doron went to the condo to meet my roommate, Glen, regarding the death of our roommate Spenser."

"That terrible accident seems highly suspicious," one ventured. The rest agreed.

When asked about connecting with them, Jon said, "I established connections with Vikram and Doron from the cybercafés in Israel. The encryption was set up by my surviving roommate, who had the codes."

The Cambridge hackers knew more about the cyber-exploits of the Stanford duo of Vikram and Doron than either Jon or Jeremy would have dreamed. One of them asked, "Have you heard about Doron's taking over the downtown Manhattan traffic center when he was 13?"

"The lights formed a massive computer game board viewable from space," another added. "The 'in' thing was to e-mail the Google satellite map of it." Jon and Jeremy couldn't help but laugh.

Jon tested the waters by asking, "Have any of you heard of the Nephil Project on the Negev Desert of Israel?"

Out of the audience a girl named Fiona spoke up. "Well, Neil and I teamed up to test his Internet Watcher program." Neil was her boyfriend and a hacker leader. "After picking up activity, we directed it into several locales neighboring the Negev Desert. We began intercepting lots of e-mail messages. The ones to friends and relatives in New York, Miami and London were invariably written in English…"

Suddenly, as if on cue, several members of the Cambridge group bunched together into an ad-lib musical ensemble, as if on stage, and began harmonizing the lyrics of David Bowie's "Scary Monsters" in mock horror. They shivered out the words and rolled their eyes in sync, then disbanded and returned to their seats. The 20-second production reminded Jon of a mutation of some Andrew Lloyd Webber musical. This motley crew apparently had talent to burn. Jon was feeling somewhat humbled.

After a pause to let things settle, Fiona continued. "The e-mail we intercepted was apparently coming from the Negev region. At least Neil's watcher was focused on that area. The message we intercepted was from a girl who called herself 'Sabra One,' who was apparently a member of some ultra-top-secret archaeological dig that had massive state-of-the-art earth-moving machinery. It sounds like what you saw when you were there, Jon."

He nodded, impressed and eager to hear more. He also felt foolish— Fiona and her hacker boyfriend had, in a weekend and from her Cambridge bedroom, retrieved more than he had found in a month's worth of traipsing around Israel's heat and sand.

Fiona continued, "Well, apparently they needed to go really deep—deeper than most ancient-culture beds. They were estimating a ground depth that would satisfy projections of the world during or before the era of some vast flood, and they were forced at times to take wild guesses. 'Sabra One' mentioned that she was not told any of this directly. She had overheard some of it, listening in on two supervisors talking privately. They were the only ones who knew what was going on and were discussing something rather odd.

"Anytime they found something significant, they were to pretend before the rest of the crew that they hadn't really found anything. So the supervisors made sure to appear indifferent or disappointed when something showed up. Well, she overheard them excitedly talking after they had apparently found something fairly significant.

"The regular team was told to leave the dig the moment it was partially unearthed. That was standard procedure. Only the supervisors and a few technicians were allowed to actually proceed. According to what 'Sabra One' overheard, they unearthed the object and then quickly moved it to a secret holding area. 'Sabra One' later tried to glimpse the ancient relic by sneaking into some storage area that was off-limits.

"Well, according to 'Sabra One,' a branch team had partially unearthed a fossilized footprint that was utterly massive. They had seen enough of it to gather what it was. That's when they had to stop and let the supervisors take over. According to what 'Sabra One' had discovered, it was way too enormous to be human, though it apparently reminded the supervisors of a humanoid footprint, as incredible as it sounds."

Jon knew this was very significant. He also knew he could have never entered the holding area.

The Cambridge hackers knew some of what Fiona was sharing and watched Jon and Jeremy for reactions. Both nodded, very impressed.

"What doesn't figure," a tall fellow named Ian interjected from near the back of the room, "is why all the secrecy. I mean it should be fair game for academia. It sounds like it might be a momentous archaeological find, something on the level of the great behemoths or beyond even that. Why try to corner the market?"

It was a fair question that was left unanswered. Fiona shrugged at Ian and went on.

RETURN OF THE GIANTS

"Everyone except the two supervisors were told to go into town for a few days under paid leave until they were recalled. Evidently, outside archaeologist had been summoned under a cloak of security, one flying in from England. We think it was Oxford." The eyes of the Cambridge group lit up with exaggerated suspicion.

Fiona then reported, "'Sabra One' had been dismissed from the team soon after. She just wanted to get away. Her message to some friend in Miami ended with, 'I think they are reading my e-mails.'"

"I wonder if she made it to Miami? Can you still find out where she is?" a group member asked.

Neil Boyd replied, "She pretty much went silent after that. Though she's probably gotten a new Internet address with a different name."

Fiona kicked in, "Yes, Neil must have about 20 different Internet addresses himself." They laughed.

"Did she indicate how big the fossilized footprint was?" Jon asked.

"I guess it was hundreds of times the surface area of a normal human footprint. It sounds ridiculous, but I guess such a creature would be eye-to-eye with the middle floors of an office building if you calculated body mass, proportional limb size and so on."

With heavy academic schedules, the members of the Cambridge Cyber gang could afford only a little over an hour for the present meeting. Other commitments awaited them.

Now they felt they had merely scratched the surface of a growing mystery. A number still had reports of "scary monster" activities to share when they next met.

Ian, who it turned out was the group president, made a motion on the floor: "Since it is a weekend, those who can might want to reconvene tomorrow, Sunday night. Let's have a show of hands."

Most of them indicated they could make it back for the second meeting. Jon was gladdened by this. They had more strange sightings to discuss that might add to the overall picture.

He noticed the full moon, and its reflection off the River Cam, shining a yellowish orange almost dead center of the large bay window. *All we need is the howl of a werewolf,* Jon thought to himself, the tune of David Bowie's "Serious Moonlight" starting up in his head.

The group ordered a final round while Jon considered the description of the giant footprint by "Sabra One." He imagined scenes of King Kong ripping up trees and throwing cars.

The group emerged on the Silver Street Bridge. Under a street lamp, Jeremy was told the location of the next meeting, at the private estate of the president of the Cambridge hackers, whose full name was Lord Ian Greville Marbury.

Jeremy informed Jon in a low voice as they headed to Trinity, "I think we are supposed to appear early. It seems we have been invited to the family dinner before the meeting."

They wandered off "into the moonlight ... the *serious* moonlight," as Jon tried to purge the Bowie tune from his head.

Chapter 9

Jon woke up Sunday morning as Jeremy was rushing off to catch up on lab work, often working weekends at an unrelenting pace. They agreed to meet for lunch at the Grad Pad.

Jon showered and, as he toweled off, stared out the rippling old-world glass of the front window onto the greens of Trinity College, prizing the rare opportunity. With the morning to himself, Jon had an English breakfast at an inn nearby, then headed up Saint Andrew Street to glimpse into some of the old church buildings.

Becoming curious, Jon entered Saint Andrew the Great at the start of a worship service. He was impressed to see the place packed. He estimated between 700 and 900 Cambridge students, faculty and townspeople were there. Jon stood toward the back, along the side wall of the nave, and listened to classic hymns, and then to a deep, surprisingly relevant sermon from Reverend Mark Ashby. Jon felt a refreshing sense of the presence of good, as though some invisible hand had been placed on his shoulder, offering solace.

He left in a reflective mood, walking slowly to the graduate union building to meet Jeremy. Certainly the rector, Mark Ashby, was an extremely gracious, humble and intelligent man, and very much on the opposite end of the scale from Jehovah Bob, whom Jon had seen flapping down the streets of Jerusalem in his Rapture suit. Banality and idiocy had supplanted dignity and honor in the church except for rare cases such as this. Indeed, the majority of the demented messengers of the Gospel, at least in the media, were ranting and raving as a means of sponging the simple masses of their money. *Is the church age finally coming to an end—not with a bang but a whimper—headed by televangelists the likes of Jehovah Bob? Stay tuned,* Jon thought grimly.

After lunch at the large, open square dining hall at the Grad Pad, Jeremy asked, "Up for some coffee?" Jon gave the thumbs-up and they crossed over to the coffee lounge overlooking the River Cam. The sun was shining in anticipation of spring, a week away. A decade back, as an undergraduate, Jon had been sitting in this very lounge, looking out, and saw Stephen Hawking—who held Newton's chair at Trinity—motoring across the backs in the direction of his home. It was a curious sight.

Thoughts of Hawking sent Jon to reflecting on the fact that he had been changing since that era. Once a hard-core atheist, Jon felt himself recently opening up to things he had abandoned in his early teens at the time, to the disappointment of his aunt and uncle. But the status quo of science had been shifting under the surface. Jon had felt it.

Jeremy looked at Jon's pensive face and queried him about what he was thinking. "Oh, the design-versus-accident debate."

Jeremy encouraged him again with a look.

Jon offered, "That the complexity we see in nature testifies to an intelligent design at work—let's just say God—versus the naturalist's view that says that everything in existence came from nothing. That random events plus time created everything that there is, the view that is offered by the 'self-appointed mandarins of science,' in the words of Professor Johnson."

"I'm familiar with the various arguments," Jeremy responded. He gave Jon a quizzical look, which Jon had anticipated. "Oh, Professor Phillip Johnson? Was once a true believer in naturalism, then switched sides. This made him especially disliked by hardliners like Richard Dawkins [Oxford don and author of *The Blind Watchmaker*]. A top legal and philosophical mind in the field of legal evidences, he entered Harvard at 15, later clerked under the Chief Justice of the Supreme Court. No one could debate him. He shot down Harvard heavies one by one—people like Stephen Gould. It reached a point where they refused to debate him. I heard him in his heyday when I was visiting Berkeley. Blew me away. In his words, the scientific establishment had been using the language of science to rid the world of God."

Jeremy nodded.

"When I heard him at Wheeler Auditorium," Jon continued, "I realized there was more than enough substance there to rock my world. I left there feeling like someone who had recently been divorced looking around for the next mate—unsettling. Perhaps there was an open universe again. And that meant the possibility of hope. Really, hope is not a bad thing!"

A suspiciously quizzical look came from Jeremy.

Jon 'fessed, "Okay, I sat through a church service this morning for the first time in 15 years. I'm wrestling with a few issues right now."

Jeremy grinned, then said tauntingly, "Now I see what's going on. I can see the headlines: 'Promising Stanford scientist busted in church. Caught in the pews live.' That's much more dangerous than being caught at an orgy. Which church, by the way?" Jon told him. Jeremy smiled and winked conspiratorially as he returned to the lab.

Continuing in his exploratory mode, Jon planned to spend time wandering the colleges and bookstores. Maybe he would even encounter some pretty Cambridge coed.

In fact, he saw a whole number of them—the Cambridge women's lacrosse team practicing near Queen's College. He sat down on a bench under a tree, to the side of the field. He was glad Jeremy wasn't over his shoulder to needle him again. Jon grinned, grateful to have Jeremy as a friend.

Jon noticed that many of the coeds playing were quite attractive. He found himself thinking, *It's so refreshing seeing feminine women*. It was like going back 40 years in a time machine. Jon loved it and realized he couldn't have spent the time any better.

A lovely-looking girl scored a goal. Jon clapped. He thought he saw the faintest trace of a smile back. Almost all of these Cambridge coeds, from what Jon could tell, had resisted the kind of sexless androgyny that had overtaken the States. The joke at Stanford was you needed legal counsel to accompany you on a date in case you were accused of rape. Beyond that, dating partners were usually hard to tell apart. Why bother?

As his eyes followed the girls running up and down the field, Jon reflected on the cultural impasse of the sexes. What was once a great polar attraction among clearly discernible opposite sexes, perhaps 60 years ago in America, had withered into something dull and uninspiring for both sexes as 21st-century culture minimized gender differences in the great multicultural equalizing process. Like the anti-sex leagues in Orwell's *1984*, the sexes were trapped in a cultural straightjacket.

Jon recalled his trip to India. Lithe, feminine, beautiful women were the ideal there. Women prized their femininity. One never saw them chop off their hair and swagger around like truck drivers. The contrast was almost too much to bear when Jon got back to the States. No wonder marriage was becoming an increasingly less attractive option these days, especially considering the fragility of most relationships. The truth was, there were few marriages Jon envied these days, very few indeed.

He felt like a misplaced Edwardian. In the late 1800s, men and women did not arm-wrestle every morning to sort out roles. They clicked through the dance steps of life in sync, each prizing the other and grateful for what they had—to Jon, this Edwardian model of sex differences and mutual attraction was one of the most beautiful things in the world, and he really wasn't sure he would ever see it.

In that great century in England, men and women were not hostile, hardened and suspicious of one another—as they were these days on the Stanford campus. Nor did they enter marriage with a long list of non-negotiables and legal contracts. Nor did they transform into some of the amazing creatures you see today—almost a cultural commentary in itself.

Jon envisioned "mall waddlers" again. Was it from genetically altered junk food loaded with trans-fatty acids in tandem with bizarre unconscious drives? Whatever it was, it created these amazing creatures—women who resembled huge ticks with turbo thighs, enormous midsections, and tiny, crew-cut-accentuated heads bobbing up and down over lumbering bodies—in all, a vision worthy of Bosch. As they rolled along, they seemed to glory in their grotesque appearance. During his freshman year at Stanford, Jon had even composed a tuned accompaniment upon seeing two Stanford Mall waddlers, wobbling like jello-mold wannabes and defiantly holding hands. *Wamper-a-swamp-wamper-a-swamp-wamper-a-swamp*, went Jon's tune.

Jon came out of his reverie, realizing he was staring intently at the girl who had scored the goal earlier. He glanced at his watch and headed off to meet Jeremy. He was still trying to get the mall-waddler memory out of his head. *Therapy for me will be more Cambridge coeds*, Jon thought to himself with a grin.

When Jon entered the suite, Jeremy was just finishing a mug of tea. "Perfect timing. We still have afternoon light as we drive to Ian's estate for early dinner." They were soon roaring through Cambridgeshire in Jeremy's restored, vintage-green '61 Austin Healey 3000.

"I really love your car," Jon said admiringly. "Tearing around in this thing, racing stripe and all, you just can't beat the unique roar of its motor." He confessed to being a motorcycle buff.

"Which cycle do you have?" Jeremy inquired.

"A BMW GS100, 1996 model—it's a near-classic at this point. Black with side cylinders."

Jeremy nodded appreciatively. "That is a classic. I've toyed with the idea of buying an old Norton Commando sitting in a friend's garage. Been untouched for decades, but don't have enough time to tinker with it under my rather grueling program."

Jeremy passed seven-foot hedges as they approached a large wrought-iron gate that had been left open. "If this is it, I am impressed." Jon remarked as Jeremy turned into the gate with a knowing look.

It was, indeed, a spectacular manor house, an absolute classic. It sat maybe 50 yards back as Jeremy drove into a large, front garden area with fountains, trees and a wide assortment of flowers, some already in bloom. It was a horticulturist's delight.

Beyond a large, circular drive was ample parking for guests. A servant outside the door motioned them inside. Ian Marbury, the leader of the Cambridge hackers, joined the servant at the front door. "Please come in. I hope you are both hungry, because we thought we might sit down for a meal before the others arrive at seven. It's the Sunday evening meal, an old family tradition, so we'll be in the main dining room. The others will be eating as well, but I think you will prefer this," Ian announced with a wink.

Jon and Jeremy entered a grand dining room, where they were warmly greeted and shown their seats. Jon was delighted to see a bountiful feast all laid out: roast beef, ham, squab, spinach and peas from the garden, Yorkshire pudding, mashed potatoes and gravy, and a large platter of fresh vegetables. He was challenged to try the homegrown horseradish in a small silver bowl. It was so strong it shot right up his nostrils like flames from a blowtorch. His eyes watered as the others looked on, amused.

"I think certain ancient clans used it to torture people," Ian offered with a smile.

At that point Jon was quietly considering its marketing potential. "It would certainly be a hit in some areas of San Francisco."

Berry cobbler with custard followed, as small talk ensued.

It turned out that Ian was a member of Gonville & Caius College, near King's College, where Stephen Hawking had attended as an undergraduate; he was not a Trinity man until he gained full stature. An after-dinner brandy followed the meal. Again, Jon went for moderation.

No doubt, Ian's family was extremely wealthy, landed gentry and nobles, going back long generations of English history. Above inherited wealth, Ian's father, Lord Marbury, had earned a fortune on his own terms, starting and directing his privately owned multinational company. He had a large London office in Belgravia and commuted to work by train or limousine when he didn't conduct business from the manor house.

Immediately after the family dinner, Ian's family vanished to their private quarters.

Evidence of the lavish meal was soon disposed of by the servants before any hungry Cambridge hackers showed up. Ian enjoyed inviting the entire Cyber gang at least twice during the school year. An entire floor had been vacated on their behalf.

Jon anticipated watching something really strange to which Ian alluded.

Chapter 10

The hacker group flooded in as Ian took Jon and Jeremy up the back stairs. The large room was set up like a home movie theater. Large banquet tables at the back contained a colorful array of foods and drinks, from sandwiches to shepherd's pie, from Schweppes ginger ale to a local stout. Jon wondered how large the staff of servants was, because it was all so top-notch.

Ian whispered to Jon and Jeremy, "This is the family entertainment lounge. We've got a digital multimedia center with state-of-the-art sound and light technology." They noticed that covering much of the front wall was a plasma screen worthy of a small movie theater. Jon nodded approvingly as Ian said, "It is high-definition, capable of photographic detail."

Jon replied, "I'm not going to ask what the whole thing cost." Then continued, "I have always admired the juxtaposition of colliding eras over here. Only the English know how to combine pre-Victorian structures with the latest technology to create the right blend."

"Just don't say it's art deco," Ian replied with a grin.

Jon replied, "Well, it would be a perfect set to film an episode of *Doctor Who*." Jeremy added, "Entering the room wild-eyed and barking at the butler to seal the door before the Daleks entered."

Ian laughed and went to the front, greeting the arriving guests, now almost in full force. With the wave of an arm toward the table of food he said, "Feast away but don't waste time. We've got a heavy schedule. Take twenty minutes."

As they ate, the large plasma screen came alive with alternating pictures of natural wonders from a Hawaiian beach to Victoria Falls in Africa, interspersed with various abstract patterns and film segments.

Jon looked over and saw Gort, the titanium robot in *The Day the Earth Stood Still*, melting earthling tanks and guns with a dazzling ray from his cyclopean eye. A few minutes later a werewolf appeared, growling at a full moon. The final image on the screen was Dr. Who, wandering around, raving about the Daleks. Ian's eyes connected with Jeremy and Jon, who nodded back. The Cambridge Cyber gang's logo was the last thing on the screen.

"We need to get started!" Ian yelled from the front. Jon and Jeremy were talking to some attractive coeds who had come up for a friendly chat. Jon remembered them from the Anchor Pub the night before. The group quickly returned to their seats.

Ian brought the meeting to order. A kind of expectant energy filled the air. Jon noticed Neil Boyd, the inventor of the Internet watcher program who had spoken with Fiona the night before. He sat behind the multimedia console, powered by Apple's latest computer hooked into fibregate.

Suddenly Ian dramatically moved aside, turning to the screen and glancing at Jon. A live, high-definition feed of Doron and Vikram flashed in front of them on the theater screen. Jon was startled when he figured out who it was. "I've never met them, but that must be Doron and Vikram," he whispered to Jeremy.

Smiling, the two waved to the group. "Hello from Palo Alto. Hi, Jon, we hope to see you soon. Take care of him, Ian, and Neil and all of you. Jon, have a safe flight back. We look forward to meeting you in the flesh. We hope you enjoy our friends at Cambridge. Neil, serious kudos on perfecting the Watcher program. We heard what you did with it—amazing." The two from Palo Alto didn't mention a thing about penetrating High Gate.

Vikram put his hand on Doron's shoulder to speak up. "Hello, Nirmalli, glad you got into the program. I know Uncle Ravindra is proud of you. Hope to see you soon." An attractive Indian girl in the back seemed to be fighting tears, covering her mouth with her hand. Doron and Vikram waved to the group and signed off.

Jon was impressed by them, two very handsome and articulate guys. A deeper look into their eyes revealed uncommon brilliance. The screen certainly matched Jon's mental impression of them. He was glad to have them in his arsenal of friends.

Ian reminded them, "Many of you recall a year back, one of us hacked into a live feed of a group of Satanists torturing a homeless man abducted from the streets. They'd broken into a house while the people were away. We forwarded an untraceable feed of it to Scotland Yard. It was on the evening news, and the torturers were behind bars." The Cyber gang clapped and cheered.

"But we don't always forward things to Scotland Yard," Ian ended with a wry smile.

Ian and Neil cut to the quick. An older-generation video clip filled the screen, showing a dark auditorium with people in the front who were barely silhouettes.

Ian noted, "Before I continue, this is an example of what can be retrieved from top-secret archives."

The image started to focus. A tall, authoritative man in a dark suit was addressing the audience from a carpeted stage. He held a thick chain leash. Next to him was a raised mini-stage, perhaps for dramatic effect. On it was what appeared to be a large dog, partially obscured by a black silk hood. Resembling a monk's cowl, it covered the animal's head and part of its body.

The camera zoomed in. The dog's head under the black silk hood had a strange way of bobbing, almost rolling around. It must have been a boxer, because it did not seem to have a snout. Jon really didn't want to see what was under the hood.

Suddenly the speaker reached over and yanked off the hood. Attached to the dog's body was a man's head. It bobbed around spasmodically as it tried to talk to the master of ceremonies. It appeared imbecilic or sedated. Jon's mind leapt with the single word *abomination*.

The Cambridge hackers looked on spellbound as the man-beast's mouth moved in a sort of stupefied way. The eyes stared out at the announcer wide-eyed and unfocused. Jon couldn't tell if the eyes were pleading or fearful. The hybrid creature seemed unaware of the audience. It and the announcer were highlighted by a single spotlight. Several people in the front row had their hands over their mouths. The clip quickly ended.

A moving subtitle gave a code number, then "Human Hybrids, subject 18, March 11, 1989, courtesy of the San Quentin Inmate donation program 6F. Subject lived 6 months. This is the private property of Hybrids, Inc., a division of Chimera, Inc., Cambridge, Mass., Palo Alto, CA, & Oxon, UK." The picture ended. A grim silence filled the room.

Neil spoke. "I discovered this digitized video clip, as some of you already know, some months ago through a difficult hacking operation.

"My point is that this comes as a shock to us because none of us knew about it. It is leading-edge science of an earlier period conducted under an absolute cloak of secrecy. I am afraid things have come a long way since then."

Ian continued, "Such projects seem to be driven by a group with considerable power and influence, acting as though they are absolutely above the law. They seem to be operating on a number of wide-ranging fronts. Can we proceed?"

On cue, two members of the Cyber group stood up to report a recent finding via anonymously posted "SOS messages."

"We have been given leads to an underground scientific complex in England—we can't say where right now—that has no official record of existing. It is in a heavily forested region. The underground complex has been secret from its beginnings in the mid-1980s."

The other member added, "Service personnel in janitorial and maintenance have been eliminated one by one, presumably because they had seen or heard things that would jeopardize the Project's secrecy. Although their access around the complex was limited, forgetful scientists failing to lock up properly or follow protocol, while wandering off for a smoke or a snack, occasionally left critical areas wide open.

"Well, some of those early maintenance staff stumbled into places they didn't belong. That's when the rumors began."

The first member continued, "One janitor—and he's the sole survivor—went underground after several coworkers had been killed in staged accidents. One multiple-truck collision near Leeds was very suspicious. In another case, the papers reported an Islamic terrorist bomb explosion in a pub. It happened precisely during the brief interlude another coworker entered one section of the pub for a quick stout. Five of these coworkers were killed within a month in diverse accidents. The surviving janitor had heard the confidences of the others before they were killed. He is frightened to say the least."

"Terrified," the other member emphasized.

"He left his job at the complex soon after several maintenance workers had died. A widower, he moved to a village in another region of England. He switched everything he owned to the name of a nephew, who has been our hacker contact, by the way. Pension checks went to a trust-fund account in the Isle of Man, and so on. You get the point.

"He's wanted to get his story out before he's done in. For that he has relied on this nephew—who happens to be the only one in a long line of laborers ever to be accepted at college. As we said, the nephew is a hacker as well."

The other one smiled for effect. "To get to the point, we've been getting the nephew's untraceable messages concerning the uncle and the underground complex courtesy of Neil's Watcher program. But we sensed we needed to meet in person soon.

"Over academic break we met the nephew—now at a technical college in Southampton. His uncle is terrified to meet anyone unless first carefully vetted by the nephew. As we are members of the Cambridge Cyber gang, he was willing to do backflips for us."

There was muted applause. We had worked out a method of contact and a safe meeting place with his uncle, the surviving maintenance worker."

The two speakers took turns reporting on the meeting with the frightened uncle.

"The uncle mentioned an earlier leak from 15 years ago that involved outside witnesses. An elephant died in the process of giving birth to something else, not an elephant. A flatbed truck hauled both creatures out of the complex by a back road. As the driver stopped to reattach a tarp that apparently had partially blown off, locals who'd been hunting in the woods got a view of it. Needless to say, stories got out in the local pubs."

The other Cyber gang member jumped in. "Well, according to the uncle, one janitor friend of his wandered into one of the massive aircraft hangar-sized rooms—apparently a birthing room. What alerted him were the terrible screams. One of the scientists was talking about needing a larger artificial womb. He saw a massive cage with the nameplate 'BAAMPTON' with that odd spelling. Way in the back he saw what he described as a terrible creature. He ran out of the complex incoherent. He died in a truck accident near Leeds. The uncle said all of them became very afraid at that point."

The other speaker took over. "After the incident, no one was allowed into the complex for a week or more. When the maintenance staff returned, two of the scientists were no longer there. The rumor was that they had been killed by something at the lab."

They ended their presentation. "We hope to meet the surviving maintenance worker, otherwise known as 'the uncle,' again soon, providing his nephew can set it up. We are quite concerned about his well-being."

Ian dismissed the evening meeting, giving his special dinner guests a warm farewell. "Jon, I hope to hear from you, Doron and Vikram when the three of you meet soon. Take courage."

Jeremy and Jon drove back to Trinity College in a silent daze.

Jon broke in, reflecting from some place far off, "You definitely did the right thing, Jeremy, by not going to the gathering in Mountain View after the event at the Fairmont like Spenser did."

"I think that could be why I am alive today," Jeremy replied almost automatically.

"I know this sounds like a Marvel Comics cliché, but I hope we can become 'noble defenders of good against the forces of evil.'"

Jeremy agreed, speeding on into the night.

* * *

Jon boarded a cab to the Cambridge railway station Monday morning. Jeremy reminded him, "The suite here is for you any time you come to town. I will insist you stay here. Please phone when you get to Stanford, and let me know what you and the others have found. This stuff will not go away. I sense something really big brewing."

The two parted like old friends, having grown very close very quickly, mutually bonded in confidences.

On the train to Kings Cross Station in London, the countryside flew past in a blur as Jon processed the meeting. It was a total shocker. He and Jeremy had no choice but to venture on in this quest.

After the recent heavy doses of horror, Jon needed to treat himself his last night in London. He taxied from Kings Cross to the deluxe Rembrandt Hotel in Knightsbridge not far from his childhood home. He was given a room that overlooked England's tribute to Edwardian architecture in all its majesty—the Victoria and Albert Museum where Brompton Road changed to Cromwell Road. From his window Jon peeked further down Cromwell Road at the Natural History Museum, where he had spent countless hours as a child.

Jon decided to walk in the opposite direction toward Harrods, that famous retail establishment that embodied the Era of Empire like no other. As a boy during his family's year and a half in London, Jon remembered getting his school uniform from the boys' department at Harrods while his mother wandered the massive marble-and-alabaster perfume hall or food courts, buying quail, prime Angus or Scottish salmon. Jon planned to next spend the afternoon exploring old childhood haunts, starting with their old house on Cottage Place.

At dinner at the Brompton Grill, a block away from the hotel, Jon vowed not to dwell on the cowled dog-man as he cut into the best prime rib and Yorkshire pudding he'd ever had.

London remained for Jon the greatest city in the world. During his final night there, he sensed he would be returning in the not-too-distant future. *Make it happen*, an inner voice urged deep within.

Chapter 11

Jon boarded the streamlined Heathrow Express for the 15-minute train ride from Paddington Station to Heathrow Airport. That part of the ordeal was easy. Getting through security was another matter.

Two hours later, Jon finally passed through the elaborate airline check-in and entered the spacious departure area, with its stores and eateries. Within an hour, the overhead monitor was flashing the gate number of Jon's Virgin Atlantic flight to San Francisco.

After a long walk, Jon was screened yet again. "Do you mind putting your laptop and shoes on the conveyer?" After more painful scrutiny, they admitted Jon into the final departure lounge at the gate.

Jon remembered how as a child he had felt the thrust of sheer joy and the sense of freedom that attended international airline travel. In those more trusting days he recalled running unobstructed from the ticket counter to the entrance and into the plane. He would be greeted by smiling stewardesses who took his boarding pass and cheerfully invited him in, making him feel like somebody of importance. It was the greatest feeling in the world. The youthful Jon would feel elated as the plane flew over the Statue of Liberty heading to London or Paris. It was a much happier world in those days.

Now it was hard to travel without feeling defiled or invaded, cast more as a criminal than a valued patron, especially when leaving from American airports. You were a faceless number under escalating suspicion. Even getting from the terminal to the plane involved being screened by scowling and suspicious guards at every point, surveillance cameras everywhere.

Jon eyed the other passengers in the lounge. They waited in silent resignation. They had learned to passively accept the nonstop invasion of freedoms—the prelude to ever-greater state control in what could be a long road to serfdom. Jon had seen the hour-hand of this clock move over the years, signaling the course of history as it slouched toward world government. Nation-states became incrementally absorbed by the global leviathan, a veneer of their former stature.

The loudspeaker blared out Jon's row as he boarded the plane. Once the door closed and they began to taxi away from the gate, Jon was truly relieved to find an empty seat next to his window seat. He slowly exhaled. Virgin's latest digital screens for TV and Internet access seemed larger and offered satellite broadband. When the flight passed over Ireland, Jon e-mailed Doron and Vikram, "I've made it past the obstacle course. Now headed to San Francisco. Thumbs up—Jon."

Jon grinned when he opened an e-mail reply from the two. It carried a live feed that filled his screen. They were waving from their favorite coffee table in Palo Alto, bathed in morning sunlight. Jon noticed a Godzilla-type toy monster stalking back and forth across the coffee table between coffee mugs to the edge of the table, where its sensor would pivot it around and back again. The cam-feed showed the two pointing at the monster and saying, "It'll lead us to the monster's lair, fear not."

Doron cut in, "Jon, we will see you at the SFO terminal 15 minutes after your plane lands. It might be quicker if we met at the upper-level departure entrance if all you have are carry-ons." They flashed a cam shot of Doron's car blasting down some street so Jon knew exactly what to look for.

Next an e-mail from Jeremy caught Jon's eye in a cluster of messages, "The girls are asking about you and when you will be coming back! Don't disappoint them." Jon grinned again.

Jon flipped through the endless channels on the flat-screen TV, looking for news and sports. He stopped briefly on a live special from Iran with Howard Stern emceeing a huge hip-hop and rap concert in an outside arena filled with U.S. occupying forces, U.S. and Israeli flags flying in the background. The benefit concert was set to the frenetic movements of Islamic pilgrims projected onto a football-field-size background screen. Cameras panned the crowds of laughing soldiers as a song from *Jo-Blow and the Muvahs* chanted, "We gonna break yo ass, you towel-headed muvahs…" A scene filled the screen from some sacred Islamic site in the desert as pilgrims danced madly, flailing about in blood-stained clothes or whipping themselves bare-chested, at times writhing on the ground. Overshadowing the pilgrims was a brief image of the American flag, soon replaced by the rap artists on stage, who made mock orgy and kung-fu movements as they screamed into microphones. Then it rotated back to Howard Stern, smiling in triumph, waving the crowd on in their frenzy, his long hair blowing in the desert wind.

Jon reflected in irony that the conquered and occupied nation of Iran was being stamped into oblivion now that it "was being made safe for democracy," in the words of the latest talking head to occupy the White House. The public had been primed to gobble up any slogan and bark like seals. A rapidly moving landscape of bodies littering a desert now filled the screen as the rap music raved on. This was a far cry from the paisley psychedelic images of the Sixties that once filled screens in the Avalon or Fillmore auditoriums to songs like "Surrealistic Pillow" by Jefferson Airplane. Those early hippies and peaceniks could never have envisioned a scene like this, never. Franz Kafka's world had supplanted their naïve idealism of a benign collective.

Jon turned off the TV as an uncomfortable thought came to mind. The ultimate outcome hinged on the public's response to the mind-boggling truth once it came out. The more likely outcome would be public apathy. Jon could envision computer games of "Man-Dog" plus other creatures hidden in the bowels of Deep Earth Lab. Raucous kids would hunt down the creatures in video games while Hollywood laughed all the way to the bank.

At that point, Jon needed encouragement. He had found a paperback at the airport bookstore and grabbed the book for inspiration. The cover noted, "Learn about the heroes of early America who had faced terrible odds and remained brave against great adversity." Jon thought to himself, *That's exactly what I need right now.*

He opened the book and read how the citizenry of New England greeted Paul Revere's warning with passion and bravery, ready to sacrifice everything they had, their homes and their lives, in the fight. He pictured colonists in New England responding to Revere as he knocked on their doors. Many offered him anything he might need as they quietly summoned neighbors to hear his warnings—that the tyrants of the day were coming in full military force to capture and end their freedoms and the burgeoning young Republic. They would pay any price to keep from coming back under this tyranny.

A statement by Samuel Adams, the Father of the American Revolution, was quoted: "While the people are virtuous, they cannot be subdued. … *But when once they lose their virtue they will be ready to surrender their liberties.*"

Jon thought, *If the same people were around today, there would be a much greater chance of heading off the approaching dark horizon.* He set the book down as his mind drifted toward the sleep zone, holding in its grasp a ray of hope—that maybe he, Doron, Vikram, Jeremy and others could expose the Project and rally public outrage. As he fell asleep, images of Paul Revere were in his mind.

Jon woke up troubled. Images of the dog-man were back in his mind, along with segments from MTV—the Bondage Sisters—that he'd seen earlier. Cynicism was back in full force. Jon grimly wondered how Paul Revere would be received in present-day America.

Jon pictured Paul Revere riding into the 21st century to warn the folk about the encroaching New World Order, approaching the door of some collective group house in San Francisco's Panhandle district off Haight Street.

He might knock on a door with a Wiccan or gay/lesbian logo. A guy would open the door with a nose ring, a half-shaved skull, purple ponytail, leather pants and a studded collar. Seeing Paul Revere, he would begin laughing loudly at the door. Through the door Revere would spot semi-clothed people passing around designer drugs while others were in the middle of a sexual free-for-all. They would greet him with raucous laughter as they dragged him through the door into the lounge, wrestling him down to participate in the orgy—straights, gays and transsexuals. Paul Revere would spot his first sexual hybrid in the nude, then someone else wearing a leather mask. He would be held down while they did a "brown-out" on his uniform after forcing him to take a hit of the latest mind-rotting designer drug. After more degradation, they would release him "buggered and bull-bujambered," to continue with his warnings to a vastly depraved and indifferent world.

He would just ride into the San Francisco Bay and call it a day, Jon thought to himself. Certainly these kinds of people were perfect cannon fodder for the most ruthless techno-tyranny. After their freedoms abruptly ended under an iron fist, they would descend into conditions inconceivable to them during their era of license. They would grovel at the feet of their new masters in shrill whines, having ignored the warnings of countless voices from Solzhenitsyn, Dostoevsky, and Samuel Adams to the ancient prophets.

The pilot announced over the intercom that they were passing over Lake Tahoe at 32,000 feet and would be in the San Francisco Bay Area and on the ground within 30 minutes. "The temperature in San Francisco at the moment is 70 degrees and the sky is clear. The time is 2:15 p.m. We should be arriving at the gate a little before 3:00."

The snow-covered California Sierras came into clear view, abruptly breaking Jon's troublesome chain of thought.

Jon was now looking forward to the rapidly approaching summer in the Bay Area. If Cambridge only days ago managed to reach 57 degrees, he relished the thought of basking in the warm Palo Alto sun. Soon they were drifting over the glistening San Francisco Bay. The Golden Gate Bridge came into view as the plane headed toward the peninsula and SFO.

Jon emerged with his carry-on luggage into the bright sunlight outside the International Terminal. Scanning the approaching traffic to the left, Jon soon spotted a car flashing its headlights.

Chapter 12

Doron swung his car up the ramp to the departure level of the International Terminal. Standing by the curb was a handsome, athletic-looking fellow in Dockers and a classic dark-blue Adidas warm-up jacket. Roughly 6'3", his sandy hair blew in the breeze as he stood out against the heralded airport and blue sky like someone in the *Collegiate Hunks Calendar*. "That's Jon," Doron announced as Vikram smiled and waved an arm out the window, and got an immediate wave back. In person Jon looked even better than the pictures they'd seen of him in the apartment when they first encountered Glen.

Jon was relieved to see two smiling faces greeting him as the car pulled up to the curb only moments after he had emerged. Before they knew it, the three of them were shaking hands heartily like old friends, even though they had never met in the flesh. Jon was glad to be back in California.

Vikram loaded the bags into the empty trunk and got in the back seat, insisting Jon take the front.

Jon had his elbow out the window, soaking up the warm golden California sun as they passed hillsides and forested areas on the 280 freeway along the top of the peninsula. He was already getting a handle on Vikram, his past, his vision and goals. Clearly this was one very gifted, very likable individual who reminded Jon of a certain Indian movie star, but for the life of him he could not remember which one. The fact Jon had been to India helped him and Vikram connect effortlessly.

Jon was forced to confess that he had lived a truly charmed life, "with trips to Europe and several family vacation houses, including the obligatory Aspen ski lodge." Meanwhile, he found humorous delight behind Doron's self-effacing disclosures; the zany childhood ventures "that were like a traveling circus in some kind of bizarre social experiment."

"It seems to me that you've emerged very much intact," Jon replied.

Doron changed the subject. "Is there any place we need to stop for supplies or anything?"

"Well, now that we're approaching the Mecca for coffee connoisseurs, I need to confess a certain addiction. How about a cup of Peet's Coffee on me?" He got nods from Vikram and Doron.

For Vikram's benefit Doron became a tour guide: "Peet's Coffee began in Berkeley in the late 1960s, started by a Berkeley grad student in the plant sciences named Peet who wanted to brew the best cup of coffee on the face of the earth. He really didn't give a rip about marketing; that's why it's a Bay Area phenom with few exceptions. So he toured coffee plantations around the world, found the best beans, got a roaster and started the original store on Berkeley's Walnut and Vine. My folks went there daily when I was a kid and we lived in the neighborhood there for a while. You could smell the coffee from two blocks away." Vikram nodded appreciatively, then reminded Doron, "We've had it together more than once, remember?"

"True, true," Doron nodded, then broke away from the 280 to head to the gentrified section of Menlo Park, where there was a large Peet's branch with outdoor tables on a side street.

They grabbed a marble-topped, circular outdoor table, claiming it with coats and bags, and headed to the order counter. Jon's moment of ecstasy came when he added half-and-half to a large cup of Arabian blend mixed with Kenyan and watched the cream swirl into flecks of rich gold.

Leaning back in the sunlight, Jon took a sip and closed his eyes. The taste was earthy, layered, complex, and strong. Jon realized the air was in the perfect mid-70s.

He also noted they didn't need to talk—a sign of easy rapport—as they melted into one of California's perfect spring days.

Rejuvenated, Doron headed down El Camino Real from Menlo Park to the neighboring city of Palo Alto. Jon watched the upscale Palo Alto mall pass by as they headed to his and Glen's condominium.

The moment they drove up to the building, Glen trotted down the outside stairs, announcing, "Jon, it's great to see you. Got anything for me to take?"

"Thanks, but I've just got the one bag. Isn't it rare for you not to be at the lab? You didn't wait for me all this time, did you?" Jon probed, humoring Glen.

Doron and Vikram could see immediately that the socially awkward Glen was in a moment of "extreme Adam's apple," as Doron thought of it, looking up to Jon with a combination of envy and almost hero-worship.

Glen nervously pointed his head in the direction of Vikram and Doron. "They told me you were returning."

Jon replied, "Thanks. Good seeing you. Let's catch up when I get my sea legs." Glen nodded and took leave, heading back to the physics lab. The others left to give Jon time to regroup before dinner.

He spent a long time in the shower. Though he liked having the largest room in the place, and though Glen was a good and unobtrusive roommate, to be sure—tidy, polite and almost invisible—still Jon felt the need to have his own space as never before. Meanwhile, Jon could see that he and Glen were way overdue for their mega house-cleanup.

Jon toweled off while staring out the large window at the nearby trees and distant hills. He was glad to be back. Then his eyes fell lower to the various family photos propped against the long picture window. Looking at them from an outsider's viewpoint, Jon would see that his family was a privileged lot: happy, healthy, bright and good-looking in picture after picture. Jon, his parents, brothers and sisters were crowding together and smiling in every photo—at the Eiffel Tower, the Great Pyramids, Victoria Falls, Buckingham Palace, Lake Geneva, Fulham Crescent, their Vermont cabin, a house in Bar Harbor and the Aspen ski lodge.

Jon dressed, suddenly feeling a stab of protectiveness for them. The haunting thought entered his mind that his ventures might cast a shadow on their lives—or, worse, draw them into a descending whirlpool of death and destruction.

He left, hoping to bicycle past his favorite haunts unrecognized. But it didn't last long. He was hailed by admiring fellow students who rose up to greet the former campus star, one of Stanford's very own Rhodes Scholar hopefuls. Jon's burning goal at one time meant heavyweight crew, lacrosse, student-body government and "random acts of kindness"—in his case, genuine.

But it wasn't just all glory days. Jon passed another bit of memory lane where a few years back he had one more break-up with a girlfriend. She made a campus scene, dishing out her pain to onlookers.

There were dark things under the surface of Jon's studly life. He realized one repentant day that he had been living a lie. He had used his popularity and good looks to pick up coeds, feeding what was then becoming a sexual addiction. That was one of the things that had awakened his conscience. Jon also dreaded being controlled by lust, knowing it could betray and compromise his whole life. He also didn't want to create a string of victims like this girl, although she and the other girls were the first to assure him that any tryst was consequence-free. That too was a lie.

The clean break with the Hugh Hefner lifestyle had lasted three years and counting. It had been like an addict going cold-turkey. So far, he was happier and more satisfied than he had ever been.

Jon biked past the crossroads where the student jogger had been killed by the pickup truck. He then entered the downtown area of Palo Alto, passing the what he was pretty sure was the upscale office of the psychiatrist Spenser visited in his final days.

Bicycling back home, Jon wondered what the psychiatrist really knew; if he'd seen howling confessions too terrible to contemplate. Or was he a front-man for some group of powerful insiders?

Jon found out one interesting detail about the Palo Alto psychiatrist from one of the Cambridge Cyber gang. During a break at Ian's, a fellow named Neville Goodwin came up, saying, "I have tried to hack into the office of your roommate's psychiatrist but have run into a serious snag. His computer had very little on it. Then I found out that the doctor's confidential data is sent daily to an offsite storage facility named DataLock, Inc., in Cupertino. It's not only large corporations doing it these days. Unfortunately, I was stopped dead in my tracks and have e-mailed Doron and Vikram—who initially charged me with the task. I'm afraid they'll need to break into the facility from that end! It's state-of-the-art storage worthy of a fortress."

Jon, Doron and Vikram went to the elegant Kashmir restaurant, the top-rated Indian restaurant in the Bay Area, in nearby Mountain View. A wall-sized mural portrayed Kashmir's Dal Lake with the famed houseboats and the Shalimar Gardens backed by the Himalayan mountains rising behind them. They all shared a love for Indian food.

After the sumptuous meal, Doron drove them to a local café. On the outdoor deck, Jon offered Doron and Vikram very brief sketches of the trip: the cybercafé in Tel Aviv, where they first made contact; the Nephil dig in the Negev; Jon's encounter with Jeremy; staying at Trinity College; and finally, meeting the Cambridge Cyber gang. Jon also mentioned Neville's remark about DataLock.

"DataLock is one of the local cutting-edge companies," Doron replied. "It's a steel-and-concrete data fortress surrounded by huge walls like a maximum-security prison, prohibitively difficult even for the best hackers."

Vikram mentioned, "Uncle Ravindra uses DataLock, and there might be a way to tour the facility and check out the fortress or find other details from my uncle."

As they left the café, Doron offered, "So it's agreed. We'll have our catch-up and brainstorming sessions over the coming weekend. One option is the cabin. My mom's on a month-long trip out of state and her cabin in Monte Rio is a great getaway. It's full of guest rooms and has plenty of space for anyone who needs to go off alone."

Jon replied, "Count me in. I know that area of Sonoma and love it. Used to take my sports car near Bodega Bay."

Doron and Vikram let Jon out at his condo by 9:30 and drove off into the night.

Jon went to bed by 10:30, troubled by a recurrent thought. He was wondering if Spenser might have left yet-undiscovered clues cleverly hidden around the place.

Chapter 13

"It" was discovered Thursday afternoon, two days after Jon's return from England, during the long-planned cleanup of the condo, now a month overdue.

With Glen intentionally assigned cleaning tasks in other parts of the condo, Jon defrosted the freezer. He emptied what he could, then rolled the large fridge out to the side balcony to thaw in the sun, occasionally hosing it down to speed the process. A mound of layered ice had built up over long months.

Old peas and vegetable bags were thrown away. Freezer-burned meats and hot dogs were carefully examined and tossed into a large garbage can.

To one side in the rear of the freezer was a large yellow plastic bag belonging to their deceased roommate. Jon had thrown out his own bag before the trip, and Glen's never-used green bag sat empty in the back.

Inside Spenser's bag was a heavy-duty clear plastic freezer bag from the lab, filled with a frozen liquid surrounding an elongated object in the middle. Once thawed, the object resembled the fibrous material of a fingernail, only much larger.

Jon hid "It" immediately. His own lab at Stanford would be way too hot to examine it. He planned to send a sample to Jeremy, who could run it through rapid DNA sequencing and other tests, far from any prying eyes on this end.

Jon wondered if there was more stuff hidden.

He next pulled a tortilla Ziploc bag out of the larger yellow bag. With Glen still preoccupied, he carefully thawed the stack of tortillas under the faucet, going through them one at a time.

Suddenly a thin silver disc appeared between two tortillas. It was a silver Super-DVD capable of holding vast amounts of data. Jon felt a wave of excitement. This could be everything he'd been looking for, compiled into one big SOS from Spenser to the world; indeed, incriminating evidence worth its weight in gold. Jon concealed it immediately, while Glen was now on the lower level, cleaning the garage.

Jon and Spenser had washed out the freezer any number of times in the past, when Glen was at the lab. The freezer bag was certainly a great way to hide things to be discovered later, especially should the owner no longer be around! Spenser had probably gambled that their cleanup rituals assured a find by Jon.

Meanwhile, there was almost no way the departmental "officials" and men in black who had rushed through the condo for a 15-minute sweep would have looked in the back of freezer compartment, all solid ice. With the grieving family packing, the officials had removed books, notebooks, and a host of things from the roommate's bedroom, including the computer. But beyond the bedroom, their hands were tied. They were not dealing with a criminal suspect, and no crime had been committed, so they did not have the jurisdiction to make a full sweep of the premises. Their mission was to look for and remove all incriminating evidence in Spenser's private quarters, period.

As for the original disc Jon had burned from Spenser's computer previously, he had planned to analyze and unscramble the various files on it after his return.

Jon remembered the moment well. The day of Spenser's death, Jon sensed an open but narrowing opportunity to back up and erase the data on Spenser's computer. Glen was gone, and it was only hours after the death, long before the men in black appeared.

Now that Jon was allied with Vikram, Doron and the Cambridge hackers—some of the world's most gifted computer geniuses—he knew he had the even-better option of giving them copies of the backup disc he originally made as well as the new disc just found in the freezer.

Make copies now and quickly disseminate for safety and security.

Jon locked his door and e-mailed Jeremy an encrypted message about finding "It" in the freezer and needing DNA sequencing. He also told Jeremy that over the coming weekend he would be at the Sonoma cabin with Doron and Vikram. They'd try to teleconference from there at some point, using a secure pre-agreed encrypted protocol.

After making copies of both DVDs, Jon headed to the FedEx office in Redwood City rather than the closer ones in Palo Alto or Menlo Park. Another gut feel. Glen looked clueless, waving as Jon left.

Jon's wideband scanner indicated no police radar activity, so he raced to the Burlingame exit, whipped around, heading in the opposite direction on the 280 and exited above Redwood City near the FedEx office. The two Super-DVDs and the sample of "It" were due to be in Jeremy's hands in England by Saturday.

After the FedEx run, Jon met Doron and Vikram at their usual café table near the campus.

Jon's espresso arrived as he was filling them in on the afternoon's big discovery. "I have to give Spenser credit. He hid 'It' and the Super-DVD where he knew the men in black would never look, but where I was certain to look—the grubbiest part of the freezer."

"I really can't wait to take a look," Doron volunteered. "My guess is he's really encrypted it, and it might end up being quite a challenge to decode."

Jon handed Doron and Vikram each a packet containing their own copies of the two discs for safekeeping. "Hide these. Let's bring other copies for the trip tomorrow."

"I think while Doron looks at the discs, I'll follow up on some ideas for entering DataLock," Vikram said. "Doron's cabin is a computer hacker's dream."

Doron reminded Vikram, "Keep in mind, there could still be records left on the psychiatrist's computer that Neville may have overlooked."

"Yes, that's crossed my mind," Vikram responded.

Doron queried, "Okay, a vote. We go in my car late morning after breakfast, agreed?" They nodded.

"I'll let you vote on whether we go the slower, scenic route or the fast route after we cross the Golden Gate Bridge."

Chapter 14

Before leaving town on the trip, the three had brunch at Palo Alto's Vermont Log Cabin, the top breakfast spot in the area, where they served real maple syrup, thin French-style pancakes, old-world-breakfast link sausages, and great omelets. Doron added, "It's a contemporary of the 1960s Fat Albert's on Old Grove Street in Berkeley."

"Which is now called Fat Apple's on Martin Luther King," Jon corrected.

"Berkeley landmarks and street names," Doron continued, "usually hold religiously to the politically correct dictum of the moment."

It seemed Berkeley was intent on outdoing all other cities in open-minded acceptance in the great cultural long-distance marathon.

Jon, who'd eaten at Fat Apple's and spent considerable time in Berkeley, began visualizing the perfect emblem for Berkeley's Court-house Square—a white marble statue of a cross between *Hellraiser's* Pin-head and Queen's Freddie Mercury, in a leather outfit with a shaved skull and Mohawk, grimacing psychotically, eyes rolled back into his skull, teeth clenched in true S&M fashion as he's bending over ready to take it. Titled "Prince Henrie La Gerbil," it would be there for every truly open-minded Berkeleyite and bureaucrat entering the Court House to gaze upon in wonder and awe.

Doron laughed loud enough to draw stares as Jon described the imaginary statue. *He's definitely getting a handle on me*, Jon thought.

They left Palo Alto, heading for the Golden Gate Bridge on the 280, the less-crowded newer highway that ran along the top of the peninsula, parallel to Route 1 and Route 101.

As they approached the Bridge, Doron was critiquing their freshman year at Stanford. "I saw the pretensions of the instructors, lisping about 'the hermeneutics of doubt' and 'meta-narratives,' robbing the universe of meaning to artificially replace it with their own politically correct dictum of the moment. It soon produced a class of empty mockers, who didn't realize they were being manipulated by the system. I had been suckered into bringing some of them to the cabin, till I woke up to the fact I was being used. The concept of loyalty was not even in their vocabulary."

Doron continued, "Since my childhood I've had a sense of purpose, but it was being infected. Vikram avoided the whole thing."

"I was just trying to survive and really didn't like what I was seeing," Vikram added. "These people were wandering into an abyss."

Doron took the scenic route toward the ocean after crossing Golden Gate Bridge, going through the Rainbow Tunnel above Sausalito and descending down to the outskirts of Mill Valley where Route 1 diverted.

As they passed Stinson Beach, Jon added a little bio of his own. "As an undergrad I used to come here and surf with a group of Stanford jocks. Student-government era for me."

After a pause, it was now time for Jon to describe the high points of his trip—Israel, Cambridge, Jeremy and the Cambridge hackers. Doron and Vikram were fascinated, taking it all in.

At Bolinas Bay, Jon feasted on the old weather-beaten cafés and bars with little private jetties, a scene that resembled an Impressionist painting.

While discussing his trip, Jon mentioned, "I saw this guy named Jehovah Bob emerging from a tour bus in his Rapture suit, raving and being followed by a large crowds. I wanted to hide."

Doron cued off Jon's Israel report to interject, "I occasionally catch Jehovah Bob on the cable channel at the cabin late at night. It's worthy of *Saturday Night Live*. The fact that people would send this buffoon millions is a true indicator of the abysmal dumbing-down of the masses."

"Call it hacker's revenge: I finally did an extensive search on him," Doron continued. "I hacked his various names—old addresses, police records, school databases, changed names, court records, government records, jobs and enterprises, and other confidential information. The court records were especially interesting, as was another record at the U.S. Patent Office."

"What did you find out?" Jon asked.

"Are you ready for the unexpurgated bio?"

"Absolutely."

"Jehovah Bob was born in Biloxi, Mississippi, under the name of Earl Bosample Shifflet; his mom waitressed in bars and nightclubs and had been married four or five times. Earl flunked out of high school. He'd been a used-car salesman until he was fired for indiscretion—being found in the back of an old Buick with a prostitute—and cash discrepancy from the till. His second wife, Arlene Bossam, still has a restraining order against him going back to the period he went under the name of Ray Bossam in Fort Worth, Texas. Ray Bossam used to enter Elvis Presley look-alike contests."

Jon shook his head. "I guess that explains his walk and body movements. His entourage ate it up."

Doron went on, "At one point Earl and his brother owned an X-rated adult paraphernalia store in Norfolk, Virginia, catering to the sailors and other military folk. Next, they rented a warehouse in nearby Newport News to try distributing and launching a new brand of sex toys. It was the idea of a customer at their shop, a navy engineer from Appalachia. Some of the info was sent as a CD recording of their discussions of various ideas to the U.S. Patent Office, hoping to get a patent. These guys didn't have a clue about legal procedure. But it is still on record in the Patent Office database.

"I hacked the Patent Office database and sent a load of info anonymously to a reporter at *Rolling Stone* magazine in New York. He did an article on Jehovah Bob based on it." Vikram was clearly amused at hacker's revenge.

"The *Rolling Stone* article included all the seedy background info, including key life-changing moments. In prison he would sit for hours watching TV preachers. Bob would imitate various movements in the mirror.

"He got his 'heavenly wings' hairstyle when he was spraying a magnesium titanium-based primer on an old Chevy. According to a partner of theirs, the power sprayer slipped out of his brother Jay's hands and blasted the pre-Jehovah Bob in the hair, creating the winged effect. He looked in the mirror and said, 'I'd be one hell of a TV preacher with this. Let's call it the heavenly wings hairstyle laid on me by the holy spirit his-self, wow. I can earn millions like Robert Tilton and Smopper Bob the Evangelist!'" Doron was virtually imitating his voice.

"Jehovah Bob went public in another region of the country with a made-up bio. In nine years he's produced two books, ghostwritten of course, and now has his own private jet and TV show."

"What was the invention they sent the Patent Office?" Jon asked.

Doron pushed in a CD and looked over to Jon.

A voice recognizable as that of Jehovah Bob announced in utter awe to the other two: "It is like unto a Barbie Doll, able to talk or sing while it vibrates. Hell, it could sing the National Anthem."

Jehovah Bob's brother Jay, in trying to flatter the inventor, intoned, "Hell, I have seen my brother, verily, watch that banana vibrating, even shaking his head to it."

Willie, the engineer, then sang in Kermit the Frog dildoese.

Jehovah Bob, clearly inspired, stepped in to continue the idea. "Or we could use the voice of Gene Simmons of KISS—you know, the guy who lashes his tongue in and out. Hell, he could talk trash to 'em if that's what they wanted. These devices could double as walkie-talkies, as genuine security backup. Why, if the women were leaving a mall, say, and one was about to be raped, she could announce it to someone on the same wavelength."

Jon and Vikram just shook their heads.

"So what was the reaction from the *Rolling Stone* article?" Jon asked.

"It caused an uproar, though I'm not sure the true believers read it at all. He seems unscathed, as popular as ever."

Fifteen minutes later, Doron pulled into the cabin's private roadway on the outskirts of Monte Rio.

Jon took a deep breath, eyeing the Sonoma cabin. Fruit trees, flowers, and vines were rich in the expansive land around the cabin, which even had a "balcony seat" overlooking the Russian River in the distance, with rising redwoods looming above it on a distant summit—Bohemian Grove.

Jon immediately could see that the cabin was people-friendly, with rocking chairs and hammocks on the porch and an expansive interior that was much larger on the inside than it appeared outside. It was a true rambling-earth cabin.

Doron said to Jon, "I'll show you the house. You may notice from changing styles that various rooms have been added over the years by previous owners."

Inside, Jon noticed warm, earthy colors, wool rugs, candles, wood stoves and at least five guest rooms, a master bedroom, Doron's room, lounges, computer areas and a large central fireplace. "That's the honorary 'Citizen Kane fireplace,'" Doron added. "I used to imitate Orson Welles in it as a kid."

"It's quite something," Jon commented.

The kitchen was a thing of wonderment. A virtual herb factory, with juicers, blenders, organic this and that. The irony was that as health-conscious as Doron's mom was, pictures of her showed that she had the same pale, anemic look as so many walking the aisles of health-food stores.

To Jon, the heaps of fresh fruit were very inviting. Doron said, "By the time it hits summer, the garden becomes 'the hanging gardens of Babylon,' with everything appearing in vast quantities, from grapes to persimmons to you-name-it. She'll eat fish, but if I happen to crave steak, I just go to a restaurant to avoid the shrill arguments. Or I cook it when she's gone."

Doron looked at Jon. "Feel free to wander."

At the end of the hall, Jon went into Doron's room. The walls were like a giant scrapbook, with memorabilia, awards, quotes, and pictures from mid childhood on. A quote from *The Matrix* hung near Doron's bed:

> The Matrix is everywhere, it's all around us, even in this room. You can see it out your window, or on your television. You feel it when you go to work, or go to church or pay your taxes. It is the world that has been pulled over your eyes to blind you from the truth. ... Unfortunately, no one can be told what the Matrix is. You have to see it for yourself. —Morpheus

A jolt went through Jon as he scanned the wall near Doron's bed. A framed article on mega-gifted children included a bit on Doron:

> Doron Swift has just won England's top annual prize in computing and will be visiting Britain with his mother. ... Doron, at age twelve, was assessed to have an IQ of 200. Now at age fifteen he has just been accepted at Stanford University on a full scholarship for ultra-gifted children.

The Prometheus Society called it "the gift of fire," which was also the name of their magazine for members, a copy of which was atop a stack. A Bay Area article reported that the Prometheus Society, like *Sigma, Sigma, Sigma, Sigma* (4-Sigma), was formed to put Mensa in its rightful place. There was a greater gulf between the super-IQ groups and Mensa, as Mensa was above the normal IQ. Doron's scrapbook revealed that Doron had joined several of these super-high-IQ groups by his early teens, evidently looking for peers.

A photo of Berkeley resident Kevin Langdon, the founder of Four Sigma, an officer in the Mega Society and the Prometheus Society, was on the wall near a framed e-mail between Langdon and Doron. An article in *OMNI* magazine near the photo stated that Kevin Langdon was a member of over ten super-high-IQ groups and had invented the classic super-IQ test printed in *OMNI*. As one article stated, "If Mensa boasts of being at the .98 percentile IQ level (2 out of 100 people), the Mega Society is beyond the .9998 percentile level (1 in 1,000,000 people).

Doron had tracked down a back issue of *OMNI*, took Langdon's test and made a perfect score. The two had exchanged emails ever since. Langdon sent Olaf Stapledon's sci-fi novel *Odd John* to the young Doron with a note: "Doron, tell me the patterns you see after you have read this book. Does the fact that it was written in the early 1930s show prescience of history and to what degree? What social dislocations and upheavals does it foresee? —Kevin Langdon."

Without being too nosy, Jon could tell Doron's search for ultimate meaning propelled him to connect with other members of these groups. One of Doron's mentors was a close friend of Langdon named George Koch, a member of 4-Sigma and Prometheus, a software whiz-kid who'd made millions by his late teens with the first interactive-database company, Thesis, that he had sold to Larry Ellison of Oracle fame. Koch later became an executive vice president at Oracle, right under Ellison. Then, surprisingly, according to a *Chronicle* article, "Koch left Oracle to found a church in greater Chicago." Doron told Jon that night, "I had been intrigued by his radical transition and spiritual journey in his quest for meaning." There was a third gifted mutual friend of Koch and Langdon who had spent years in India, but left after a surprising awakening or conversion. Doron had a few of his books as well.

Jon found Doron's room fascinating, endearing and humbling. *Certainly the same search for meaning has been key in my life as well. He's a kindred soul*, Jon thought.

Jon then drifted along the long central wooden hallway, a mosaic of variant laminated woods. It was a virtual gallery of family photos, assorted pictures, newspaper clippings, Doron's childhood drawings, and bric-a-brac. One yellowed article showed Doron's mom, Linda Swift, in San Francisco's "Summer of Love," her face painted, dancing around in Golden Gate Park with Timothy Leary and the Grateful Dead in the background. *What a contrast with more recent photos,* Jon thought.

Another yellowing news clipping with portions highlighted came from the August 1999 *Sacramento Bee* by Suzanne Bohan:

MONTE RIO — The Bohemian Club's Annual Summer Encampment came to a close here Sunday, ending a two-week retreat for the rich and powerful that President Herbert Hoover once called "the greatest men's party on Earth." The club's famed annual gathering has been held for more than 100 years at the 2,700-acre Bohemian Grove in Monte Rio, about 70 miles north of San Francisco in Sonoma County. This year's event drew in notables such as former President George Bush, Texas Gov. George W. Bush, Henry Kissinger, retired Gen. Colin Powell, former House Speaker Newt Gingrich and Dow Chemical Chairman Frank Popoff...

'...There are often public policy speeches,' said Mary Moore, with Bohemian Grove Action Network, a protest group. 'And the American public is not privy to it.' Thus, it was at the Grove, it is said, that the Manhattan Project was set up and that Eisenhower was selected as the Republicans' candidate for 1952.

Doron's mom had a wicker magazine-holder mounted on the wall with various articles about Bohemian Grove—clearly one of her causes. Jon took a moment to sift through some of them. One in particular drew his attention. It was Anthony Sutton, a British scholar and a former Hoover Institute scholar at Stanford. His Phoenix Letter, quoting various sources, stated:

Up to a few months ago, we had limited knowledge of Bohemian Grove, the exclusive, elitist hideaway by supposedly adult wheeler dealers, a.k.a. Washington statesmen and prominent people (all male).

We dismissed the behavior as immature, even pitiful by emotionally disturbed juveniles and not worth attention. This is where Kissinger, Ford, Nixon, Bechtel, Bush, Cheney, Hoover and their friends (2600 members) hang out and relax. And if they want to behave as little boys that is their privilege, it is private property.

… For decades, there have been vague rumors of weird goings on in Bohemian Grove in more remote parts of its 2200 acres. Reliable reports claim Druidic like rituals, druids in red hooded robes marching in procession and chanting to the Great Owl (Moloch). A funeral pyre with 'corpses.' (Scores of men work in the Bohemian Grove as servants so this party is fairly well established.)

An article in a local community newspaper, *Santa Rosa Sun* (1993, July) reported on the Cult of Canaan and the legend of Moloch at Bohemian Grove stating, 'The Moloch Pagan Cult of Sacrifice is human sacrifice.' … In the mid-1980s there were rumors of murders in remote parts of the property. A local police investigation went nowhere.'

According to an observer and near-victim, who can describe the Bohemian Grove's inner hideaways, the closed sanctum, even the decor at secret locations, places where no outsider goes (or servants according to our sources) there is an UNDERGROUND lounge (sign spelled U.N.derground) a Dark Room, a Leather Room and a Necrophilia Room."

[quoting an observer regarding the underground room] 'Slaves of advancing age or with failed programming were sacrificially murdered at random in the wooded grounds of Bohemian Grove and I felt it was only a matter of time until it would be me.' This potential victim survived. Others reportedly did not. —Anthony Sutton

Jon continued examining the wall exhibit in the hall. There were various protest pictures featuring Doron's mom and her friends. One in front of Bohemian Grove showed a long line of limousines entering. Doron's mom held a placard about "elite businessmen pig/perverts." One of her friends, equally wasted-looking, had a photo of a giraffe with the words, "Stop flying in strange animals for your orgies. Leave these pristine creatures alone." Another placard read, "For God's sake, don't sodomize the animals." The next placard: "Stop Your Human Sacrifices Now."

Jon next noticed a small newsprint from what he assumed to be an underground paper about the sighting of a hybrid dog-man spotted walking the aisles of a local supermarket at 2 a.m. in Monte Rio with its handler. It was mid-July, during the climax of Bohemian Grove festivities. It tallied with the footage Jon had seen at Cambridge. Jon felt a distinct chill.

Chapter 15

Back from an early dinner in Monte Rio, the long-awaited moment to penetrate Deep Earth Lab had arrived. Jon was sitting slightly behind Doron and Vikram as they brought up the screen that they had not dared show a soul.

Jon watched as the fierce Indo-Tibetan gatekeeper appeared. Then came the query about the footprint of Vishnu, and then the greeting, "Welcome to the land of giants." Jon froze but didn't say anything. *This is precisely what Jeremy passed through*, Jon thought.

Next, live sequencing of DNA filled the screen with the vast flowing patterns of colored genetic material. Doron and Vikram had guessed that to venture any further required an extensive knowledge of DNA-specific molecular biology and more esoteric passwords for individual entry.

The moving screen was immediately recognizable for Jon, who was able to read DNA sequencing. His blood turned to ice for a second time that day. He now fully realized that he was looking at the identical screen that Jeremy had brought up at his secure lab in Cambridge.

Jon exerted supreme self-control, wondering to himself before injecting any of his doubts: *Is it possible that Jeremy is an insider playing me along? Or is he being used, unaware that his work is being appropriated by some stealth project? Surely it is the latter.* Jon was burning with alarm.

He also knew that Jeremy's character, his love of the good and his sacrosanct sense of honor—all clearly revealed during their mutual covenant of trust—made it virtually certain Jeremy had been used. Jon said out loud, "Jeremy has to be warned as soon as possible, for his own safety. He is being used."

The two looked stumped. Jon clarified: "I'm certain this is the identical screen that Jeremy pulled up from his secure lab at Cambridge and showed me in utter confidence, taking a considerable risk, maybe more than he was aware. I remember the cyber-sentry on that end also asking a query about the footprint of Vishnu. We need to send a QuickTime video of this to Jeremy as soon as possible. We should also tell him to be extremely cautious from this point on."

They agreed, stunned.

Doron made a digital video of the cyber-sentry and the moving DNA screen, and sent it encrypted to Jeremy. Jon imagined Jeremy's shock upon opening the file.

Though it was Friday evening in California, it was presently 4 a.m. Saturday in Cambridge—not a good time to call. But Jon wanted to have a secure conference call with Jeremy soon after he got up and had a chance to look at the file.

Doron reminded Jon, "The job of getting any farther into Deep Earth Lab's network involves the task of backing down into the broader network. We've been working on this to no avail. It's become a sort of bad joke. We don't doubt there's more, but is it worth the effort and time commitment when other approaches could bear more fruit?"

Jon reminded them, "That may be true. Also remember that the sample of 'It' was sent yesterday and is due to arrive in Cambridge in eight hours, Saturday by noon. I'm hoping Jeremy can do a quick sequencing of the sample in time to tell us something while we're still here at the cabin."

It was now 9 p.m. The three decided to take a break in the large "earth lounge"—a warm and expansive circular room with walls and ceiling built entirely of oiled and shellacked wooden panels. Half the ceiling was comprised of six large, pie-slice-shaped skylight windows that formed a grand circular window overhead, opening up the night sky like an observatory. Adjacent to it was the open kitchen.

Doron added, "Considering Mom's preoccupation with UFOs, this extra amenity comes courtesy of one of the earlier carpenter-owners, who happened to be an amateur astronomer."

In the center of the large room stood an oversized coffee table fashioned from the cross-section of a giant local redwood tree, the top laminated with clear-cast plastic over an inch thick, giving the eight-foot-diameter surface a rich, almost multidimensional look as earthy shades of brown glinted out like some ancient fern encased in amber. Surrounded by large plush lounge chairs, it was the perfect place for brainstorming sessions after they emerged from their various nooks and hideaways to regroup.

An 80-inch HD plasma screen was centered on the main lounge wall. "I won it in a contest in high school and used it mostly for video games," Doron remarked. "Mom uses it to watch the latest inverted soap operas and *Bizarre Realities* TV series (transsexual romances, couples on their 14th marriages in live therapy sessions telling all)."

The "honorary Citizen Kane" fireplace was burning pungent, aromatic wood, perfect for the cool evening. Vikram was staring off at one of the huge redwood cones mounted on the wall, formulating a kind of cathedral to nature theme for his future techno house.

Jon was contrasting the whole scene with where he had just been. *What a diverse world!* He appreciated the Sonoma cabin as much as Ian's suite in Cambridge. So utterly different.

Jon proposed, "While we're sitting here, if you've got a moment, let me show you something I have only glanced at. From what I have seen, it could provide some insight."

"Feel free," Doron and Vikram responded. Doron connected Jon's laptop to the big plasma screen.

Jon gave them some quick background perspective. "Got this off the first DVD I copied the day he died. This file was not encrypted, so I looked at it on the road. Keep in mind my roommate prided himself on being an agnostic. But suddenly he's commenting on a number of ancient documents, mostly religious, which seem far afield, at first glance, from molecular biology. I think this is seminar material. And I think it's from his earliest days with the Project. It has the feel of neophyte all over it."

The two nodded with interest, stretching back in their chairs.

The latest voice recognition software had revolutionized classroom note-taking, turning lecture material into readable text right on a laptop screen.

Projecting sequences of text from his laptop on Doron's giant screen, Jon noted, "There's one big theme here, no pun intended. Most of it seems to be in random order." The screen lit up with text.

There were giants in the earth in those days; and also after that, when the sons of God came in unto the daughters of men, and they bear children to them, the same became mighty men which were of old, men of renown.

And God saw that the wickedness of man was great in the earth, and that every imagination of the thoughts of his heart was only evil continually. And it repented the Lord that he had made man on the earth, and it grieved him at his heart.

And the Lord said, I will destroy man whom I have created from the face of the earth; both man, and beast, and the creeping thing, and the fowls of the air; for it repenteth me that I have made them. But Noah found grace in the eyes of the Lord —Genesis: 6:4-8

Jon moved to another passage from the same chapter six of Genesis.

And it came to pass, when men began to multiply on the face of the earth, and daughters were born unto them, that the sons of God saw the daughters of men that they were fair; and they took them wives of all which they chose.

And the Lord said, My spirit shall not always strive with man, for that he also is flesh: yet his days shall be an hundred and twenty years. There were giants in the earth in those days; and also after that, when the sons of God came in unto the daughters of men, and they bare children to them, the same became mighty men which were of old, men of renown.—King James Translation, Genesis 6:1-4.

Jon noted that Spenser would either highlight a special portion of a quote or simply quote it along with commentary to himself. One commentary conjectured, "Goliath—possible descendant of the Nephilim? Were there tribes of Nephilim in Canaan before then, or pre-Flood?"

Jon looked over at Doron and Vikram, and said what was obvious: "The Nephil Project!" They nodded.

"Had I read this before the trip, the project's name would have made more sense. Evidently, the Negev region was layered with history, specifically descendants of the Nephilim."

Jon next showed a short passage from the famed ancient historian Josephus:

There were left a race of giants, who had bodies so large, and countenances so entirely different from other men, that they were horrifying to the sight, and terrible to the hearing. The bones of these men are still shown to this very day, unlike any credible relations of other men—Josephus, *Antiquities:* 5.2.3.

Jon next showed a bizarre account from Frank Edwards, *Stranger Than Science*, footnoted "(New York: Lyle Stuart, 1959, p. 129)." It read, "In 1833, soldiers digging a pit at Lompock Rancho, California, unearthed a 12-foot giant with a double row of teeth, both uppers and lowers."

Jon then showed another one of his roommate's comments:

The ancient prophet Amos describes a race of ancient giants as being as 'tall as cedars'— (Amos 2:9). That would be over forty feet tall. How could such a creature be controlled or managed?

"That's something taller than a four-story building!" Vikram noted.

The following margin notes were loaded. Jon paused for emphasis, reading out loud the text on the screen, imitating his dead roommate's speech patterns:

Is there a recessive Nephilim gene pool? Need the ability to check for genome echoes in various population groups by mass genome indexing—this is a must. Need a breakthrough in this technology. Or, option two, go to the primary ancient pre-flood source— would involve deep earth layers. Deep Earth. Need expertise on where to go in Near East. Note earth's topography shifting, thus need algorithms to account for earth shifts in the hunt for dig sites. Quantify pre- and post- flood earth movement and shifting sites. Feinberg opts for former option. Others divided. Northrop has pushed for expediting this at all costs.

Next Jon showed a series of digital outlines of men: first a normal six-foot man, then several basketball greats in the seven-foot range, then a digital guesstimate of Goliath at 10 feet tall, which towered above the basketball centers. The next speculative outline was an "Anakim post-flood Nephil remnant." The outline approached 18 feet and utterly dwarfed all the others. The margin query continued, "Forty feet in height equals treetop height, thus conforming with the statement in Amos."

A man-sized creature was depicted in digital outline, eye-to-eye with the treetops towering over all the other giants. A deepening horror returned to Jon as the margin notes of the dead post-doc continued: "Antediluvian Nephilum? Source? Size? Genome base? Calculations followed comparing bone density, weight, size."

Doron and Vikram were taking it all in, hunching forward, muscles tightened.

Jon stated the obvious. "He's calculating—with respect to gravity, weight, mass and other variables of 'Nephil class giants'—the reason why such a creature would need muscle strength many times that of men on an ounce-for-ounce basis to deal effectively against gravity. Simply put, that means incredible strength. Elephants are strong but they cannot leap up into the air and click their feet. Their strength ratio to gravity grounds them."

Vikram took it from there. "A gnat with proportional strength boosted up to elephant size would be able to toss an elephant 50 city blocks. Therefore, not only was the 30-foot prototype perhaps hundreds of times heavier than a normal man, but its muscle strength per ounce of muscle, like that of a huge grizzly bear, has to be many times more powerful just so that it can stand up. This must have been a formidable creature."

Jon showed them a rather baffling margin note from the dead roommate: "Feinberg is way over his head. What a Pandora's box. Rots of Ruck in the play area."

They filed it away. Jon then showed a digital reprint of a newspaper story of a hiker in Montana who went to sleep in her tent with a package of bacon under her pillow so the bears wouldn't find it. The headless torso was discovered the next morning. It seemed the grizzly had swatted the head with enough force to send it like a hockey puck about a hundred yards.

Jon noted, "Again, a number of memos are dated around the time my roommate was first brought aboard the Project after the Fairmont event. Now, I found what I think is a much later memo. And this is a real mind-bender. It says, 'Have I seen one of these things? Can't re-

member. Missing time? Blocked memory? Are we programmed to forget?'"

This hit all three of them.

Doron challenged, "I'm dumfounded. Let's take a break and if I
come up with something, get ready to regroup." The DVDs from Jon
were a mouthwatering challenge for a super-hacker, and Doron could-
n't wait. He was fascinated with a deepening mystery.

Doron headed to his room, determined to crack one of the really
large files—which could only be a high-definition video file, considering
its size. It was on the DVD from the freezer.

Sooner than expected, Doron yelled, "Okay, I think we've got a hot
one. It's a video file. Are you ready for our Friday-night movie?"

Chapter 16

As the hour-hand in England approached 7:00 on Saturday morning, the three at the cabin were getting ready for their Friday night movie. In Cambridge, Jeremy emerged from the shower, toweled off, dressed and sat at his computer, coffee in hand. He noticed a high-priority message from Doron carrying a large attachment titled "a mystery being unveiled." It downloaded in seconds over his new fibernet connection.

On the other side of the world, the three expectantly watched the big-screen in the lounge as the hour-hand approached 11:00 Friday night. They were anxious to see what Doron had just decoded from the DVD only minutes ago.

Simultaneously, Jeremy stared at Doron's video of hacking into Deep Earth Lab's highly secure access screen. He saw the familiar Tibetan cyber-sentry, then the broiling DNA waterfall of fast sequencing. Jeremy sat stunned as he watched, feeling puzzled at first, then betrayed. The hacked entry was identical to the secure gateway he had always accessed at his Cambridge lab.

He e-mailed the three at the cabin, "Yes, it is identical in every way. What a shocker." He speculated, "We may be dealing with a top-secret multinational group conducting illegal experiments. Let's talk later, say 6 p.m. my time, so for you 10 a.m. tomorrow morning. Jon knows the code we agreed on."

Jeremy then retrieved the message Jon sent before leaving Palo Alto. Jon warned that the sample of "It" would be arriving at Cambridge by noon that day, Saturday. The message related how the mysterious sample was found hidden in the freezer.

Jeremy shot an e-mail back just minutes after his e-mail to the three of them: "Jon, I plan to be at the Trinity College porters' lodge by noon today to intercept the FedEx package. Will do an immediate DNA sequencing of 'It' and should be done before our conference call later today. As you said, it would be wiser to run the sequencing from this end at Cambridge rather than for you to suddenly appear at the Stanford lab during your leave of absence. That would draw immediate attention. I also agree with your warning about my using absolute caution on this end from here on out."

He added some troubling news. "Ian told me yesterday that the former maintenance worker, whom the two Cyber gang members previously met with, has been killed in a road accident. He was en route to his second meeting with the same two Cyber gang members. He promised to bring hard evidence. The two awaited, but the maintenance man never showed. They later discovered in the news that he'd been killed."

"The group here is in high alert and increasingly passionate about unmasking what is going on," Jeremy continued. "Jon, we need you to comeback to Cambridge!! In fact, all of us agree, we need all three of you here! Please think about it. I know it's barely been a week. More when I get the specimen sequenced. Cheers—Jeremy."

Only moments later, the three in California were soon equally stunned.

In clear, haunting detail the original film clip of the dog-man came on the screen. It was not the pixilated, badly done "copy of a copy" Jon had seen at Cambridge (which Ian also sent Vikram and Doron that night), but the razor-sharp original.

They could now see the facial expressions and quiet gasps in the audience when the hood came off. The odd expressions on the man-dog's face showed that it was clearly under some kind of trance or hypnogenic drug. "That's the face of a subnormal man," Doron observed. The dates and credits rolled by in sharp, professional detail.

"Well done in unscrambling this, Doron." Jon continued, "And I'll bet there's a lot more if Spenser was creating a databank of whistleblower stuff for life insurance. No doubt he had access to archives of the original material."

The next film clip was also of very high quality, taken on Spenser's expensive miniaturized recorder. His commentary—a low whisper— was either live or later dubbed into the digital clip.

An ornate amphitheater came into view, perhaps the same one as the earlier presentation, but redecorated.

Spenser whispered into the camcorder: "It's peak season here at Bohemian Grove, and I am at one of the most elite of the private lodges. It has an underground auditorium, where we are now, and I'm surrounded by the rich and powerful."

The master of ceremonies emerged, tall, slightly bearded and dressed in a "weekend for millionaires wardrobe for slumming it up in the wilds," as Doron observed.

A floodlight came on, directed at a dog-man dramatically caped in a black hood. It did not resemble the earlier creature. A controlled front paw brushed the hood away as the human head popped into clear view. Spenser's nervous breathing could be heard as he held the camcorder.

The human head began to talk in an almost metallic voice, attached to what appeared to be a genetically altered dog's body. The head did not flop around spasmodically, but seemed alert and more clearly part of the whole creature. Spenser speculated in whispers, "I think this is either a volunteer from the Army Rangers, or a Navy SEAL."

Then the announcer confirmed, "The major has done this as a noble act of sacrifice for the nation."

It's amazing to see the extent to which patriotism can be invoked to get men to do almost anything, Jon thought as Spenser's powerful camera zoomed in uncomfortably close.

The talking head attached to the dog had a military-type buzz cut and tough facial features common among top Marines, Seals and Special Ops Commandos. He joked with the audience, "The next time I'm with you I will be in full military dress and promise to join you for drinks." There was nervous laughter.

The emcee broke in, "The major's body is being kept alive, awaiting the reattachment procedure."

Spenser added in a later dub-in, "I learned subsequently that a sizable monetary gift for the soldier is being held in a private Swiss annuity."

The master of ceremonies admonished the audience, "We are at a place in history where we need to transcend the limitation of human forms. We need to think inter-species with open minds because great horizons lie ahead. We want to complete what some call Creation has left out. And frankly, our *Chimera program* is only one of the frontiers we are working on. The more ambitious programs need to be perfected before we bring some of our results out into the open for you to see—and, frankly, you will be astounded by some of them."

Then the emcee announced, "Fellow Bohemians and renowned guests, I suggest we all take a walk with Major Sanders, who has so bravely volunteered for the interspecies project. He will lead the way as all of us head toward the sacred owl."

Spenser whispered, "The main Sacred Owl ceremony already took place a few days ago. We had a similar feast tonight—like every night. Glad I had enough champagne to handle this!"

The master of ceremonies and the man-dog (or dog-man) led the crowd up wide stone stairs to the outside. As they emerged into the night air, towering redwoods, illuminated with spotlights, came into view, creating a sense of vastness. "It's approaching midnight, an untimely Halloween in July," Spenser intoned with an ironic whisper.

The digital camcorder was activated at various times as the assembly moved along roadway cum-nature paths, weaving through the redwoods toward the lake.

Suddenly the rumored 50-foot-high stone owl loomed into view, indeed resembling some ancient Babylonian god. The whispered narration pointed out, "It's kin to Moloch, god of the ancient Canaanites known for fire sacrifices of infants. They did that in effigy here a few days back."

The video switched to an earlier shot. Images appeared of an outdoor feast.

The next scene portrayed a massive lakeside crowd facing the huge owl on an opposing bank. It zoomed to a boat moving toward the owl. "This is the Cremation of Cares ceremony—we are seeing the effigy of a man in the boat." The effigy was placed before the massive stone owl and burned as a sacrifice.

The camera swept the onlookers. The mood of the all-male audience reminded Jon of that raucous bravado seen at post-game parties at alumni football games. Then an over-dramatized, slightly high-camp voice, worthy of a '40s ringmaster, narrated the event in a showman's hollow voice. Jon could sense his roommate was overwhelmed. "I think the count here is 800 or so VIPs participating, including three former presidents and any number of premiers, ministers of state, captains of industry and the super-rich."

Jon commented, "Well, this is the crowd that Spenser always wanted to join."

His old roommate dubbed in, "Notice the digitally highlighted participants." All of a sudden, digital markers formed glowing auras around certain individuals in the crowd as the roommate commented, "Highlighted are those whose membership in key exclusive groups intersect at least three times. They are unimaginably powerful—an inner circle within an exclusive group. Thus they would each have a three-way membership in the Bilderbergers, Trilateral Commission as well as IATA/CFR roundtable groups."

Jon thought to himself, then announced to Doron and Vikram, "He's rigged this almost like a newscast to be shown or inserted over the TV networks."

The dubbed footage concluded with, "For perspective, it has been important to view the owl ceremony. We will now return to the *Chimera* demonstration."

The camera was now at the front of the moving assemblage, with side shots of certain people as it moved ahead. Near the front, the camera revealed that the human head of the man-dog was now wearing a military-type beret.

Moving powerfully out of the shadows, the dog-man's body seemed to match that of a large Rottweiller.

The master of ceremonies was gesturing in a wide open area. The crowd began forming in a circle. Night-vision was on and Jon noticed that the area had been cordoned off with guards so no Bohemians would stroll into the demonstration.

The dog-man began marching in military fashion, like one does during a parade review before the officials' box. With both back legs marching in place, it saluted with its right front paw. Then it did several side-step marches in both directions, returning to the regular march after that, knees coming up high. It shifted to trotting in place. The emcee commented, "As some of you may be thinking, the addition of human-like arms would help, and various options are on the drawing board at Chimera, but the present prototype can still do plenty of damage, with claws closer to that of a raccoon that have great prehensile strength."

The MC continued, "This prototype can run at the enemy at roughly twice the speed of an Olympic sprinter, knock them to the ground and disembowel them quietly in seconds. It's a major breakthrough for Special Ops in ongoing global conflicts."

The whispered commentary noted, "Under present post-PATRIOT Act legislation the home front is now fully open to military incursion. The enemy could be the house next door, or you, for that matter."

The moment the emcee mentioned its speed, the man-dog tore at full speed off into the distance, then sped back, stopping and barely panting.

Off in the distance the camera zoomed in on a man wearing a padded training suit—the next target. The man-dog was on him in seconds, flattening him on the ground, and for dramatic effect it started to tear apart one of the protective cushions effortlessly, freezing as the flesh level was reached. Both got up and saluted in the direction of the crowd. There were a few controlled gasps, and Spenser shivered into the microphone.

The camera turned off in the distance. A large bull had been released from a truck and was starting to wander.

The emcee cut in, "One thing that Chimera, Inc. has done is significantly increase the strength of what would be an ordinary large Rottweiller. With hyper-dense muscle-growth factor originally based on the musculature of several high-strength animals, it now has explosive capacity. For endurance, a secondary muscle gene has been introduced from the gazelle. The present prototype can run for two hours straight at a fairly fast pace, basically matching an Olympic sprinter going at full speed. Special Ops has never known anything like this. And, of course, there are non-military applications as well."

A question was asked that was hard to hear.

"Yes, we *could* have done all this using a tiger's body, but neck disparity was a problem. We started with the Rottweiller, breeding it for human blood types and other functions decades ago. The Russians were actually ahead of us on some of this. So, yes, a tiger is possible at some point. But as you will learn down the line, there are prototypes lined up that are almost unimaginable. But they are a different project altogether, and I am not at liberty to discuss them."

With theatrical timing, the man-dog took off like a bullet toward the bull. It jumped on the animal from behind and began tearing flesh off its back in great chunks. It reached around its head from behind, and tore the throat out. It jumped off as the bull hit the ground, turned it over, and had its guts and entrails out in seconds. Quiet gasps could be heard over the mini-cam.

It raced back toward the crowd on three legs, one prehensile front paw holding an organ of some kind. The man-dog deposited what turned out to be the bull's heart in front of the emcee, who picked it up wearing latex gloves, then held it high. "Do I need to say any more?" There was stunned silence and a few mutterings. The digital clip abruptly ended.

Jon said to the others, "We've got to send Jeremy this as well. I am willing to gamble he has seen the master of ceremonies at the black-tie event at the Fairmont."

Doron added, "I bet that if I scanned the Forbes 400 list, I could come up with the announcer as well as others on this footage."

Doron then had a morbid vision of his mom finding the DVD, slipping it into the player while she sipped chamomile tea, then seeing the man-dog trotting up toward the camera. She would go howling out into the night like a banshee, needing extra aromatherapy and Rolfing over the succeeding weeks. The next Bohemian Grove picket line sign would say, "Leave the Severed Heads Alone."

It had been a long day, and midnight had since passed.

Doron proposed, "Sleep in and regroup at your leisure. That's assuming you can get to sleep."

Chapter 17

By 8 a.m., as the others appeared, Jon offered up his morning gift—Peet's ultra-fine-grind blend of Java & Kenyan coffees slowly dripped through a paper filter, with Maui large-grained unprocessed sugar, topped off with Horizon organic cream. "This is the one addiction I have left," Jon volunteered.

"This might be the best cup of coffee I've ever had," Doron confessed as Vikram gave the thumbs-up.

It was a clear, warm, spring morning, and after they'd wandered the garden and orchards drinking their coffee, they assembled in the den. Doron hit the Play button as they sat back in their chairs.

It was Spenser's second large file, decoded from the freezer DVD that morning.

On screen, a large, airy, elegant room flooded with bright sunlight coming in through multi-windowed wall sections, half open. People strolled in and out from the garden.

The video cam zoomed outside, revealing a perfectly manicured lawn bordered by flowers, exotic trees and fountains stretching off into the distance. "Estate … old money…" the three chimed in. It was the private world of the elites.

It was a familiar world to Jon, who had grown up as a member of the Social Register, with extended family in Connecticut and New York. Jon had attended similar gatherings in some of the most elegant estates in the country. He had a feel for what was on the screen. What they were seeing was impressive. It also reminded him of how old money found various ways to touch the darker side of existence.

Forty or so people were returning to their seats. The chairs and couches were diverse and elegant antiques, predominantly bright, silk-covered, 18th- and 19th-century French period pieces.

The host walked up to the podium. Donned in an expensive silk shirt and ascot, he resembled a character out of F. Scott Fitzgerald. He signaled an end to the recess, beckoning stragglers back inside with a grandiose motion as the outside loudspeakers played reveille.

Turning to the very upper-crust-looking fellow beside him, the announcer said, "Well, back with us again—and I am not including his brief words last night at the Fairmont—is Lord, or should I say Professor, Northrop of Oxford University. He is one of our very own guiding lights, who has from the early days of the Project provided us with that vital bridge between his fields of paleontology, anthropology and archaeology, and the specialized field of the rest of you present who are not among our billionaire supporters—molecular biology." Awkward laughter from the academic have-nots provided a pause.

The host continued, "I might add that Lord Northrop is not only an internationally recognized authority in his academic specialties, but he is also a member of England's nobility—an earl, no less—and quite a landowner, I might add, should you ever get the privilege of grouse- or duck-hunting on one of his estates. Lord Northrop has supplied us with material far more valuable than gold or diamonds, as those of you who are new with us will find out soon enough.

"Lord Northrop is presently chairman of the department of anthropology at Oxford University. He fits neatly into that English tradition of aristocrats who have pursued knowledge for its own sake because money was never an issue. Let me move aside and relinquish the microphone." Polite applause.

In patrician English, the English lord and Oxford don smoothly began with an Etonian lilt, "Trusted and valued colleagues, I am here to give you the latest report from the front lines of our various digs in the Near East. I also hope to give you some perspective on our mining of the earth's deep riches, truly riches far more valuable than the treasures of King Solomon. The riches we are speaking of have for so long been hidden away deep in the earth's soil. They don't glitter like gold, and in prior ages someone finding them, ignorant of their value, would most likely toss these unremarkable objects back into the soil. That's the riddle, isn't it!" He paused, looking around.

Lord Northrop continued, "These very rare, unremarkable-looking, sepia-colored objects that emerge from the earth harbor the power, vastness and inexhaustible range of DNA, but a special DNA, seemingly programmed by the gods. The DNA we are searching for, I will argue today, is in some ways vastly superior to our own. As such it can be spoken of as a kind of Holy Grail." He paused to take a drink.

"He's definitely gaining a hold here," Vikram remarked. "Reminds me of a stage hypnotist."

With a note of distrust, Doron added, "At minimum he gives a pretty good upscale Amway pep talk."

Rapidly moving subtitles—a running commentary courtesy of Jon's old roommate Spenser—flashed past in the lower part of the screen. It was an effective way to include information-laden background material.

"I'll send this to Jeremy and Ian when we're done watching it," Doron cut in. "We need to direct them to his estate for information mining."

"I wouldn't be surprised if they've already preempted us on that," Vikram responded. "Nirmalli e-mailed me that they'd identified the British archaeologist that 'Sabra One' spoke of. I'm sure it's this same fellow."

The don now divulged the true value of the hidden DNA: "The Flood was the great event that hid the DNA deep in the earth. I have mapped probable hot-zones using Oxford's computer department in tandem with my own department. None of them has the slightest clue as to what is going on. I have created a coded map, and that, dear colleagues, is what guides our various digs. Our search for antediluvian DNA will bring back to the earth some awesome, even terrible powers—the power of extended lives, what we call Methuselah DNA, and the ancient race of giants, the ancient gods of lore, who walked the earth and had unspeakable strength as well as other powers. I imagine they could throw together the great pyramids the way a child makes a sand castle on the beach.

"You can imagine how such strength could be harnessed today, from the war front to space exploration. Yes, I have even thought of having a few of these recreated ancient gods at the gate of my estate. Then you don't need to post 'no trespassing' signs. People would run as fast as they can." Nervous laughter.

Jon commented, "Lord Northrop is going beyond theory at this point. The old boy has seen a giant or two already, I'll bet."

Northrop outlined the trail of evidence from ancient mythology to fact. "I have spent a lifetime looking beyond bits of mythology and eyewitness accounts in ancient documents. Hidden in these texts are great possibilities. The ancient gods, whether Greek, Vedic, Egyptian, Babylonian or Mesopotamian, were convenient religious images to describe a truly baffling phenomenon; how these gods were produced by something very strange—the cohabitation of spiritual beings, who had somehow materialized, with earthly women." The speaker let an extended silence punctuate the moment as he pursed his lips again after a sip of burgundy.

With a kind of depraved excitement, Northrop went on: "The byproducts of these so-called supernatural copulations were inevitably described as giants or gods. And by their physical size and stature, they must have been terrible to behold. The ancient record in Genesis describes it the most clearly. It says that 'the sons of God saw the daughters of men, that they were fair, and entered them.' It is a tenable theory that these so-called 'sons of God,' often described as angels, were another magnitude of beings, most probably very superior to us. The result of this union was a race of giants. Does this mean we accept biblical authority and belief? Not at all. They were merely overlaying the myths of their time to explain a certain phenomenon."

Earl Northrop paused again, and then continued, "Probing beneath the myths, we have a being mysteriously created by the melding of substance from what are called spiritual or interdimensional beings able to enter our world and humans.

"Their progeny, the giants, had to be very intimidating; in fact, so powerful there is the biblical myth of a jealous tribal god sending the earth a flood to wipe them out. Freud explained how this tribal god was simply a primitive projection. The disaster hits, the giants perish, and the name of Jehovah is invoked." He took another long swig from the wine glass as his lips remained slightly more wine-colored.

"He's beginning to resemble Willem Dafoe in *Nosferatu*," Doron intoned.

The Oxford professor kept eyeing a group of younger men to the front on one side. "It is natural that these mysterious giants are spoken of with religious language. The more powerful they are, the more godlike they become. Maybe this was the early beginnings of a master race had they survived—but they didn't. Something killed them. Now, the biblical report tells us that God killed them because—and here we get the worst sort of biblical language filled with all kinds of moral value judgments—they were judged as 'abominations,' or 'evil.' God's judgment is then displayed when these beings perished in a natural disaster, a flood."

"Or, perhaps it did happen just as the biblical record explains—because these creatures *were* in fact evil," Jon muttered, thinking of his missionary aunt and uncle.

Northrop soon entered new territory: "I want to talk about another jewel we are after, lying beside the other fossils. The Methuselah account illustrates another kind of antediluvian DNA. It seems people at one time lived much longer lives. I don't know about you, but I would love hanging around the old estate for another 500 years or so without having to undergo transfusions from Dracula." He winked.

Jon pictured the earl at age 800 at his crumbling estate, a face like a mummy, senile as a pickle, and ranting at the unworthy while spitting on them from his balcony, a butler poised behind him with a wheelchair.

Doron yelled at Northrop on the screen above, "What about Alzheimer's? That can ravage your brain in only a few years. So what do you think you'll do hundreds of years after the fact? Blither and drool in some padded cell? Sounds more like hell to me."

"Mad dogs and Englishmen, out in the noonday sun," Vikram half intoned, from the era of the British Raj.

Northrop—oblivious of his critics at the Sonoma cabin—continued his excited sales pitch after a large swig on the old goblet following a fourth filling. He pursed his lips and told them, "Finally, we in the Project believe that fossils from the Methuselah era harbors the holy grail of DNA! The intersection of the ancient world with modern science could bring us this miraculous treasure. It could revamp our genetic makeup, extend our lives and give us powers unimaginable!" Applause.

"How many of these people have made their initial down-payments on the immortality serum?" Vikram wondered aloud.

"You mean the Muthboozallahh Formula," Doron replied, his mouth twitching in mock senility.

Northrop gave the closing challenge: "Some of us who have vision may live to see not only the next century, but a number of centuries to follow. We can live life to the hilt, invest in the market not just over decades, but centuries, providing untold wealth. We can master literature, we can span the vast range of human thought and stretch our earthly senses to their limits, and we, my colleagues, *will be as gods upon the earth.*" His voice shuddered with delicious expectation, his eyes now lowering to trouser height of those young men on the front row.

The date at the end of the video confirmed it was filmed right after the black-tie affair at the Fairmont.

Doron sent Ian and Jeremy the video of Northrop, along with a message from Jon: "Keep a lid on this. We can't chance any leaks, too risky."

Jon confessed to Doron, "I definitely don't want to see Jeremy reported in the news as a suicide found strung up under Blackfriar's Bridge."

They retired to the garden after going off to lunch. The scent of flowers, fruit trees and aromatic herbs wafted around them in a gentle breeze—a safe zone that none of them wanted to leave.

Vikram reflected out loud from his deck chair, "The earth could soon see the appearance of these giants."

"Technically it would be *the return of the giants*," Jon corrected.

"For that matter, the giants may have already returned," Doron added.

He then reminded them, "Conference call with Cambridge within the hour."

Chapter 18

Half a world away, Cambridge had been ramping up as well.

When Jon was doing the mega housecleaning, the core leaders of the Cambridge hackers discreetly gathered in a lower room at the Anchor Pub. Ian had called the meeting suddenly, just hours after the retired maintenance worker had been killed en route to the rendezvous with the Cyber gang—the latest in a grim string of events.

The core leaders sat at Ian's favorite corner table beneath a large poster of a WWII RAF pilot in a leather bomber jacket, giving the thumbs-up from the cockpit of a vintage airplane.

As he looked up at the poster, Ian challenged them, "Most of these brave RAF pilots and British commandos gave their lives when they were the same age as most of us! ... Vikram and Doron never boasted about penetrating what none of us could hack. But I discovered that their motivation had shifted from gaining some dubious trophy on the scoreboard of hacker superstardom to something far larger and more noble. And this is what we need to remember for ourselves.

"We need to find this beast, then drag it out into the sunlight, and we need to do this by remembering those virtues that once made England great. Intelligence alone won't do the job."

He shifted gears. "It is beginning to look like Britain has been where the really outrageous stuff has been going on all along—and not the States.

"The dog-man project was one thing; true giants another. Britain's forested areas are still shrouded. In England, most forested land belongs to the government or private estates and is strictly off-limits to the public."

"One communiqué I retrieved was taken from the DVD Jon brought with him on his trip, the backup of his dead roommate's computer. Jon gave it to me briefly when he and Jeremy had dinner at my place before last Sunday's gathering. It stated, 'Britons are still under a lower surveillance level than Americans and are able to put up with more aggravation and inconvenience while remaining less likely to pry or protest—a safer cushion for the Project, especially should unfortunate incidents occur. California, especially the Bay Area, has no cushion. Furthermore, given the predatory and opportunistic nature of the American media, any breach would become instant news; the more shocking, the more obsessive the media would become.'"

Under his solemn challenge, Ian looked at each member at the table and asked, "Are you willing to put your life on the line, like this RAF pilot pictured here on the wall, to root out this enemy?"

Each answered, "I do, for the love of England, I do," then they had a final toast.

Before going to bed, Jeremy e-mailed Jon just as he was racing off to FedEx "It" and the DVDs to Cambridge: "It was time for the core leaders of the Cambridge Cyber gang, plus yours truly, to ante up for the nation that we have loved so dearly in that almost mystical way common among Englishmen. It's the politicians, not the people, who have transnational allegiances and secret pacts, auctioning off our land and heritage to the Euro State for a pittance. Our heritage, as you know from having lived here, is unique in all the world. Our tiny island once governed an empire over which the sun never set. But, we've lost our national soul and barely get glimpses of the sun these days.

"Things are moving quickly. The third floor of Ian's manor house has been converted to resemble one of those British code-breaking facilities from World War II. More soon. Take Care—Jeremy."

* * *

By Saturday evening in Britain, Ian and Jeremy awaited the video conference with Jon, Doron and Vikram, who had just come in from the garden and were ready to go.

Ian and Jeremy had just watched the newer version of the dog-man in Bohemian Grove as well as Lord Northrop's talk, whose estate they had been closely monitoring for some time. The Americans had no idea of this.

The screen in the Roundtable room at Ian's (now called Roundtable East) suddenly came alive. Ian and Jeremy saw Jon, Vikram and Doron seated at a large redwood table in a kind of nature sanctuary. They waved.

Ian and Jeremy switched the video cam at their end to remote so that Roundtable West could see the grand hall.

Vikram and Doron realized they were seeing an old English Roundtable from the era of jousting knights. On the wall behind were mounted broadswords; to the side stood two full, glistening suits of armor.

Doron said, "That is definitely a Knights of the Roundtable room! Impressive. It looks like something out of the British museum."

"Yes, this is all family heraldry," Ian countered. "Our little bit of English history." He then began, "Jeremy has e-mailed you about the secret meeting at the Anchor Pub and the vows among our inner-circle members to maintain absolute secrecy. Though Jeremy has not been a formal member of the Cyber gang—'I'm not really a hacker,' Jeremy confessed—he is a trusted advisor and an honorary inner-circle member."

Ian continued, "Most of us would be blind guides in the field of molecular biology without Jeremy."

"Ditto for Jon and his range of gifts, among them molecular biology," Vikram and Doron confessed.

Anticipating a question from the Northrop video, Jeremy spoke up: "First of all, in case you are wondering, Lord Northrop was at the black-tie affair at the Fairmont Hotel. I met him briefly. And I think I've seen him lurking about some of the high-level meetings here in Britain. I just didn't really know who he was then. … I am assuming Northrop's lecture was nearby after the Fairmont event."

Jon nodded. "That's right. We think it was at the Mountain View estate where some went after the Fairmont."

Turning toward Jeremy on the monitor, Jon asked, "Did you get the sample?"

"Yes," Jeremy confirmed. "It arrived by noon, and I went straight to the lab earlier today."

"We're all ears."

"I got results, and it's a bit of a shocker. I did an age analysis before the sequencing and found out, first of all, that it was a recently living sample, ten or 15 years old at the most. The second thing I found out was that it is identical to one of our 'benchmark genome configurations' that the rapid sequencer is programmed to run comparisons against. These are genomes of such unique configuration that the rapid sequencer is constantly looking for anything close! When a sample comes within range, it sends off a loud buzzer. Such 'benchmark genome configurations' are *almost* human. At the same time, they have properties that have never been found in the human genome. I have assumed our benchmark configurations were ideal equivalents, or perhaps based on some primeval X-sample."

He confided, "Keep in mind, just because we can strip down the DNA doesn't mean we see the big picture right away. When I saw the video clip today of Northrop, I immediately realized he must have been the source of the samples for our lab. The lab treats this as a top-secret project. Those in the lab have not asked questions in the past; we've merely worked hard in processing samples that have come in. We're never told where they come from. It's been a 'for God and country' sort of thing."

Jeremy paused, searching for the right way to phrase it: "We have hit what we call the alarm buzzer perhaps 15 times in two or three years, as far as I can remember. I don't know whether these buzzer samples were antediluvian or not. I gather that they were from the ancient world. After hearing Northrop discuss the Nephil digs, it's obvious from where these top-secret samples have been coming all along—the Negev and places in the Middle East."

Moving into speculation, he continued, "We now know those alarm buzzers went off when a sample had been detected with either the Methuselah gene or the full genome of some ancient giant. I figure the lab has wanted to use my search algorithms for DNA shadows to build a mock-up genome of what we could call pure DNA from a pre-flood-stage Nephilim. I will guess right now that such a sample then goes to another lab for replication and to be cloned."

Jon, who had guessed the whole process with a glimpse, felt a powerful urge to ride his BMW motorcycle as fast as he could—to wind back the recording of time and history itself, hit pause, and start the sequence all over again, hoping that this time he would find that recent events had never happened. When he got home, he would just say "hi" to Spenser, hardly skipping a beat, just glad that the cosmos hit the big Replay button and averted a total disaster.

He was brought back as Jeremy concluded in regret, "I feel as though I have been an unwilling accomplice in this whole thing. My rapid sequencing and single-minded efforts have served only to hasten the Project's goals."

There was silence as the five mentally raced through options and solutions—five geniuses going at near-light speeds, a continent apart, connected in thought and purpose. Most assuredly, they would use their collective talents. For now they needed to continue what Jon's former roommate had begun before his death—gathering sufficient and undeniable evidence in tracking down the beast.

Jon broke in, "The second DVD, the one I found in the freezer, is now declared open season for all hackers. Jeremy, you've doubtless given a copy to Ian. Let your trusted inner circle have a go at it as well."

Vikram was asked about progress on his end. "I am close to entering DataLock, thanks to my uncle. He has a DataLock account and I have permission to piggyback his computer. He also gave me critical passcode information."

In a comedic break, Ian showed a brief segment of surveillance video of Lord Northrop at his estate. "We've known of him for some time," Ian said, hitting the Play button.

The earl was dressed as a true dandy, mincing down some hallway. It ended with a shot of him lecturing his dog, making exaggerated facial expressions of disapproval. Jon could tell this was a databank rich with material.

"Think of this as a diversion courtesy of the Cambridge hackers. Anything involving Oxford is fair game to those of us at Cambridge."

"I'm not sure Oxford will ever live this down," Doron replied.

Ian and Jeremy then made an urgent formal motion: "Gentlemen, given the nature of what we are dealing with, the three of you are needed here in Cambridge as soon as possible."

To lure them more, Ian sweetened the pot. "Gentlemen, I offer you my family's most regal guest quarters of your choosing, from grand individual rooms on one discreet hall to a stately cottage on the grounds, surrounded by a private, gated garden. I will even throw in private butlers, if it takes that!"

Jeremy added his confirmation: "They are truly stunning. But, Jon, I expect you to stay with me at Trinity." He again reminded Jon, "And keep in mind, the girls have asked about you a third time now."

Vikram and Doron turned their heads toward Jon in mock surprise. Ian grinned on the monitor as he watched the two react.

Vikram confessed, "We need time to tie things up—at least for Doron and me. We are in the accelerated doctoral program, and it tends to be top-heavy. Let us see what we can do. Also, don't forget, the second DVD might shift the entire equation back to the States, depending on what we find."

"True enough," Ian admitted. "I haven't had time to get to it yet."

It was now 10:00 Saturday night in Cambridge and 2 p.m. at the Sonoma cabin.

"Let's regroup again tomorrow, Sunday, perhaps a few hours earlier?" Ian probed. The others agreed.

Ian and Jeremy signed off. "Till tomorrow, gentlemen. And seriously, please consider coming to England!"

Jeremy e-mailed Jon later that night, "The Cambridge hackers here know they have huge talents in their midst, but they are also realistic enough to recognize the sheer brilliance of Doron and Vikram. They see your brilliance is of a different nature but of equal magnitude and equally as crucial. Now think about a return trip, eh, Mate?"

After the video conference ended, Jon pictured Jeremy in his Austin-Healey 3000, speeding in the late evening through Ian's gate and down country lanes back to Trinity College.

Chapter 19

An hour and a half after signing off with Ian and Jeremy, Vikram announced, "It's done!"

Doron and Jon looked at Vikram as he entered the den.

"I just penetrated DataLock and accessed the psychiatrist's files. So far, it seems to contain scanned written notes, voice records and a stream of separate video logs of the live sessions filmed from a remote mini-cam—I would guess hidden in the wall of the office behind a painting, the lens camouflaged in the painting."

"You are a true wizard," Jon responded. "I can't wait."

Doron made a gesture of obeisance.

As the others gathered in expectation, Vikram hooked his portable computer to the 80-inch HD plasma in the lounge. "I made a very quick entry and exit, downloading what seemed the most relevant file data, hopefully leaving no footprints behind."

All of them knew stiff federal laws were now in place, after America's long-standing war on terrorism, that could easily get Vikram incarcerated, if not kicked out of the country.

The screen in the lounge lit up with a wide-angle view of the psychiatrist's office in Palo Alto.

Jon felt an immediate jolt as his deceased roommate, Spenser, appeared on screen. He was sitting in a leather lounge chair, facing the psychiatrist. He was cradling his head in his hands as though either weeping, fighting a headache, or in grief. They were conversing about the recurrent nightmares, which were getting worse.

"I just think I saw a monster, a real monster at some point," Spenser insisted. "I believe the nightmares are a memory trying to get through."

All of a sudden the psychiatrist uttered a cryptic phrase— *"The truly gifted are able to walk on rainbows."*

Spenser's demeanor instantly changed. He lifted his head, sat back, and appeared to be under a powerful trance.

"It's almost like watching a multiple personality," Doron interjected.

Dr. Lederberg addressed Spenser: "What you think are memories of monsters appearing in your dreams are no more than just nightmares. You have not seen any monsters in real life; you are dreaming them. ... What did I just tell you?"

"My memories of seeing monsters are just nightmares. I never really saw them."

"That is correct—you never really saw them. They are only dreams. Now we need to go deeper, so I will begin the countdown." The psychiatrist started to count backward as Spenser's eyes closed.

"Have you shared these thoughts with anyone?"

"No. I have kept the vow. I have not spoken to anyone about any matter relating to my work at Deep Earth Lab."

"You know that your vow is for life. Should you ever try to break it or run from it, you are to phone me for advice. You know you can always come to me about any matters. Never forget, you always have a safe place to go. You can take Exit One, Exit One, I repeat, Exit One."

"Yes, I can take Exit One."

"Doubtless he means Route One over the cliffs and into the sea," Jon commented. "No need for hired assassins." The others nodded grimly.

The psychiatrist continued, "You have a safe place with Exit One. It is always there waiting for you, should you need it. If you get an indication from me that it is now time to take Exit One, what does that mean?"

"I am to drive to Exit One and take it."

"That is correct. You will enter a zone of total safety. It is a doorway safe from all things frightening. They cannot get to you once you have taken it. What did I just say? Confirm, confirm, confirm."

"Exit One is the doorway to safety, safe from all monsters."

"That is correct."

The psychiatrist continued: "The giant you think you saw in England was only a nightmare. It was a result of food poisoning. Remember, you ordered mussels and they were contaminated. That was the cause of your first nightmare. Do you remember eating mussels for dinner?"

"I remember now, that is what happened. I ate mussels, then got food poisoning. That caused my first nightmare."

"That is correct. It had nothing to do with Deep Earth Lab. It was just a nightmare from food poisoning. ... Remember that the imagery of your nightmare came from a movie you saw as a child. It was not real.

Deep Earth Lab exists to help people, to help people, to help people. …
Deep Earth Lab has accepted you as a member of the family. It will protect you. If you have questions, phone me."

"I will phone you."

Dr. Lederberg suddenly opened his armrest and hit a button on a
control panel beneath it. A door behind his desk, presumably to a private
office, opened as five men entered quietly. They sat around the subject
in surrounding chairs.

Spenser was commanded to look at each man for five seconds and
repeat, "I un-remember this face. I have never seen this face before."
This ritual took a few minutes.

The young Stanford scholar again closed his eyes as directed. The
five men silently exited out the same door. Doron made a mental note to
capture the faces and run a rapid digital comparison through various
databases. Jon had the same idea, only sending them to his brother at
the FBI instead—indeed, sending the whole series of sessions to him.

"You know never to reveal anything to those outside the Project,"
Dr. Lederberg commanded. "That would compromise the very important work of Deep Earth Lab, and you have promised total secrecy. Do
you remember your blood oath? Would you repeat it?"

"Yes, my life and my honor reside within the covenant. I am to tell
no person anything pertaining to Deep Earth Lab outside the covenant
as long as I live, as long as I live, as long as I live."

"When you wake up, you will have no memories of this session. You
will recall the Model 15 session that you have enjoyed watching, the
Model 15 session, the Model 15 session. That will be our session, the
Model 15 session. You will now wake up feeling true peace of mind. You
will feel pretty good, pretty good, pretty good." The countdown began
as the roommate awoke as though catching himself dozing off and feeling apologetic about it. He yawned.

"How do you feel?" the psychiatrist asked, smiling benignly.

"I feel pretty good. I am sorry I may have nodded off," Spenser responded apologetically.

"That's okay, you've been working hard. Remember, there are no
problems we cannot solve together. Go out and have a great day. I will
see you next week at this time?"

"Yes, I will come next week at the same time," Spenser confirmed.

Vikram stopped the video.

"For one thing," Jon speculated, "he would certainly look for objective evidence beyond his nightmares—say, in the archives of the Project or from fellow workers. Any clue that it was real would cause him to doubt the psychiatrist."

Doron added, "I also wouldn't be surprised if his initial trance was caused by one of the latest hypnogenic drugs, courtesy of our military spreading democracy."

Jon agreed. "My brother has seen these compounds at work in the FBI. They can crack the mind wide open. Planting a suicide command would be easy, and they've done it. That was what the House Committee investigating this new drug group discovered."

"There was one cryptic note on the disk about 'Can't trust him. Need a second opinion. Is he toying with my brain?'" Jon then related. "His diary notes mentioned his concern over missing time and odd fitting memories of the sessions as though spliced together. He called it 'trick-time.'"

Pondering this, Doron said, "It makes sense that, at one point, Spenser may have recorded the audio portion of these sessions with the psychiatrist as a means of double-checking them later to see what was really going on. Miniature digital audio recorders would be easy to hide."

"I've wondered about the same thing," Jon elaborated. "A hidden recorder would solve the dilemma regarding tangible evidence. If he heard the shrink initiate the programming mode or plant a false memory, I'm sure he would go into survival mode. He would play dumb as he gathered evidence on the sly. He would also start looking for an escape route other than Exit One."

Vikram wondered, "Could hearing his stealth recording of the hypnotic session undo the programming—like breaking a spell?"

"Probably not," Doron replied, "but it would scare the life out of him. Once he discovered the suicide programming, he would be aware that he was in reality walking a minefield."

"He would need to find a way to defeat the suicide programming," Vikram amended. "He'd also realize that if he stopped the sessions, it would signal the psychiatrist."

Jon paused in thought. "Spenser may have found a way to get around the literal command. Remember, the covenant was to speak to no *person*. He could talk to an inanimate object like a video recorder, fooling his mind and telling himself that it was intended for no one. It might have eluded the psychiatrist who programmed him to whistle-blow on him-self for talking to a person."

Vikram mused, " By the time he left the DVD in the freezer, he must have felt the powers of hell on his back. I wonder if he went to another shrink to see if he could be reverse-programmed or de-hypnotized?"

"Maybe, if he could do this without awakening the whistle-blower programming," Jon responded, blotting his brow. Seeing his former roommate so vulnerable before this unspeakably evil mind-trap filled Jon with outrage. Jon thought of the fragile, bird-like Rosemary in *Rose-mary's Baby* trying to flee the Manhattan coven, but winding up back in the office of her obstetrician, Abraham Saperstein, a leader in the coven. She was caught like a fly to flypaper.

The session quickly ended after jumping through several other video segments.

Vikram sent what they'd just seen to Ian and Jeremy in Cambridge. "Confidential for now."

It was time for a radical change in atmosphere. Jon, Doron and Vikram went speeding off to Sebastopol, through 40 miles of prime Sonoma countryside, to a beer-and-burger joint for dinner.

On the return trip home, Jon was asked about his brother, Jack, in the FBI.

"First of all, don't think I haven't had Jack in mind for when the time is right. He's already agreed to check into the suspicious circumstances surrounding Spenser's death. Jack joined the FBI around the time I first started grad school at Stanford. He's an honorable guy, the type who al-ways comes through in a crunch, just like my father. He did a tour of duty in the Marines before law school. He chose the FBI over private law practice after seeing America's taste for frivolous lawsuits, bank-rupting businesses and wrecking lives. His big mantra has been, 'The legal system and courts are not about the truth anymore.' Jack's an old-school idealist."

Jon then confessed, "You may as well know this in case anything hap-pens to me. Dad arranged sizable living trusts for me, Jack and my sis-ter to be in diversified accounts offshore. My first trust monies were put in a Swiss annuity set up by my father when I was in my teens and we were living in London. There are other trusts. I used one of the trusts for my last trip."

Getting to the next point, Jon said, "I've been pondering about making a secure contact with Jack, to tell him the whole story in case any of us, or all of us, mysteriously disappear. Our challenge will be to secure evidence that is admissible. That's where Jack comes in. I think we already have enough data to give probable cause. We need to provide Jack a way to discover the evidence and legitimize it through the FBI without any trail leading back to us."

"I think we can do that," Doron concurred, adding, "Speaking of evidence, as a security backup, I want to send the decoded files from the second DVD to Jeremy and Ian before we leave the cabin tomorrow morning. I meant to tell you both I'd decoded most of the stuff. I'll tie things up before we go to bed, if I have the energy."

As Doron pulled up to the drive at 10 p.m., Jon challenged, "Will you guys think seriously about going to England?"

"Well, apart from finances and papers, we should be good to go, at least I would," Doron replied.

"Truthfully, I would love to go. But let me think about it," Vikram answered, heading to his bedroom.

Chapter 20

At 10 a.m. Sunday, as the video conference with Ian and Jeremy began, Jon announced, "Gentlemen, we accept your invitation. It seems we have no choice but to head your way as soon as possible."

Before anyone could say more, Jon looked at Doron and Vikram and added, "I will be covering the cost of the trip and will not take 'no' for an answer." The two shrugged a "well, okay," looking cheerful.

Ian didn't waste a second. "Your rooms will be ready here at the manor." Now adding further temptation to mock-lure Jon and play with Jeremy's mind, "Would you like private butlers?"

Jeremy immediately cut in and looked at Jon. "Don't forget, your room at the suite is eagerly awaiting your return. No defections to Ian's manor, even though it may be far more glamorous than anything I can offer!"

Jon graciously assured him, "I am honored to return." Then before breaking off, he reminded them, "We're about to watch the what may be the main segment from the freezer DVD before returning to Palo Alto. This may be Spenser's ultimate message in a bottle."

And it was. The three drove back in stunned silence. What they had just watched was unthinkable. "It's truly out of some alien universe," Jon remarked, breaking the silence. "It's really more than I ever bargained for." Doron and Vikram barely managed a grunt, their faces lost in thought.

* * *

Vikram sat in a prime window seat looking out as Virgin Atlantic Flight 120 to London passed above the California Sierra Nevadas in the initial climb. Clear streams, lakes and pure natural springs flowed across a pristine wilderness far below. It was unlike anything in Vikram's native India, where pollution and overcrowding sullied even the most remote areas.

To Vikram, the rock faces below spoke of the thousand ways to die that the early gold prospectors faced crossing these slopes—all for a few ounces of gold. The present journey was for far greater ends than gold and probably no more risky. His heart kept racing in nervous expectation. It wasn't the risks and horrors that lay ahead; it was the *beauty* that lay ahead, the object of a secret affection.

Nirmalli, Vikram's pretty cousin, whom he loved like a sister, e-mailed him the news. "Sharmilla has just been accepted here at Cambridge for a year in the exchange program with Bangalore University. Isn't that great! I get to have my best friend as a roommate, starting in the fall. You must visit us when we're all set up."

Sharmilla was *the* one Vikram had virtually fallen in love with from the first time he'd set eyes on her. He recollected being spellbound. It was right before he left for Stanford at 15—*his reward for being a computer genius*—to leave India beset with the pain of separation at the moment of his crowning glory. What irony!

He had her old photo hidden in his hands, away from Doron's probing eyes. He'd sneak peeks when no one was watching. Sharmilla had that classic, haunting beauty of those rare, high-bred Indian women who seemed to descend into the world like goddesses. Stunning and intelligent, she had deep, sensitive, soulful eyes, like the classic film beauty Sitara Devi.

Vikram caught himself picturing the two of them walking arm-in-arm like two Indian film stars. *Don't jump ahead of yourself. You're sure to spoil it*, he reminded himself. He began sinking into that familiar Asian melancholy that had beset him over the years, a distant yearning coupled with a deep sadness. Would it all just vanish in thin air like an illusion?

Doron was on the aisle seat at the moment, channel surfing. And Jon was at the other aisle seat across from Doron, with another empty seat between himself and a petite woman passenger unobtrusively napping. He was reading the *International Herald Tribune*.

"I love the idea of just slipping out of the country to England, the land of my ancestral roots," Doron told Jon.

"You were here before, as I recall," Jon queried.

"Yes, I'd won a national computer contest. Had to go with my mom because I was 15. I was greeted by the London media as the latest phenom. We were chaperoned by hyped-up hosts to endless boring tourist sites. Mom gloried in it; I detested it. That's why I love going incognito."

Meanwhile, Doron could read Vikram's mind. He knew exactly what his handsome Indian friend was pining over. This got Doron to reflecting on his own zany encounters with girls, though not nearly as innocent as Vikram's.

He remembered himself at a local indoor mall—the old food-court routine gave him an escape route. This girl had claimed in the Internet chatroom to be a *femme fatale*. Maybe on another planet! Hiding behind a column, he spotted a vampirish, Goth waif of a girl, punked out in all-black, including black lipstick, black nails, weird makeup, strangely cropped black hair and a shaved skull. In elevator shoes, she was over six feet tall. Doron slinked back around the corner, down the far escalator and out of sight as fast as possible. His e-mail to her would "confess" that he was really a GI stuck in Germany and that he'd look her up once he got back to the States, no kidding, really and truly. Phew.

Doron glanced over and saw Vikram absorbed in some vintage Indian film in Hindi—*he's looking melancholy, all right*.

After a nap, Jon noticed Doron viewing the film classic *Frankenstein*, starring Boris Karloff—the original tale of a man-made monster terrorizing the countryside. The monster's ugly features, huge size, raging, unstable mind and superhuman strength made it all the more terrible. Still lethargic, Jon was up to little more than watching Doron's screen from the side as the film was nearing the end.

The two watched angry villagers forming a mob in growing numbers as they marched toward Frankenstein's castle, waving pitchforks and torches to hunt down and destroy the monster.

"That's what we need to do in England," Jon commented.

Doron nodded. "The thought has not escaped me."

Frankenstein's castle was now in flames. Jon looked on with growing satisfaction as an angry populace, pressed to the limits, was rising up to destroy this fearsome horror. Bravery replaced fear, the crucial transition. Doron and Jon looked at each other, then back at the screen again. They didn't need to say anything.

Later on Jon ordered a ginger ale and scanned the sports news. Doron reached across the aisle and tagged Jon, pointing to his screen. Jon looked over. Doron had found one of the new religious satellite channels. An infomercial was underway. It was Jehovah Bob, gesticulating and ranting in his holy ghost talk, his hair out to the sides like wings, slightly metallic-looking. A new product was being "unveiled for the first time," the advertising promo stated as it flashed on the screen. "Not *him* again," Jon said in disgust. Doron nodded.

Jehovah Bob was strutting up and down the stage in the same exaggerated manner he did when Jon first saw him on the streets of Jerusalem.

Then he stopped and pivoted toward the camera with a huge, wild-eyed grin on his face. His eyes rolled heavenward as he declared the gift he was bequeathing to the public. "I want you to be the first to get my little dancing and praying angels." He stepped back, and from behind his back he thrust his arms forward, clutching what looked like vibrating "angels" with attached halos (apparently with no arms or legs, just tubular bodies) about nine inches long and wrapped in some kind of gossamer white cloth. Doron looked at Jon with a sneer.

Then the camera turned toward a side-stage where the faithful were holding up these vibrating "angels" as they smiled ecstatically. Scrolling text announced that the angels were on sale for "the special introductory price of only $29.95 plus shipping and handling." As the subtitle repeated the message at the bottom of the screen, Jehovah Bob proudly marched his over to the group on the side stage and held his own vibrating angels high in the air.

"Well, it looks like he's finally found a way to unload the inventory at the Newport News warehouse," Doron quipped. "This should be fresh material for my contact at *Rolling Stone*."

Jehovah Bob began twitching and rotating his arms as though heavenly energy was passing through him in a kind of *shekinah glory* moment. Jon had no doubt how his missionary uncle would react to this debased psycho-extravaganza.

Doron couldn't take it for a second longer and immediately switched channels, muttering, "Any group dumb enough to believe this deserves to be used as fertilizer. The herd is long overdue for some thinning."

Dinner was announced as people were encouraged to lower their tray tables. The navigator then mentioned that in several hours the plane would be flying toward an early dawn at 10:30 p.m. their time.

Shafts of daylight streamed through the windows when it was close to 11 at night California time. Looking red-eyed and feeling groggy, the passengers were encouraged to awake as coffee was being served before breakfast. The big day had officially begun. They would essentially be pulling an all-nighter.

As Virgin Atlantic flight 120 approached the runway, England looked almost surreal. Well into spring, it was a clear, sunny day with a blue sky. The countryside surrounding Heathrow Airport was a lush emerald-green. There was something reassuring about farmlands that had remained unchanged for generations.

* * *

In little time they were through customs and took the escalator down to the underground tube station, soon heading for Kings Cross. The air smelled different; the people were different; the sights and sounds were very different.

At Kings Cross Station they hurried toward an out of the way group of platforms in a separate building pointing to Cambridge. They grabbed a whole section to themselves, with a window table between their seats in an almost-empty train car. It was the reverse commute taken by the hundreds of Cambridge to London bankers and consultants. Jon started to feel a deep relief. At least this part of their quest had gone smoothly and without incident.

Jon studied the brightening faces of Vikram and Doron, sitting across from him as the train sped by towns and farms toward Cambridge. They seemed cheered and energized by what they saw. Soon they arrived at the quaint Cambridge station and rushed to a cab, heading to the Cambridge Graduate Union for a proper lunch. Jon was famished, and a hearty lunch should tide them through the afternoon until dinner at the Varsity Restaurant, where they were due to meet Ian and Jeremy for dinner.

After coffee in the upstairs lounge of the Grad Pad, overlooking the River Cam, Jon left a message on Jeremy's phone that they had just eaten at the Grad Pad and that he would be playing tour guide to Vikram and Doron till dinner. "Jeremy, I am very glad to be back."

Jet lag seemed to peel back their souls, temporarily removing normal defenses and leaving them strangely open.

Each of them had their own unexpected moments of revelation as they wandered Cambridge.

Doron got hit first when standing in the marble antechamber of the Trinity College chapel. The room memorialized the titans of history who had gone to Trinity; an assemblage of some of the greatest minds of all time were immortalized in marble, their names covering two walls. The greatest, Francis Bacon and Isaac Newton, were memorialized in life-size marble statues. Yet the room's connection with the chapel was not accidental. Above the ceiling of human intellect rose a far higher ceiling, represented by the lofty chapel and stained-glass windows.

The point was inescapable to Doron. It spoke *not* of a chaotic, fragmented cosmos, but one that had order and meaning that could only come through a Supreme Being. A stanza from William Blake rang out in Doron's mind as he recalled Newton's final years studying Scripture. Doron "got it" and was speechless.

Vikram's moment of vulnerability came in one of the gardens along the backs, as Saint John's College loomed in the background. A majestic line of swans passed slowly by, their beauty and elegance reminding him of Sharmilla as they swam in quiet formation. Suddenly he broke into tears as he walked toward the banks of the River Cam, his back to the others as tears coursed down his face. The deeper Vikram's feelings went, the more private he became. Vikram had been that way all his life. It was a sacrosanct moment, a doorway to the eternal, as he realized how little he knew about ultimate reality. He quietly wept in silence, bathed in Cambridge's fond sunlight.

Jon too was taken by surprise. It crept up on him unannounced as they walked up Saint Andrews Street. He had this haunting feeling of a need to be alone as they came up to the sanctuary of Saint Andrew the Great, which he had attended the last time he was in Cambridge. The sanctuary was empty, sunlight pouring through a stained-glass window. Jon's soul hungered for something. Vikram and Doron, sensing Jon's need for solitude, agreed to meet him at the nearby mall behind the church.

So there Jon sat alone in an empty pew and, in a fumbling sort of way, said a prayer in his mind. He, like Vikram, felt like weeping when he saw the words cast in marble, "Greater love hath no man than he who would give his life for a friend."

A hand fell gently on Jon's shoulder as the rector smiled at him, apparently on his way out of the sanctuary. It was Reverend Mark Ashby. When the time was right, Jon planned to query him about the ancient giants, the Nephilim. Jon got up soon after the rector left, noticing that something within him was deeply moved.

By the time they stood in front of the Varsity Restaurant to meet Ian and Jeremy for dinner, all three of them were on their second wind, having survived the strong waves of drowsiness that hit them mid-afternoon.

Surprising all of them, a military-style Hummer jumped the curb, stopping within inches of Jon as it took half the sidewalk in front of the restaurant. Ian and Jeremy were beaming with wide grins as the three travelers of Roundtable West laughed at the audacious sight.

"Just grab the big table in the second room and we'll be right there," Jeremy yelled as Ian pulled away to park. It was a perfect dinner of laughter and light banter.

A long day was ending for Jon after he and Jeremy went on their ritual evening walk as the others headed to Ian's. At Trinity, Jon sprawled out on his familiar bed in the honorary Tennyson room, reflecting to Jeremy, "This is what fellows do in the midst of battle. They engage in ordinary talk just moments after seeing fellow soldiers blown away into eternity. Because they must survive, they must go on."

Jeremy nodded. "I don't know what I would do without you, Jon." As the hour hand passed 10:00, Jon fell into a deep sleep. Jeremy turned out the lights and retreated to his bedroom.

At Ian's manor house, Doron and Vikram were in shock as Ian walked them through their own individual suites. Worthy of London's famed Connaught hotel, they came with private, marble bathrooms, heated towel racks and separate marble shower chambers with large brass shower heads on the ceilings, capable of creating a virtual waterfall of water. The main rooms had huge beds, spacious antique writing tables, a small library, lounge chairs, wall-mounted widescreen hi-def plasma TVs connected to satellite, spare computers in the closet, broadband access, phones, small private refrigerators with a range of drinks and snacks, and anything else under the sun that anyone could ever possibly want.

Ian indicated a button to summon a butler or servant any time of day or night. He opened the curtains to reveal an expansive, center bay window, overlooking elegant gardens and distant fields.

Vikram and Doron, jaw-droppingly grateful, stuttered a thanks to Ian, who smiled graciously and responded, "It's really my honor to have the two of you here." If they had been feeling somewhat like wandering nomads in recent days, now Doron and Vikram felt like temporary royalty. At 10:30 p.m., in their own separate suites, they sank into the deepest sleep imaginable. *This is the quiet before the gathering storm,* Doron thought.

Chapter 21

Sunlight patterned the walls of the suites like a gentle alarm as Vikram and Doron woke up after a fully rejuvenating sleep, their body clocks almost reset to English time.

Vikram opened the linen curtains of his room, stood back and looked through the bay window overlooking the rear gardens. The beauty of spring played out as songbirds and butterflies swarmed fountains and flora of every variety, the morning sun painting everything it touched with a golden light.

Inside his door sat a silver tray with a sampling of fruit, coffee, tea, a newspaper and a card announcing an ample breakfast: "Good morning. Breakfast will be served in the main dining room at ten. Join us."

In his suite, Doron was briefly appreciating what life was like in the veiled world of the aristocracy. He was showering in an elegant marble chamber in Greek motif under a warm waterfall that washed away the fragrant soap. He noticed Ian's family crest on the large bar of Royall Lyme made by Fortnum & Mason.

Soon cologned and toweled, Doron wondered in mock irony how he could have survived this long without such luxury—and how he would ever adjust back to life the way it was before. He noticed a silver tray inside the door. Then Vikram knocked moments later, and the two headed upstairs for a breakfast like no other.

Hoping to postpone the darker realities they had come to combat, both Doron and Vikram maintained their traveler mode at breakfast.

Ian sensed their need for a break and said, "No heavy stuff for a bit! Jeremy and I will show you what this region has to offer. It's only fair your first day here. And if you need more time to unwind, it's yours, though all of us are desperately curious about that final segment!" The two guests looked haunted for a moment. But they also knew that, for strategic purposes, they needed to know the region.

At Trinity College, Jon started the day with a strong cup of espresso, very glad to be back.

Over breakfast at a nearby spot, Jeremy told Jon of recent developments. "As I e-mailed you, I've decided to ante up in full like the rest. Pledged my all, like the others, at the Anchor Pub—no holding back. This thing's too big. All of us meant it with every fiber of our being. So I am disengaging from the lab. I've already told them—with convincing reasons—that I will be severely curtailing all work until further notice. I've felt used, and it's given me a ruthless resolve, quite honestly."

Jeremy confessed, "I feel more like putting on my brother's old commando outfit, boarding some Rover and blasting things up there. Or at least rounding up the traitors. Excuse me for venting my frustration. I am very aware that we need utter discretion for the survival of the mission. I am also under no illusions that we couldn't be hunted down by this adversary."

Jon replied, "Well, as I've discovered with my own leave of absence, something this big requires our full attention. No soldier in the full heat of war is there part-time between classes!"

Jeremy nodded. The two finished breakfast as Ian, waiting for them to arrive, was giving Doron and Vikram an elaborate tour of the manor. Naturally, they passed through the baronial Roundtable room. Doron stopped to examine a centuries-old suit of armor. "The heraldry is awe inspiring. So much here that didn't come through in our videoconference."

Ian confessed, "Our family roots have existed here for many generations. I suppose our love of this soil is almost imponderable to those who have moved about."

"Your family's continuity on this land for 800 years would be unheard-of in America, especially for the majority of us who relocate every four years, jumping about like grasshoppers," Doron added.

Jon and Jeremy arrived and were escorted to join the others. Ian took his guests to the dedicated Cyber wing on the third floor that they had been using of late. "For now, this is one of our main battle stations."

"It really is reminiscent of England's code-breaking operations of WWII, hidden out in rural farms and estates," Jon commented to Doron.

Doron pictured Ian's manor in a scene out of *Enigma*, the film about cryptoanalysts at Bletchley Park, Britain's top code-breaking center, hidden in rural England.

"Well, as a matter of fact," Ian related, "my father recently revealed that for a period during WWII, some of England's best code-breakers, many Cambridge dons, worked here in this manor house in the very rooms we're now using."

"An impressive legacy," Jon replied.

The group headed outside to the large garage-cum-storage facility that housed the Hummer and a fleet of other cars, including a Bentley, two Jaguars, a Rolls-Royce, a restored vintage Austin-Healey, and a Land Rover. It reminded Doron of a vintage-car museum. He gave up trying to resist and sat in the driver's seat of the Rolls-Royce, turning to the others as he gripped the wheel. "I'll let you take it for a spin later, if you want," Ian added.

Then he announced, "We'd better not lose any more time. We think you will like what we've lined up, especially getting a handle on the layout of the region."

Jeremy insisted Jon start out in the front passenger seat of the Hummer and they would all swap around during the trip. Vikram and Doron grabbed window seats in the second row, perfectly content.

"The rest of our group isn't due till tomorrow, Saturday," Ian reminded everyone, "and won't come unless I give the word based on how all of you are feeling. So let me know if you're up to it tomorrow." He tromped down on the Hummer's gas peddle as they lurched out the gate to parts unknown. "We need a little encouragement," he noted cryptically.

An old biplane noisily flew over the Hummer as it sped on the M11 near the exit for Duxford. The Yanks knew something was up. When the Hummer entered the gate, an air show was well underway, with planes on display on the ground as well as ongoing air maneuvers above them, sometimes buzzing low, other times flying in formation and doing aerial stunts.

The Flying Legends Air Show was at the nearby Duxford Imperial War Museum. Jeremy and Ian saw the half-page article en route to the Varsity restaurant the previous night. The newspaper announced, "Spitfires, Hurricanes and German fighters will be on display this week in one of the biggest-ever gatherings of World War II planes. Also present will be the world's only airworthy Bristol Blenheim and an American B-17 Flying Fortress."

The lesson for the day was "heroes in battle" and the sacrifices it required. No one missed the point.

Jeremy yelled to Jon that a specially good Taunton cider—cold, tasty and potent—was being sold. Wasting no time, the five lifted their pints, already starting to feel like RAF pilots and commandos. What a way to begin the quest.

By the time the Hummer pulled up to the Anchor Pub on the Silver Street Bridge after a very full day, the three visitors privately shared an unspoken conviction—that there was a very real chance all three of them would *not* make it back to the States alive, considering what they were up against. That was one reason they left California quickly and quietly, without any long goodbyes. They hoped if they left quickly, they would somehow return home.

Ian sensed it, knowing the same sentiment held true among all of them at Roundtable West. He lifted a mug at the table beneath the RAF pilot poster, saying, "May God grant us victory!"

Chapter 22

It was finally time for the private viewing of what Jon, Doron and Vikram saw before leaving the cabin. The select group of Americans and the Cambridge hacker leadership were now assembled in Ian's home theater where Jon and Jeremy first saw the dog-man.

The doors were locked, and all staff were told to stay out of that wing of the manor.

The English members were asked to look for regional clues.

Jon announced, "I am not absolutely sure that my former roommate, Spenser, was involved. What we do know is that what we are about to see was on the DVD hidden in the freezer."

The large plasma screen covering the front wall came alive. Pin-drop silence replaced all discourse.

* * *

The view was from within a moving car, looking out of the front window through a wide-angle lens. The angle suggested a high-quality mini-cam was attached to the dashboard in front of the steering wheel. The camera also seemed to be in a remote tracking mode, as though matching the eye movements of the driver, fully replicating what he was seeing.

It looked to be early afternoon on a sunny spring day. The car seemed to be on a private road. There were no other vehicles or road signs, while the road itself had slightly different markings from standard public roads. The vehicle was driving on the left-hand side of a wilderness road through a setting that looked "English." The car traveled at normal speed, passing in and out of thick forest to relatively open areas.

The car emerged from a stretch of dense forest. To the right there was a wide area of open space, a clearing. But there was something odd about it that jarred the mind. An anomaly came into view that took up the camera's entire field of vision. The thought *counter-natural* again came to Jon's mind.

As it came into clearer view, a vast forested area appeared in the background of the open clearing. But it was odd. It was a sort of "island," apart from the large open field between it and the car, composed of dense trees, all strangely bent inward at sharp angles.

The bent trees formed a ring, a natural wall, around the outside of the "island." It was the oddest sight in the world. The digital lens followed the eyes of the driver. It fixated on the inward-bent trees, scanning at a low level.

The car slowed to a crawl. The closest outer tree wall of this fortressed anomaly was maybe a football field's distance away.

The recorder started to pick up the strangest sound, everywhere and nowhere in particular. It began to sound like a conversation between an adult and a child. The adult voice sounded metallic, like it was coming over a large stadium's PA system. The replying voice, something like a child's, was heard at equal volume. It was wondering, musing, but lacked the metallic quality of the first voice. No loudspeakers.

The eye-cam pivoted to the forest on the left, looking for the origins of the sound. Nothing. Straight ahead. Nothing. Back through the rearview mirror, nothing. Where was it coming from?

The shifting viewpoint slowly rose upward above the bent-tree-lined area creating the "island." It rose higher and higher, looking up and up.

A sound of whimpering terror issued from the driver.

Then something utterly unexpected popped into view with terrible impact as Jon realized, *The eyes are conditioned not to see it. It's been there all along.*

An immense humanoid form rose up into the sky—a giant.

What was previously camouflaged by its very incongruity with nature and all learned expectation, was a child giant, now in clear view, towering over the bent trees within the "island" and reaching beyond the halfway mark of the natural trees behind it.

It looked almost like a normal child, maybe with the proportions of a four-year-old boy, perhaps the size of a giant blue whale from tail to head; as tall as a five-story building, maybe even taller. It had to weigh tons. The mind rolled and leaped at the sight.

The giant was big enough to kick a full-sized African elephant like a soccer ball. It could probably stride over the bent trees and reach the car in a few more strides.

The sense of paralyzed vulnerability—like a tiny bird trapped in a small cage—was overwhelming as most of the viewers in Ian's home theater echoed the driver's sheer terror. They felt their mouths going dry, their blood turning to ice. The horror was palpable. Jon looked around. Ian had his hand over his mouth, frozen, shocked.

The child's eyes were strange, probing, different. They searched out from high up in the air—looking around, down, searching.

The metallic voice from the stadium speakers seemed to be trying to coax and reason with the child. Jon thought, *If most parents have problems getting **ordinary** four-year-olds to obey—not to speak of rebellious, psychotic or autistic children—**here** is a challenge of titanic proportions.*

The child's eyes again focused on the car, sweeping the area from a great height.

Now the eyes were lighting up with interest as what appeared to be a small toy slowly moved along the road. The musing sound became louder.

Within the car the videocam caught the whimpering of sheer terror from the driver, who seemed to be frozen, helplessly edging forward. The speaker system drew the child's attention back again, as it turned away from the car. It was now looking down.

Giant curved mirrors, of the type seen in stores used for security, were mounted on some of the normal trees within the "island." The digital cam auto-zoomed in on the mirrors to see inside the complex. Standing far below the massive child in a "play area" on an unprotected stage was a man in a white lab coat. He was evidently trying to control the child with dialogue, now speaking commandingly through the speakers to get the child giant's attention.

The child was emitting a sound of wonderment, to itself or to the tiny man below, in a strange voice—that seemed to cut through nature itself. The eyes again returned to the car as the driver started whimpering again, the car still barely moving forward. Jon perceived a level of sheer helplessness that few can ever imagine. *What a time for a breakdown*, Jon thought.

The eyes, the eyes, high above the trees and searching like a lighthouse.

Fearless, curious, uncontrollable, all-powerful, unstoppable. A child giant in a vast playpen now fixating on a distant toy slightly beyond its grasp—the car on the nearby road. It looked down. It saw. No sufficient barrier existed between this immense creature and the car. Nothing to stop it. Nothing but speed, the ability of the car to outpace it.

The voice over the speakers again pulled the giant's attention back to the compound. Its massive head turned away from the tiny car again.

The child giant made a frustrated grunt, the way children do when a toy won't respond or breaks in its hand. The massive face creased with irritation. The voice on the speakerphone cautioned, cajoled. An inscrutable look flashed across the huge face towering above the compound. Then something happened.

A deep boom, like thunder, resounded.

The car shook with the rumble of an earthquake. It shook again.

Jon was reminded of the sound of *T. rex* walking in *Jurassic Park*. Then the deep booms came in waves, shaking the landscape, shaking the trees. The cam showed the child defiantly jumping up and down as it looked at the insect-sized man on the platform.

Words came out of the loudspeaker banks in a garble. A shrillness of tone began to rise with a frenzied pitch. Fear, unmistakable raw terror. The voice was now beginning to lose control.

Suddenly, in a single motion, the massive child giant moved forward and stomped on the man in the lab coat. The scientist in the play area was crushed. It was like a normal child stomping down on a two-inch figure made of modeling clay.

A massive thud rumbled through the earth like waves rippling across a pond. It reached the car with terrible force as the car lurched after the "BOOM!" It shook as if in the middle of an earthquake, maybe a 7 on the Richter scale.

The scene was now replayed in high resolution, zooming in on the mirror on the tree. It showed the stage area. They could clearly see the forced bravado of the scientist looking up to the child giant towering above him.

The scientist, on an elevated platform in the back area, was addressing the child through a row of microphones, the bank of speakers behind him. His voice turned into sheer terror—*a kind of terrible unmasking of reality*, Jon thought.

Now they could see the child with both feet together as he took a small leap, coming down on the stage. The thud was deep. The man in the lab coat was obliterated, squashed to a pulp.

The cryptic note on the first DVD came to mind. Jon had tried to make sense of it at Doron's cabin before they'd seen this. Now it made sense—"Feinberg is way over his head. Rots of ruck in the play area."

What a prescient remark and how true it became. On the same DVD was a newspaper article with photos about Feinberg's untimely death. The pulped body, it explained, had "been run over by a massive bull-dozer near the M1 extension."

Jon thought, *Spenser knew this stuff, then they brainwashed him to forget—the source of his conflict.*

A distant alarm went off from some rear building in the complex. The child giant again looked down at the car, now unobstructed by the irritating voice below. It mused to itself, its voice uneven, rising and falling in fascination at the tiny, slowly moving car.

Inside the car, the driver's voice started begging in shrill incoherence. The hands were fluttering about, desperately attempting to get the car to move. But the faceless driver seemed paralyzed.

Jon considered the challenge. Do you move the vehicle slowly so as not to draw too much attention to yourself, or stomp on the pedal and speed off as quickly as possible? Speeding might draw greater attention, along with the challenge of a good chase. A speeding car, limited by the narrow road and a turn ahead directly into the woods, might barely be walking speed to a creature of this height. A few strides and it would be all over.

The giant started to move in the play area, fixating again on the car. At this point the car was finally speeding, careening back and forth, as the driver tried to stay on the narrow, two-lane road. The videocam was soon beyond the "island"—now out of view.

As the digital recording ended, a barely audible synthesized voice was on the periphery of Jon's perception—perhaps an overlay. Jon couldn't be sure. But one word kept repeating very slowly, drawn out: *"Trans...mutans, trans...mutans, trans...mutans, trans...mutans."* Jon wasn't sure whether he was the only one hearing it.

The film ended.

* * *

A stunned silence filled the room.

Ian announced, "If you're feeling as shell-shocked as I am, then let's regroup when we've settled a bit. I'm going outside for some fresh air."

Jeremy whispered to Jon, "The mandarins of science are playing God again and engaging in the biological equivalent of the Manhattan Project. This is the new atomic bomb."

"That's my thought exactly," Jon replied.

When they reconvened, Jon stood up and confessed to the group, "There isn't enough recognizable voice beneath the shrill whimpering to really identify the driver. I somehow doubt it was Spenser, my former roommate, but I could be wrong."

"And the locale?" Ian spoke up, "Most of us to lean toward England for a number of reasons."

Another added, "Unfortunately, the 'island' in no way resembles anything we've gathered on the underground complex in New Forest. It's doubtful the maintenance worker's surviving nephew would be of any use on that score, but we can check."

Doron suggested, "If we could patch in on one of the Earth Horizon military surveillance satellites, there is a remote chance we might catch the odd-looking 'island' in some forested area, starting with the general region rumored to have the underground complex. But patching into a military satellite is very risky."

"There may be another way we can track this," Ian suggested. "If the man in the white lab coat was a scientist on loan to a British university, such as Oxford, we can try to scan the news and university records. It is certain any stealth project would plant the body to avert attention from the real base of operations. It would corroborate with a media suicide story. We can match the digital image of the scientist and look for news reports of his death. ... Jon, any observations about the giant?"

Jon responded, "My guess is that the child-giant was destroyed soon after the incident. He was more than they could control, and if he got out from where they were containing him, the game would be up."

Doron reflected, "Certainly burying it would require vast earth-moving equipment. And dismantling the body and cremating bits of it would be a huge operation."

"Whatever secret complex this happened in, if the car had been intercepted by security, the driver would have been terminated if the giant didn't get him first," Vikram ventured. "A breach of security by a potential whistle-blower would have been fatal for the witness."

Jeremy speculated, "I'm guessing that the child-giant we saw was not a pure Nephilim, but an oversized mutant, perhaps a hybrid of human DNA and 'shadow' DNA retrieved from one of the digs. I have to tell all of you that if rapid shadow sequencing has been used, my efforts have made me an unwilling accomplice in this horror. Hopefully, what we saw predates any work that I have done through Cavendish lab."

"You're absolved," Ian pronounced.

The meeting broke up, the participants left dazed and stunned.

Chapter 23

Jeremy and Jon sped out the gates of the manor immediately after the session ended. Jeremy felt this powerful compulsion to race his Austin-Healey back to Cambridge at full throttle—"Either this or I stand on the roof at Trinity and just scream at full volume." Jeremy sped through Cambridgeshire's winding country lanes like it was the Monte Carlo Rally. By 10 p.m. they crossed the private bridge on the backs into Trinity's reserved courtyard parking area.

Jon turned to Jeremy, "I've way too much adrenaline in my system to even think about sleeping."

"Anchor Pub?" Jeremy challenged.

"Absolutely. Let's walk there. I need the exercise."

In fifteen minutes Jon and Jeremy had full pints at a private table, feeling like inmates who had just escaped the asylum.

Jon took a deep draught, then confessed, "I'm still doing mental replays of being in the driver's seat of that car—then suddenly seeing the giant come into view. The shock of discovering that this massive creature has been there all along. Then I begin trying to out-race it in the car as the engine stalls. Jeremy, it's the primal nightmare."

Jeremy nodded, "I've been doing the same replay! I am afraid we could easily end up in a similar situation if we're not careful."

Jon suddenly had a disturbing fantasy:

Jon's in the caves near the underground facility, navigating a vast overhanging cavern. The ropes slip, and Jon falls into the open mouth of a sleeping giant. It snaps its mouth shut as he's immediately cut in half by razor-sharp teeth. His body, severed and gushing blood, slides down to the cavern floor.

Phew, this could be a tough night to sleep, Jon thought. *Better not share that one with Jeremy.*

Jeremy interrupted Jon's vision. "If we engage the enemy less than fully prepared, we will end up like Don Quixote, charging windmills—except that in our case, we would be charging giants with cardboard swords and shields."

Jon shared a different perspective: "One interesting thing about the world that existed at the time of the Nephilim, according to my uncle, was that there was a kind of burgeoning sorcery spreading among the people."

Jon paused. "My uncle speculates that some kind of mass dalliance in the occult somehow gave the ancient Nephilim a gateway of permission to enter the earth. Interestingly, witchcraft and Neopaganism are having a huge revival in our time."

"You may be on to something," Jeremy confessed. "Our hackers who have been spying on Northrop's estate have already found a sizable collection of occult artifacts. Northrop's Aleister Crowley collection alone is worthy of a museum. He's got the early pentagrams, Crowley's sketches of himself as 'the beast,' and the famous hat he wore in Tibet in the early 1900s. It's perhaps the greatest Crowley collection in the world. This is no idle hobby. I know Ian has footage of Northrop's that he wants all of you to see."

Jon answered, "Yes, Ian sent us several segments of Northrop at his estate. Bizarre stuff."

Jeremy now broached a plan he and Ian had concocted. "We've discovered that the 'Clockwork Earl,' as your group has named him, has an account in Liechtenstein containing many millions of euros. He has other accounts in the channel Isle of Guernsey, another in Grand Cayman, one in Gibraltar, and, of course, a hereditary account in Switzerland. Ian mentioned hacking into the earl's accounts and using it against the Project. Ian says we cannot do it without Doron and Vikram."

"Great idea. I'm sure they would be glad to assist."

The two downed their pints and walked back to Trinity College, hoping to find sleep.

* * *

The horrors of the night before had noticeably ramped up their group purpose and intensity at the Cyber wing the next morning.

With everyone else distracted on projects, Ian crept off, careful to make sure nobody followed him. He had to do this alone. He unlocked the thick door of the steel-lined room on the second floor of the outside storage facility.

Ian rarely entered his father's arsenal, but knew that there was enough serious weaponry inside to provide all they would ever need when the time came.

As Ian knew, Doron had already downloaded the top military weapons-simulation programs. As the military had learned with helicopter simulation programs, costly mistakes were no longer expensive or deadly, and trials could be repeated quickly.

In a VR theater, the Cambridge hackers could simulate intense battlefield training in the use of grenades, Semtex, and the various shoulder-launched rockets and anti-tank weapons, including the French Eryx missiles. After Ian and Doron tried the anti-tank missile-simulation program a few days earlier, they saw an impressive learning curve.

Ian sat on a crate of Stinger missiles with the door closed. A hard decision was at hand. His dad's trust meant the world to him. Gravely he began considering the fact that he would have hell to pay unless he could convince his dad that this was the only recourse left in a courageous patriotic act that required utter secrecy—and the only means left to counter a serious threat to England. Ian could hear himself say, "Dad, you just never would have believed me. I had to keep you from knowing."

I'll have to convince Dad after the fact, Ian realized. *There's no way I'll ever get his permission.* Ian had made sure his father didn't know what the dedicated wing was all about apart from normal activities. His father joked after Ian gave him the standard walkthrough, "I guess I'm secretly gambling on the fact that amidst such creative ferment, radical new innovations might arise that could provide serious investment potential." Ian smiled and said, "I hope we can come up with some good stuff."

As Ian was stealthily transferring weapons from the arsenal, Jon and Jeremy—the only real non-hackers present—were off by themselves in a comfortable corner room called "the map room," with atlases, spinning globes of the earth, and shelves of topological and historical maps of Britain—old and new. They were looking for hints of where the "island" might be.

Jeremy stood near the window and remarked to Jon, "For one thing, the government and private estates still own over 70% of England's forests, making most of the forested land off-limits to the public—which is a perfect cover for the Project, especially if its facilities are deep enough in some private reserve or governmentally protected zone."

Jon ventured, "I imagine that clues to look for would include fortified and electrified fences, severe warning signs about trespassing and other signs of hyped-up security."

"We also need to consider forests of sufficient size, density and proximity," Jeremy replied. "Three come to mind that could be hiding our 'Island.' There's Rendlesham Forest, in Suffolk's coastal heartland. It was where the famed UFO sightings took place around the American Air Force Base in the early 1980s. Then there's the Kielder Forest, Britain's largest forest, near the Scottish border. But I doubt this is the one. Then there's the option we've been concentrating on almost exclusively—and I still think this is the one—and that's New Forest. It's in South England, it's huge, and it is a stone's throw from one of England's biggest ports, Southampton. And, as we all know, it is where the maintenance workers were killed."

Just then, Neil knocked on the door. They looked up as he asked, "Know where Ian is?" They shook their heads. "Well, our two hackers who went to meet the uncle the day he was killed just got off the phone with his surviving nephew. The lad's been increasingly struggling with a deep sense of guilt for his uncle's death. He's offered to be of use any way he can. He's gone to check out where his uncle might have stashed evidence. He believes the 'accident' was to remove not only a potential witness, but to see that evidence remains buried. He fears that his own e-mails to friends might have put his uncle in jeopardy."

"For now, he's checking on a local underground, of locals who were once connected to the facility," Neil continued. Apparently they've been trying to blow its cover. He thinks they could be of real help."

Jeremy mentioned, "Perhaps we should pursue that cautiously. Meanwhile, considering that New Forest has got 30 villages in and around the complex, we should certainly be able to find some place away from prying eyes."

"What if I as an American fronted as a seasonal tourist and rented a vacation home?" Jon offered.

"Not a bad idea at all, Jeremy responded. "It would create almost zero suspicion."

When Ian appeared in the hall, he gave Doron a conspiratorial wink. The two joined Jon, Jeremy and Neil in the map room.

Jeremy mentioned their thinking to Ian and Doron: "Why not get a place in New Forest as an outpost for us to probe?"

Ian noted, "Great minds think alike; been thinking the identical thing. We need a way to pay with untraceable funds, and cash makes people suspicious."

"I have that covered," Jon told them. "Remember, I can be an American tourist."

"A generous offer," Ian added. "For now, several have volunteered to act as a front party looking into New Forest resources. Their venture would be called something like 'the annual Cambridge computer geek grouse-hunting expedition.'"

Jeremy noted, "As Cambridge students, the advance party can't go wrong if they claim to be there for regional sports, such as spelunking, canoeing, walking the trails and hunting."

Ian called Neville on the wireless intercom. Neville gave the door a loud rap and came in smiling. "Conspiring?"

They nodded, all looking slightly paranoid.

Ian challenged Neville, "Tell them what you've found."

Neville replied, "I have found that there is an enormous underground facility right there in New Forest owned by a trust. I've also confirmed our suspicions that a secondary Northrop estate, thousands of acres in size, has direct rear access to where we believe the underground facility is located."

"That pretty much gives the whole game away! I've got several connections in the area. This includes my old girlfriend," Ian concluded with a truly perverse grin.

"Tell all, Ian," Jon goaded. "Don't hold anything back."

"In case she sees us, I have preemptively done damage control. I've prepped her for a planned 'hunting expedition' and that the group—including me if I can make it—might be in the region. That just gives us deniability should any of us run into her. She also knows it's very iffy."

Jon commented, "Certainly a hunting expedition would provide the perfect excuse for wearing camouflage outfits and carrying the occasional hunting rifle!"

"Nothing would be said of any T-4 explosives, grenades, rocket launchers or other 'hunting' weapons," Ian commented with a wry look.

"So it's on?" Jon probed.

Ian winked and nodded, "We're loaded up and good to go with the best weaponry available."

Neville mentioned, "By the way, the nephew has reported that he found out from locals that some very odd-looking machinery has been routed around the township in the last few days."

As evening arrived, they went off in groups for dinner.

Ian, Jeremy, Jon, Doron and Vikram decided to have dinner at the Anchor Pub. Ian said, "Dad is out of the country; Mom is with friends. Besides, we need to unwind."

On the way out, Doron, who had been buried all afternoon till Ian appeared in the hall, commented privately to Jon, "There's something on your roommate's DVD called 'The Diary of Dread.' Do you know anything about it?"

Jon shook his head, feeling another wave of encroaching horror in the pit of his stomach. But he knew he had to see it and tried to disguise a deep sigh of pain.

Chapter 24

By mid-morning Monday, as Vikram was hidden away with a "Do Not Disturb" sign on his door, Ian approached Doron, Jeremy and Jon and said in a near whisper, "Let me show you a vehicle that's far more suitable for the mission than the ostentatious, military-green Hummer, which would serve only to draw attention wherever it went—that is, unless we used it as a decoy."

They entered the garage complex. Ian walked to the back of the garage, stopping by a vehicle that easily passed for a large civilian van. "This is loaded up with weapons and gadgets of all types, and, believe it or not, this is far more expensive than the Hummer. It's called a SmarTruck, a low-production model made by Ford for the NSA, CIA and special ops missions."

Ian sat inside. "I'll demonstrate some of the things it can do." He grabbed a trigger. "The powerful pepper/tear-gas spray ejectors are able to saturate a large area in proximity to the vehicle."

"Next, an oil-slick ejector that covers the road behind the van can throw any pursuing car off the road." Hitting another button, he continued, "The tire flatteners are ejected out onto the road and instantly flatten any and all tires."

Ian went to another bank of controls. "This is the most serious weapon of all, a laser cannon. It ejects from the roof." He hit a switch and it started to raise into view. "It's supposedly able to cut through the barrel of a tank and bring down a helicopter within a certain range."

Jon felt like he was in the middle of a James Bond episode, being briefed by Q. He pictured the laser cutting the arm off a giant.

Ian rapped hard on the van's body. "It's bulletproof. It also has night-vision goggles as well as a secondary night-vision periscope, which offers normal viewing, extreme telephoto; plus, it can go into an infrared mode to read heat signatures." Ian raised the periscope five feet out of the roof. "It can go higher."

He hit another button. A huge metallic antenna opened out on the vehicle's roof. "This can act as a super ear, able to pick up sound across incredible ranges. But the main feature is that this antenna is really a satellite hookup for direct communications on globalphone, broadband Internet, or commercial radio and television satellite uplinks."

Doron noted with a glimpse, "The satellite hookup could be our strategic ace-in-the-hole. We can broadcast to the world with this."

Ian continued, knowing Doron got the point. "TV networks commonly use these antennas for satellite uplink feeds of live reportage. This van can do this from almost anywhere in the world."

"With potential penetration that could greatly surpass Orson Welles' telecast of *War of the Worlds*," Doron observed.

"Yes. Which crippled the Atlantic Seaboard, if I recall," Jon observed.

Doron added, "Yes. It was in 1938, the night before Halloween, and it paralyzed the East Coast as listeners heard about a 'Martian invasion' presented as breaking news. Major media mischief." He knew the van could be the very thing to implement his backup plans—ideas he had told no one.

Before leaving the garage, Ian confided in a low voice, "We must immediately start training on the weapons simulator in the VR room. It's going to get very real very soon. We'd better know our stuff."

When the group returned to the manor house, Vikram announced he had just successfully hacked into the Palo Alto psychiatrist's DataLock records for the second time and had downloaded more files. From England it was an even greater challenge. He'd glanced at only a few of the downloads, but still caught some of particular interest.

They all rushed to the upstairs to the theater, needing a break.

An image filled the screen as Vikram announced, "This is Walter, the Stanford molecular-biology dropout. Doron and I visited him in San Diego. Most of you know about that rather strange visit."

"Yes, I recognize him," Jeremy said.

"Walter is now being screened for the Project. I am guessing he had never been made a full member of the Project. Here he is being given a total memory-block by the psychiatrist."

Fast-forward, next scene: "Replacement Memories."

Fast-forward again. The shrink is talking: "Walter, you are to leave the program, go home, and not come back. You are to remember the following: You have not been approached by Deep Earth Lab, and have never seen or heard of it. You now realize that you are most comfortable teaching on the high-school level. If you hear my voice over the phone, you are to return immediately to this state. I will count down."

"No suicide instructions," Jon observed.

"At least not on this segment," Vikram responded.

Doron announced, "When we dropped the words 'Deep Earth Lab,' as we told you, Walter suddenly got a faraway look in his eyes and got up and left the table. When we phoned him, he didn't remember."

"Walter never stood a chance," Vikram replied.

"Maybe we can give him some kind of life after all this is over—that is, if we are still around," Jon remarked.

The next segment involved the Palo Alto psychiatrist performing deep programming in a large, darkened room—not his office. One audience member had a "Cremation of Cares" T-shirt, hiking shorts and a large drink. He had a decidedly military look.

"That's the 'U.N.derground' room in Bohemian Grove," Doron announced. "It's almost in earshot to my mother's cabin. Some bizarre things have taken place in this room during the distraction of Grove activities, including S&M, torture and alleged incidents of human sacrifice."

The Palo Alto psychiatrist injected the dog-man. "A hypnogen," Jon guessed out loud.

The dog-man had the same wobbly head-movement as the older prototype they had seen at the first showing at Ian's. The battered and bruised face suggested someone from the "San Quentin Inmate donation program." The dog-man was eerie as always, but, compared to the child-giant, this barely raised their pulses.

Lederberg began fully erasing the creature's human identity with all the attendant memories. The psychiatrist next began programming it to have an "inter-species consciousness" so it would adjust to its new look without going into shock.

Of special interest were the faces of various onlookers caught on camera in the different segments.

"This will add to our gallery of faces, many of which we've isolated and digitally enhanced."

"Call it a gallery of rogues," Jeremy instructed.

A figure in the shadows, lounging about in an oversized chair, suggested Lord Northrop, but they couldn't tell for certain.

145

"Can we highlight that?" Ian queried.

"He's certainly a Bohemian Grove type of guy," Doron commented.

Jon challenged them with a secondary plan. "What if we sent the whole gallery of faces to my brother, Jack, at the FBI? He's trustworthy to the ends of the earth."

Ian replied, "Let's see what we can come up with on this end first. The rule holds that the broader the circle of those who know, the probability of something getting out goes up geometrically."

* * *

After lunch Jon worked up the courage to tackle his old roommate's "Diary of Dread." He got first crack for obvious reasons, being the surviving roommate and the only one there who knew Spenser.

The others were on the third floor, doing broad searches of the enhanced faces and other leads from Vikram's morning venture, while Ian and Doron practiced in the weapons-simulation VR chamber.

Jon appreciated having use of Doron's large, elegant suite to watch the video diary in privacy. He was in a vulnerable mood and needed solitude.

Jon hit the Play button. On the suite's 55-inch wall screen, Jon's old roommate, Spenser, smiled with sad irony into the camera as he spoke. He was sitting in a chair with a neutral background.

"Jon, I guess that if you're watching this, it means that I am no longer with you. Glen, if you are watching this and Jon is alive and well, please give it to him and shut it off immediately. Don't feel insulted, Glen, but if you want to risk it all and open up a Pandora's box of violent conflict—which I know you don't—by all means, take on the Project yourself. But I think you and I know that Jon is best suited for handling this sort of challenge. It is bigger than anything you can imagine. So *adios*, Glen. Walk away and live. Don't *ever* breathe a word of this to anyone, or you will wish to God that you had never heard about any of this."

Jon was just glad that Glen had never found the DVD in the first place and remained clueless.

"Jon, I did my best to set up hiding places that only you would find. I hope you found the decoding sequence of this DVD that I hid." Jon had never found the decoding sequence. *Thank God for Doron*, he thought.

"Jon-man, this DVD has been updated periodically, then replaced in the freezer whenever I have added evidence. I have no idea what stage it's at for you now. Sorry, Jon, the files are not in order, they are random—but they are self-explanatory. The same is true for my diary folder—this is the lead part with some written bits, recorded audio bits and more camera shots.

"My goal has been to assemble the most incriminating evidence against the Project possible. But it has been very hard for me to do, for reasons you will learn later. So let me get right into that.

"You may wonder why I never talked to you about what was going on in Deep Earth Lab. The answer is that if I had broken my vows and verbally spilled anything directly to you, *anything*, our lives would be in immediate danger, and this includes people you don't know: Some of my accomplices in the Project have turned in horror against the Project, sharing with me their deepest confidences. They would be wiped out the moment that I leaked *any* of these findings to *any* outsiders! How is this possible? Because I have been programmed. So have the others.

"Certain things I did or said would cue this programming into action. The moment I revealed the secrets of the Project to an outsider, a sequence would begin, over which I have absolutely no control. I am talking about the most cutting-edge technology of mind control. I would automatically phone the psychiatrist who programmed me and confess everything I had revealed, and exactly who I'd revealed the information to, address and all. In hours, Jon, that person would be dead. The Project is that powerful. And, of course, I would be history as well."

Jon second-guessed how Spenser discovered his own programming—with a concealed recorder.

"The missing memory after the sessions was a clue. I had a backup set of ears that could not be hypnotized—in the form of my miniaturized digital recorder hidden in my pocket. I needed objective evidence of what was going on with Dr. Lederberg, because I kept leaving the sessions feeling that my mind had been scrambled, that something much deeper was going on.

"I first carefully jumped through the recording for clues. I figured there was a post-hypnotic suggestion, a code word. So that I wouldn't be hit by the code word, I used dictation software that turned the audio file to a text file and then read the session. That's when I saw it all, including the fact I'd been programmed for suicide.

"If I stopped going to the sessions, that alone would signal Lederberg I was out of control, and the game would be up. I have dreaded going, but I have had to go. I'd already begun collecting stuff on the DVD but have never told a soul. Had I spoken to you or Glen or anybody, that would have been it.

"I can anticipate your question, Jon. Yes, I have been planning to get deprogrammed by another therapist. But there are other obstacles. Finding the right expert and keeping this from the Project's psychiatrist will be hard, if not impossible.

"This is risky. I am planning to make a break for it and leave the area, maybe even the country. I want to put as much distance between myself and the Project as possible, leaving no leads. If I do, I will contact you. But I am afraid that if I attempt to leave, a programming sequence will be triggered. Yet I can think of no other options at the moment."

It hit Jon with full force. Before showing them the video diary, he told the others, "My roommate had been forced into a kind of mental prison that denied him all freedom to speak. Should he even mention his nightmares or inner conflicts regarding the Project, he feared the programming would be triggered. It was the consummate inner war. It revealed both the horror and the heroism in what my roommate was really up against."

In the upstairs showing later that day, Jon paused it and explained: "Evidently the suicide command had been triggered the moment he made a run for it. Whether he drove off on Route 101 toward Santa Barbara and Los Angeles or in the opposite direction, the suicide program would be triggered. It took more than the *thought* or *desire* of escaping; it took the actual *act* of escaping, at which point the programmed autopilot took over. At that point, I believe, he headed to Route 1 fully in a trance. He took EXIT ONE, the final destination over the side of the cliffs."

To most of them it was a sobering, inside view of a chilling world of power, ambition, false hopes and seduction.

Earlier that day, Jon had sat back in the chair as he watched the video for the first time. After a pause, he hit Play again, watching the screen intently. The videotaped message continued…

"Go with your conscience, Jon. Use your own best judgment about how to expose Deep Earth Lab. Use this information wisely. Be careful who you trust. Remember the movie *All the President's Men*, with Robert Redford? He walks into a major newsroom with undeniable proof of a major conspiracy. It's on the evening news as a major story. This may be tempting, but don't try it. The Project has a wide reconnaissance network. I believe some of the players behind the Project are owners in the major media conglomerates. The story would stop right there, never making network news. The reporter or anchor you gave the DVD to would smile, shake your hand and thank you sincerely. Both of you would be dead in 12 hours. Remember how we used to joke about how Orwellian the news was? It is, more than ever.

"If I recall, you have a brother working for the FBI. That could be key. I expect the Project will quickly grab my computer and anything else they can lay their hands on. That's why most of the files on my computer are encrypted. That's also why this DVD is so important: It has all the evidence I have managed to collect.

"Jon, I need to confess something. I have been taken for the ride of my life—and I have been a willing participant from the very beginning. In truth, I have been nothing more than a useful idiot to the Project, a prostitute. To put it bluntly, my ambition to make it to the top, for greatness and recognition, was so out of control that I was willing to make any compromises. I sacrificed all the values I once held dear as though they meant nothing. You know the mindset at Stanford. Those headed for the top prize will gladly walk over others' faces to reach the pinnacle.

"But the Project is way beyond that league. Being a genius is not enough, never was. Being inventive is not enough. The virtues are never rewarded. These people are different. You've never met any people like these, believe me. Jon, they can cue in on your greatest weaknesses like vampires smelling blood. Those at the top will share their power, their greatness, their bounty with no one. Any player apart from them—and they truly are an inner circle—is usable, disposable. To think otherwise is naïve. They have the best and brightest in the world's food chain of minds who are no more than useful idiots who naïvely serve them.

"At gatherings they appear as anonymous faces. You never really know for sure who they are or where they come from. They disappear without trace. Oh, I have met a few, such as an Oxford Professor, named Lord Northrop. But most stay far in the background.

"In some gatherings they even wear masks, no kidding. Did you ever see the film *Eyes Wide Shut*, the last film Stanley Kubrick made?—He died literally two weeks after it was done! Funny coincidence, eh, Jon? That's more than a film, Jon. That was Kubrick's last warning. Those are the sort of people we are dealing with here. It's beyond the pale of the man on the street to ever understand. These people can get you to sell out in ways you never imagined.

"Jon, I have never felt such terror and remorse as I have since I gave a blood oath at Bohemian Grove in an underground room. I knew I had entered a covenant with evil; that's the only way I can describe it. I literally walked out feeling like a slave."

Spenser's face on the screen became haunted with a profound sadness as he described these things.

"Jon, as soon as I made the vows, I got to taste the bounty of *their* world, their pleasures and, frankly, their depravities." He stopped to compose himself.

"Lesson number one: Once you have done certain things, call them rituals, it *changes* you within, and the more they are able to control you.

"Lesson number two: As you degrade yourself, their power over you increases. I am sure this is the same principle by which certain insiders have controlled American presidents ever since the early 1900s. I now believe that most public figures are bought and paid for—the willing vassals of an inner circle. I finally started thinking, if there is this much evil, maybe there's also a God.

"I hope my efforts have not been for naught. Jon, I hope you use your brilliance to expose this dark horror. Drag one of its tentacles out into the light of day for all the world to see.

"The biggest tentacles I know—like nothing on Earth—are absolutely enormous creatures you will see on this DVD. One of these monsters surfaced in one of my nightmares, and I finally realized it was more than just a dream—but only after I got a recording here—which I'll tell you about. When I was in England, I was taken to some facility where I am pretty sure I saw one. It was at least a three-hour drive from Oxford. That's all I can remember at the moment."

"Well, the recording of the giant on the DVD I've left you was taken by a member of the Project who became an ally of mine. He was in the forest area, trying to spot wildlife. He drove where he was not supposed to go and was taken by total surprise when he saw this creature looming at treetop level. Oh, yeah, and you will see Feinberg killed in the play area. It was shocking when I saw it.

"The fellow who recorded this is a New Zealander. He actually made it out through a rear-approach road, then e-mailed the digital film segment to himself, then me. He is among a number of us who have turned on the Project. I was told he went home. Frankly, I think he is no longer around. Be careful.

"Jon, I hope I live to tell you all these things in person. You are one of the smartest, most noble people I have ever known. I always felt like an incomplete shadow compared to you. So people like me compensate privately to be accepted, even admired. How hollow. After the event at the Fairmont Hotel I was briefly at the pinnacle—and, oh, how my pride was fed. That was the bait and I was caught, finally, like a salmon on a three-pronged hook, never to be released!

"Jon, don't ever sell out. I feel like a lost soul, trying to avoid perdition. Jon, use this and don't fail."

It abruptly ended. Jon was drained, but determined more than ever not to fail. *Spenser, you will be vindicated.*

Chapter 25

After the others watched the Diary of Dread, several bio segments followed, taken on the sly by Spenser. One chronicled an earlier trip to England during Spenser's grace period with Deep Earth Lab, the "wine and dine" era. His visit to Lord Northrop's Oxfordshire estate had absolutely classic scenes worthy of a *film noir*:

It begins outside the huge front door. It seems Lord Northrop wants a moment of privacy with his American guest.

Livecam is on.

The Clockwork Earl, as Roundtable West has named him, banishes his chauffeur in an accent that changes from Upper Crust patrician to an effeminate Etonian, la-di-da that if it were ramped up any higher would no longer be English, but a controlled, convoluted squeal. Northrop tells Spenser to "join me in the front seat of the Bentley," idling in the drive, "I'd like to show you around a bit." The stealth camera remained on and was clearly out of view of the earl.

They drive hither and yon, engaging in light banter. The message to the young American from the Project was clear: *You have entered the rarefied air of the world's elite—rejoice in being selected as few are, and know that this does not come without costs and sacrifices.* The tour of the grounds is an unbridled display of lavish wealth and conspicuous consumption.

At one point they pass an all-weather Arabian tent at least 100 feet long with one side opened out, facing the road. It's the sort of banquet size used for outdoor receptions, grand parties, fox hunts and other equestrian events.

Within the center of the tent stands an unexpected oddity: a gigantic, gold-leafed crown large enough to fit a head at least 10 feet in diameter. On the top of the crown, where a large gem might have been, is a life-sized, regal-looking armchair. The earl grins to himself as he hums some unrecognizable tune.

While the earl is driving past a long field of vegetable gardens, he suddenly reaches over and lays a firm hand on the young American's thigh. One can sense the utter embarrassed awkwardness of Jon's former roommate.

"He's feeling trapped and revolted," Jon commented.

Lord Northrop then goes from humming this rather odd tune to singing it. Curiously, his pronunciations become distorted in the oddest sort of way as he sings:

"The Maustery of the Whole Human Rausssssss,
The maustreee of the wholllllle humannnn rausssssssssssssssss,
The maustry of the whole, the maustry of the whole,
The Maustry of the Whole Human Rausssss."

A flurry of comments speculated the song had double or triple meanings. One Cyber gang member put in his bid: "I'll bet a pint of stout the earl plans to take him back for buggery."

The earl then initiates the guided tour of his palatial manor, a regal dwelling worthy of a Rothschild.

The Cyber gang so far has been unable to access a number of the rooms because the earl's security cameras were off-limits—and for good reason. As Ian had said earlier, "Northrop wants privacy from the probings of a curious and voyeuristic staff, above all when he is 'making maustery.'"

Ian speculated that X-rated events had taken place over the years that would make half the ears of London burn with delicious curiosity. As Ian was of the privileged class, his comments made sense.

Ian said the obvious: "From the earl's viewpoint, the possibility of any staff member selling certain things caught on camera to some tawdry, gutter-level paper would be a nightmare."

No, the earl needed privacy. That's where Jon's roommate's tiny mobile camera was so useful in showing rare footage. Curiously, in his diaries the American visitor was positive that when he first saw two of the main servants at the door, there was an instant mutual recognition, at which point the two nervously left. He recalled he had seen them leaving the Palo Alto psychiatrist's office as he entered!

"The two servants were unmistakable. I also recall spotting them at the beck and call of Lord Northrop at the black-tie affair at the Fairmont Hotel," Jon's roommate narrated.

The earl was now leading the way to some of "my prized private exhibits and art collections." They pass an art exhibit in a large gallery with black ceiling and walls and narrow beamed lights directed on the various paintings. The artworks, he narrates, were undoubtedly commissioned by the earl and produced by well-known artists. Some were reminiscent of H. R. Giger, the Swiss surrealist and alleged Satanist who did the creature design for the film *Alien*.

The earl stops at one curious painting near the beginning of the exhibit so that his American guest can take it in.

The painting is titled *Bringing Forth the Dark God*. It's hi-def on the giant screen. A giant whose features resemble a fusion of Satan and Siva stands towering above the city of London at night. Jon's roommate later wrote in his text diary that he felt a terrible apprehension.

Another curious painting nearby shows a huge giant striding down a street, towering above the houses. A closer look reveals it is wearing a crown with a throne on it and a man sitting on the throne—a man strongly resembling the Clockwork Earl. The crown-rider is cowled and has a magician's staff.

The next painting shows the same giant approaching Stonehenge under a black sky and a full moon, with a vast assembly in druid robes spanning out into the fields. It hits Jon with the impact of a meteor.

Ian and Jeremy look at Jon, rolling their eyes.

"Oh, boy does this ever up the ante in what we may be facing," Jon whispers back.

In the painting, a large fire burns in the center of Stonehenge, and certain details suggest preparations for a sacrifice, a human sacrifice.

Another painting depicts the same giant wearing the crown, but nude this time, walking across some wilderness bordered by forest. The giant is sexually aroused, and the man on the throne seems to be wearing the Clockwork Earl's special phallic nose, the one he was seen wearing on the balcony in the video hacked by the Cambridge group. This painting is titled *The Hunt*.

The next painting portrays a massive homosexual gathering, a kind of Sodom and Gomorrah, with another nude giant doing unmentionable acts. The paintings now become progressively more hideous and grotesque as the exhibit ventures into scenes of an ancient, pre-Babylonic world, depicting people shattering every moral barrier on Earth, including bestiality, in some ancient precursor to witchcraft.

One of the last paintings is titled *The Father of the Nephilim*, and resembles Lucifer in some other period of history, people quavering beneath him, an idol representing him in the distance. This creature is immense, clearly "the god of this world," as the description beneath the title declares.

The earl had been caught on tape more than once declaring to others, "We need to bring back the dark god. We need to find his bones and bring him back."

At that point in the segment, Spenser stated in a voice dub, "Northrop, I believe, is trying to fulfill what Aleister Crowley originally set out to do. But Lord Northrop is doing this with far greater means, and this includes a genetic invocation. He has helped finance any number of digs to find the Nephilim burial grounds. His real goal is their original ancestor, 'the dark god.'"

After the exhibit, the lord entreats his American guest to stay over for the night, having previously shown him a lavish guest room. Jon's roommate is now desperately making excuses. "That's so kind of you, Sir. But if I do not get back to London by late tonight, a critical experiment I am working on for the Project could be lost, with drastic consequences."

The Clockwork Earl reluctantly accepts the American's excuse—this wildly gifted new talent that the Project has been drooling over from the moment one of its unwitting spies in the Stanford molecular-biology department told them what Spenser was pioneering.

Lord Northrop bids him good leave with an invitation to come back and stay a few days. The American nervously accepts while hurrying out the door. He leaves in his rental car, racing back to London while nervously dictating his various thoughts and impressions into the mini-cam.

The showing ended, and Ian disbanded the group in time for dinner. On the way out the door he hinted to Jon and Jeremy, "Give me a call on the cell phone if you decide to head to the Anchor Pub later on." They agreed.

Jon unwound as they drove back.

"I'm beginning to appreciate how Spenser had parallel talents to yours. Whereas you have been able to find genetic shadows in the human genome and have discovered ways to vastly speed up sequencing, he innovated radically new ways to scan DNA, then digitize it. With this, someone could send a digital file anywhere in the world. And here's the kicker—Spenser had found a way to program a certain type of tissue—in a kind of DNA soup—to absorb the DNA impression that had been digitized and sent. You could literally transform the transmitted digital file into living tissue. Hence, even an embryo could be produced. This would be a huge leap for Deep Earth Lab."

Jeremy nodded in stunned silence. "I never realized he was able to do that. No wonder they were after him. Crikey."

Jon went on, "Thus, a Nephil artifact could be scanned, digitized and live flesh fully reprogrammed and transformed, including the embryo of a giant—this from almost anywhere in the world. That could easily have been what was going on at the Nephil dig in the Negev. You certainly don't need to worry about customs. A DNA sample is digitized and sent from the dig. The digitized DNA could then be sent instantaneously to any of the Deep Earth Lab facilities, anywhere."

Jon then observed ironically, "My old roommate did not have a clue as to how great his contributions had been."

Jeremy amended, "As is often true with the wildly talented and super-gifted, they assume everyone looks out on the same universe with their level of genius. The baffling gulf for so many geniuses—some successful, some half-formed—is understanding the far more diminished consciousness of the common people. Insights they glimpse in a fraction of a second, the normal person might be lucky to see in years, and then only if given the insight time and again."

Jon added, "Indeed, the gift of fire. I have no doubt that most, if not all, of the group in Ian's manor have this gift in one form or another. Doron is top-heavy with it."

Chapter 26

The next morning, at Saint Andrew's, Jon went through the door to the rear study. The rector's assistant, a student trainee, told Jon to have a seat, that the Reverend was on the go continually but was taking time out to see Jon. "Americans must have pull," he quipped. "He's postponing his regular squash game with his best friend John Newsome in physics." He said it with a smile and left.

Mark Ashby soon rushed in, smiled, shook Jon's hand vigorously and said, "I'd forgotten about my squash game when I made the appointment with you. Apologies for being a little late."

"I'm the one sorry to have messed up your squash match!" Jon interjected. "Should we postpone till later, would that be easier?"

Reverend Ashby shook his head. "Not at all, we're set to play tomorrow. Being here is my first priority. ... I have learned that if I keep physically fit along with the usual mental and spiritual rigors—part of my daily routine when I was a student at the Royal Military Academy in Sandhurst—I gain the stamina to take on a very full workload." Then he added with an ironic grin, "My father was a military man and was preparing me for the military at Sandhurst, not the ministry."

"What made you wind up here?" Jon pressed.

"Well, after Sandhurst I went to Oxford, got one degree, then went to Cambridge and got another degree. I knew by then that the ministry was to be my future."

Far from being some bespectacled, milquetoast vicar, the rector was a vigorous, well-conditioned man's man, who, you got the feeling, would be equally comfortable out on the field doing maneuvers as preaching in the sanctuary. Local legend had it that Ashby often took mile-long swims at night in the cold River Cam, but he would only grin and shrug his shoulders when confronted. His wife also maintained a stoic silence about her husband's intensive physical rigors.

Jon got to the point. "Because I know we've only got a few minutes, please excuse me for jumping into it. A question has been dogging me as a scientist. If I might ask, how do you explain the Nephilim? What were they? Were they real, or mythical constructs?"

"Before we get to the Nephilim," Reverend Ashby noted, "let me provide a bit of perspective." He collected himself thoughtfully.

The reverend said right off the bat, "The Bible stands on its own as the Word of God. ... One of the humbling aspects of biblical revelation is accepting the upper limit of the human mind and being willing to live with mystery. We can't always have all the answers on our terms. The temptation is to fill in all the gaps prematurely from whatever the reigning conventional wisdom of the era happens to be. A 19th-century romantic will insert one thing; a 20th-century modernist or a 21st-century postmodernist, another."

Ashby went on: "Divine revelation is the communication from an eternal God with infinite intelligence disclosing realities far beyond the mortals to whom He is speaking, mortals with brief life spans, narrow perspectives and limited aptitudes. As science has repeatedly discovered, following a long period of skepticism and doubt, revealed truths later make sense scientifically."

"Jon, should you and I somehow time-travel back to the ancient world and try to explain some of the things of our day to them, in describing realities of our world we would be limited to the language and metaphor of that time period."

Jon nodded.

"For instance, imagine the challenge of trying to explain artificial intelligence, nanotechnology, or even a microwave oven, to an ancient audience 2000 years ago! In years past I've talked to Stephen Hawking about singularity, and even we have problems communicating." He smiled wryly.

"If you and I are in the ancient world, we face a much greater challenge than Stephen Hawking trying to describe singularities to Mark Ashby. Our challenge is to use ancient language because the technical words don't exist and won't for millennia. So we describe things in childlike pictures—the upper limit of language in the ancient world. Are you still with me?" Jon nodded, fascinated.

"Now, let me give you an example in reverse. A prophet in ancient times peers into the future in which completely alien technology exists.

He would be overwhelmed and at a loss for words simply by a glimpse of London or Manhattan from a helicopter as it moves over the city.

"The Apostle John's Revelation depicts what may be an apocalyptic figure able to summon fire from the sky. Well, to me, that could be any number of things, from the miraculous—and I don't discount that—to some technology in the distant future, say, laser or particle-beam weapons fired from military satellites. In simplest language, they would be literally bringing fire down from the sky."

Jon was nodding, eyes deep in concentration.

"Now consider the Nephilim, those huge giants walking the earth before the Great Flood. We may never understand the genetic mechanisms of what happened when we are told that spiritual beings—let's call them angels, in this case, fallen angels—were able to fully enter our dimension and procreate with women. But we can perhaps picture some of it. We are told the final product, the Nephilim, were so terrible that God declared them evil, a threat to life on Earth. We are told that God removed these creatures by causing a cosmic calamity, a flood. Perhaps ten thousand years from now we will know some of the genetic details—if the human race can manage to survive that long! So far we are giving the Nephilim a good run for their money with our own brand of folly and destruction."

Reverend Ashby continued, "All we know is that the Nephilim once existed. I believe the biblical revelation about them at face value. I may not understand all of it, but I believe it. On the authority of the scriptural account, I also believe that these giant creatures were up to no good. What little we get from the Bible is that they were a new class of creature that were extremely powerful, extremely violent and completely immoral. It seems they were intent on destroying the race of men. They might have destroyed it a secondary way as well by genetically corrupting it—therefore ending it—which was something God would not allow."

Jon nodded soberly as Reverend Ashby went on: "Jon, if the Nephilim had destroyed or polluted the entire human genome, an interspecies hybrid would replace man, and that was not what God originally intended. We are entering deeper issues of theology—but if that happened, God's plans and decrees for the human race, His sovereign will, would have been nullified, making Him no longer God."

The reverend took another approach. "Things are getting a bit ontological at this point, but follow me. God, who is Truth and who cannot lie, is suddenly made a liar by proclaiming outcomes as certainties that can no longer come true—then His very nature is undermined. There can be no future Messiah if the race of man is abolished. With no human lineage to act as the vehicle, the promised Messiah cannot be born. So the Nephilim presented a compound threat!"

Jon nodded, realizing the reverend could have gone on for an hour more, but had already made some heady points in an economy of time.

"Jon, I hope this has been helpful. Forgive my limitations in presenting a very spotty and incomplete picture. But take this at face value; the Nephilim would be creatures you would want to avoid at all costs. And let's pray they stay buried deep in the earth's crust, never to return!"

Ashby smiled with warm sincerity and intelligence. After a firm handshake, the two men agreed to meet for tea in the near future. Jon said he would try to show up again for the Sunday service.

"I would love that," the reverend responded, and gave Jon a manly pat on the shoulder. He waved to Jon as he crossed the street.

Jon left with much to think about.

After they had brunch and were now heading to Ian's, Jon appealed to Jeremy for a bit more time on the road.

Jeremy winked, took a radical turn on a country road, and accelerated. Roadside trees whisked by in a delightful blur as they passed fields and glens, spring flowers lighting up the countryside.

The top was down, the air was clear, and it was a warm, sunny day in Cambridgeshire. Jeremy and Jon decided to head off to points unknown. Jon phoned Ian on his cell phone and let him know what was going on.

"You need it and deserve it," Ian encouraged. "Have a great ride and come here when you feel like it. If the two of you are up for dinner at the Anchor Pub or the Varsity, drinks are on me."

* * *

Courtesy of Ian, Vikram and Doron were awarded a car for the afternoon—the Rolls-Royce. After a nice country drive, they stopped at an overlook of a regional park, by now deep in discussion.

Vikram was asking provocative questions about the world of power players, hidden in the shadows of history. "Is there really an agenda of insiders steering things?" he challenged.

Doron complied. "Okay, be patient. Maybe I'm jaded from living next to Bohemian Grove, a playground for global insiders, especially with a mother obsessed by their antics."

Trying not to sound too paranoid, Doron ventured, "Okay, this is it in a nutshell. Figureheads acting as presidents and premiers—mere actors on the stage of history—serve the true rulers of nations. The figureheads are men on a short leash, allowed into office because the insiders know all their weaknesses. They'll protect their image over anything.

"Consider Woodrow Wilson, who was willing to pawn the nation merely to cover up his adulterous affair with a faculty wife when he was president of Princeton—a scandal that would have ruined his presidency. The era wasn't exactly as tolerant as that of Bill Clinton. After paying off the faculty wife a substantial sum, Wilson's 'friend' merely asked for a 'favor,' knowing Wilson didn't have the funds to ever repay him.

"The favor? Woodrow Wilson agreed to sign into law the Federal Reserve Act, creating the debt engine for America. Now growing national debt with compound interest could eventually bankrupt the nation, its currency becoming worthless. Woodrow Wilson, because of a moral indiscretion, allowed the genie of fractional reserve banking out of the bottle. Our sovereignty ended. The U.S. Treasury no longer printed dollars; they were now Federal Reserve Notes.

"Meanwhile the riddle of debt is that 'the borrower is the slave of the lender.' National debt operates like a ruthless game of Monopoly. All the players have to do is drive up the national debt—wars being the quickest means—disenfranchising a trusting populace. The masses, inexorably, become indentured servants as the nation becomes bankrupt. The players don't feel a twinge of remorse.

"Their plans for our future? Most probably a global feudalistic system of total control. They become '*the mausters of the whole human raussss*,'" Doron sang in high Etonian falsetto, imitating the Clockwork Earl.

"On another level, as technology becomes more powerful, the rise of techno-tyrants overseeing police states is the intermediate stage to World Order. The State can spy on, and control, its citizens. Any crisis can invoke government involvement, or, policing. Power over the individual expands till the individual becomes like Winston in George Orwell's *1984*—under total surveillance, with no appeals to freedom.

"And useful crises? Look at the endless war on terror. It became a pretext for the freest nation in history surrendering long-held freedoms without a shot being fired. More effective than an invading army.

Doron ended, "I don't believe these developments have been accidental. They've been as orchestrated as a complex chess game, but most people don't want too look. They lack the will and intelligence to see the pattern."

Vikram shook his head. "I've seen India's version of these same dark forces at work. I've wanted to look the other way most of the time."

Chapter 27

Manhattan gleamed like a smoky topaz beneath a clear blue sky as the day began with endless espressos being served at sidewalk cafés from Greenwich Village to uptown Manhattan. May had arrived with the up-tempo energy of spring, intoxicating New Yorkers with that sense of boundless expectation. Pedestrians took off their coats and rolled up their sleeves to stroll in the sun, the inhibitions of winter banished to the distant past.

Gleaming especially that day was the Trump Empire Center, Manhattan's most impressive and luxurious building complex, finished in the second decade of the 21st century and surpassing Rockefeller Center in its heyday.

Donald Trump's self-described "lifetime achievement" boasted an unobstructed waterfront view of prime Manhattan as it jutted out from the shore, offering a sidelong view of the city. It had an unhindered view of the World Trade Center being rebuilt, methodically rising into the sky well along its ten-year building effort that began in 2005.

The exclusive residents of Trump Center couldn't help but stare at the World Trade Center's progress with mixed emotions. Soon it would surpass them in height, but certainly not in class. If the Trump complex melded the best Regency Empire architecture with streamlined con-temporary design, then by comparison the World Trade Center of the 21st century was as alienating and dehumanizing as the vast crystal cities of the comic-book planet Krypton.

Adin Mocatta's arrival at the Trump Empire Center that morning in a stretch limo got the usual attention of onlookers expecting to see a rock star emerge. To their disappointment, the limo headed to the under-ground garage. Adin got out and headed to the complex's most presti-gious suite, the penthouse, on a private elevator with state-of-the-art recognition technology.

Among the onlookers was Jon's brother, Jack, the FBI agent, sitting innocuously in the shadows at an upscale café. Dressed down to blend in, he had been sitting there for over an hour, drinking coffee, reading intel and monitoring the entrance of the Center. On his laptop he'd earlier gotten a message from Jon, passing on more info from Doron and Vikram. "You guys are a gold mine," he wrote back to Jon. "The limo just arrived. Gotta move soon."

Using a special filter that could penetrate glass, Jack discreetly filmed the limo arriving with Adin Mocatta inside it. He sent a digital image to Jon.

Jack had recently contacted the manager of Trump Center under the official seal of the FBI. The manager was informed that if he squealed, he could go to jail. Jack was quite sure the manager was an informer and well-paid by the dummy companies of Deep Earth Lab.

Jack already knew that there were passageways so secret that they did not appear anywhere in the architectural plans. He needed to check them out.

The centerpiece of the grand suite was the massive chamber modeled on the secret upper chamber of the world Masonic headquarters in London. A prismatic Eye of Horus was etched on a thick, pyramidal window that reflected across the water when the sun hit it. Inside the grand chamber, where the board of Deep Earth Lab met during their U.S. meetings, were ancient occult symbols blended into the fashionable decor.

Jack knew from Doron's report that Lord Northrop had visited the Project's offices over the years in various grand buildings before they moved to Trump Center. The earl's diary showed he always loved coming to New York City, especially in the spring. He and the other directors of Deep Earth Lab—still unknown to the Cyber gang—oversaw a shadow enterprise, its name nowhere to be found in the world's stock exchanges. According to Doron, Northrop was not coming to Manhattan this year. Something really big was brewing on his end. But other things were happening in New York as well.

As Jack emptied his coffee cup, Adin Mocatta entered an elegant, expansive office in the Empire Tower's premium suite covering most of the top floor.

Mocatta, as Jack learned from Doron (who had hacked into Northrop's vast private records more than the earl could ever imagine), was the rising star of Deep Earth Lab—a mid-fortyish, former Rhodes Scholar who was appointed to oversee a consortium of its U.S. companies. His entry bid to gain inner-circle access had been to donate three of his companies to the Project, companies he had created and controlled since college.

Vikram had already penetrated the suite's security cams, discreetly hidden in crevices around the room. Jack had just reviewed them: Pictures of Oxford University with an Oxford diploma lined one side of a rear wall. A framed picture of Oxford's Balliol College hung at midpoint beside a photo of Yale's heavyweight crew rowing at Henley on the Thames. Adin was pictured rowing for Yale in the third oarsman's position, straining and grimacing behind wraparound designer sunglasses as the boat was mere feet from the finish line.

Handsomely framed pictures of Yale, including a Yale diploma, lined the other half of the wall. On an adjacent wall hung gilded frames displaying various honors and awards, including stories about him from front-page articles in *The Economist*, *The New York Times* and the *Wall Street Journal*. Even *Parade* magazine published a cover story on him as possessing the business acumen and foresight to rival billionaire Larry Ellison, Oracle's founder and CEO.

Naturally, there was no mention of Deep Earth Lab anywhere in the articles. In truth, as Doron informed Jack, Adin Mocatta was the Chief Financial Officer for the American operations of Deep Earth Lab; this was off-record. Those companies he ran for Deep Earth Lab listed him on the masthead as either the CEO, president or chairman. He was on a fast track to be admitted to the director level of Deep Earth Lab, the most exclusive of inner circles.

Though he had excelled at Yale, Mocatta was proud of the fact that he was by no means the common New England WASP, Yale's perennial poster-boy image.

Doron had been fascinated to discover that the Mocatta lineage extended across Europe in high finance back to the Black Nobility of Venice, then further back into the mists of the ancient world of Babylon, creating a legacy of a long line of merchant bankers spanning across time. His father's powerful uncle, Jacob Mocatta, in the City of London—the old financial city within the city of greater London, with its own Lord Mayor, before whom even British royalty had to bow to enter—would sit with five other men every morning to set the price of gold for the entire world at N. M. Rothschild. The firm of Mocatta & Goldsmid had remained the key bullion brokers to the Bank of England since the 1700s. Adin's distant family in Europe were tightly intermarried with the aristocracy of high finance.

As Doron had told the others two days before, "To say that Adin Mocatta has powerful connections would be a profound understatement. I think we may have our lead horse in a race of invisibles. We've got to run with this guy, watch him more than he can imagine."

The grand chamber, from which Mocatta's office was off to one side, was the centerpiece of the suite. It was occupied only very occasionally by the secret director of Deep Earth Lab. No one but the inner circle knew his identity. This much Doron knew—he entered the top-floor suite fully out of view of the public. Doron's theory was that if they hot-wired this passage, then "when the rat passes the sensor, we'll know." He gathered from Northrop, who never once divulged his name, that Donald Trump was one of his golf partners whenever the director was in New York. Yet not even Trump, who had negotiated the lease on the penthouse suite, had a clue as to who Mocatta really was.

Northrop's private diary reminisced their first meeting. The earl addressed Adin's class of Rhodes Scholars during orientation week. The earl, by sight alone and without a clue as to Adin's name or background, quickly recognized his obvious brilliance, ambition and ruthlessness—in short, he recognized a kindred soul. The earl was still proud of this score.

Recent activity had been traced to Mocatta. Jon got an e-mail from Glen, saying he was being watched and that strange things had been happening around their place, including a phone tap, visits from overly talkative cable and phone-repair men, roofers and environmental inspectors, among a host of constant invasions of privacy. Glen didn't like this at all.

Jon replied, "Lie low and be smart. We know nothing, and that's the bottom line." Jon commented to the others, "I'm glad I followed my intuition. Glen knows absolutely nothing about what's really going on. His total ignorance is our greatest defense."

On this sunny May morning, overlooking the tip of Manhattan, surrounded by water, Adin Mocatta needed some unhindered time to undergo altered consciousness. This meant total solitude. He was virtually the only one present in the vast top-floor suite. He and the directors had sole access to the upper suite. The penthouse suite did not exist as far as outsiders were concerned. If anyone had inquiries, the lower floor was where an assortment of hired talking heads could answer questions.

With lights dimmed and the massive doors locked, Adin Mocatta stared through the expansive plate-glass window while diverting his attention from the World Trade Center—to him a bad futurist painting. As Adin unfocused his eyes, the alien structure blurred in the periphery of his vision. From his control chair he selected auto-tint and darkened the view of the Trade Center.

Perhaps someday he would be able to unmake it by willing it out of existence. At the moment, before consciousness expansion, the first step was to relax and let his thoughts unwind. Memories always helped.

For the moment he reflected on a childhood moment. A very pleasing one. As a child, Adin was one day deep in thought in a corner of the living room of the large family manor house during one of those noisy seasonal celebrations, the house packed with relatives. He hoped the raucous crowds and small talk would end and the people would just go away, above all the overly affectionate older women.

One particular uncle who had studied the Kabbalah under the famed Adin Steinsaltz in Jerusalem announced out loud to the others, "Watching him think is one of the most beautiful things I have ever seen. Do any of you have any idea how bright this child is? Mark my words, he is like a young Maimonides." A host of relatives glowed around the young Adin, then promptly forgot it all. Not the uncle, though—*he knew*. Adin was given his name in honor of his uncle's great mentor, a genius among geniuses.

Adin had an unprecedented bridge to higher consciousness.

He took out a vial of liquid, which he swallowed. He was careful to put the empty vial in his pocket, which he would destroy off premises. Adin reflected that this elixir didn't come easily or cheaply. Far from it. Once it was discovered by the others at the helm of the Project, they would see that this breakthrough, once produced, could enable Deep Earth Lab to eclipse the Oppenheimer diamond mines in ultimate value.

Over the past few years the Project's stealth labs, most underground and far from public view, had been able to isolate from various giants a number of neurochemicals, brain proteins and hormones that had never been seen in nature before. But these discoveries came at great cost. The Project had been forced to kill nine of the giants so far, invariably finding most of them too violent to control. Not even the hypnogen approach on the giants had fully worked. Temporary mind-control would be established, but then things would go haywire. A worker would get crushed, then costly damage-control was enacted under emergency situations, each time further endangering the Project.

But as Adin had noted, the giants had evidenced extraordinary mental abilities quite apart from their massive size, strength and fierceness.

Adin alone was the explorer of this new terrain of consciousness. He was also the only member of Deep Earth Lab engaged in this effort, courtesy of an ambitious scientist willing to do anything to please him. He'd been sending Adin vials from the key British facility in New Forest near Southampton.

Benchmarks in his diary were recorded. Adin managed to glimpse what he called "the plane of the gods." His old Oxford mentor called this the real basis of the ancient accounts of the gods and demigods.

Adin had also managed to mind-meld with one of the giants, literally seeing through its eyes.

Once he was inside the mind of one of the giants—not a pure Nephilim, but a Nephilic crossbreed of the Anakim class—it suddenly jumped up and completely mangled one of the scientists beyond recognition. It had been one of the strangest thrills of Adin's life.

This creature could think thoughts that could be heard miles away. But this oversized giant was an aberration and a danger to the lab. It had already killed three people, and if it had grown any more powerful, it could have sabotaged their effort, breaking out into one of the local towns in the perimeter of New Forest. No protection from their friends in Parliament or MI5 would be able to provide damage control at that point.

But there was good news. It seemed one of Northrop's crews had located a genuine Nephilim burial ground in the sub-Sahara. This might be Adin's big breakthrough.

The elixir finally began kicking in.

Adin made the successive leaps from the relaxed state, to contemplation, to non-thought, then to "broadbanding," a kind of hyperthought he had been able to do since childhood, though it had been greatly enhanced by using the elixir.

Adin suddenly detected a "watcher" within the building's perimeter, some individual aware of him. This adversarial energy field, by the laws of consciousness, could bring unwanted consequences.

The assassin level of damage control, as Adin had said from the beginning to other members of the Project, was an absolute last resort.

A fairly safe compromise had been the hypnogenic mind programming, but that too had downsides. Highly gifted people could detect its patterns, both live and dormant. Remote suicides were also very risky. Now it seemed that this awakening process was already underway.

Adin's broadbanding started to take a demonic detour at about the time Jack and the manager of Trump Center were navigating the secret passageways. He was now feeling accelerated levels of rage.

In another periphery of his consciousness, Adin became deeply bothered. Way off in England, a group *knew*. He feared that they could see him but he couldn't see them.

Chapter 28

The two men who were the Cyber gang's sole liaison with the nephew left Cambridge early in the morning to meet him in New Forest.

One of them, who was a member of the Cambridge Spelunking Society, commented, "A key objective will be to learn about the network of underground caves—and whether it's possible to enter the underground facility by means of them. I'd love to get in one in due course." This meant maps.

"Keep in mind that newer maps have been edited for security reasons," Neville cautioned. "However, older cave maps should show whether cave structures run beneath the facility. My guess is that large caverns may even lie below. Oh, and beyond libraries, try antiquarian bookstores."

Ian then warned, "Remember, meeting the nephew, especially in New Forest, involves considerable risk. If your cover is blown, do not approach the manor here or any of the Cyber gang members till you are cleared. You *can* send encrypted e-mail. But under no circumstances physically return to this manor and drag possible watchers behind. This will jeopardize the entire operation." They understood completely. "Wish us luck."

Heading to New Forest, they drove via Kent, picked up a rental car and left the older car behind—avoiding personal info that might be recorded by New Forest street cams.

Before noon, the two parties met in Burley, the closest village to the underground facility, where the uncle had lived when working as a maintenance worker.

As agreed, the two Cyber gang fellows and the nephew showed absolutely no signs of recognition as they passed one another on the street. The nephew went over to his car and slowly drove far enough ahead of them so as not to draw suspicion. He led them circuitously toward the long forested road leading to the underground complex.

Back at the home base, not having heard from the two Cyber gang members for many hours, Doron and Vikram found an excuse to field-test something they planned to use extensively.

Britain's dalliance with Big Brother technology involved elevated street monitors from one end of Britain to the other. The catchphrase invoked by the State to placate the public was, "Secure Under the Watchful Eyes."

With Ian standing behind them, Doron and Vikram penetrated the "Secure Watchful Eyes" national surveillance system. In little time they were watching activity on the main street of Burley on the outskirts of the largest and densest forest area of New Forest.

Burley's main street was a three-block stretch, with pubs, restaurants, an inn, a pharmacy, a café or two, a bakery, a food chain and several other places. Watching the constant crowd flow, dull faces going hither and yon, became incredibly boring. So they ran a fast digital replay.

Then bingo—jumping back to 11:30 a.m., they saw the green rental car of the Cyber gang parked on the main street with the stuffed Cambridge Enviro-Owl hanging in the back window, the cue for the nephew and the street-cam experiment of Vikram and Doron.

Next they spotted their two members strolling Main Street, looking like tourists.

"There they are," Ian said excitedly.

Doron spotted a black van with tinted windows parked outside the main café after they jumped two corners further along Main Street. Not a good sign, one of the Cyber gang observed. "It may be nothing. Underground facility personnel, scientists or members of the security force are bound to enter the local village for meals, snacks and supplies."

They jumped video cams back up the street to where the two Cyber gang members were slowly wandering.

At that point they spotted a fellow with a green jacket and red bag, who walked right by them. The two immediately turned around and started heading for their car.

"Well done," Ian blurted.

The fellow with the red bag was the nephew. He got into his car on Main Street and made a U-turn heading out. Then the two Cyber gang members pulled out as one of them was pretending to look at maps. Soon both cars were gone. Contact had been made.

The two were now with the nephew, eyeing an impenetrable entrance with a huge gate. It was connected to a very high steel-and-cable fence running the entire perimeter of a vast property. Apart from the entrance, the property was almost impossible to differentiate from the regular forest. It blended in perfectly and seemed to go on forever. They took pictures as they drove along in a commercial vehicle the nephew had borrowed. Occasionally they stopped along the side of the road.

They studied the main gates from a distance. The nephew told them, "The actual underground complex is a mile or two within this large tract of land, dunno how large, but extremely large. The actual facility is out of sight and out of hearing. I reckon this is one of the few places in Britain where one could pull off an undertaking of this type." They zoomed in on the main gates and shot pictures, then left.

There was an unexpected change of plans. On a private farm where they'd left both cars to drive in the commercial van, the nephew confessed, "We've a network of allies that has formed among the residents of this region. We call it the New Forest Underground. I think you'll find them worth meeting."

"Let's not waste a second," the two responded.

"I didn't tell them much, but I did tell them I was meeting some important blokes from Cambridge who had met my uncle and knew about some of the horrors going on."

The two Cyber gang members followed the nephew through the farmlands. By now they were well beyond Wi-Fi reception and any chance of contacting the home base. Due to tracer technology, regular cell-phone contact was considered too risky to try. Neil had told them about that.

Meanwhile at Ian's, the group was becoming increasingly worried about foul-ups as the afternoon moved toward tea time, still with no word back. They hoped the two hadn't been abducted, now kneeling in the dark, handcuffed and blindfolded—either awaiting execution or being tortured while revealing the identities of everyone in their group!

Not by a long shot. The two Cambridge travelers had been abducted—to high tea!

By 3 p.m. the two Cambridge students—now honored guests to these country folk—were enjoying a full spread of high tea. Afterwards, they listened to their hosts, and were glad they did. The generous hosts owned a sizable spread of farmland and were long-established residents whose family had lived in the region for centuries. The nephew had known them since he was a boy, and it was clear they considered him one of their own. Lines of trust were crucial, and it was happening naturally.

The nephew introduced a man at the table as one of his uncle's close friends. The close friend spoke up: "Many of us here have lost either friends or relatives at that underground facility. Most of us here believe something unholy is afoot. We don't like what's going on and never have."

Another member at the table said, "Many of us have felt endangered ever since the deaths."

A round of speakers at the large table began adding perspective on a decade of local horror stories—monster sightings, wailings, things in the night, suspicious activity around the Project.

"In these parts, it doesn't take long for secrets to travel from the local pub to the community," the host observed.

One of the Cambridge guests set down his tea cup and asked a rugged-looking older man sitting across from him, "So you've talked to people who have actually seen some of these things? Monsters and whatnot?"

The man's angry, veined eyes were staring out the window off into the distance. He replied, "Indeed I have, lad, indeed I have. Scary monsters? You bloody well believe it, mate! Things you could never imagine, that's whot!! Unnatural, it is, unnatural. Makes Frankenstein look like a warm, lovable puppy, it does. You could give Frankenstein a good kiss on the lips compared to some of these things."

In silence, the faces around the dinner table suddenly filled with fear.

Their guests from Cambridge now realized that they had found the most valuable resource possible from this trip—committed allies. And this discovery came as a total surprise.

* * *

When the two Cambridge visitors drove out of New Forest after saying goodbye to their hosts and new friends, night was falling. Gnarled ancient oaks that had stood from the time of England's kings of old were quickly transforming into cowled monks in the approaching darkness.

Dominated by the woods, regions of New Forest opened out into heathland, extending for miles where deer and other wild animals roamed free. Farmhouses richly dotted the region, their lights coming on. One they named "the hobbit farmhouse," their unexpected find.

"I think our real purpose in coming here was to meet the New Forest Underground. I also believe we have evaded detection," the driver announced. "If we have somehow gotten on the Project's radar, so have ten thousand other tourists swarming the area today. Common sense dictates that the Project would need a surveillance team the size of a battalion to monitor things at that level."

His companion replied, "Beyond all that, our new allies may have already saved our lives. Remember how one of them told us about the invisible cameras around the perimeter of the underground complex?"

"Yes, and our original plans were to sneak around the facility on foot after leaving them," the driver blurted. "The cameras would have caught us, and we might not be returning to Cambridge now—or ever!"

The next morning after a good sleep, the two travelers walked into Ian's manor. The others were relieved to see them and were all ears.

"We come bearing gifts. But we've more than that, we've got some good news."

When the two finally described tea at the hobbit-like farmhouse and the older ruddy farmer blurting out, "Scary monsters? You bloody well believe it, mate! Things you could never imagine, that's whot!!", Jon couldn't help but smile over at Doron. He pictured the local townspeople of New Forest becoming those angry villagers storming Castle Frankenstein as fear turned to rage, then to fearlessness, and again to courage.

"We mentioned meeting some Yanks who had lost friends from an American base of the underground facility. This further shocked and enraged them. They asked to meet the Yanks if at all possible.

"But we can assure you that the locals of New Forest have no concept of the advanced technological doorways we are privy to, nor the potential wealth and materiel on hand. It's better for our mission, as we all agreed, that they don't know."

They took turns speaking and felt the visit to New Forest had, indeed, created a radical change in plans, much for the better.

Vikram remarked, "Rather than the initial option of descending on New Forest with various vehicles on a likely suicide mission, we may have a whole underground army in place and waiting to go into action with us."

Jon was able to tell the others, "We might actually survive this conflict and have some kind of a life afterward."

"It's the first sign of hope on the horizon in some time to those of us who have privately resigned ourselves to the worst-case scenario," Neville concurred.

"Having already drawn up our wills with goodbye letters to family and loved ones," Neil remarked, having recently rejoined the group after being away.

Jeremy announced, "This has been a major coup," as Ian slapped them on the backs, repeating, "Well done, mates, well done."

Jon brought up the inevitable. "What about sending a more substantial group of us to meet the Underground?" Some were skittish about this.

"We don't need to break cover. But the reality is that you can't stay in hiding forever. Life demands risks, and we can't wage this type of war safely hidden behind our computer monitors forever."

The group nodded as Ian replied, "I agree. In fact, I'm ready to go almost immediately. I'm thrilled at the fact there's a New Forest underground already in place."

One of the returned travelers made an untraceable phone call to the "hobbit farmhouse." After he hung up, he told Ian and Jon, "They can't wait to meet you. They especially want to meet the American." He winked at Jon then gave Ian all the phone numbers and contact information.

At the others' insistence, Ian, Jeremy and Jon soon left the manor in cheers of encouragement. Jeremy insisted on the back seat of the old Land Rover to give Jon a good view of England in May. "We can get our stuff at Trinity in about five minutes," Jeremy told Ian.

Ian later confessed as he got on the M4, "I've decided I don't want my old girlfriend to get wind we're in the area. On reconsidering, I realized she would blow our cover one way or another."

He paused. "Neil reminded me that even an indiscreet phone call to one of her friends would go through the surveillance station of Echelon in nearby Dover. If she mentions the wrong thing, we're toast."

Ian was now formulating a quick excuse should he bump into her (he could just picture her—looking skeptical, hands on hips, betrayed yet again) as he announced with clearly fake enthusiasm, "Oh, my heavens, how good to see you! I was just passing through to look at the birds in their habitat. Why didn't I visit you at *your* habitat? Well…"

He grinned morbidly, again only a few clicks away from some of their abusive games they used to play on one another. He had loved taunting her. She would accuse him of being insensitive, a sadist; then they would make up. He'd have a kind of sensitivity conversion until the testosterone kicked in once again, and the games began all over again. Ian, near the end of their relationship, had started to despise what he was becoming— a taunting bastard. He always knew he was a bit of a madman, and his "relationship" with her had been bringing out the worst in him. He smiled again—*I'm merely here to observe the local birds.* What a line!

Chapter 29

Ian pulled up to the hobbit farmhouse at the expected time for tea with the host and his closed circle of leaders in the New Forest Underground.

As Jon approached the front door, the host extended a hand. "Please do come in. So you must be the famous Yank named Jon, is it?" the ruddy-complexioned man probed. "My name is Gerald, and when the others enter, I will introduce you to the others."

The tall, handsome American won them over with a single smile as he waved to nine others.

Moments later, Ian and Jeremy entered. Jon watched his two friends from the viewpoint of the locals present. *Quite impressive.*

Ian was under the spotlight first. Unable to hide his evident nobility, he created a quiet awe, the reaction of most Englishmen when a titled aristocrat enters their midst (Jeremy introduced him). Some of the older ones present knew the family name. The tall, dark-haired Englishman with the brilliant emerald eyes had an uncanny resemblance to a certain famed English actor. "Yes," one of them blurted, "that's it. Timothy Dalton."

Jeremy was next under the spotlight as Ian introduced him as "a Trinity College science scholar and occasional lecturer." Jeremy had the classic English scholar look, typifying the best and brightest among what Cambridge had produced over the centuries. Jeremy was as gracious and humble as ever, further endearing himself to the group.

Jon later told Vikram and Doron, "The New Forest Underground received us like knights of the roundtable. You would never get a reaction like this in America. And what a beautiful region this is. You'll love it."

When the group moved to the den after tea, the visitors cut to the chase when probed about their needs. "Until we find just the right rental place somewhere within greater New Forest, we feel it wise to stay in nearby Southampton, where we can pretend to be tourists."

Ian confessed, "Please don't go to any extra trouble on our behalf, but since you asked what we need, I will tell you. Ideally, we need a large farmhouse to rent some distance from the underground facility. We've been unable to penetrate it, but believe that once we are here in the area, we will be able to do so."

"Specify in more detail," the host encouraged. "We really want to be of use."

Ian smiled, "Okay, the house should be quite large, able to board up to ten of us. It should have a large barn and plenty of land. We plan to bring maybe seven vehicles, including a truck. We'd like to hide at least four of them in a barn or other large structure, so they would be free of satellite and drone surveillance."

The local leaders looked at one another, their features brightening, while Gerald interjected, "Well, as a matter of fact, your two mates who were here yesterday had already mentioned the possibility of your needing a safe place to conduct operations. So I think some of our fellows here have already had a bit of a look around."

The host eyed one man, a pleasant-looking fellow across the room, who spoke up: "Well, it so happens that our family has been doing vacationer rentals for a long time in these parts. We also act as caretakers for the estates of a number of very well-to-do families. We've been doing this for a long time. There is one place in particular that has been vacant for over a year, and it more than fits the description of what you want. The owners are in Kenya attending to their coffee plantations. I heard from them recently. Because of some local problems in Kenya, they are not due to return to these parts for quite some time, I would imagine up to a year or more. Would you be interested in seeing it?"

Ian and the others were flabbergasted. "We would be honored! Thank you so much."

Gerald's friend continued, "To put your minds at rest, the owners of this estate have given me free reign to use the property while they are gone. I can speak for them. I am certain they'd back your venture, indeed, *our* venture. They detest this facility."

Ian responded, "We'll be most happy to pay whatever it will require."

"Not on your life," the man responded, "We would never accept it. We all sense that you are sacrificing your own lives and taking considerable risk in the process. We're only too honored to help."

Gerald the host spoke up, "If the truth be told, in our view, the lot of you are like a visitation of angels."

The three assured their New Forest allies that the same was true for them. "We never dared entertain the idea of an underground group of allies such as yourselves. You've given us cause for hope that we never expected."

Gerald's friend asked, "Can I take you to see the place now?"

"Absolutely!"

"Then let's not waste a minute more," he said, getting up from his chair.

Those in the den smiled warmly at their honored guests from Cambridge, as Ian said to all of them upon leaving, "Please know how grateful we all are."

On the way out, Ian promised Gerald that they would call back within a day.

Gerald assured them with a very earnest look, "We are ready to help you in any way we can at any time, day or night. In fact, I'm hoping you won't even need to go to that hotel in Southampton."

They didn't. After being given the keys to the estate, they raced back to Cambridge. Jon rarely remembered being so encouraged.

And the estate? Heavens, it was out of some classic film. This unexpected boon broke months of grave sobriety for Jon, ever since seeing Spenser's car smashed at the bottom of Devil's Slide.

I think we can do this, Jon said to himself.

Chapter 30

Three days later, under cover of night, an impressive convoy was making its way to one of the region's most expansive estates.

Ian led the way as the convoy of vehicles entered the back side of New Forest at the farthest point from the underground facility, maybe 40 miles away.

The convoy, consisting of the three Americans as well as the Cyber gang inner-circle, were traveling under a cloak of silence—no cell phones, walkie-talkies or anything else. They were going low-tech.

Ian was driving the SmarTruck with one passenger. Jeremy drove his Austin-Healey 3000 with Jon accompanying him. Vikram and Doron operated the Hummer—"as Yanks, it's only fitting," Ian announced (and, yes, Vikram was now an honorary Yank, which he grinned about). The Land Rover was being driven by Neil, who had pioneered the Watcher program, with Neville joining him in the front seat. The two Cyber gang members who had come to meet the nephew drove a large truck packed with supplies and key equipment from the Cyber wing of the manor house. Other members of the inner-circle task force operated various assorted vehicles, including a refrigerated truck with food and other supplies.

Ian's servant staff had packed the truck with at least three weeks of the best food one could hope for. As his servant staff was packing, he remarked to Jon and Jeremy, "The plan here is to protect ourselves from having to go on any forays into local food marts. We must try and avoid *any* possibility of being spotted. The backup plan will be to send our least-identifiable members out for supply runs. Luckily, this is prime tourist season, so the whole region will be flooded with new faces. We just need to exercise caution."

"Two of the family cooks will join us within a day or two to take care of the task of feeding us," he added. "We're able to bring the food supplies because there's an outside storage shelter with freezers and various iceboxes." It was a facility worthy of Britain's super-rich, Jon had noted.

Ian hit the button on the small pad as the convoy approached an impressive high gate with the words "The Wellstone Estate." As the huge iron gates swung open, the convoy entered a long road with open land and intermittent clusters of forest. The gate closed behind them as Ian hit the button again.

At least half a mile along the main road they made the final approach to what could only be described as a massive residence in elegant rustic design with various side buildings nearby, including a large, six-car garage. Further in the distance stood a huge barn. "That's big enough for all our vehicles," Ian had said upon first seeing it three days before.

Before leaving, Ian told the others, "Don't stop and gape. Just follow me behind the house to where we can unload. Then park either in the garage or the barn. I will give you a tour of the premises once we are done."

Ian parked the SmarTruck and stood outside smiling as he motioned toward their prize. Those seeing it for the first time gawked in amazement. Doron and Vikram quickly trotted around the outside.

They flew into action. The house had ten guest rooms plus a master bedroom. As Ian headed with his belongings for one of the smaller bedrooms, Doron, Jeremy and Jon grabbed him and guided him to the master bedroom, insisting he take it. It took a while, but finally he obliged.

Jeremy said, "Ian, with the huge resources you and your family have put into this, if you don't take it, all of us will camp out in the woods." Ian nodded graciously as they slapped him on the back.

As Gerald's friend told them when he showed the place to Ian, Jon and Jeremy, "The Wellstone family has the means to build a replica of Windsor Castle if they'd wanted to, but they didn't. They also have a huge London mansion bordering Regent Park as well as a flat in Knightsbridge two blocks from Harrods." The three then just shook their heads at their good fortune. He looked at Ian then and said, "I'll bet the owner knows your family."

"Kenya it is, mates," announced Jeremy, who had been there as a child, as had Jon. Pictures galore lined the walls—coffee plantations, smiling servants, animal hunts, 19th-century family members holding large rifles, along with some more-contemporary shots.

Mounted on the walls were stuffed animals, an old pith helmet or two, and posters from old colonial Kenya. One display had brilliant butterflies, another had multicolored coffee beans, another the labels of their various brands of coffee, including Jon's favorite, Peets. It was like a massive museum.

The bedrooms were no less ornate or interesting. Some of the walls in other rooms were deep burnished woods of all sorts, from cherry to maple.

Ian announced, "Since it's after 1 a.m., let's sleep in. I'll handle the kitchen detail in the morning if I can have a few volunteers. Then we can set up the grand old cyberwing. Maybe we should call it Cyberwing New Forest."

Though Doron and Vikram confessed to being utterly spoiled at Ian's, this was not a bad substitute. Both of them wondered what on Earth they would do when they returned to the plebeian world of Palo Alto. "I'm certainly in no hurry to go back," Vikram confessed to Doron.

Before leaving for New Forest, Ian explained to the others why the two Yanks were holed up in their rooms for a day. "Both of them have arranged to submit final projects and papers to their faculty advisors via the Internet. They should be through soon." Both of them aced their tests in absentia.

"Now we're freed up," Doron told them upon leaving for New Forest.

Doron now discovered that the New Forest house had premium satellite television, including channels from the States. "Signs of a dying culture," one of them intoned.

Before they turned in for the night, Vikram and Jon wandered by Doron's room at the end of the hall (like his room at the Sonoma cabin). "Close the door," Doron said in a low voice.

On the screen was a familiar character. A figure dressed like a combination of a TV wrestler and a comic superhero swaggered across stage with a crusader cross and sword emblazoned over a Star of David. It was Jehovah Bob, live from the States, drumming up a grandiose "crusade against evil," as the bottom of the screen announced.

Jehovah Bob yelled into the microphone, "It is taaayuummm to deal with the evil forces around the world-ahhh. It is taaayum to deal with the creatures of darkensssss-uuuhhhh. I cannot-uuuh reveal where they are-uhhhh. But I will battle them. We need prayer-uuhhh. We need do-nations-uuuhhhh for this crusade against evil-uhhh."

Vikram and Jon, on the way out, looked over quizzically at Doron, who was trying to hide a perverse grin.

Back in his room, Jon opened a large window and felt a fresh scented breeze from the orchards and gardens as he lay down. He was grateful for how things had gone so far; an adventure he would not have thought possible a year ago. He also knew that aspects of himself, long dormant, were coming back to life.

Chapter 31

Ian and three volunteers were serving up a "proper English breakfast" of fried eggs, ham, rashers of bacon, bangers (sausage with meal), fried mushrooms, baked beans, fried potatoes, baked tomatoes, buttered toast, marmalade, strawberry jam, tea, coffee and juices. "We've learned why English breakfasts are the main meal in Britain," the Americans confessed. There were hails of appreciation in the large dining hall.

After breakfast, Neville and Neil immediately grabbed a few volunteers and started to set up the cyberwing. Fiber-optic cable was laid between the SmarTruck, hidden in the barn, and the house. In little time they set up the bank of computers.

With feeds from the SmarTruck, broadband Internet access was tested.

"The reception is extremely powerful, rivaling the bandwidth at the manor. We have full access," Neil yelled down the stairs.

"Welcome to the New Forest cyberwing," Neville announced as the whole group ran upstairs.

As Ian and Doron stood behind him, Vikram performed an undetectable test and verified they could connect their various remote cameras to a satellite uplink for broadcast-quality television transmission to anywhere in world. Vikram and Doron had previously rigged it at Ian's manor so their feeds from the SmarTruck would override major network television in the States, Great Britain and around the world. He'd given it a two-second test before at the manor. He did it again. Vikram announced, "We can do live feeds. Test confirmed."

Doron reiterated an earlier warning: "A live feed intercept is not our first option or preference. But if our lives are in danger, whatever's happening can be televised far and wide. It may end up being our ultimate defense—especially if the major networks black out news of events from here."

Jon then cautioned, "I heard from Jack. One of the worst-case scenarios all of us have discussed are commando units in helicopters blanketing us should we be discovered. Jack warns that a containment operation would be the minimum if they get wind of us. Even a search-and-destroy mission is possible if we are perceived as 'enemy combatants' under present anti-terrorism laws. That's why we need to be wary and keep a very low profile. If Deep Earth Lab discovers us, they could use their political operatives to launch commando operations against us. To justify such operations in case of public backlash, they are certain to plant evidence."

Ian fessed up, "Unfortunately, they don't even need to plant evidence. The straight fact is we're hot, very hot. We're not going in like Dirty Harry with just a 44 Magnum. I've raided the family arsenal and brought some very incriminating evidence—not only guns, illegal in themselves, but Stinger-type anti-aircraft missiles, grenades, as well as plastique and Semtex explosives, easily enough to blow the gates of the underground facility and its buildings to Timbuktu. I made sure we had enough to blow a giant's head or leg clean off, which we intend to do, especially if one of these things gets on the loose in New Forest."

Ian and Jon chimed in, "Remember, we've been tiptoeing around for a very good reason—to keep off the radar."

"With new search-and-seizure laws," Doron mentioned, "the police can plunder anyone's possessions, presuming them guilty. That's what has become of America, once the land of the free. And Britain is close behind. I've seen SWAT teams—no longer with any need for search warrants—assault houses in Palo Alto, dragging the inhabitants out into the streets and confiscating their personal effects. Let's assume the same could happen here."

Doron added, "One powerful countermeasure against these anti-terror police sweeps has required us to establish remote protocols on servers hidden in various locations; several are offshore."

"These remote servers can be activated by individual coded commands that are easily triggered by notebook computers, SmartPads, even Internet-ready cell phones," Vikram said.

Neil told the group, "Whether all of you know it or not, Doron and Vikram have been working their bloody heads off to set up some of these remote units. Keep in mind, it is a last resort."

The group applauded with appreciation.

185

Vikram continued, "If a raid takes place, down to the last two seconds—assuming everything is working and we have battery backup—we can trigger an auto remote."

(Vikram had privately told Doron, Ian and Jon several days earlier, "I've set up a fourth tiered auto remote server in Bangalore in an ultra-secure location." With delicious irony Vikram continued, "My cousin has hidden a Wi-Fi laptop computer in an antique Indian sandalwood trunk that is used for the family puja altar. No one ever opens the trunk, so it's a perfect place. The auto remotes will absolutely wreak havoc once given the password.")

Jon predicted, in the language of mathematical chaos theory, "I have no doubt that the exploding drama will take on a life of its own."

Ian assured the group, "These auto remote protocols will go out like ripples in a pond across cyberspace—if we are raided or interdicted or shot dead, nothing can stop them from going into action. Let me now challenge you with something that needs to be included. We need recorded bios of each of us that can be broadcast to the public. There are some very good reasons for this."

Neil followed up, "Could you take a few minutes, each of you. Some of us have already completed our televised bios. We did it before leaving Cambridge for New Forest. Jeremy set the tempo and agreed to have his segment played for you to hear."

Neil paused and hit Jeremy's recording: "Hello, my name is Jeremy Saint John, and I am a graduate fellow at Trinity College and was a Churchill Scholar during my undergraduate years at Cambridge. I work at the Lab of Molecular Biology. I pioneered the ultra-fast DNA sequencing program called ManEater that has been appropriated by a transnational group known as Deep Earth Lab. I have evidence that all of my innovations have been used by Deep Earth Lab to unravel the genome structure of some of the abominations you have seen in this broadcast. ... My parents live in Surrey at the following address. ... And my father is a retired aeronautical engineer at EuroAir ... Inc."

"With these bios," Ian added, "the public would indeed wonder about our group being unfairly imprisoned or terminated by the government. Public outcry may become key for our survival and the ongoing exposure of Deep Earth Lab."

Jeremy added, "As you can see from my statement, each biographical statement must be sufficiently in-depth so the public is concerned about what becomes of each of us. They must get a sense of who we are. The individual does matter."

The bios were completed before lunch.

After sandwiches and soft drinks, most of the group reclined in a densely forested outside area near the house, "away from easy surveillance, especially drones," Neil warned.

"Get ready for a very full afternoon. Our allies in the Underground are due to be here soon," Ian remarked, hoping for a fifteen-minute nap on the lawn chair under the trees.

* * *

Neville looked at the gate monitor and yelled, "They're at the gate."

"Buzz them in," Ian responded. The Underground were tracked on the estate driving ordinary vehicles.

"I think they plan to transfer to the service vans in a safe place away from here in case the EuroDrones pick them up, though I haven't seen too many drones lately," Jeremy interjected.

"Remember," Ian announced, "we have two groups going out today that we will call Group One and Group Two. Group One will head to the underground facility in the care of the New Forest Underground regulars who work there."

"Group Two is the gardening group heading to Lord Northrop's estate."

The day before, at tea, Gerald had told an excited Ian, Jon and Jeremy the fortuitous news: "One particular family in the New Forest Underground has been tending to the gardening needs of the rich and powerful land-owners here for decades. So getting some of your members onto the Northrop New Forest estate as 'gardeners' is now possible. You fellows won't have to break in!"

Ian gave both groups bags of sophisticated bugging devices, probes, micro-cams, mini-cams and transmitters ready to plant. "These are our eyes and ears."

Dressed as gardeners, by 2 p.m. three of the Cyber gang boarded one of the vehicles and headed out the gate.

Group One drove through the front gates of the complex in their utility vehicle by 3:15 p.m.

Whispering to Ian on the secure cell phone, an excited Neville announced, "We're in. The road here seems to go on forever. We are heading to the tarmac near the aircraft hangar, which houses one heli-copter and several smaller planes. I see it. Near that is a vehicle building." He switched on the tiny cam function.

Ian responded, "I see it. It's clear on the monitor here."

Neville continued, "The underground complex proper is some dis-tance away. I hope to at least get a glimpse of it."

Ian, Doron, and Vikram watched from the home base. The two Cyber gang members, dressed in the same maintenance outfits as their New Forest hosts, helped the others clean the hangar, change a tire on one of the vehicles, perform an oil change on a small shuttle bus, move refuse to the large outside waste bin, and other assorted maintenance tasks as they planted bugs.

The home base heard the hosts joke, "We should hire you, mates. Makes our jobs easier, that's for sure."

Neville announced, "A single transmitter has been placed under the dashboard of each vehicle, including the planes and the one helicopter."

"We've tested the plants They're good to go," Ian responded in Neville's earpiece. "These new prototypes are very hard to detect dur-ing standard bug-sweeps."

The home base watched as the maintenance vehicle left the tarmac area, entering a road that looked familiar. Neville's blood froze when he realized why it looked familiar. He said to Ian, "Can you see this? I'm al-most certain it was the one taken by the New Zealander who filmed the child-giant."

Neville swiveled the cam. Ian said, "Describe to the driver the 'is-land' of inward growing trees and the play area."

The driver replied off the cuff, "Oh, that's no longer here. They re-moved it after an incident. The trees were cut down several years ago, and everything in that area was bulldozed. Though, believe me, mates, there is plenty happening here. This is the main place."

"We've glimpsed a giant or two in our time," the driver mentioned, looking over to the other worker in the front seat.

A look of fear overcame the worker in the passenger seat. "I'll do all I can to avoid seeing one of those things again. In two bloody strides these creatures can pick you up as if you were a small toy and do anything they bloody want."

Ian, Jon, Vikram, Doron and Jeremy looked at each other in alarm.

Neville ask the two workers up front, "So the giants are hidden from view these days?"

"Yeah, I reckon, mostly. I've been told they come out under controlled circumstances. Some kind of mind-control maybe, don't really know. But they are around, for sure. I can't imagine what these bloody scientists plan to use these creatures for. Bloody boggles the mind, it does."

Neville queried the driver, "I'm feeling a nervous tingling in my hands. It just started." The driver responded, "Yeah, that's what we get. Hard to explain really, but we get it as well. I can feel a tingling right now, as a matter of fact." His mate in the front seat said, "Me too."

The home base saw through the mini-cam. In the distance appeared a dark fortress, surrounded by trees.

"So that's it, eh?" Neville asked.

"Most certainly is, most certainly is. You don't want to go into that, mates. I've bloody well never been in there, but I know some blokes who have, some of our group who we've lost to so-called accidents."

The worker in the passenger seat apologized to the others as he took out a pack of cigarettes. "I always have to have one when that building comes into view." His hands were shaking as he lit it. He looked plaintively at the driver, who assured him, "Don't you worry, we're just driving near it and we'll be away from this thing in three blinks. I just want our friends here to be able to put one of their little devices on one of the bushes or wherever it's supposed to be."

He turned to Neville behind him and said, "Best we not come any closer than this or they'll get suspicious. They have big monitor cameras around here. I think it best I place your device on something. I think my mate and I will stand outside and take a quick smoke and relieve ourselves. That way it won't look suspicious even if we are being observed. We do this sort of thing all the time." His mate nodded.

Neville gave him a micro-cam glued to an artificial leaf.

The maintenance man relieved himself against a tree. While leaning on it, he placed the miniature camera precisely where Neville had told him. The tree had a new leaf, indistinguishable from the others, with a clear view of the underground fortress.

As they headed back, Neville whispered to Ian through the mic, "Micro-cam now in place. Can you see through it?"

Ian responded, "Yes. Well done. That thing looks horrific, like some kind of massive fortress. From now on we'll call it *the Fortress*."

Neville told the home base, "We've been here less than an hour, which is their standard clean-up sweep. We should be heading out the gate in moments."

Group One headed out the gate into New Forest proper, then barreled along various roads. Soon they entered a farm where their vehicles had been left.

Back at the Wellstone estate, taking a ten-minute break, Ian, Jon and Jeremy sat around a Damascus brass table in an upstairs den for a coffee. Ian listened to Jon and Jeremy's proposal. He was amazed as his eyes fixed on a wall-mounted 19th-century tribal mask from Kenya. Ian finally replied, "Your idea is what we've really been waiting for. We tech guys have completely missed out on the nuances you bring from the biological sciences. Could you explain it to the group tonight?"

Group One was returning to the Wellstone Estate in a private van. The driver said to Neville, "If any of you needs to go out on errands, wants a pint or a tuck run, or just wants to hang out at the coffee bar, we can take you."

Neville was relieved to hear it. "You read my mind. Some of us will need to get out now and then so we don't feel like trapped animals."

Jon looked at Ian, who gave a fearful and nervous nod as he reminded Jon in a low voice, "We must be very careful. We just can't jeopardize the operation. A little slip and…"

After a few minutes, Ian remarked to Jon, Vikram, Doron and Jeremy, "Now watch this."

In clear view they now saw Group Two, the "gardeners," at Northrop's local hunting estate.

"They've already planted a number of these micro- and mini-cams. Let's see if we can switch through at least a few of them," Ian stated.

The screen shifted to a live cam shot taken in the back of Northrop's estate in a densely wooded area. Neil came into view.

Ian asked him over the secure cell, "So that's the rear gate. It looks like an access point into the underground complex. Is it?"

"Looks like it to me. We're just now trying to figure out how to spring the servo-lock," Neil replied.

It was a thick gate. Attached to it from both sides ran the high cable fence capable of being electrified.

"It seems the Clockwork Earl has his own VIP entrance that's out of view from everything. Let me move the cam. Can you see the gravel road from here leading into the dense woods on the other side of the fence? I'm sure it leads through to the underground facility."

"It's the perfect stealth entrance," Jon observed.

The mini-cam focused in on one of the Cyber gang members with a tiny computer connected to the electric lock. They heard a springing sound. They heard "bingo" as the lock loudly clonked open. "We've already deactivated the alarm," he said.

Smiling like a stage magician, he and Neil nudged the gate open a few feet to prove what he had done. He then swung it back and reset the lock.

"We're done gardening," Neil whispered to Ian and the others over the live cam. "See ya soon," he said with a triumphal smile then turned the cam on the others who waved, grinning, into the live cam.

Chapter 32

Dinnertime was approaching. Just as Ian was about to phone Gerald and the others at the hobbit farmhouse about joining them for the evening meeting, they were at the front gate, pressing the buzzer. Ian saw Gerald and his wife smiling on the monitor.

"Now, this is a welcome surprise," Ian told them gladly.

"We're just bringing a few goodies," Gerald replied.

The group met them at the garage as they opened the rear of their van.

Gerald announced, "You don't need to waste your time cooking dinner. We've brought it for the lot of you."

"You shouldn't have gone to that much trouble. That's much too much," Ian and others chorused.

Gerald's wife announced with a smile, "Several families cooked the meal this afternoon. It's the least we can do for our guests."

Ian implored, "Will you at least join us for dinner? We have some interesting things for you to see at our evening meeting. It's been a hectic day, as you know."

"We would be honored."

Ian watched the lavish spread being laid out on the banquet table. The timing of this gracious offering was perfect. The two groups had come back dog-tired. Those who'd stayed with Ian at the estate had been way too preoccupied with monitoring events to undertake tackling dinner.

These people are a godsend, Ian thought.

The dining hall applauded the generous offering of the hobbit-farmhouse hosts and their friends.

"It's the best solid English country cooking I have tasted in a long time," Neville remarked. "Thank you so much."

"Hmmm, apple crumble, treacle and custard," one of them remarked. "I think we're ready to pay homage."

After dinner, the whole crew and their hosts collected in the den to hear the reports from the two field crews. They had been waiting for other members of the New Forest Underground to appear. And they did, right on time.

Volunteers had previously mounted a large plasma screen in the front of the den.

As members of Group One and Two spoke, Ian and Vikram began clicking through every single bug, micro-cam and sensor that had been planted. It was a field exercise worthy of England's famed MI5 intelligence service.

They were amazed at the clear views around Northrop's estate, even the hidden rear entrance leading into the back of the underground facility. Another view showed the outside of Northrop's manor from the side, next a massive private garden area with lawn like Wimbledon. At the front was an altar of some kind. Another view from the rear showed one of the servants sitting on the stairs, having a cigarette.

Neil mentioned, "We can access the interior cameras in Northrop's manor itself through a stealth chip connected to an outside wire. We also need the ability to override their security cameras with replacement images. We can get the cameras to record a full, uneventful day and night, with which we can feed them the images at whim. Even if an African safari were to come through Northrop's local estate here, the cameras would register no such event, and none would be any the wiser. Want to test it?"

Ian performed a test, sending back to the Northrop security center, from one particular outside camera, an endless tape loop of a five-minute segment of a nonevent they'd just recorded—in this case, a bug that kept returning to the same nearby flower. It was perfect.

Neil concluded his report. "Those monitoring Northrop's estate will see only what we allow them to see."

Ian came to the front. "I would've never believed we could get so much done our first day here. Bravo, mates, bravo. Very impressive. But we could not do a thing without our brave hosts sitting amongst us."

Gerald and the other New Forest allies nodded graciously.

Ian agreed with Vikram that the last shot on the screen would be from the plastic leaf pointed at the Fortress.

The group looked in hushed silence. The ominous Fortress was lit up with a strange greenish light, eerily now standing out against England's extended spring twilight.

The New Forest Underground all had looks of amazement. "It's utterly incredible," Gerald blurted.

"Now," Ian paused, "we may have something on hand even more impressive than what you've seen so far."

Ian looked to Jon and Jeremy to join him.

"While the lot of you were out planting these sensors, and it was a jolly good job, Jon and Jeremy presented me with a remarkable option to greatly enhance our surveillance capacity. Remember, they may not be official hackers, but they are our resident biologists and geneticists, and I reckon there's few better than them." There were shouts as the two walked to the front.

Ian headed to a seat, saying, "I've asked them to emcee for a while."

Jon and Jeremy turned and watched the stationary image while asking the audience, "Any observations?"

Neil spoke up. "Well, I was there when we fixed it to the branch. I felt the problem was that it's stuck quite far away from the Fortress with a fixed view. It also may be vulnerable to wind and rain."

Jon and Jeremy applauded from the front. "Exactly."

Jeremy observed, "When we were monitoring all of you placing stationary sensors around that, I told Ian that's where they will stay. They're good as far as they go, but they are stationary."

Jon took over, "What Jeremy and I are talking about is a remote-controlled mobile unit using a small animal, such as a rat or a squirrel, as a carrier."

Loud hails began.

"A bit of history," Jeremy broke in. "The concept of animal relays was pioneered by the CIA and by us. It allows a rat's eyes and ears to become our remote sensors as we guide it around. One can also use squirrels, the second common option. Rats can go where it's dark and dirty, places where squirrels would never go. Though squirrels definitely have some advantages."

Jeremy paused. "Some of MI5's greatest breakthroughs have come through remote-listening squirrels at such places as Hyde Park, where heads of state would walk from Embassy Row to sit on a quiet bench away from the crowds. A harmless-looking squirrel was able to record every word, whereas the appearance of a rat would simply have caused pandemonium and would be a dead giveaway."

"Even a rat imitating a squirrel?" Ian ventured, mocking a squirrel's posture. They laughed.

Jon took over. "A specific biochip can be implanted that allows you to control the animal like a remote toy. The rat, in most cases, becomes a movable digicam that can access all sorts of places. Let's call it the 'rat servo-cam.'" More excited laughter.

Jon continued, "A rat, for instance, would be able to *penetrate* the Fortress." He paused for dramatic effect.

"Once inside, the rat could go almost anywhere within the building, including *beneath it*. If there are, indeed, huge holding areas beneath the Fortress, a rat would be able to access it far better than any human cave-climber. Squirrels have impressive access within a forest or anywhere there's lots of trees, like a park. So they are an option for outside viewing. Let's say one of these creatures comes out. We can watch it from a tree or on the ground. With a squirrel, we can follow it."

Ian asked, "Can you create such a thing here, and what do you need to prepare it?"

"The good news is that I have already brought a good sampling of these bio-implantable chips as well as something else we will need to make it work—high-density virtual-reality goggles and a guidance joystick. Jon and I, with your assistance, plan to create an operating theater upstairs in the taxidermy room. We can perform the whole implant procedure right there. Both of us have done it before."

The crew from Cambridge, like soldiers showing bravado before battle, applauded and yelled. Jon predicted that this would surface as tensions mounted.

Jeremy and Jon looked toward Gerald as they challenged, "If our local allies could lay their hands on a Norway rat or two, we'd be set. They are in most large dock areas such as Southampton."

Ian remarked, "I gave Gerald a call earlier. I believe he's already got some people working on it, yes?"

Gerald gave the thumbs-up from his chair. "Rats are no problem for the New Forest Underground. It's some of the people we worry about," he announced with a wink. "On a similar note, you fellows don't need to go shopping at pet stores and local pharmacies for supplies, because our mates in the Underground will do it for you."

"That's terrific news," Jeremy responded.

"You many not appreciate them very much, but Norway rats can scale any wall, swim any sewer, climb any elevator shaft and enter places well nigh impossible for ordinary folk," Jon remarked.

Jon finished the thought. "These rats would make the perfect mobile cam for inside the Fortress."

Another loud applause. *More bravado*, Jon thought.

Ian announced, "We will take a ten-minute break, then Jeremy has a film to show us that he brought from Cavendish Lab."

Ian looked over to Gerald and the others from the New Forest underground who had arrived en masse after dinner. They were flabbergasted.

* * *

As people returned to their seats, Jeremy announced, "This film is about what Jon has called 'servo-rats.' It deals with squirrels as well and should answer scores of questions."

Gerald and his wife moved to the front, as did their friend, who had secured the Wellstone Estate for their visitors from Cambridge.

The film begins.

A grain-sized biochip is shown being injected into a squirrel's cranium through a hypodermic needle. Moments later it is outside, scampering up a tree, completely unfazed by the procedure. Now the perspective is reversed.

The scene is repeated through the squirrel's eyes as it passes bark on the tree trunk with knots, whorls and small details. A small bug emerges from a tiny hole as the squirrel jumps to an upper branch. Then it looks down from the tree.

Two men are sitting on a park bench near the tree. They can be heard talking through the squirrel's ears as it looks down at them. It can see the *London Times* sitting on the second man's lap.

Now digital interpolation takes over. It zooms in on the newspaper to the point that single letters fill the entire screen in sharp detail. For dramatic effect, a tiny Egyptian hieroglyph appears beside a section heading of the paper. The second man takes out a small business card, turns it over, and the same Egyptian symbol appears.

Jeremy paused the film and mentioned, "We can see the two spies connecting—and it's been by means of the squirrel. No cameras, no equipment."

Neil asked, "How is the squirrel moved about?"

Jeremy answered, "This is a bit technical, so I'll be brief. By point-to-point 'goal programming,' the squirrel, of its own accord, 'wanted' to go where the red indicator dot designated as its next destination."

He fast-forwarded. The red pointer is placed over a leaf on the ground directly behind the bench. The squirrel scampers down the trunk of the tree next to the designated target leaf, where it begins digging for acorns behind the bench.

One of the men in the film demonstration whispers to the other sitting beside him, "The code word to retrieve the money wired from Riyadh to Geneva is Atilla-828-342, but you have to appear in person at 11:30 a.m. sharp. Go to the teller wearing the blue pendant."

It came through as loud as a yell through the squirrel's ears. Nothing was missed.

Jeremy paused the film, and awed faces nodded. Gerald looked dumbfounded. "My crikey, I don't know what to say."

Jeremy made another point: "The latest miniature chip implants are so tiny, they're undetectable. Now get ready for the rats!"

The audience now saw through the eyes of a gray rat. It scales a high interface in an old building to enter through the attic. Another segment has the rat running on top of a pipe, jumping to another pipe near the furnace in the basement.

The third segment begins. The rat is in a sewer conduit. The screen goes black for a time. The rat emerges and jumps on a toilet seat, looking about a bathroom. It scampers into the bedroom of someone sleeping.

"Do you see why we have trouble keeping them out of our homes?" Jon asked.

The final section of the film portrays a British commando unit using a joystick to guide a rat into what appears to be a terrorist hideout in some Middle Eastern country. The rat is hot-wired with explosives. It scampers into a back room; the camera shifts to an outside view of the building. In seconds, the building explodes as an SAS unit surrounds the building.

Jeremy paused the image on the plasma monitor and simply looked across the audience with a "do-you-get-it?" expression.

The whole group applauded enthusiastically as Jeremy told them, "We can be up and running very soon. All we need are the animals."

The New Forest folk were clearly mind-blown at this whole new world of technology.

Gerald spoke up: "Anything you need from us, just give the word and you'll have it. We have two of our people right now in Southampton looking for those Norway rats you want. I'll check my cell phone and see if they've come up with anything yet. Should be a message."

He put away his cell phone and nodded at Ian. "Three large Norway rats! Paid someone at a dock warehouse who trapped them in cages."

"Great news."

As the meeting ended, a volunteer group carried out all the cutlery and containers they had washed, putting it all in the back of Gerald's van.

Gerald climbed into the driver's seat to head back to the hobbit farmhouse with his wife. He looked at Ian and the others and said, "We have been hoping and praying for fellows of your caliber for longer than you know. Your group of blokes are like a godsend to us in New Forest, make no mistake about it. We've been in fear for a long time—too long. We know you have much to lose and have come here willing to risk all of it. No, we are the ones that are grateful."

"It would be much tougher without them," Ian said to Jon and Jeremy, as Gerald drove away.

Chapter 33

Adin Mocatta was bothered by recent rumblings from below.

A tip-off from the building manager of Trump Empire Tower was given to the dummy office on the lower floor. The manager approached his contact, whom he believed to be the corporate vice president. and who had paid him handsomely in the past. He knew this tip-off would result in a generous reward—and it did, in a stack of crisp hundred-dollar bills.

Lower staff were never allowed near the upstairs executive penthouse suite—immediate termination was the result—so the dummy VP sent a secure e-mail to Mocatta. It included several shots of an FBI agent, filmed from the Trump Tower monitors, as well as a scan of the official FBI letter.

The e-mail read, "The building manager has just reported that an FBI agent in the anti-terrorism unit has been prying around the complex. He asked about architectural plans as well as some invisible passageways."

The letter to the building manager, on official FBI letterhead demanding full compliance, read in part: "We have grounds for concern that there may be a terrorist group acting within the premises of Trump Empire Tower."

That's all it took. It was a long shot, but they could actually lock down the entire massive complex and sweep it.

Adin could not afford to have FBI agents blundering into the penthouse suite. It would open a can of worms.

He thought for a moment. His gut reaction was that this was typical FBI blundering and misdirection. *If a terrorist in a headdress goes through one door, you can be sure the FBI will take the other.*

However, he thought, *a **mistaken** search of the premises would be as bad as being directly fingered.*

Adin sent a dispatch to the Project's stealth security team to forward the photos of the agent to the Project's undercover agents in the New York bureau. They were ordered to monitor the agent (Jack) and report back to the stealth team. The directive also had a second order: "Trail Lederberg 24/7, but do it without footprints. He must not know. Lederberg could be the source of a leak that has awakened FBI interest. Find out."

Sitting back in his lounge chair, Adin eyed the Manhattan shoreline as he pondered possible indiscretions by Dr. Lederberg. *Was it the programmed suicides that has awakened the FBI? Has Lederberg slipped in ways I don't know? Has his office been broken into and something incriminating found? Has he blabbed to a colleague after one too many drinks?*

A final icy thought pierced his mind like a dagger. *Could I have been given a hypnogenic cocktail at that early Bohemian Grove retreat when I, new to the Project, first met Lederberg? If so, is it possible that I had been programmed in the black room? If so, could a single phone call from Lederberg…*

* * *

Jeremy and Jon had been given three Norway rats early in the morning by the locals, who had gone to Southampton the night before. They dropped by the rats on their way to work, smiling proudly as they handed Jon the cage.

The two men drove away, speculating where the rats might end up in the Fortress. "Let's hope one of those bloody monsters doesn't just crush 'em, though I reckon they would be hard to catch, eh?" The other one nodded in silent reflection as they went out the gate.

As the operations were underway, the others looked on in their *ad hoc* operating room, a rearrangement of the Wellstone taxidermy and butterfly-mounting room. A boar's head had been stuffed and now sat in one corner, waiting to be mounted somewhere in the house.

An injection stand held a hypodermic needle that could be precision-guided. The barely visible biochip had already been loaded into it, held by a gel medium.

Jon turned a metallic crank as the needle moved very slowly down toward the top of the rat's skull. He and Jeremy decided to see the results before they tried it on the other two rats.

Ian's computer was connected to the receiver that could pick up the chip's special signal. Unlike the older chips, which needed relays every five or ten miles, the new-generation chips could be received from more than 20 miles away. Yet there was an added option. The new chips could also find any Wi-Fi hotspots within their 20-mile radius.

Jon told the others, "Any of us have the ability to be in the SmarTruck, monitoring broadband and Wi-Fi, and connect to every chip out there on the field, whether stationary or implanted, whether they are in New Forest or Ian's Cambridgeshire manor."

When the rat awakened, it began sniffing around a large holding box, scampering across the newspaper laid on the bottom.

Jeremy put on the headphones for auditory input and yelled, "I can hear you fellows whispering back there!"

Nervous smiles appeared on some of the rear faces, at which point Ian taunted, "Maybe we need some of these mobile microphones around the house just to make sure everybody's on the level!"

Jon put on a virtual-reality helmet and stood silently for a moment. "I can see through its eyes," he announced, while reaching over toward the joystick on the countertop, stretching awkwardly and fumbling till his hand found it.

"I can hear through its ears as well. I'm going to try to direct the rat." He moved the joystick. "When you see the rat move, describe to me what it does, when it moves, and where it goes."

They told Jon that it scampered to the side and walked around all four sides inside the box.

"Good. I'm going to run the same type of test outside of the house. If I get into trouble, I'll stop the rat, and one of you may have to collect it. Okay?"

"Give it a try, Jon."

Several followed the rat outside while Jon and the others remained in the operating room. It went out the front door, took a left and ran along each side of the house, staying within six feet of the outer walls. It ran haltingly at first, then at a more deliberate, natural-looking clip, without stopping as many times. Those looking at the monitor concurred with Jon's perception—he was getting the hang of it, and the animal was behaving more naturally.

Finally the Norway rat reentered the front door and scampered back up the stairs. It stopped in the hall, returned to the taxidermy room and stopped beside the large box.

"Better than I'd hoped," Jon announced, echoing the others' enthusiasm.

Jon and Jeremy implanted the two other Norway rats, then asked, "Do you think you could manage to find us some squirrels?"

"We'll get right on it after lunch," the others responded.

Ian phoned the Cambridgeshire manor and talked with the cook and house servant, who soon headed to join them at the Wellstone estate. They agreed to come in time to cook the evening meal, the next day at the latest.

Ian spelled out a list of things needed, then confessed, partly joking, "I'm having one of my characteristic cravings. Can you bring five pheasants from the local market?" He gave the others nearby a guilty shrug. "The depraved tastes of peerage," he confessed.

* * *

By afternoon, activities at the Wellstone estate resembled a mini-rally of animals racing around the house. A motley of squirrels and rats took turns running the course.

The squirrels were as entertaining as the rats. As it turned out, one of the Cyber gang members, Cyrell Smythe, a former video-game addict, was unusually adept at putting the animals through the paces. He and Doron were the two best at it.

A squirrel ran up one side of a tree, jumped from branch to branch to branch until it had gone around the entire tree from the top, then scampered down the opposing side, stopped, and ran around the base of the tree. Loud clapping ensued.

"It's starting to look like Harry Potter's Hogwarts School around here," Jeremy remarked, smiling as he leaned back in an outdoor chair, looking at one of the squirrels staring down from a branch. A moment later Jeremy turned and saw the squirrel now beside his chair, sitting up on its haunches in an almost worshipful pose.

"It's paying you homage, Jeremy," one of the onlookers quipped. Jeremy grinned and reached out and patted the squirrel's head.

Then Gerald and his close friend, Clive—who had gotten them the Wellstone estate—arrived. They had come in SUVs to transport the whole group to dinner at one of the New Forest Underground houses.

The group looked on expectantly as Gerald and Clive rounded the corner and walked head on into the "cyber-rat" and "smart-squirrel" demonstrations in the rear gardens. They were stunned.

Gerald kept shaking his head. "With those ordinary-looking animals, you can go anywhere you please in the underground facility, can't you!"

Upstairs, one of their ace game-players—in this case, Doron—took over the controls. The next moment, the squirrel ran up Gerald's body and sat on his shoulder, paws up. Gerald, startled and amused, looked on as it jumped to the ground and headed for a tree.

Ian signaled out the window and invited the two visitors upstairs to see something else. The guests entered and froze upon seeing the image on Ian's large monitor. It was Lord Northrop, whom both men recognized immediately. They had never seen the vast Oxfordshire estate, where the earl currently was.

"Is that Lord Northrop at his private estate?" Gerald asked. "I mean, are we seeing him through his own monitoring cameras there at his castle or whatever that place is?"

"Yes, we hacked into his main surveillance system over a month ago. You are seeing him live."

"This is just bloody amazing, just bloody amazing."

In truth, it was one of their most incriminating recordings of the Clockwork Earl, but the visitors didn't know that.

Northrop was practicing some kind of regal walk in the hallway, taking steps with exaggerated motions like a dwarf riding an oversized bicycle. Stately music playing in the background.

Doron was fighting hard to suppress a chuckle as he quipped to the dumfounded visitors, "I believe the earl's greatest accomplishment is not being an Oxford don. I believe he secretly heads up the government's Department of Silly Walks." Most of them had seen old replays of *Monty Python's* John Cleese, in utterly exaggerated movements, act out some kind of preposterous walk as he left the Department of Silly Walks. The Clockwork Earl was coming close.

"What in the world could he be up to?" Gerald asked again.

"Believe us, this is tame," one of the Cyber gang responded.

Jon told the group, "Looks to me like he's excitedly preparing for some kind of grand event."

"Getting ready to ride the 'dark god,'" Doron amended.

Vikram told the visitors, "He actually has a huge crown with a throne in it. It's big enough to fit on the head of a giant. I think Northrop actually plans to ride it."

The mouths of their shocked guests were hanging wide open.

Ian then gave Doron a wink to play for the guests another previously recorded segment of the Clockwork Earl.

"This was taped a few weeks back," Ian confessed.

It's the Oxfordshire main estate. Northrop's back is to the camera on an expansive upper-floor balcony above the back gardens. It is dark outside, and his silhouette becomes visible as he turns sideways, still leaning against the railing. A protuberance is sticking out where his nose should be.

The earl is wearing a phallic strap-on nose almost identical to the protuberance worn by Malcolm McDowell's character in Stanley Kubrick's *A Clockwork Orange*.

Northrop is leering over the balcony. He holds up a wide-rimmed champagne glass and takes a long draught as an effete scream issues from behind him. He wiggles his rear and then looks around menacingly, holding out his arms ready to stalk. The earl's nocturnal games of extreme nastiness have begun.

A vague form resembling the earl is seen creeping around in the shadows along the hallway. The cameras follow the Clockwork Earl as he begins stalking after a taunting, effeminate voice that is out of view. Down the hall, his hunched form creeps forward. It is dark. He stumbles, tripping over something and falling to the ground. There are more crashing sounds, raves, then falsetto screams. A door bangs shut. Two excited screams.

"I could never imagine something like this," Gerald reacted in a shocked tone. "A man of that wealth and position doing such things. I just cannot understand it." The blessed cloistered moral naiveté of the ordinary people was refreshing to Ian and Doron.

Gerald clearly felt betrayed. "We try to serve people like Earl Northrop; we give it our best efforts. They live like gods compared to us, then look at what they bloody do with it all. I reckon with the horrors we have seen around here, it should come as no surprise with folks like him, eh?" He was looking at Clive, nodding grimly.

He tilted his head in Clive's direction and said to Ian and the others, "Well, I guess it's best all of us leave so we're not late for dinner. Don't want to keep the others waiting, do we Clive?"

Clive continued, "We'll be going to my house for a change. What I have may not compare with Lord Northrop's, but you can certainly add anything I have to your battle chest! With enough of us locals pitching in, I bet there are some valuable assets we can use!"

Chapter 34

Clive owned a large, rustic house surrounded by fields and several barns—another great hideaway.

After dinner the guests moved to the family den. Others from the local underground soon showed up and joined the main group, where Taunton cider was being served.

Neville and several others met with the New Forest Underground spelunker, an athletic and agreeable-looking fellow in his mid-thirties. He worked for the national park service. They grabbed a small table some distance from the main group.

The local cave-climber showed photos taken at various points of the New Forest cave systems. One cavern in particular appeared almost limitless.

"I would definitely like to see this one," Neville volunteered, "but as you know, our real interest is the system that goes near the underground facility. Is that where this cavern is located?"

"It's fairly close by. Just give me the word and we'll go."

Ian, standing in the middle of the room so he could monitor several groups, turned to the cave group and teased, "Neville's been badgering us for days to go down into the caves. If the lot of you are up to it, I can think of nothing better. In fact, I might join the outing myself."

Vikram jumped in. "Count me in as well. I have explored the caves in the region of Maharashtra's Ajanta and Elora Caves, as well as one huge one in the jungle near Mysore City."

Neville gave him a smile and a thumbs-up. "You're always welcome."

Neville related to his new friend his ordeal of trying to get cave and topographical maps of the area. "Each office I visited, I discovered that either the geographical records appropriate to our query were no longer to be found—'somehow misplaced'—or that the specific pages dealing with the cave networks close to the underground facility had been removed. There was nothing—not in the county offices, not in the

Forestry Commission's main office, not in the land surveying office, our last resort."

Mike, the New Forest spelunker, replied, "I don't think this is accidental. I tried to get the very same cave maps a few years ago. They were gone then. In fact, their absence was one of the things that alerted me to the fact that something was going on. One of the first things I did after that was team up with my old mate—a fellow cave explorer who's been at it with me since we were boys. We learned the network of caves led to an absolutely huge cavern much further along. It's beneath what you call the Fortress."

He took a long sip of Oxbow Cider and paused. "Do you know what we found when we got down there? We found a man-made wall that was impregnable. It totally blocked our passage to the cavern. My mate had done his military service and reckoned a direct missile attack wouldn't breach that wall. It was the type used around missile silos he had seen before—reinforced concrete and steel probably four foot thick. That absolutely told us something big was going on."

"Amazing," Neville replied. He paused. "Okay, but what about this—you were working from the front side. What if we approached the cavern from the side of Northrop's estate, from the rear?"

"We've wondered about that," Mike confessed, "but never dared enter from that side."

"Well, it will take us a few days before we have a way of breaching the Northrop estate," Neville responded. "Would that interest you?"

"Count me in! By the way, to answer your earlier question, I got my cave maps from one of the maintenance men shortly before he died."

Shaking his head, Neville said, "We'll make good use of those maps in his honor." He then announced, "The spelunking group is now called Group Three."

Jon and Ian turned and smiled.

At that point, Group Three (making Neville a leader in two groups), joined the larger group as a heated conversation became noticeably louder. Gerald was describing the time a close friend saw a giant standing outside the Fortress in the rear area.

"My mate who had worked there had seen these things several times. That's how I learned about them. He decided to sneak around to that back area of the Fortress where the huge door exists. The giants were let out after the maintenance staff had left. But he managed to get a look. Undone, he was.

"Mates, it was holding a cow with one hand and devouring it as though it were a breakfast sausage. Somehow the bloody ground opens up. The earth moves. That's how the giants get out. I can't quite describe it."

He tried to use his hands to explain. "You can't bloody see it from the air because the forest is too dense in the area, and, beyond that, there's a covering over the Fortress that hides it from above." His hands, palms down, went in a curve from left to right: "There's some sort of massive, painted camouflage fabric. I reckon that from the air it looks no different from the forest!"

Gerald looked for words. "Big enough, that entrance in the ground was, my mate told me, to lower a bloody house in."

He returned to the giant. "At any rate, this giant was almost as tall as the trees as it held a cow with one hand, and with one bite it chewed off at least a third of the animal. It just held it as its guts spilled out, with blood pouring all over the place. Two bites later and the cow was completely eaten. Then this creature gave out a deep roar of a type that would chill your marrow. I know that a number of people have been killed by these things. The body might end up on the side of a motorway or in a field where it's been moved by the facility."

Eventually someone changed the subject.

Jon then asked the group, "What do you know about Druid history and Stonehenge close by?"

"This whole area is known for its Druid relics, especially in the caves," Clive replied. "It's also famous for present-day warlocks and witches. You can go down the main street of Burley and find the 'Olde Witche's Cafe.' The locals refer to the town hall assembly as 'the coven.'"

Clive continued, "During a summer solstice ceremony, a friend's son was hired to help serve the food at Lord Northrop's. He hires temporary local help during these bigger events. Any rate, the boy told me and his dad that they had a huge bonfire in the back gardens after midnight and people were dressed in robes and hoods just like the ancient druids. Rumor had it that it turned into an orgy."

Doron added, "Northrop's been seen at Bohemian Grove, an elite club know for strange rituals close to where I grew up."

Clive observed, "He's a man who seems to like to wear what I would have to call extreme encumbrances, hooded robes and all, indeed, outfits I dare not mention—certainly after seeing what you fellows showed us before we left to come here."

"Why, that balcony scene with him wearing that protuberance—it can't be anything other than what it resembles, or I'm a horse's ass," Gerald elaborated. He described the scene to a few friends standing nearby, who shook their heads.

"Extreme encumbrances indeed," Clive uttered, shaking his head in amazement. "How depraved men like Northrop could pursue diverse evils while risking the lives of others boggles the mind."

Someone mentioned a worker at the facility walking into a gelatinous crimson humanoid-jellyfish, its lower appendages bright translucent and able to sting.

As everyone began leaving, Gerald observed, "Who needs the devil. These folk have done a pretty good job creating monsters that look like devils. Act like 'em as well."

Chapter 35

Group Three explored the sealed-off cave complex. They were guided by Mike, the spelunker, a recent member of the New Forest Underground. Neville reported on the day's events:

"Not even a rat can make it through what I'm pretty sure is a spherical super-wall. The massive cavern has been turned into some sort of anechoic chamber—fully sound-insulated—through whose walls not a single sound can penetrate, even a giant screaming. We have no choice but to attempt to approach the Fortress from Northrop's side. Can we get assistance from Group Two?"

It was a done deal.

Later that night, Ian gave Neville an amazing combat suit for upcoming ventures.

With Doron looking on, Ian said, "Super night-goggles will allow you to see within the cave almost as though it were daylight. Your mini-cam can also switch into full night mode. You've got super-amplified hearing that, like most of the other features, is accessible by this hidden keypad."

Neville stood by the window, hit a button and looked into the forest while wearing the night-vision goggles. "It's like day. Greenish but clear. I can see details. This is amazing."

Ian went on, briefly imitating Q from the *James Bond* movies. "The combat outfit can immediately sense any monitoring device or bug from over a mile away with bug-detection equipment worthy of MI5. It can also block the functioning of these devices."

Ian paused. "Now, Neville, give me your full attention. There is a reason this suit costs tens of thousands of pounds and is very hard to get. It has an 'invisible man' function."

Looking amazed, Neville took over: "Let me guess. With ultra-miniature diodes coating this outfit, one is able to become almost invisible as the outer layer duplicates any background, relaying it from the back side to the front, much like a chameleon. Background is transmitted through the suit as though one were no more than a glass window."

"Yes," Ian replied, "but let me caution. Keep in mind that the wearer is never fully invisible. The key thing to remember is to remain stationary. Movement is what gives you away."

* * *

Group Three left the next morning with Group Two.

Ian and some of the others at the Wellstone estate had taken over the security cameras of Northrop's New Forest estate. Monitoring was now underway.

The spelunking group arrived hidden in one of the local gardening vans and remained out of sight till the van approached the thick, wooded area, which extended behind the manor in both directions for several thousand acres, much of it pure forest. The fence line to the underground facility, directly to the back of the manor, was maybe five acres deep and fully out of range of the house but for security cameras at the hidden gate. That too was now under complete Roundtable control. The Cyber gang could breach the electric lock of the gate into the facility at any time.

Neville was examining the old map with Mike. "That's it," Neville pointed. "The entrance to the cave complex is close to the high banks of that stream, the one branching off from the Avon River."

Group Three quickly headed due east, carrying Kevlar ropes, cams, powerful LED explorer flashlights and other high-tech gear, including miniature sensors to be planted. If they needed to blow a hole in a cavern, they could do that as well—though it would be a dead giveaway, and was obviously inadvisable except as a last resort.

Vikram was the first to find the small, hidden cave entrance near the river.

"This is not a virgin entrance. I am sure that, apart from those who made the cave maps, this has been breached in recent years," Neville told the group.

"If not Lord Northrop, I would imagine the Project forces have been through this," Mike concurred. "I think we should also be extremely careful for traps, detectors, even trip mines."

Neville, as only Vikram was privy to, was wearing something that Ian's two servants had recently brought from the Cambridgshire manor—the highly touted U.S. military ops, Army Ranger, and Navy SEAL cyber-warfare combat outfit—among the most prized items of his father's arsenal. Unless someone knew what it was, it looked like the typical camouflage outfit until it went into action.

Neville was soon discovering that these remarkable suits lived up to their reputations.

He did a mock, "Can you hear me now?" He was connected visually and audibly to Ian and Doron via the SmarTruck's digital satellite feed.

"Confirmed," Ian replied. "We, the Wellstone command center, can see and hear everything you do. Can you test the GPS?"

A small global-positioning chip gave Neville total directional awareness in the cave. He read the triangulation numbers. "Spot-on," Ian said. "We've got you down to the centimeter."

Ian was looking at various members of Group Three on the large plasma monitor via Neville's live mini-cam as they stood near the cave entrance.

Ian cautioned Neville before they entered the cave mouth: "Please relay this to the others. If the facility security forces have already breached the cave—and it is only too predictable, given Northrop's connection to the complex—it will only make it easier for us to use their own equipment against them. But be very careful. Look out for invisible cave-cams or monitors. If they pick you up heading toward the complex, all hell will break loose. Your built-in scanner detectors should tell you if there is a visual sensor up ahead or hidden—then, hopefully, they will automatically disengage the sensor.

"Now, remember our plan. As we discussed, we will take over their various sensors as we did with the security monitors on Northrop's estate. We can record, then play back through them inactivity in an endless loop. At that point you can scream and it won't matter."

Neville concurred with a whisper.

Vikram was the first to enter, then stood aside so Neville could move ahead to scan for detectors. There were none in the immediate vicinity. Vikram, carrying a backup portable bug-detector, also found nothing. They put on low-light goggles upon entering the cave. A small, infrared beam could light up a cavern.

With Neville and Mike leading, the group walked carefully down a gradual incline until they were 60 feet under the surface, at which point the cave network leveled out. The cave widened so they did not need to stoop as they walked.

"We've got you on GPS," Ian's voice instructed. "Take the middle cave network that inclines downward."

The cave was a good twelve feet across. They passed through a smaller cavern. Vikram paused to probe for sensors. As he did, he looked up and admired the stalactites. Neville was looking for Druid relics. Nothing so far.

Vikram whispered to him, "Tell them I think I have found a good drop-off point for the special-ops package (a biochip-implanted rat)."

Ian confirmed via Neville's earpiece, "He's absolutely right. This would be a good place to let it go. Remember to hide food as you go along. Though we hope to wind this thing down long before it runs out of food."

The rat was let out the box, at first sniffing about and wandering aimlessly. Then it went up on its hind legs.

Doron took over, joystick in hand. Ian and the others could monitor it within the cave network by means of a red dot.

He was seeing through its eyes and ears. "Good to go," he whispered to Ian. The rat slowly circled around a large group of boulders that the group was sitting on near the middle of a cavern. It again stood up on its hind legs and froze. "That's the signal," Neville said, giving Ian the thumbs-up while waving to Doron through the rat's eyes.

Doron tried to make the rat wave back but couldn't quite pull it off.

The rat left the cavern and quickly moved along in the direction of the Fortress. Years of interactive video games allowed Doron to appreciate the sheer irony of what was going on—though this time it was a real rat in a real maze with a real danger zone at the end. If he had scored record numbers as a child, surely he needed to do that now.

Group Three headed swiftly back out the cave.

* * *

The group was about to see the great secret hidden beneath the Fortress revealed.

The large monitor lit up with images seen through the rat's eyes as surround-sound speakers in the den played sounds picked up by the rat's ears. They searched video footage of Group Three recorded earlier, searching for clues, then jumped to the live video feed where the rat was right now.

Group Three was caught on videotape earlier, wandering in the cave. As they stumbled along in the direction of the rat, it sounded like an army.

"Were we that loud?" Neville asked.

"Well, I'm sure you were quiet as far as your own hearing was concerned. To the rat you sounded like giants on a rampage!" Jeremy retorted with a grin.

Soon the audience in the den was amazed to see what Group Three could not have seen—the secret journey of the biochipped rat after it was deposited and had left them.

"I still can't get over seeing through the rat's eyes since we let it loose in the cave," Neville admitted to the group.

On a separate monitor, a red dot progressed through the map of networked caves, indicating the rat's progress toward the Fortress.

Doron mentioned an important fact. "The great thing about point-to-point guidance is that you leave a very capable animal on its own resources to get to its goal without micromanaging it. It can re-route its way until it gets there. A determined rat is very hard to keep out, as I think you can now see on the screen!"

Suddenly the screen showed a vast overview of something as large as the main hangar at Cape Canaveral Space Center.

"Our package made it," Neville announced in wonder.

"That chamber really is huge," Jon remarked.

The reinforced wall, on the other side, covered much of the enclosure. They saw air vents, ducts and open cavern areas and natural rock below—almost in an Art Deco fusion of ancient and modern.

From the rat's vantage point, more than halfway up on a ledge, it was like looking down from atop a ten-story building.

Ian noted, "Do you see that massive cage in the distance, the one that's empty at the moment? I think we can guess what that's for."

That rat looked around again.

A true shocker came into view. The group collectively gasped.

"Pay dirt!" Doron yelled. "Bingo."

There it was—an enormous giant. It was reclining, apparently hooked up to various tubes. There were tractor treads on the tremendous platform where the giant lay.

Jon remarked, "The platform looks like what NASA uses to transport rockets to the launch pad."

"It's definitely for moving what I'm going to guess are sedated giants to their cages, or holding areas, or perhaps the lift," Jeremy observed.

In the distance, in an adjacent super-chamber, the group saw the vague outline of what looked like a floor-sized lift.

Ian said, "My guess is that above it ascends to the huge opening above ground."

Doron zoomed in on activity far below. "The computer is enhancing what the rat is seeing."

Jeremy and Jon watched carefully. Someone in a white lab coat was using a syringe to extract liquid from a glass container connected to tubes coming from behind the giant's ear.

"Can you zoom in more?" Jeremy asked Doron. "He looks familiar just by the way he moves."

Doron zoomed slowly in as the pixels reformed on the screen, blurring at first, then clarifying.

Jeremy sounded aghast as he suddenly recognized the fellow in the lab coat. "Good Lord," he exclaimed. "So the mole at Cambridge has been Elliot Wezelby all along! He's the one everybody calls the Weasel. I was down to about three suspects. Turns out this is our guy."

"So you know him?" Ian asked.

"He's in my department. Like many of the molecular-biology faculty, he makes frequent trips, so I couldn't go on that alone. But he's always been a manipulative weasel of a fellow. I've never trusted him. Every time he's tried to ingratiate himself with me, I've walked away, repelled."

Jeremy probed, "We're recording this, right?"

Ian nodded, "Absolutely! *Everything* goes into our database in case something hot appears. That includes the Clockwork Earl doing his fingernails."

"Wezelby does resemble a weasel," Ian then admitted. "Dreadful-looking fellow, with those pinched eyes and odd glasses."

"Maybe we should give him a cameo appearance on the BBC, randomly overriding a news broadcast," Doron teased.

Not having a clue that a group at a nearby estate were watching him live, the weasel-like scientist looked around, then carefully stepped behind some unidentifiable structure. He injected some fluid from a syringe into a small vial, then tucked it in a pocket beneath the lab coat. He quickly stepped back from behind the structure and walked away in a things-as-usual manner, discreetly looking around. A finger twitched on the giant's hand as he passed. "You'll get your walk soon enough," the Weasel replied.

The rat's sharp ears picked up deep rumblings from some other area. Vaguely in the shadows on a far wall was the silhouette of a massive chair and a sedated giant sitting on it. The giant was fully the size of Egypt's famed Colossi of Memnon on the West Bank of Luxor—two ancient gods of stone sitting on their thrones facing off past the Valley of the Kings.

Off to another side they spotted an airport-hangar-sized opening leading to another chamber.

"I suppose we should navigate the rat inside those areas as well," Neville remarked.

"It may be wiser to do this during the late hours of the night," Doron responded. "There's no telling what we'll find."

Jon felt the same gut-wrenching combination of horror, fear, dread, revulsion and evil so hard to describe. As he had said before, "abomination" was perhaps the most fitting word.

"Take a final look," Doron announced. "This could go on all night. It is nonstop, and I know we are tired. I will fast-forward it in the morning to see where the rat wanders. Meanwhile, good going, Neville and Group Three. We're red-hot. Never dreamed we'd get this far by evening."

Ian hit the switch as the large plasma screen turned black.

The group arose from their chairs in silence. No war whoops, but a mood of quiet foreboding.

Later that night, as the three of them sat on lawn chairs under a starry sky in the rear garden, sipping beers, Jon remarked to Jeremy and Ian, "If the giants possess psychic powers above and beyond their vast physical strength, there's no telling what we may be facing. That's the unknown I fear the most."

"That, and the possibility of a fatal slip-up," Ian countered.

"Or a mole in our midst," Jeremy added. "Not even the other members of the Cyber gang have a clue as to what we are doing. For security we have shut them out, all of them—we've been as secretive as MI5, but not so with the New Forest Underground. Let's hope the older members at the top keep a careful eye on newer members. We're taking them on faith—a necessary risk."

Ian added, "I can't imagine what we would have done without them. They have completely changed the odds on what would have certainly been a suicide mission."

Suicide mission, Jon thought, as he pictured himself in climbing gear, a bomb in a knapsack, grappling down a wall of one of the underground chambers near a sleeping giant. An alarm goes off…

He could feel the inevitable battle looming, so heavily weighted in favor of Deep Earth Lab and its seemingly limitless resources.

Chapter 36

Adin Mocatta lay back in a leather gravity-chair facing the tinted windows overlooking the Manhattan shoreline and its expanse of water. He had just emptied one of the vials, waiting for its contents to kick in. The neurochemicals extracted from the giants were a whole order of magnitude beyond any known substance in producing altered consciousness.

Adin's eyes jumped to his inner eye. His mind leapt from a bright, sunny noon in New York City to an overcast 5:00 in the afternoon in England.

He entered one of his best-ever mind-melds with a giant, as objects rapidly came into focus. He saw several people standing fearfully in the distance, including his useful idiot "friend" from Cambridge who held the shut-down switch. The giant's neck and upper spine had electro-circuits that, if remote-activated, would disable all motor activity beneath the neck. It was a final resort should a giant lose control and go on the rampage. The scary thing to those standing near the giants and observing from ground level was that it did not always work. Some giants appeared to have a growing ability to defeat the electro-circuits.

There were just too many unknowns with these creatures, especially as they approached the original Nephil Class giants and the "Alpha Parent." As Northrop observed, "One just might be the dark god himself."

Adin noticed that among the bystanders, looking on in religious awe, was none other than Lord Northrop himself. Then he spotted Wezelby, the Cambridge geneticist in the white lab coat, moving over obsequiously beside the famed earl, who had just arrived. Only he and the earl were privy to what Adin Mocatta was trying to do.

He saw Northrop hiss at the Cambridge geneticist, "Close the bloody device so your finger doesn't trigger it by accident."

The Cambridge man, indeed, Jeremy's nemesis at the lab, nodded obediently. No doubt, he was in terror. Yes, the huge giant was getting its walk that day. And the Weasel knew that it could pick him up like a bug, chew his head off and spit it the length of a football field.

Adin watched the two men through the giant's eyes. Small, puny. One fearful, the other reverent. He was now feeling like a giant god. It was no longer fantasy. The sense of power was absolute. It was an addicting feeling. No one in history had ever done this. The rare neurochemicals, in tandem with his genius, were creating an unprecedented situation of mind-melding.

The secret agreement between Adin and his older mentor, Lord Northrop, was that when the true dark god arose from within the stable of giants, Adin would acquiesce and surrender control. Adin convinced Northrop that he would be able to spot the dark god when it arose, because it would be a consciousness like none other in history. It would be powerful, and it would know things only an angel could know. Long an adept in mysticism, especially the Kabbala, Adin believed he would be able to identify this in an instant. Though it knew things, the creature he was now overshadowing was probably not the dark god—or at least not yet. The dark god could awaken in this giant, or in an even more powerful creature. And it could awaken at any time.

* * *

The moment the machinery rumbled at the Fortress around 4:50 p.m., a buzzer at the Wellstone estate sounded. Doron and Ian dashed over to the monitor. Doron immediately put on the VR helmet and grabbed the joystick. Ian leaned against a large oak table, looking on transfixed.

The chip-implanted squirrel shifted to a branch with an open view overlooking the moving ground. Its ears picked up a deep rumbling engine from the opening in the ground. The squirrel moved to a higher branch to feel "safer." It also offered those at the Wellstone estate the best perspective of unfolding events.

The ground kept disappearing, leaving a crater-sized opening that continued to grow. The grinding continued as the vast alien world beneath the earth came into clearer view, with artificial light emerging.

A separate engine sound could also be heard. "It's got to be the lift," Jon said as Doron nodded, still wearing the helmet.

To the squirrel's eyes, a new kind of earth had replaced the other one, this one bright and shiny. On it was a tree-sized being resembling a man. It was not as tall as the squirrel's giant oak, but as this being stood up, its eyes seemed to go well above the halfway mark of the tree.

Doron acted on the squirrel's scream response. It was given point-to-point order to scurry up to a higher branch that might be out of reach of the huge creature.

"Do you see it has six fingers?" Doron asked for Ian's verification.

"Yes, I believe you are right. ... Yes, confirmed, you are right. This thing's horrible."

"An apt image of it ascending, as though from out of an abyss in hell," Doron said. "Try the helmet on—you'll get a sense of what it looks from the squirrel's perspective." He handed Ian the VR helmet.

"Horrors," Ian managed to blurt out. The giant's eyes swept around. Every time they scanned the nearby tree, Ian felt a jolt of dread. "I'm giving you back the helmet. You may need to put the squirrel through the paces here."

Doron saw the giant looking around slowly, as though waking from a dream and trying to orient itself. What made Doron uncomfortable was the sense that it was looking for something, almost as if it sensed being watched. Doron did not have that comfortable "I can see you, but you can't see me" feeling that he'd anticipated.

High up the tree trunk, Doron's squirrel found a hole and climbed inside. *The searching eyes, the searching eyes*—like those of the child-giant they had first seen on the DVD—but these were more terrible, more knowing, deliberate and older. How old? It was hard to tell; adult or close to adult was his guess. The eyes were looking into the tree, searching, searching—*but why, for what?*, Doron wondered.

Wearing the virtual-reality helmet in an upper room at the estate, everything Doron was seeing was interpolated with depth perception. It was also recorded in high resolution—for the group to see that night, and for public exposure. Ian watched the large monitor as Doron saw through the VR helmet. They zoomed in on those watching the giant. They then examined the shaft leading to the huge hollow earth below the Fortress for every clue, every bit of incriminating evidence they could find. Soon Vikram entered and joined them.

No, the Cambridge geneticist would not be awarded the Nobel Prize for this, not by a long shot. "He will get fame," Jeremy announced, "but not exactly the universal admiration he has sold his soul for."

Through the squirrel's sensitive ears an inhuman voice filled the air at ear shattering volume. The words were hard to make out. It was as though multiple vocal cords were trying to join up with that buzz-saw, super-thought effect. The result was an unholy voice.

Vikram pondered the ancient gods walking the Gangetic flood plains and addressing his terrified ancestors, so small, so helpless. "They would fall obeisantly before such a creature, memorializing it with temples and images," he said with a note of sadness and alarm. No doubt, something like it was on the puja altar of his relatives—beneath which sat a computer at stand-by, ready to initiate a terrible protocol if it came to that. *How ironic*, Vikram thought to himself.

Doron felt relieved that the giant's eyes temporarily ended their probing when the immense creature turned to address Northrop, who nodded to it in response to something it had said.

Trying to hide the fear in his voice and instead sound robust, the Clockwork Earl asked from far below, "Do you feel like going for a walk?"

It made a loud, indecipherable sound.

"Maybe it is speaking in another language," Doron theorized.

Jon, who had also joined them soon after things had gotten underway, replied, "Yes, maybe the primal tongue that existed before the Flood. Let's do a language analysis after we get it all recorded. We could be hearing the ancestor of all languages."

"Or it's just really bad elocution," Ian added.

At that point, to their utter surprise, the giant turned and tore off a clump of large branches connected to the large tree below where the squirrel was hiding in its hole.

"I have a strong gut feeling that this creature senses something about the squirrel," Doron said in a low voice. "It has been probing the tree, giving the tree an undue amount of attention. I am also concerned about the possibility of something we have not fully considered, the possibility of paranormal powers in these giants."

He was intently looking through the squirrel's eye's hidden in the hole in the trunk two-thirds up the tree. *Is it possibly within reach?* Doron wondered. He then envisioned the giant pushing over the whole tree, crashing it to the ground. Or it might just snap off the top third of the tree and hurl it into the distance. This was utterly frightening power. In the distance, Doron saw that the three or four humans looking on were nervous.

The giant then barked another indecipherable phrase in Northrop's direction.

"We really need to analyze the language and translate it," Ian said.

"We have a number of sentences already," Doron responded. "We can start doing that soon."

* * *

Trying to hide his fear, Lord Northrop knew he had to walk near the giant once they commenced. He and Adin spoke earlier on the phone. Northrop and Adin agreed that the ongoing remote-guidance experiments, Adin's broadbanding, would make possible the earl's up-coming inauguration ceremony at his New Forest estate. Northrop was now feeling the summer solstice coming upon them fast.

Northrop grabbed the remote from the shaking Wezelby standing next to him. To the earl, Dr. Wezelby was an unattractive fellow who re-pulsed him as a man. He was a bleeding sycophantic worm of a man, and the earl would like nothing better than to see the giant flick him across the landscape like an annoying tick. Yes, he'd fantasized it more than once. A quick flick and off goes the head, soaring past the branches into the trees.

The giant moved ahead, still under the camouflage awning several hundred feet high, held up by massive poles and cables and covering the aerial view of the Fortress. It had a chemical coating, thwarting any satel-lite or drone penetration—and even if that did happen, the Project had allies at the top of the government who would intercede immediately. The area fell under military- and government-related defense technol-ogy. Any prying bureaucrat and ambitious whistle-blower would get roasted by his superiors, if not taken out by a convenient accident. And Northrop knew all of this; after all, he had helped the inner-circle fash-ion the fail-safe levels around the Project.

Northrop's theory was that the present giant before them was a gen-uine Nephilim within a few generations of the original dark god. One prototype in particular, developing quickly in the bowels of the Fortress, might be the one the earl had been looking for. This created dizzying levels of expectation.

What the earl was also certain of was that no one could control this god of the distant past. He secretly believed that when Adin tried a mind probe, he would be eaten up, all his circuits fried. Northrop pictured being given the shocking news by one of Deep Earth Lab's directors after finding Adin Mocatta drooling like an imbecile, his eyes wide open in shock—that would be the final signature of the dark god. Then the Clockwork Earl would kneel before his deity, and together they would make mastery, "Maustery of the Whole Human Rauss." He almost squealed, till he saw this foot, larger than an automobile, shaking the earth by his side. What power!

Earl Northrop and his scientific entourage accompanied the giant for a 40-minute walk as Adin gave the earl various pre-agreed secret signals. Once they were near the back gate to the Northrop estate, they turned around and headed back with the giant to the massive lift. Adin kept probing its psychic gifts as it walked—abilities much like the ones the neurochemicals were giving him.

When the giant returned to the Fortress, it straddled the huge flatbed on the lift. With a touch of the remote by the earl, the giant seemed to fall into a deep sleep. The parting image through the squirrel's eyes, now on a different tree, was the lift taking the tree-sized creature down into the bowels of the earth.

What further bothered the group looking on at the Wellstone estate was that the giant ignored the original large oak tree altogether upon its return. It had immediately eyed the exact tree where the squirrel had relocated during the walk and was presently hidden—watching the giant from a high branch. It even started approaching the tree until Northrop signaled it to head to the lift.

"I think it knows something," Doron told the others. "And this worries me." This would include any chip-implanted rats hidden in the massive underground region below. Perhaps it had learned to tune into one of the rats below in its holding area. A giant able somehow to detect consciousness—a frightening thought.

* * *

As the lift slowly transported its massive cargo back into the bay in Chamber Three, Adin Mocatta ended an absolutely exhausting two-hour broadbanding session and was now feeling a terrible headache coming on. He got up from his gravity chair and lowered the shades, darkening the office suite to keep out the painful light that only intensified his sharp headache.

The penthouse office complex had three apartments kept ready for the directors. Adin, who rarely used them since he had several residences in New York, decided to appropriate one of them and lay down. He would try to ride out the headache.

There were a number of things bothering him—leading to his fear that the Project may have finally come under scrutiny. He was haunted by the odd sense of something watching from the tree, a secondary consciousness layering itself on top of the animal consciousness. He had torn off the limbs of the oak tree while watching for a blip and detected two response levels.

From his earliest days with Deep Earth Lab, Adin had foreseen that when the Project meddled sufficiently with the order of things or took certain risks, it could no longer maintain full invisibility; this was especially so with recent "accidents," such as the one involving the Stanford post-doc driving over the cliffs of Route 1. It was too soon after other rigged suicides. This could have tipped the scales, which was what Adin feared as he lay down.

Then there were the earlier deaths of those maintenance workers who had seen too much at the underground New Forest facility. There were also others in the bloody trail of bodies—including Dr. Feinberg—who had been turned to pulp by that odd child-giant Adin had so detested. That was before they learned to implement rapid maturity. Until they destroyed it, the child-giant had created a bloodier trail than any of them had foreseen.

Adin Mocatta was now beginning to assume the worst and wondered about erasing some of Deep Earth Lab's incriminating fingerprints. He had devised a protocol for such a situation. But that too would involve risks.

His headache slowly diminishing, Adin decided to leave Trump Empire Tower. Rather than taking the usual limousine to his Central Park West residence right there in the heart of Manhattan, Adin decided to take a helicopter from the rooftop helipad to one of his private estates. He entered one of Deep Earth Lab's invisible exits, an elevator, and exited onto the helipad just above the penthouse.

At his country estate near Chappaqua, Adin wouldn't have to see a soul as he pondered the next move in the necessary peace and quiet.

The next few hours could be critical, he thought, as the helicopter left the pad in a loud whine, its rotors beating far above Manhattan as it moved across the sky, heading to Upstate New York.

Chapter 37

Adin's helicopter moved over a rich green forest of trees before landing on the helipad at his Chappaqua estate. It was a little after 3:40 p.m. local time in New York, or 12:40 p.m. in Palo Alto.

He was on the upper sun deck, reclined in a lounge chair, his cell phone and computer nearby. Adin made a secure call to his team in waiting in Palo Alto: "Confirm target, only then begin." He then got under the waterfall of the shallow pool on his rooftop deck, feeling the headache ease away under the cascading water. After twenty minutes, he emerged, toweled off and returned to the lounge chair.

The warm June air of upstate New York hugged him like an Abercrombie & Fitch bathrobe as evening approached. The headache that had started at 1:30 at the Empire Tower had almost disappeared. He took a brief nap.

At 6 p.m. Adin turned on the evening news. Reports were coming in about a massive explosion in downtown Palo Alto at 2:20 p.m. local time. Adin studied the plasma screen on the wall. There it was, almost as clear as his being there—the cratered building of Lederberg's offices.

"Right now the possibility is being considered that this is a terrorist bombing," the newscaster speculated as the building was being cordoned off. "The local FBI is now on the scene and has taken over the investigation."

The FBI agent caught on camera at the Trump complex most likely would be heading to Palo Alto, Adin had gambled. With the agent preoccupied, Adin would have more freedom to operate in Manhattan as the big event in New Forest rapidly approached. Agent Jack was also a prime target of the security team. A head shot in Palo Alto would have no connection to the Trump Empire Tower.

But the main benefit of the explosion was that Lederberg would never be able to phone Mocatta and initiate programming. That threat was gone forever.

From his secure rooftop garden, Adin called Northrop on Secure-Cell and gave him the news. It was a little before midnight in New Forest, and the earl, a late-nighter, responded. "Well done. At least he can't phone us anymore. By the way, I thought that we had a good session today. I was amused by your dropping the large branch near the Weasel. I loathe the bastard. Keep me in the loop regarding Palo Alto and that bloody FBI agent."

"The Project's security team ran an intensive background check on the agent," Adin replied. "We got his name, bio info, including his high ranking on the FBI's counter-terrorism team. I am sure he will be visiting the blast site. I still think he's a lone ranger looking for terrorism leads and a promotion. I'm sure that was what he was doing when he stumbled into the Trump Empire Tower."

"Nevertheless," Northrop said, "this agent could quickly become a danger to all of us if he should suddenly decide to enter our executive offices with a team. Almost anything found could be used to justify a full probe. And you don't want to be under this kind of magnifying glass, not with what we've got ahead."

Adin agreed with the earl, and had his middleman contact the security team a second time, congratulating them on a successful mission. He had already issued a full watch for Jack's arrival at both airports, New York and San Francisco. Mocatta gambled that Jack would have no clue he was being watched. All arrival gates would be under tight scrutiny. They would either arrange a fake terrorist incident or follow him and take him out later.

Evidence, Adin thought, recalling Northrop's warning that almost anything tagged at the executive offices could justify a full probe. He would sweep the offices soon.

Over the telecom, Adin ordered a martini.

Sitting back in the lounge chair, he looked at the plasma screen. He studied the cratered building again, took a sip of the martini, and smiled. Awaiting dinner, he did a quick self-evaluation, looking for slip-ups. He had done an excellent job on the Project's behalf. For one thing, the entire Nephil dig in Israel was only possible because of his family connections in the Knesset and higher up. The only possible slip-ups for Adin were his private experiments with the neurochemicals.

He prided himself on being very cautious. Apart from the obsequious Cambridge scientist at the underground facility—ever trying to please Adin to gain more favored status—no one else connected to the Project had direct knowledge of Adin's experiments with the neuro-chemicals.

Even if Northrop—who had known about Adin's broadbanding since his Oxford era as a Rhodes scholar—had some idea about the neu-rochemicals being used to enhance his natural ability, there was ab-solutely nothing to worry about. Adin had enough on the earl to blackmail him to the end of time. Parliament might even consider re-opening the Tower of London if they knew of all the horrors Lord Northrop had engaged in.

And Northrop was by no means the only one on whom Adin had in-telligence files. For years he had kept records on anyone who was any-thing, above all the Deep Earth Lab directors, who were each potential rivals. He had even used the Mocatta family's influential European branch to get at the Mossad's exhaustive files, ever ready to be used for political blackmail and intrigue. Adin knew much more about Deep Earth Lab's board members than they could ever imagine.

Adin Mocatta smiled to himself, emptied the martini, and ordered a Kobe filet, asparagus, creamed potatoes and a good wine.

On the TV a newscaster speculated, "It is not official, and we can-not confirm the full number of deaths so far, but the body of a well-known Palo Alto psychiatrist has been found in the rubble."

Lederberg's been taken out, he thought with relief, as he lingered over a glass of premium vintage wine.

Chapter 38

The next morning, Jon woke up haunted by a nameless anxiety. The first thing he did was check his e-mail.

Sure enough, there was an urgent message from Glen, who reported a huge explosion that rocked downtown Palo Alto around 2:20 p.m. It would have been 10:20 p.m. local English time, just when Jon was going to bed. This confirmed yet again the accuracy of Jon's hunches.

Jon downloaded the live news reports and hastily called a meeting in the den before the groups left for the field. "I just heard from Glen, my surviving roommate. What's being called a terrorist attack took place yesterday afternoon in Palo Alto at the office building of the psychiatrist who programmed Spenser's death. The whole building was blown up.

"I am guessing the explosion was intended to kill Dr. Lederberg, who undoubtedly knew enough to sink Deep Earth Lab. It is certain that countless people in the Project had been programmed and controlled by him. It was during prime office hours, when Lederberg was most likely to be there working."

As news segments played on the large screen, the group looked on in fascination, looking for clues. In one major piece, a newsman was standing in front of the cratered building hours after the attack. Smoke was still pouring out as fire crews overran the rubble. "A group called 'The Servants of the Prophet' has taken credit for the attack," he reported. "Experts assume that 'the prophet' is Mohammed and that the attackers come from yet one more terror cell that has escaped detection. The FBI has now come on the scene." The segment ended with a guarded reference to the psychiatrist's death.

Doron cut in to answer an earlier query. "Whether those behind the explosion knew about the psychiatrist's backup records stored at DataLock, Inc., is an open question. I frankly doubt it."

Vikram, the first to penetrate DataLock, mentioned, "I have no doubt that a main purpose for the records hidden at DataLock were for

Lederberg's own protection, should Deep Earth Lab turn against him. Someone asked earlier, 'What if DataLock were targeted in a secondary explosion.' Okay, I think this is doubtful at the moment. And remember, we still have a full backup of all those records anyway."

"And what we have should be legally incriminating evidence that could expose at least the U.S. side of Deep Earth Lab," Doron interjected.

Jon remarked, "I'm now wondering if Jack's inquiry at the Trump Empire Tower might have set things off. I'll bet the so-called terrorist attack will lead back to Adin Mocatta, who Jack has been monitoring. Either that, or just bad blood between him and Lederberg."

Jon's cell phone beeped. "It's Jack," he signaled to the group, as he headed to the porch.

Ian took over, showing the remaining news segments and pausing for comments in between.

A news anchor announced, "Witnesses saw the well-known psychiatrist enter the office early this afternoon, and no one saw him leave. His car is still trapped under the collapsed ceiling of the underground garage. Agents from the FBI crime lab appear to have confirmed his death. Again, this is not official."

Doron quietly realized an interesting aspect to Lederberg's death that few would appreciate: *Those in the Project who know about their own programming will now believe they are finally free from ever having it activated again, since Lederberg's dead—and this could be their greatest vulnerability.* Doron's stealth plan was very much in effect.

He changed gears and mentioned something weighing on him to the group. "I've mentioned this before, but when I was seeing through the eyes of the squirrel, I felt watched by something within the giant—call it a presence or a consciousness. I had a dream about it last night. I saw a secondary awareness looking back at me through the giant. This has been bothering me ever since. I guess I'm worried that something could have been alerted, maybe even compromising our cover. I say this in light of yesterday's explosion."

Vikram unknowingly came perilously close to solving a conundrum when he tried to reassure Doron, "I don't think you've really alerted anything. But if you mean, as Jon was just saying, that Adin Mocatta implemented the explosion, sure. But I believe that he has no real idea of our existence. He may sense something on the periphery, but nothing tangible. It's only enough to keep him paranoid, which can only open him up to further mistakes and miscalculations. The Palo Alto explosion may just be indicative of his increasing paranoia. Remember, it was Jack snooping about at their office complex. And he's been warned of the FBI."

He paused. "Let me make another educated guess. I'll bet Mocatta does not have a clue about Lederberg's backup records at DataLock. To repeat what I said earlier, DataLock is most probably Lederberg's insurance against the Project. This could be a huge plus for us."

Jon returned from the porch with more news. "That was Jack calling on the FBI secure-line. He has just been given full sanction to investigate this 'terrorist' act in Palo Alto. It falls under his jurisdiction. He's due to fly from New York City to the Bay Area later today. He left agents on his anti-terrorism team ready to penetrate Mocatta's suite at a moment's notice. But Jack wants to leave Mocatta undisturbed, so he'll act with no awareness that he's being watched. But it may be too late for that. Jack found out that his picture was leaked to Mocatta."

Jon went on. "The main thing he's been trying to do is link Mocatta to Deep Earth Lab's front companies, money laundering and other irregularities."

The group disbanded for the various missions for the day. Jon was suddenly hit with an acute need to escape, to get away from the estate just for a brief break. Unlike most of the others who'd left the Wellstone estate regularly, Jon had been homebound and was beginning to feel like a trapped animal.

He signaled Jeremy as he headed out to the verandah. "I don't know about you, but I'd love a run in the old sports car to some café. The Underground gave us a list of safe places."

Jeremy agreed. "Yes, this whole thing has been intense, and we've been stuck here far more than the others. Let's check with Ian."

Ian looked nervous, but said, "Just take care. The good part is that you're both legitimate tourists and we are in the high tourist season. But leave where you are if anything seems strange."

He gave them a parting reminder: "Summer solstice is under two weeks away and quickly approaching. We need the both of you around because I think things are going to blow wide open."

* * *

Jeremy and Jon headed out the gate to a "safe" coffeehouse owned by a member of the Underground. "It's on the outer periphery of New Forest, away from Burley on a country road," Jon reminded Jeremy, as he examined the local map. "It should be back roads all the way."

Jon had his arm out the window. He felt the trapped feeling quickly leaving him as the wind massaged his head. The country roads were stunning in late spring.

As they drove up to the rustic coffeehouse, it reminded Jon of some weather-beaten café along the coastal redwoods. They grabbed a table on the porch. Both hadn't seen a paper in weeks, so Jon grabbed a stack from a basket.

Jon took a sip of espresso, responding with a look of blissful relief. Then his eyes stopped dead on an inside headline of the *Telegraph*: "Award-winning Belgian journalist killed by stray fire near Gaza. Israeli soldiers apologize for mistake." It was what Jon had feared would happen from the moment he left the Belgian in the Arab Quarter of Old Jerusalem. "Now he's dead," Jon said, barely audibly.

Jon reflected on his brother as he watched the geese flutter in the distance. Jack's voice on the phone was still fresh in his mind. He wondered how much Mocatta might have probed into Jack, his family and thereby learn of Jon. Could he be aware of the suicide of Spenser, then connect Jon as a roommate? Adin could then link Jon with Jack. If so, it would change the whole game—and not at all in their favor!

They drained their cups, thanked the owner—whom they had seen at the last Underground meeting at Clive's—and left with several pounds of French roast "on the house." On the drive back, Jeremy drove slowly to stretch the time out.

Describing a cartoon in one of the papers, Jon said, "It depicted federal agents doing a full-body tackle on some 75-year-old grandma in a park and handcuffing her. Fumbling American agents—too dumb to tell good citizens from criminals and terrorists. The terrorist is hiding in the bushes. Meanwhile, we're reminded of the constant over policing of honest citizens in police-state America. Even Jack thinks it's part of an agenda. The public is being tenderized for something far more draconian."

Jon went on as Jeremy listened. "Growing portions of the American population are relocating overseas to find the very freedoms that America once stood for. I've considered doing it myself."

"England is well along the same fatal course," Jeremy responded. "I feel it every day. The street cams are enough to drive me crazy, quite honestly."

Voicing another concern, Jon added, "Jack has spoken of a civil war in the FBI in which the corrupt agents could soon be in total control. He's considered quitting a number of times. Dad and I have told him to tough it out, that he may even be running the agency one day."

The two pulled up to the entrance of the Wellstone estate. Jeremy pushed the button. Ian's voice over the intercom sounded relieved as the gate opened.

When they entered the house, Ian asked them to follow him upstairs. "Can you join me as I flash through all our sensors and implants?"

"Of course."

Ian quickly flashed through the first tier. At the moment, the rat in the underground facility was eating from a mountain of food stored for the giants. The squirrel was some distance from the Fortress, nibbling on acorns.

Next, at the second tier, Ian blipped through the countless stationary bugs the groups had planted. All was in order.

The third tier involved the elaborate surveillance of both Northrop estates.

At the Oxfordshire estate, one of the butlers and a maid were "getting it on" in one of the bedrooms. In another wing a servant was putting a piece of silverware in his pocket.

Ian clicked to Lord Northrop, now at the New Forest hunting estate. Northrop was in his Etonian accent mode as he spoke to a servant over the phone. A member of the superior British upper class was addressing an underling. The earl became imperious, shrill: "What would you do if I invited His Majesty the King? Would you serve the King shepherd's pie and scrumpy, or caviar, lobster and champagne?! Think hard; I know this is an intellectually taxing question."

Ian jumped through all 30 or so monitors to see who was on the other end of the phone line. He found the quavering servant in the kitchen of the Oxfordshire estate, a frightened rabbit of a man virtually standing at attention while on the phone. "Lobster, sir, and caviar and champagne. I'd never serve scrumpy to a royal, Sir."

Never a dull moment.

"We should serialize this on TV. It would blow away most reality TV shows," Jon interjected as Ian and Jeremy agreed.

"We may yet be televising Northrop in ways he would never imagine," Ian replied.

Chapter 39

An hour after returning from the café, Jon ran into Doron. "I need to share some intel that could save Jack's life."

Jon immediately passed it on to Jack. "Been thinking of you, Bro. Talked to Doron just now. More info you need to be aware of. As I think you know, Adin Mocatta has seen the shots of you on the security cam at Trump Empire Tower. He also saw the official letter you gave the manager—who passed it on to the dummy office below. No doubt Mocatta has ordered background checks on you. And that could lead to me as well.

"Jack, now this is important. It's almost certain his team will be looking out for you at both the explosion site as well as at the gates at Kennedy as well as San Francisco. Watch out. Need to see you alive again, so don't walk into a setup. Doron says use utter caution around explosion site in case they use a sniper option to take you out. Keep me updated as much as you can when you're in Palo Alto. Love, Jon."

Jack replied before his secretive and exhausting journey to the West Coast, "Confirmed, dear Bro. Will alter plans and take appropriate measures. Will approach Palo Alto by a rear entrance. Will stay in touch at least by secure line." He added cryptically, "Thank Vikram for what he just did."

Bewildered, Jon asked Vikram, who responded, "Oh, when you were out with Jeremy, I arranged it so Jack can be met by my Uncle Ravindra at the small regional airport of Monterey. That way, there is no car-rental database and no exposure at SFO, where they will be expecting him to arrive."

"Vikram," Jon replied, "I am deeply grateful. You may have just saved my brother's life."

"Amazing foresight," Doron amended. "Hey, you never told me."

Vikram replied with a grin, "You were off somewhere."

* * *

Vikram's Uncle Ravindra stood on the tarmac as a very "un-Jack-like" fellow emerged from a small plane at the Monterey Airport. Jack came on a private plane service from Nevada, having already crisscrossed the country on flights to avoid the main routes.

It was now the morning after the Palo Alto explosion.

Ravindra shook the hand of a forgettably ordinary man (the whole point of disguise in the intelligence agencies).

"You are Agent Jack, is it? How was your flight?"

"It's made me appreciate the large commercial airlines, something I never thought could happen. Thanks so much for coming here to meet me."

Ravindra's private limo was waiting. Jack threw his stuff in the back as Ravindra said, "Please feel free to use my residence. Vikram told that me that you and your teams might need to use it as a base to stay off the radar of these terrorists. After traveling all night I'm sure you would like a good shower and change of clothes, yes?"

Jack nodded. "I'd love it."

When Jack took off the disguise at the Indian millionaire's mansion, Ravindra became "most impressed," as he e-mailed Vikram. Jack could look formidable. He had fearless, chiseled features, stood 6'4" and weighed 240 pounds, much of it from weight training and prior years in elite military service.

Jack, having showered, felt new again. Then he made some calls.

His teams had the luxury of coming on commercial flights and traveling business class, preceding Jack's arrival by many hours. Under FBI orders, police had cordoned off the area and kept it under 24-hour guard. The FBI had sole access at this point.

Vikram, who'd hacked into Lederberg's office, forewarned Jack, "Depending on the damage and what is still standing, try to find the camera that was in the wall, as well as the small fireproof safe that was hidden in the opposite wall. In all likelihood, the safe holds the contract Lederberg signed with DataLock. If you find it, as we've discussed, you'll have legal cause to raid DataLock and seize the original evidence with no trail leading back to us."

At the moment, one of Jack's most trusted and able men was heading a team at the gutted Palo Alto building. He was searching the blown-out office. Jack called and asked, "How's it going?"

"Fine, sir—nothing yet."

"Okay, as I told you, important documents are often in things like fire safes, hidden away for obvious reasons. I want you to take your time. Sift the walls if you have to."

"Yes, sir. I'll call the minute I find anything."

Jack's man spent half an hour pounding apart the already-broken and collapsed walls. He noticed a shiny lock glistening from amidst the rubble, and discovered a small, fireproof safe. He dusted it off and immediately secreted it as evidence as he called Jack. "I've got the safe."

"Well done. Take it to the FBI lab in Redwood City. Call me when they pop it open. Don't leave the safe alone with anyone for a second. Do you understand? I want you there the whole time."

Jack was back on the phone. Ravindra overheard him say, "But I don't need that agent. I don't care if he's with the Redwood City crime lab. I've got the best two teams I've ever had. … They insist? … But I don't need—okay, but I want to go on record protesting this. Understand?"

Doron had previously warned Jack about several FBI agents who could be moles for Deep Earth Lab. The one assigned to Jack's anti-terrorism team was one of these agents.

Jack now ordered a secondary team to go to the Palo Alto site soon after the agent left with the safe. Jack instructed his top man on the secondary team, "You're to pretend to be looking for evidence. Divide some of the team outside the immediate building area. Comb the area for outside observers and possible snipers. Keep the area busy. The raid on DataLock must be a total surprise. So part of this mission is confusion and misdirection."

As he headed to Palo Alto, Jack got a call from the new agent who had been thrust upon him. Jack ordered him to join the peripheral team fumbling around the building now that the safe had been removed.

Jack next called his head man at the site. "Okay, now spread the word that the higher-ups are insisting we take a compromised agent. He's local. I've had intel he's not to be trusted. Warn the others about this new guy. I'll tell you the plan later."

"Roger."

On hand at the explosion site was one of Jack's handpicked agents disguised to look like Jack. "You'd better be wrapped in Kevlar in case snipers are looking for me," Jack called to warn him. "Keep your eyes out. Also, keep an eye on the new agent assigned to the team. Don't trust him for a second."

Jack's man called him from the Redwood City crime lab. "Sir, they got the safe open. We got some evidence, including a signed contract with some company called DataLock."

Of course, Jack could show no prior awareness of this key piece of evidence. He tried to hide his excitement, keeping an even tone: "That could be good news. You and the others have the lab photo the evidence, then bring the original stuff to me immediately. We have no time to lose. Get me the driver. We'll give him the directions to where I am right now."

Jack handed the phone to Ravindra, who gave directions.

While his men were en route to Ravindra's with the DataLock contract, Jack called his trusted superior at the New York office to report the evidence from the safe.

"Excellent, Jack. The DataLock source could reveal what the terrorists were after, eh? I think you should raid DataLock. Go for it. I'll give the order for all the backup you need. And, yes, I am already aware they are tagging you with one of their own. We discussed this possibility. You know the options."

The moment the contract arrived, Jack left the residence in Ravindra's limo, the other agents now joining them. They sped to DataLock.

Twenty minutes later they were outside a huge, gray fortress of high, thick, concrete walls. At the security gate, the guard let Ravindra's limo in upon seeing his customer ID. Nothing could be seen through the tinted windows of the limo. Jack and the others were still hidden in the back.

The gates closed behind them. The building had no windows and stood in the center of the compound, with an open concrete area surrounding it at least twenty yards wide. They drove to the director's office on the ground level and pulled up to the outside door next to an expensive BMW. Ravindra had made an appointment to meet the director.

As the director emerged to greet him, Ravindra and a tough-looking agent wearing a dark-blue FBI jacket got out of the limo as more agents followed.

The startled director looked up as he heard the roar of helicopter rotors. Two dark-gray FBI helicopters swooped down and landed 30 yards behind the limo near the corner of the building. More FBI agents came out.

Ravindra told him, "Sorry, but there has been a terrorist incident, and I agreed to help the agents visit you undercover. I hope you understand."

The black helicopters were all the director needed to be in the most conciliatory mood possible.

Jack handed the frightened director the official FBI documents authorizing a full search. Also included was Lederberg's DataLock contract.

Jack told him, "Your client, Dr. Lederberg, we believe was the target of a terrorist attack. As you may know, his building was blown up yesterday, and he was killed."

"I was very sorry to see it in the news. I'm most eager to help. Perhaps I can save your team the equivalent of looking for a needle in a haystack. My engineers will open up Lederberg's storage data and retrieve it in full. Would that be okay?"

The director of DataLock was painfully aware that the other option would be for the FBI to invade the vast storage databases in a ruthless search. This could be ruinous for DataLock. The search alone could lock down the facility for weeks as endless terabits of stored data came under FBI scrutiny. Once this got out, the director knew, the company could be hit hard.

The FBI team, headed by Jack, soon found Lederberg's backup of data. At that point, the FBI's cyber-expert on the team (whom Doron knew about) quickly made multiple backup DVDs of the files.

Jack sent Jon a secure "got the contract and we're in DataLock" text message with the single hit of a button while his agents and the director were busy recovering data.

They let out a cheer at the Wellstone estate.

The FBI teams left soon after they secured the evidence. Jack had the primary DVD, while several of his men, now joining the helicopter teams, had the other DVDs. One was to be FedEx'd to Jack's immediate superior in New York, whom he'd talked to earlier.

* * *

Now came a critical stage in the plan.

It was mid-afternoon. Ravindra waved as Jack left with a trusted agent who'd brought the evidence from the crime lab. They were in the agent's rental car to meet up with the others, who were bringing the agent who had been thrust on them by the New York higher-ups.

The suspect agent had spent fruitless hours with Jack's team at the cratered building site—the purpose being to keep him fully in the dark about the DataLock raid while it was in progress. Just one call to a Deep Earth Lab contact could jeopardize the operation.

Now it didn't matter, especially with data backups separated and secured.

Jack had his stealth cameraman, who'd recorded the DataLock raid, now document what was about to happen next.

As he gave him the encrypted fake DVD, Jack told the new agent, "Take this to the crime lab, and see what you can find out. It may provide us with the reason terrorists hit the building." Jack was filmed giving the DVD to the agent. It contained bogus evidence—useless encrypted data that Vikram had sent to Ravindra, who burned the DVD.

As the agent drove away to the Redwood City crime lab, members of Jack's team discreetly tailed him.

The suspect agent, en route, decided to take a quick lunch stop at the food court of a new mall near Redwood City.

"Watch for a hand-off," Jack told his key tracker over the cell phone. Jack was in a rear car. He had earlier warned his teams privately, "He may try to make a copy of the evidence and slip it to someone. We need this on camera."

The agent was filmed talking on his cell phone as he looked for a remote space in the mall garage. He found a darkened area, parked and sat for a few minutes. He looked around, then copied the DVD on his laptop in the car. That was recorded on camera. The agent then left the car with the original DVD in an attaché case and the copy in an inside pocket.

Next, the agent went to the food court, got a burger and fries, then sat down at a table in an empty section of tables.

On camera, he was recorded slipping the copied DVD under the half-eaten food on the tray.

Moments later, a fellow dressed as a food-court employee took the tray, palmed the DVD while throwing the trash away (the crucial evidence Jack wanted caught on camera), and quickly disappeared by some back stairs out of the mall with the useless DVD.

Jack grinned. He assumed—but could not tell anyone on his team—that the bogus food-court worker was Deep Earth Lab's contact, not a terrorist.

Moments after the hand-off of the dummy DVD, Jack's team swooped down on the compromised agent, seizing his attaché case with the bogus disc they gave him. That part of it was on camera. He was filmed being handcuffed and taken away.

Off camera, Jack and his team substituted one of the genuine DVDs for the fake one in the agent's attaché case. Then three of Jack's key men took the attaché case with the genuine DVD to the Redwood City lab, and that, too, was filmed, including when they took out the DVD and gave it to the crime-lab technician.

What the Redwood lab tech found on the DVD was red-hot.

Meanwhile, as far as the FBI knew, the DVD that had been handed off by the compromised agent contained the identical evidence as the one at the Redwood lab. This was important. From here on out, any leak would be blamed on the suspect agent and his FBI superiors, who insisted he be included in the operation.

It was the perfect coup for a large-scale media leak.

Jack also knew the suspect agent would be run through truth tests and proven to be compromised. This would uncover further pockets of corruption in the agency, if not Deep Earth Lab infiltration. *Let the thinning of the herd begin,* Jack thought.

Jack was amused by the fact that the stolen DVD was full of gobbledygook. He pictured an infuriated Adin Mocatta examining pages of meaningless encryption that seemed to carry deep meaning—like an entry out of Nostradamus. Then the paranoia would mount up. *If we keep the heat on him, he won't have time to do background checks on me or learn about Jon,* Jack thought to himself.

* * *

Three days after the raid on DataLock, Jack was back in New York City in the hallowed halls of the FBI, giving his report. He stood before his superiors, explaining how he had caught the agent in the process of an otherwise successful operation. "I'd been tipped off by reliable sources that Agent Polling, assigned to our team against my wishes, was not to be trusted and already under suspicion. You remember that I went on official record protesting his being put on our team.

"I felt I had no choice but to put a tail on him to record his actions, and I'm glad I did. I believe you've seen it all on film. My team did manage to get the DVD back from him, but unfortunately, not the one he copied and passed on to the unknown contact. I believe all of you have reviewed the contents of that DVD. It is very valuable information. Unfortunately, I think we can anticipate further damage from the DVD that got away."

Some coup, Jack thought, as he was excused from the review session with the words, "You are to be congratulated on every aspect of this assignment, especially the raid on DataLock."

Now the next step in the plan could begin.

Doron and Vikram sent a digital image of a well-planned DVD of incriminating information to their contact in the Stanford hacker underground to burn to disk. It was now ready for the media leak.

Drudge Network had offered the Stanford hacker a handsome sum once they reviewed a segment. The deal was on. It also assured that those at the Wellstone estate remained completely out of view.

Chapter 40

Drudge Network's week-long series titled *Terror Target or Terrorist of the Mind?: The Dark Side of a Palo Alto Psychiatrist* climbed the Nielsen ratings nightly till viewership rivaled Super Bowl levels. The major networks had diligently side-stepped the story, again losing ratings and credibility.

Lederberg's mind-control sessions were now appearing on Drudge Network's primetime special across the nation. The public was devouring the series and sensing a malevolent agenda.

The Stanford Medical School disavowed any knowledge of the hypnotic programming sessions, urging the media to look elsewhere for answers. Ditto with peers in the psychiatric world.

Drudge Network's crowning Sunday evening finale of the series pulled in a record audience. The network had already agreed to play the final segment unedited from their anonymous source if it passed minimum standards. In truth, it was a masterpiece of film editing, produced in the shadows of New Forest by Doron and Vikram with editorial oversight by Jon.

The much-anticipated final Sunday night documentary was broadcast live as millions watched the following:

The Mazda Miata was shown lying at the bottom of the 300-foot cliffs of Devil's Slide. Enhanced by light-amplifying commercial cameras, the view was quite clear. Huge waves rocked the sports car, trapped in the boulders below. The camera then panned up, then along the coastal highway at Half Moon Bay (Doron had edited out Jon standing nearby, oblivious of the news camera). Next the car was shown briefly being hoisted up the cliffs.

Then came an inset of Spenser, the dead Stanford scholar.

Digital maps showed a moving dot, representing the route from the student's Palo Alto duplex to Half Moon Bay. Then a real-life recreation showed the car going over the cliffs and crashing below on the boulders, a terrifying plunge. It replayed from various angles. Previous deaths from the Devil's Slide area of Route 1 were quickly reviewed.

Then Spenser's background was explored: the hometown where he grew up, his Midwest family roots, his family home with insets of his parents, siblings and relatives, the high school he attended, local newspaper reports of his scholarships and achievements, and interviews of old friends still living.

A Drudge commentator mentioned, "This was the third Stanford post-doctoral molecular-biology student killed in what had been explained away as a string of disconnected suicides and accidents. But is this really true?"

A random Stanford student on University Avenue in Palo Alto was interviewed about the unfortunate series of coincidences. "Sir, what do you think?" The student answered, "Well, most of the students I know at Stanford are of the opinion that these were not disconnected coincidences, but part of a bizarre pattern of murders."

Asked to speculate about who or what would cause such murders, he replied in a low voice, "Many of us believe it is a very powerful global company operating behind the scenes known as Deep Earth Lab." (Naturally, the "random" student was actually a member of the Stanford hacker underground, and a trusted friend of the go-between.)

The on-street interview was now followed by Drudge Network's chief commentator at the scene of the accident. He looked into the camera from the cliffs of Devil's Slide, his hair blowing in the breeze of the Pacific Ocean—"We have asked previously why someone who seemed to have it all would commit suicide, in a particularly grisly manner, at the very prime of life.

"We would like to caution our audience to get ready for a startling revelation. We have found evidence from the very records of the Palo Alto psychiatrist whose building was recently blown up in what has been called a terrorist attack. The evidence we are about to show you is truly macabre.

"The following segment—and we cannot reveal the source but assure you it is reliable—should answer the suicide question once and for all." (Part of the deal with the go-between was that the network reporter would be adding commentary for dramatic effect. But they were forbidden to edit anything out of the film.)

Live on screen was a view from the hidden wall-camera in Lederberg's office, showing a side shot of Spenser. He was sitting in a leather lounge chair facing the psychiatrist. Both had their sides to the camera. The young scholar was cradling his head in his hands as though either weeping, fighting a headache, or in grief. He and the psychiatrist were conversing about his recurrent nightmares as a result of something he insisted he saw in real life—a monster, a real monster at some undisclosed location. He was desperately trying to convince the psychiatrist that he had seen it, that it was not a dream. Others had seen it as well.

All of a sudden, the psychiatrist looked intently at the subject and uttered a cryptic phrase—*"The truly gifted are able to walk on rainbows."* The Stanford scholar's demeanor instantly changed. He lifted his head, sat back, and appeared to be in a trance or was becoming a different person.

The psychiatrist addressed the patient: "What you think are memories of monsters are no more than just nightmares. You did not see any monsters in real life; you are dreaming them. What did I just tell you?"

"My memories of seeing monsters are just nightmares. I never really saw them, I dreamed them."

"That is correct, you never really saw them. They are only dreams."

It was time to go to the deepest trance level. "Now we need to go deeper, so I will begin the countdown." The psychiatrist started to count down in reverse as the roommate's eyes slowly closed.

"Have you shared these nightmares with anyone?"

"No. I have kept the vow. I have not spoken to anyone about any matter or event relating to my work at Deep Earth Lab."

"That is good. You know you can always come to me and speak to me about any of these matters. Furthermore, you always have a safe place to go. You can take Exit One, Exit One, I repeat, Exit One."

"Yes, I can take Exit One."

The mini-documentary showed an inlay of the Route 1 highway sign. The commentator remarked, "Experts are positive that 'Exit One' is a programmed command. The subject is to drive to Route 1, then perform a programmed act."

The segment returned to the psychiatrist's session.

"You have a safe place with Exit One. It is always there waiting for you should you need it. If you get an indication from me that it is now time to take Exit One, what does that mean?"

"I am to drive to Exit One and take it."

"That is correct. You will enter a zone of total safety. It is a doorway to heaven, a doorway safe from all monsters. They cannot get to you once you have taken it. What did I just say, confirm... confirm... confirm."

"Exit One is the doorway to safety, the doorway to heaven, safe from all monsters."

* * *

Adin Mocatta was watching the Drudge primetime special from his spacious Manhattan apartment in the famed Dakota House overlooking Central Park West. He was sitting in the very living room once occupied by ex-Beatle John Lennon and his wife Yoko Ono. It was the same Gothic building where the horror classic *Rosemary's Baby* had been filmed by Roman Polanski in the mid-'60s. But this was no movie, as Adin was painfully aware. It was a growing horror, now out of control, live on camera, being aired before the whole nation.

Adin felt panic as Lederberg's secretly recorded mind-control session reached the point of the programmed suicide instructions. The unimaginable had happened. The now-dead subject had mentioned his "vow" as well as "Deep Earth Lab."

He felt palpable terror. The explosion had somehow unleashed the very thing it had been geared to cover up. Rather than burying evidence, it had blown it into the light of day. Adin would need to do damage control with the Project's directors. His mind, running helter-skelter, was looking for scapegoats.

What also bothered Adin was information he didn't know about that had been kept secretly at DataLock. His heart was racing. What else did this fool have on film? Deep Earth Lab confessionals? Code words? Bohemian Grove events, including the animal-human hybrid displays? Now-dead employees showing their faces? Reports of the various giants with locations, names and addresses? Could he, Adin, somehow be on film as well, visiting Lederberg and giving him instructions? He had indeed visited the psychiatrist's office to give him directives.

Adin now realized, in the aftermath of the Palo Alto explosion, that it had rebounded on him like a witch's curse to the power of ten.

Apparently the stealth team never even saw Agent Jack, which eliminated the possibility of a friendly-fire incident or a "terrorist" sniper bullet to the head. So Jack was presumably alive and well and still a menace to Adin—indeed, more of a menace than ever.

The Project's food-court man who retrieved the DVD was already out of the country, courtesy of the ever-open Mexican border. He was en route from Honduras to Malaysia.

Adin could not afford even the smallest thread leading back to Deep Earth Lab. The task at hand was to make Deep Earth Lab no more than an urban myth, a convenient code-word used by the psychiatrist, who would be cast in the role of a modern day Jekyll-and-Hyde figure, a white-collar serial predator who was a free-ranging individual inventing conspiracies on the fly.

Adin assumed that the various news leaks were the result of standard FBI fumbling or that someone in the agency was leaking the evidence for a large cash payoff from some media group.

"Corruption is the perfect cover," Jack had told Jon.

* * *

Drudge Network was thrilled at Sunday's record audience. They had agreed to pay the secret source, and it was a considerable sum. The network wired the money to a numbered account overseas. Part of the money was then relayed to the Stanford hacker underground for a job well done. The rest went to the war chest in New Forest. None at the Wellstone estate liked the idea of Ian fully absorbing the incredible cost of the operation.

Beyond that, as Doron put it rather succinctly, "There's nothing like displaying the evidence on national television and getting paid for it!"

In their evening session, those at the Wellstone estate watched the final news documentary of Jon's deceased roommate, Spenser, which was shown on national television in the States that day.

Releasing pent-up energy and again forcing bravado, the group loudly applauded the first evidence of rewarded efforts.

Jon had to choke back tears as he felt his roommate's vindication. He had ached to see this moment on national television. And he knew there was more to come.

As the evening wound to an end, Jon got before the group and shared Jack's latest e-mail. "Jack wants me to thank each of you. He has just been given command over an entire FBI section—a formidable promotion. He wants you to know this could never have happened without your efforts. The directors at the FBI who have trusted Jack as an ally told him today they have been amply rewarded by his stunning success in Palo Alto. They feel the tables shifting in the ongoing civil war in the agency. Jack gratefully acknowledges that the information edge he was given by you was what made the difference in what up until now has been a very discouraging struggle."

The evening meeting broke up in a very positive mood.

Jon and Vikram headed to their rooms at the end of the hall. As they passed Doron's room, they glimpsed Doron lying on his bed with a conspiratorial look on his face. Naturally, Jon and Vikram entered to have a look. It was the late-night evening news on ITV.

On the screen was a shot outside the arrival gate at Terminal Three at Heathrow Airport as a huge crowd packed the gate.

Hastily walking out and waving away crowds and reporters was a familiar figure dressed in a costume that was a cross between a Marvel Comics hero and a TV wrestler. Emblazoned on the front of his caped outfit was a Crusader Cross and a Star of David. As his face came into view, the platinum winged hair appeared, as did the wild expression on his face. It was Jehovah Bob, arriving in England earlier that afternoon.

A microphone was poked near his mouth as he rushed on. He sped out of view, followed by his entourage.

Trying not to smirk, a British reporter wondered what "America's most successful and colorful evangelist" was up to in this, his latest crusade. The news segment showed a fleet of buses waiting for Jehovah Bob and his ever-overweight, outlandishly dressed followers who, as the British commentator observed, "looked like residents of a Los Angeles trailer park."

The camera zoomed down to the group boarding the buses on a lower level. On the sides were painted, "Jehovah Bob, God's Great Warrior."

The televangelist didn't board any of the buses but climbed into a large limousine waiting nearby. Presumably, he was headed to more luxurious quarters as the faithful were transported to one of the large lower-star, mega-hotels on the outskirts of London.

The brief segment ended with the reporter asking, "What could Jehovah Bob be up to?" as he over-pronounced the televangelist's name. "Stay tuned."

Chapter 41

Vikram heard a familiar groan coming from the den, a mixture of outrage, disgust and incredulity—a unique sound that could only come from Doron.

Vikram rushed in and looked questioningly at his old friend, who, with a pained look, pointed to his laptop screen. Vikram knew what was ahead. It was Doron's oldest, most debilitating battle.

Doron was ready to explode. "Maybe she'll have a road accident before she gets to the plane."

Vikram rushed over to read the message on Doron's laptop. The e-mail was shimmering before a rainbow background bordered by animated flowers and herbs. It announced:

"Peace n' Joy! I'm off to England to take part in the Summer Solstice ceremony at Stonehenge! Can you believe it. It's the biggest Stonehenge ever, and the biggest event in the world. It'll be truly tribal (truly herbal)—finally, a genuine human be-in! Wish you would join me and see it, experience it. The moon will be full. They expect over a million pilgrims. Earth-Harmony will be very strong, Rosa my astrologer tells me. Remember when we went to Stonehenge when you were a boy? (sorry we got split up for so long in the crowds) This time I expect the true light to come down. This will be inter-dimensional! Love 'n hugs, Mom."

Vikram was shaking his head in sympathy as Doron said, "Thank God we made sure that she has absolutely no idea where I am. I've never wanted to be more invisible in my life."

"Yes, fortunately, she thinks you are still in Santa Barbara at an unlisted address," Vikram responded. "I am really sorry about this. The timing is too much."

Jon and Jeremy moved closer, having overheard Doron saying to Vikram, "I can picture her flapping about semi-clad while giving sidelong grins to what she calls bare-chested, 'earthy, warlocky men.' Considering her propensity for 'writing self-destructive life scripts,' as Grandma called it, having her show up only miles from here is the last thing I need. How diabolical is that?"

Doron's normally sunny disposition was turning acrimonious. "I can see her engineering the whole thing. She ends up in the jaws of a giant as it bounds across the landscape, chopping her in half as she screams dramatically." *The high-school play of her mind downshifting toward the abyss,* Doron thought—*thespianism meets reality.*

Doron turned and confessed to Vikram, Jon and Jeremy, "For months I've been blissfully free of feeling like a burned out co-dependent. But she triggers it every time and my rage level goes off the chart."

The vitriol was mounting as Doron continued. "My grandma once remarked, 'Even when she's giving, under it all, she's really taking. She's a negative force, unable to give.' I hate to hit you guys with all this family garbage, but I need to work through it, and the fact is, she will be coming at our most critical time." He became incoherent and they understood. Right now Doron was in meltdown.

Doron regained composure as he remarked to his friends, "Remember the Clockwork Earl's painting of the towering giant approaching Stonehenge with surging crowds in Druid robes stretching across the landscape? That scenario could be the big surprise at the upcoming Stonehenge. And guess who'll be there to greet the unexpected guest? Mom!"

Doron also feared that his mom would vibe him out, sensing him nearby, and show up on the doorstep. Inevitably, it would be during the peak of battle when all hell was breaking loose, indeed, at the critical moment Doron was unleashing protocols that needed split-second timing. Yes, at that moment he was under peak pressure, somehow his mom would appear with a giant in tow. That paranoia alone was the last thing Doron needed.

As those departing to the field filled the den, Doron, switching gears, announced, "I know this may come as a shock, but we've been here over three weeks now. And guess what's upon us? I was just reminded by my crazy mom—the Druid and Wiccan celebration of Summer Solstice. And you know what that means."

Then for dramatic effect, Doron added, "Northrop's big event is the night of the Solstice. And we'll be out and about with our lives on the line. It's only days away!"

A moment of sobriety came upon the group as they caught Doron's tone of irony—death was a real possibility for each of them.

They also saw another aspect of Doron they'd never seen before. His vulnerable side and his pain. Genius often came at a stiff price. And that was true of others there besides Doron.

* * *

The gardening crew at Northrop's contacted Ian early in the afternoon. "We just found out the earl's begun a desperate hiring binge. They're contacting the usual locals that serve at such events—plus recommended friends. That's us. Sorry, but American accents will give the game away. Check with the other crews and give us names."

Group Two, now on the field, assured Ian that at least four could be on hand as support staff serving Northrop's gala event. "Put our names in the pot."

"Done, mates," Ian replied.

"This is made to order," Jon commented.

"What better way to be on Northrop's estate than as paid staff the very night things blow wide open. We'll be there to serve 'em, all right!"

Those at the cyberwing control center worked feverishly, knowing that time was running out.

Ian observed to Jon and Doron in a low voice, "I am considering whether the SmarTruck should be nearby Northrop's in case things take a strange and unpredictable turn. It could be risky. On the other hand, the region will be filled with distractions."

"Well, if things suddenly go ballistic," Doron reminded them, "we will need the SmarTruck close enough to uplink for live television coverage. Considering the recent media revelations Stateside, this could create a whole new feeding frenzy. Whatever we do, we must get one of the giants on national TV."

Doron and Ian left the room to head outside for a break, discussing the hi-tech military outfits with the invisibility functions.

"The truth is," Ian said, "we can enter the earl's estate dressed in these outfits, the invisibility function on, and roam at will with camouflaged TV cameras. I assure you, we can walk right through the gates and nobody will know."

Ian, who had already seen the extent of Doron's genius and cunning, had no doubt that Doron was the one to join him in this most important endeavor. They'd spent extra hours on the weapons simulation programs for that very reason.

"This could be delicate," Ian said to Doron, "but let me be the one to push the case for your inclusion in a way that would allow the others to vote for you in joining me."

"Agreed."

The two returned to the cyberwing control center as Ian clicked through the 60 or so monitors on both Northrop estates to assess the situation. They briefly flashed by the earl, ranting and raving over the phone about money disappearing from one of his offshore accounts.

Northrop screamed, "It was done so cleverly, one of your men told me, that there is no trail of evidence. Yet it's been debited from my account. I want those funds back. Do you understand?" Ian acknowledged kudos to Doron.

The earl complained, "This is absolutely the worst time for this to happen. I have too much on my bloody mind to bother with it at the moment." He slammed down the phone.

"Considering Northrop's vast wealth," Doron told Ian, even a few hundred thousand pounds is a mere pittance."

Ian repeated, "Well done!"

In a return sweep half an hour later, Ian and Doron saw the Clockwork Earl, this time passionately lecturing a bewildered dog about etiquette while squeezing its head tightly with both hands as their noses almost touched, the dog eyeing around nervously, Northrop's face flushed, eyes ballooning out.

Doron quoted one of his mother's alien aphorisms: "I would say he is in a state of extreme psychological." Ian laughed.

Things appeared to be in high gear at the main Oxfordshire estate. Ian spotted a number of full-sized flatbed trucks lined up, some already packed and moving out the gate. The Arabian tent was still there but the massive crown was gone.

Ian next clicked through the various monitors around the New Forest estate and spotted a flatbed truck that had pulled into the rear side of a multi-acre remote garden bordered by seven-foot hedges.

Ian remarked to Doron, "This is where the Clockwork Earl has his annual midnight Druid festivities." They watched as workers using a small crane unloaded strange looking polished hardwood objects the size of roof beams.

Doron approached it like an IQ puzzle, rearranging the beams in his mind, and saw immediately what they were.

Doron turned to Ian, "They're parts of a gigantic throne."

By afternoon Doron was proven right. Work crews had assembled a massive throne sitting off to the side of the secret garden, tucked in a freshly cut-out section of dense forest and looking out. A camouflage curtain was now being hung in front of the opening of the area, effectively hiding the throne.

Doron added, "The giant will be able to look out at the festivities while fully hidden from view, especially in the dark of night."

Ian responded, "Who on Earth would've ever believed this a year ago? I wouldn't have believed it if you'd told me."

Doron looked at Ian, confirming their earlier conversation. "There's no doubt that we need to be right there in that secret garden, suited up in the invisibility mode with two TV cameras and explosives nearby— Semtex remotes at the very least. That's where the action's going to be."

Ian nodded, his eyes lighting up as he replied, "This event will be sufficient for the satellite uplink to Drudge Network. Wait till the curtain is withdrawn and they see what's sitting there. I can't think of anything more dramatic to stir up the situation, I really can't."

Doron nodded, grinning mysteriously as he looked off in thought.

That evening, Ian pushed the vote. "I need a show of hands whether Doron joins me on Northrop's estate in the invisibility suit." Unanimous.

"Okay, it's agreed," Ian acknowledged. "Doron, are you up to it?" An obvious nod from Doron sealed it.

Ian went on. "Next vote, I propose that Vikram should be the one to stay here running the controls and monitoring the event in case things go awry. If so, Vikram will be the one to begin the critical remote protocols."

"I don't want to be left out of the action," Vikram protested.

Ian and several others assured him, "Vikram, your role might be the most pivotal of all, and we're not exaggerating."

Vikram responded, "I feel honored."

Ian and Doron returned to the cyberwing as Doron remarked in irony, "Entering Northrop's in those suits will be like going on a spy mission to some *Beaux Artes* ball in hell."

Ian answered, "I expect things could get very strange and truly dangerous. I hope we survive it. Because TV cameras are not going to be the only thing we will be carrying."

Chapter 42

Across the Atlantic, Adin Mocatta was in the Dakota House brooding as he looked out his living-room window over Central Park West, the constant crowds of New Yorkers and tourists flowing like ants below. Some would inevitably look up, awed, as they scanned the Gothic structure towering over them.

Adin was in an especially bad mood. In America, it was a fact of life that you could not click through the channels without eventually running into Jehovah Bob—now the most prominent in a rash of vulgar TV evangelists. Adin especially hated this character, always had. And Adin just had a "twofer."

He had watched the final Drudge segment showing his old nemesis, Dr. Lederberg, hypnotically programming a Stanford scholar, whom Adin recognized. The name of "Deep Earth Lab" had been mentioned, then the programmed suicide was shown in graphic detail. This left Adin beside himself.

He switched channels and ran right into Jehovah Bob, exaggeratedly shadow-boxing some pretended creature, hips shifting and hair flapping like bird wings. The televangelist then pivoted his hips *à la* Elvis Presley and began his overblown victory-walk, now that the imaginary creature was defeated. This mockery in Adin's face made him blow a circuit.

Almost insane with rage, Adin seriously contemplated putting a hired assassin on the televangelist's tail and paying him extra to torture the man (and, oh, could he ever visualize this part) before he killed him. Then Adin suddenly got hold of himself. He'd struggled more and more to downshift these violent moods ever since he started taking the elixir. He also knew self-indulgent passions could jeopardize his whole mission in the world.

He decided to indulge his loathing for this seamy redneck in a future broadbanding experiment—perhaps creating a catastrophe of some horrendous sort. But considering what was now at stake, Adin could ill

255

afford to have his attention divided by this unworthy creature. But oh, it would writhe like an earthworm some day, but not yet.

* * *

Most recently, Jehovah Bob had acquired some powerful invisible backers. It gave him a new audacity. One anonymous donor had given the televangelist's manager funding as well as the idea for the present crusade, which was "guaranteed to bring in more money than the past three years combined by capturing the public imagination as never before."

True to the prediction, money, indeed, came pouring into the ministry in record amounts. Most of the donations came from the anonymous donor himself, who used an untraceable numbered account from Liechtenstein, one of Europe's oldest banking havens. Invariably a note followed these direct money wire-transfers to Jehovah Bob's manager.

The most recent note, in semi-Chaucerian English, cryptically instructed the manager:

"Not far from Stonehenge, the ancient creature awaits in its lair near Burley, deep in the ancient woods of New Forest. A great celebration is planned. Only Jehovah Bob can battle this ancient enemy. We the faithful await his arrival before the first day of summer when the witches celebrate the Summer Solstice. We will reveal the secret stronghold of the ancient foe."

A map was included with an X and the words "meeting place" beneath it. The marking appeared to be on a sizable tract of land surrounding Burley, perhaps a private estate.

Jehovah Bob, with his large band of American followers, was now answering the call of the faithful as preparations were underway for the overseas crusade. "Jo-Bob," as his manager called him, had asked, "Are there any hot young maidens (wink, wink) in the New Forest area? See if you can provide me with a late night *visitation-uhhhh...*" When the great battle against evil was over, Jo-Bob would verily be rocket ready for his buxom lass.

* * *

The New Forest Underground crews arrived a little early. Gerald was with them this time.

Ian, Jon and Jeremy looked out the window of the Wellstone estate and spotted Doron uncharacteristically hanging out alone with the Underground. They were laughing over something. Gerald then drove away, laughing and waving.

A few hours later, Ian got a call on his cell phone. "We've been hired. Just been given gate passes and parking spaces. We're in."

As Ian clicked off he told Jon, "The Trojan Horse will be in the gates for the big party."

Group Two, directed by Neil, attached leaf micro-cams on trees surrounding the giant's throne. Like the other chips planted, they could ride on the local Wi-Fi over the Internet using encryption streaming.

In the closed-off Druid garden, Neil placed cams with several views of the central bonfire pit area.

By the day's end, Group Two had successfully installed micro-cams for a broadcast system that was fully independent of the roaming TV cameras—still the primary system. Also, more implanted "roaming mini-cams" were released, including a bio-implanted local field rat.

At the Wellstone estate, Jon assisted Ian and Doron in a side garden, practicing trial maneuvers with the invisibility suits. Doron and Ian would move slowly ("yes, I can barely see you"), or, freeze in front of hedges, trees and rose bushes ("now I can't see you at all"). Ian and Doron quickly got a handle on the strengths and limitations of this new technology.

* * *

With Jeremy standing behind him looking on, Doron showed one of the new rats in the underground facility, watching Jeremy's unpopular Cambridge colleague known as the Weasel.

The rat peered from behind a stack of books as the Weasel was putting away lab equipment with quick, agitated movements. Doron turned around and looked at Jeremy's sneer. "We're actually watching a recording from earlier in the afternoon."

"Either way, it's rough on the eyes," Jeremy remarked.

Doron ran a fast-forward to several hours later, returning to normal speed. Now the rat was on a higher shelf, looking down. The Weasel walked back into the lab—which from overhead resembled a doll house as it sat in the immense underground hangar—and nervously eyed around.

The Weasel took out a vial from his pocket and, in quick movements, vacuum-sealed it in a mirror-finish Mylar bag used for shipping pharmaceuticals and lab specimens. He opened a cabinet and took out a slightly larger, 3x4-inch, foam-reinforced, quick-seal mailing envelope. He slipped the smaller bag with the vial in it, then added a small amount of dry ice and quick-sealed the envelope.

Trying to maintain a things-as-usual look, the Weasel slipped it in an inner pocket and walked out of the lab.

"Caught in the act," Doron announced as he looked back at Jeremy, who nodded.

"Behold," Doron said. On street cam the Weasel now had a large overnight FedEx Tyvek padded envelope. He entered a tobacco shop next door to a mailing store. Then he darted into the mailing shop.

Doron hacked into the records of the Ibsley shop, from where the Weasel had sent the FedEx envelope. It was mailed to to a Mr. A. Poole, 112 West 72nd Street West, #13, New York, NY, 10023—the address of a MailExpress in midtown Manhattan, mere blocks from the Dakota House.

Doron explained to Jeremy, "I scanned the *New York Times* story on Adin Mocatta's purchase of John Lennon's old place. I then retrieved the store-cam picture of Adin picking up the most recent package from the Weasel at the midtown Manhattan MailExpress at the above address." Jeremy was in awe.

Jon, just joining them, urged Doron to send Jack the segment of the Weasel preparing the package as well as the one of Adin Mocatta picking it up from the 72nd Street store.

"Somehow I knew you would ask that!" Doron replied. "Rather than send it straight to Jack, we've got to get it to him via a back door, with no footprints leading back to us. I don't want to risk e-mailing it." Jon nodded.

Doron sent the digital segments of the Weasel and of Adin via the Stanford hacker who was their go-between. The hacker, using an "anon" at Mail Boxes Etc. near Palo Alto, then FedEx'd the DVD to Jack at the FBI offices.

* * *

Jack got the DVD in less than a day and e-mailed Jon a cryptic confirmation.

Jack had already gotten recordings of Adin Mocatta arriving in a limousine at the Trump Empire Tower, the secret entrance to the penthouse office suite and much more. On the latest DVD Jack got that day, Adin was picking up a FedEx envelope at a New York mail drop near the Dakota House.

A trusted member of Jack's team asked Jack, "Okay, what do you think is in the package?"

Jack just shrugged. "Since it's addressed to a fictitious name, it must be something he doesn't want others to know about."

With the latest evidence arriving that morning, Jack had FBI approval to monitor Adin Mocatta coming and going to his various residences, and to move aggressively on Mocatta at his own discretion.

Jack explained to his team of agents, "The Chappaqua estate is where Mocatta almost always spends his weekends. For us, this is the preferred time to enter the Trump Empire Tower penthouse offices. The Dakota House is Mocatta's preference when he is working during the week. If we need to bust him midweek, Dakota House will be at the top of our list."

That night Jon gave his brother Jack more background info in an e-mail: "Try to follow me, Bro. Doron went on a knowledge binge. He fast-reviewed the backup of Northrop's phone conversations. Doron found that Northrop, a director of Deep Earth Lab, has had high regard for Adin Mocatta, who he sees as a future heavyweight. Doron just encountered references to Adin's "broadbanding" ability. It's a psychic ability. Now, whatever Adin Mocatta is being sent at the mail drop was extracted from the giants. It may be a hormone or a neurochemical. Stay tuned and be safe. Jon."

Jack had been given yet another gift by his brilliant brother, Jon, and his band of geniuses. Jack's plan, as they had all agreed, was to uncover Deep Earth lab "by accident," while innocently looking for "terrorists."

* * *

Those at the Wellstone estate began to approach each meal as though it was their last. So they savored every bite. Tonight it was beef Wellington cooked by Ian's servants.

After dinner, Ian announced, "This afternoon, Vikram hacked into the firewalled computer at the estate in Mountain View. The owner, as we all suspected, is one of the directors of Deep Earth Lab. From his computer Vikram managed to download a virtual black book of contact info, Deep Earth Lab locations in various locales, cell phone numbers, private unlisted numbers, unlisted addresses and all kinds of incriminating information. Some of this we think is for blackmail in case defectors and rogue workers suffer attacks of conscience."

"Bravo, Vikram, well done, mate."

As the meeting came to a conclusion, Ian held up one of the gate passes to Northrop's estate that Group Two had been given that day. "Neville, I am going to guess that since one of your claims to fame was to create perfect duplicates of Wimbledon center-court tickets, these should be no problem, right?"

Neville grinned and nodded. "I will print enough to get at least six of us into Lord Northrop's famed hunting estate." Youthful indiscretions did come in handy now and then.

As everybody got up from their chairs, Doron had one more point. "I am guessing that they will probably transport one of the giants to the throne, have him sit down, then hook him up to the anesthetic or at least a tranquilizer."

The two molecular biologists, Jeremy and Jon, nodded. Jeremy added, "I would guess a low dosage of anesthetic. Unless they have fully succeeded in hypnogens and mind-control over these creatures."

"During the event we may need to cut the tube for a surprise wake-up. Any thoughts?" Ian probed.

Doron responded, "I would volunteer the field rat. It can gnaw through the tube in seconds."

The group concurred.

On the way to bed, Vikram and Jon looked into Doron's room. He was watching a special news flash on the secret journey of Jehovah Bob. Vikram said tauntingly, "He's headed this way, isn't he!"

Doron waved goodnight as he switched the TV off and rolled over. He knew some plans must remain entirely secret.

Chapter 43

Jon could feel Northrop's solstice celebration fast approaching, "like a comet heading for the earth," as he remarked to Vikram, Ian, Jeremy and Doron. "Collision time is this Saturday by midnight." The tension in the air was palpable.

Vikram observed, "The throne in the side garden certainly suggests that the time of the unveiling of Northrop's dark god will be Saturday night at the latest."

"Whether the Clockwork Earl plans to ride the giant to Stonehenge after midnight is another matter," Jeremy speculated. "If Northrop's planned unveiling of the dark god takes place, I suppose he'll have to. But is it even possible?"

"It's definitely doable," Doron replied. "We've built a model and calculated that the giant can walk at over 40 miles an hour and that means a little over an hour stroll from New Forest to Stonehenge going in a straight line."

Jeremy added, "Yes, but such a trip would hardly go unnoticed. And which giant—the one at Northrop's? The three creatures we've seen in the vast enclosure are unimaginable, formidable. It could do nothing but draw attention. Talk about outing yourself."

"I think when you believe you are the equivalent of a time lord, able to inaugurate a new age on the earth," Doron remarked, "then a public outing is part of the package."

Vikram continued, "Meanwhile, we will be more like the wasp in the grasslands of the Serengeti that stings an elephant on the eye, creating a thundering charge of elephants felt across the plains. It's a hundred-million-to-one ratio of forces."

Adding another perspective, Ian said, "We must prevent any power from covering up or obscuring the evidence—and I hope that those who dare to do so will be implicated and destroyed in the process.

"If the media and government agencies can't or won't follow the leads, we will do it for them. Even if we have to e-mail the whole bloody world," he added as he gave the thumbs-up, resembling for a moment the World War II RAF pilot on the poster in the Anchor Pub.

* * *

The time had come for the first of the secret protocols devised by Doron and Vikram. The only others present to witness the event were Ian, Jeremy and Jon.

The group were upstairs in central control. The others were out on the field.

A phone started ringing over their headphones as the group listened.

"Hello, Elliot Wezelby speaking." They could see the Weasel standing at his desk in the underground enclosure.

"Elliot, it's Doctor Lederberg calling you from Stanford. Now, before you go into shock, let me just tell you that the reported explosion was a ruse planned by the Project. I will go into it all later. But just be assured that I am alive and well. How are you doing, Elliot?" It was clearly the voice of the deceased Palo Alto psychiatrist.

The Weasel faltered, "Uhh … quite well, sir. I am doing quite well." Long pause. "I am very relieved to hear that you are alive, Dr. Lederberg."

"Thank you, Elliot. Now listen carefully. There is something I need to tell you. *Walking the heather can be a transporting experience.* Acknowledge, Elliot, acknowledge." The psychiatrist's voice was perfectly simulated by Doron as he invoked the unique code word to initiate the programming mode they had hacked. Vikram was running the digital voice synthesizer.

The Weasel responded in the subdued monotone voice of every subject they had seen go into deep trance, now repeating the key response: "I have kept the covenants of Deep Earth Lab and have never violated any of my oaths."

As Doron spoke into the computer's microphone, the Palo Alto psychiatrist's unmistakable voice came out on the phone line.

Jeremy whispered to Jon as he nudged him, "This is absolutely incredible."

"Elliot, I want you to remain in New Forest until I tell you to leave. Is that understood?"

"I understand. I am to remain in New Forest until I am told by you to leave."

"That is correct. I want you to work normal hours at the Project the rest of this week until Saturday. On Saturday, you are to be at the lab from noon until midnight, is that understood? Acknowledge, Elliot, acknowledge."

The Weasel repeated the command, then vowed obedience. Queried about opening the various gates of the facility, Dr. Elliot Wezelby of Cambridge responded, "Only I and seven others have full access to opening and closing of all the gates, including the big outer door. I will await instructions."

Doron now engaged a confirmation test. "Elliot, I want you to go to the village of Burley at 2 p.m. this afternoon, purchase a single rose from the florist on Main Street and leave it on the dashboard of your car." A street-cam test later confirmed that this was carried out to the letter.

"When you hang up, you will not remember this conversation, nor will you remember receiving this telephone call."

"When I hang up, I will not remember this conversation, nor will I remember receiving this telephone call."

"You are to remain ready for further instructions."

"I am to remain ready for further..."

"You are to keep your cell phone with you at all times day and night."

Elliot performed the repeat confirmation.

"Elliot, I will begin the countdown. When it is over, you will automatically turn off your cell phone and put it away. After you have put it away you will soon fully awake, feeling healthy and positive. Listen, Elliot, listen. ... Fifteen ... fourteen ... thirteen ..."

When the phone was hung up, the observers were in awe.

Ian mentioned, "When the time is right, we can tell the others. But the smaller the circle that is aware of these things, right now, the better." Several of them had been concerned that a mole may have infiltrated the group, most likely from the New Forest Underground.

* * *

Doron, Vikram and Jon watched a late-night TV news special at the end of a very full day in Doron's room. In one segment, TV crews had been following Jehovah Bob's traveling caravan like bloodhounds. Now they were showing the British public—ever fascinated with American vulgarity—the tour highlights.

Jehovah Bob dolls were pictured on sale at Piccadilly Circus, Trafalgar Square, and along King's Road in Chelsea. A doll demo showed how they would "drop trou" occasionally as they vibrated. They were selling like crazy.

The TV special briefly explored the *Rolling Stone* revelations on the evangelist's shady background. On screen was a shot of the Newport News warehouse with the sex toys—"the birthplace of what we believe are now the singing angels," the commentator mentioned. "Fully deserving," as one Oxford sociologist on camera pointed out, "the Darwin Award."

Next came live interviews of several of Jehovah Bob's seedy cohorts from the past.

One toothless man in Mississippi drove off in a lurching, beat-up old Buick, smoke pouring out the back. A zoom shot into the rear seat showed liquor bottles and other interesting things. This fellow and Jehovah Bob (under one of his earlier names) had been accused of gang-banging several underage girls.

"Low rent is an understatement," another commentator said as they panned some of Jehovah Bob's old dwellings and garages, especially the body shop. "This is where he magnesium-sprayed his hair, creating the present winged effect, a virtual trademark along with his walk."

Next they showed a long line of buses following the evangelist's limousine across the south of England, heading in the general direction of the Port of Southampton.

The commentator noted, "No one can really guess where he is going and what he's up to. He certainly won't say."

En route, they showed Jehovah Bob stopping the caravan at a "spiritual center of darkness" to rebuke the dark powers "in-thu-nayumm-ahh—of Jeezzusss-uuuhh," vibrating like a demented Elvis as his followers, mostly overweight women, stood swooning.

"One hot spot is Glastonbury and the wooded area nearby, where Druid altars once stood," the commentator added.

A helicopter view, circling from above, showed Jehovah Bob in his superhero outfit, walking off toward the woods by the side of the road. The mob behind him broadened out like a cape. At this particular roadside exorcism, the evangelist held two vibrating angels in his hands, each roughly ten inches long, and pointed them at the "enemy," supposedly the site of another Druid altar. The followers imitated him as they prayed *en masse*, rebuking the demons.

The news special reverse-zoomed from the helicopter, showing hundreds surrounding Jehovah Bob, pointing the vibrating "angels" and babbling fanatically. An audio microphone amplified the gibberish over the air. *"Shushumna num, shumna num, **shumba shumba shumba!**"*

A language expert commented that it followed no known laws of syntax but seemed rather to be contrived glossalalia.

The final scene depicted the words *"shumba shumba shumba"* on T-shirts for sale in Earl's Court, Chelsea and Hammersmith. The commentator held one up, and pressed it over his front. "Well, shumba, shumba, shumba for now, and we promise to update you soon on this most amazing phenomenon."

Doron switched off the TV as the others headed for bed.

* * *

A considerable distance from the Wellstone estate, Doron quietly instructed his reception party of New Forest Underground volunteers. He was at Gerald's on a fabricated excuse of running some errand. They were meeting in the large barn, and the group of 30 was having problems staying serious.

"The plan is to meet his caravan at the perimeter of New Forest, and lose the public with a decoy. You will enter the earl's estate via the back gate as we discussed. It will be in late evening, so most people will be preoccupied. It will also still be light."

Gerald, the original host at the hobbit farmhouse, agreed to be the leader of the reception party. He remarked, "I reckon this religious showman in all his Elvis Presley glitter will get much more than he ever bargained for. They'll confront the real monsters this time. Then we'll see what kind of courage he's got."

"Remember secrecy," Doron again reminded the group. "The others have too much on their minds. And we need this distraction. It will help them."

Gerald knew the region like the back of his hand, and that included Northrop's hunting estate. He reminded the others, "The earl's estate has five separate private roads of entry from various directions. The road we will use is completely out of view. It goes right through the earl's private forest. Some of you know that it begins near the Arundel River, where there is an obscured older gate. The private road ends up at the mansion just out of view of his garden where they do their bloody midnight ceremonies."

Doron added, "When Gerald and Clive approached the television people, they agreed to keep absolute secrecy. Several commentators and cameramen will be included with us as we lead the caravan on the private road. Network news helicopters will be in wait till we summon them. We're being given field phones to communicate with the pilots."

Doron provided his secret team with another perspective. "The main television producer/commentator, who's been following the caravan, senses a huge story brewing and has agreed to do anything we require of him. He believes he'll win the British journalism award denied him in the past. And he's ready to do backflips.

"Now strategy," Doron instructed. "The team at the Wellstone estate, as most of you know, will need the help of the Underground in what I will outline. We've worked out a pincer movement. One is to take place at Northrop's gala event; the other at the gate of the underground facility leading to the Fortress. I'm afraid that this part we will be playing by ear. There are just too many unknowns. But we will have a load of contingency plans. At minimum, we plan to create absolute pandemonium."

He ended the meeting with the challenge, "In Jon's words, 'Those approaching these terrible creatures must become just like the emboldened villagers approaching Castle Frankenstein.' Fear must turn to courage. We will have arms."

Perhaps trying to subdue their fear and nervousness, hearty cheers of bravado rang out in Gerald's barn as the meeting came to a close.

Gerald remarked to Doron as they drove back to the Wellstone estate, "I can't tell you how excited we are. This is what we've been waiting for, mate, be assured of that."

Chapter 44

It was Thursday in Manhattan, the big day now only two days away. Adin planned to start broadbanding at noon, but he needed to talk to Northrop before that.

Adin had become increasingly anxious about having the neurochemicals in Trump Empire Tower, where an FBI raid could jeopardize everything. So he spent increasing amounts of his time at the Dakota House, where he could do his broadbanding in safety with little chance of Agent Jack blundering through the door. He also felt more safe here when talking to Northrop. Planning was becoming intense.

Security at the Dakota House was in high alert to show Adin shots of anyone inquiring after him. He had plans to get Agent Jack out of the picture as soon as possible, courtesy of several former members of the Russian Mafia, who now had the info on Jack. It would not involve the Deep Earth Lab team. This too gave Adin a sense of peace.

Adin and Northrop began their planning session for the big event via secure-phone. He told the earl, "I am now able to overshadow the giants for up to three hours at a stretch. Maybe longer if need be. But beyond all that, there are some big issues bothering me—the greater consequences of the unveiling. We've both known time was running out for this thing to go public ever since the first leaks by the maintenance workers over there."

"That is correct," Northrop responded. We can keep a lid on them for only so long."

"So the way we introduce these creatures to the world also becomes a PR issue."

"Yes, it is. We need to proactively go public with something too great to remain a secret for much longer." The earl agreed.

Northrop paused. "Look, Adin, some of the old holdout members of the board are clinging to an outworn strategy. Our dirty little secret was going to get out sooner or later anyway. ... I believe our supreme PR move can be synchronized with Britain's rapidly changing culture. We can capitalize on the wave of Britain's massive pagan revivals. Druids and Wiccans are in a passionate search for their ancient gods. A new tolerance to the alien and the occult is in the air. I say we ride the wave.

"Listen, Adin, instead of terrifying monsters, the giants will be introduced as the returned ancient gods of old, now riding into the world with messianic timing, heralds of a coming age. I have media people in tow who will push this angle strongly."

Adin added, "Of course, neither of us has consulted with the more rigid directors!"

"Of course not," Northrop replied. "You create the situation and let the pieces fall where they may. We must engage the dialectic of history itself. The directors can all take a flying leap if they can't see our moment in history."

The earl paused and added, "Then there is the considerable amount of money going to the both of us that the others don't know about. The investors are drooling over this breakthrough. A live demo will clinch it for us. I am going out of my way to have them on hand Saturday night."

Knowing he needed Adin's ability to mind-meld with the giants in order to make the unveiling work, the earl continued: "Adin, the religious demands of the pagans to have their gods can be compared to the liberation of various minorities in recent history. I have key Hindu leaders who will speak out."

"And the scientists who had made it all possible can now come out of hiding and be given the highest accolades," Adin added. "The media can call them the new Einsteins."

The earl continued, "I've invited a "who's who" guest list. They'll use their powers of influence, but only if it is done right. That's why you and I have to choreograph this like the Bolshoi Ballet."

Earlier, Adin had worked hard to convince Northrop of the need to have the creature "sitting on the throne at the unveiling, like an Indian guru peacefully giving *darshan* as the curtain is raised."

Adin again reminded Northrop, "The initial shock and horror can be transformed into religious awe and adoration."

"Yes, yes, so you've said, and I fully agree."

After hanging up, the Clockwork Earl was observed by Ian, Doron, Vikram, Jon and Jeremy on a Wellstone monitor telling his bewildered dog, as he pressed its head between his hands, "This beats living in total boredom! *A rumma-ding, and a rumma-dumma ding-dong.*" It was now nervously wagging its tail.

* * *

Adin began his deep breathing as he closed his eyes. As he settled down, he thought of the three main creatures in the underground complex.

Two of these giants were not that difficult to control. But one, the oldest prototype and Northrop's favorite, was becoming increasingly powerful in resisting the overshadowing process. This one seemed to have an unusual range of paranormal abilities, though Adin hadn't figured out what all of them were. Northrop was sure that this was a perfect clone of the dark god. It was from a dig in the sub-Sahara, where the great burial ground of the Nephilim lay, according to Northrop's research.

Adin, who had more than enough neurochemicals on hand for repeated sessions, had already decided that before the great day—in two days—he would take incrementally larger doses from here on out.

As noon approached, the din of Manhattan traffic became ever more faint and distant as Adin began broadbanding.

He entered the mind of giant number two and was soon looking through its eyes around the underground facility from its immense cage. Its own consciousness stirred and shifted beneath his own. Off in the distance he saw Wezelby, whom he secretly detested, and fantasized luring the obsequious fool over in payment for sending him the vials.

Adin had used people like this all his life and always felt contaminated afterward. It made him detest these useful idiots even more. At some point, once he was in the giant, he would just trample Wezelby and that would be it.

Adin caught himself, aware that a new kind of violent rage had returned. Was it the chemical or the giant's mind influencing him? He wasn't sure which force was the more dominant.

Now mind-melded, *he/it* got up from the giant's chair and walked its quarters. Wezelby gave it a nervous sidelong glance. Lord Northrop soon appeared in the holding area and ordered the staff to prepare it for the lift. They planned another rehearsal walk to the throne area, then back.

A number of those at the Wellstone estate were monitoring the event live through the three implanted rats below and the squirrels above. They also planned to test the wild field rat once the giant was near Northrop's in a trial run.

The giant rode up the lift as the ground seemed to open up. It was sitting rather than lying on the platform. The squirrel remained some distance away, looking on. The giant stood up. Wezelby and others stood in the distance. Wezelby gave Northrop the remote so that if the giant did anything wild, they could stun it, put it to sleep or paralyze it. Or, with a button under a lid of its own, kill it. There was a poison injector as well as the exploding collar around its neck.

The forest floor shook under the canopy as the walk began. Taking a rear road, they headed for Northrop's. This time, he followed behind in a small, fuel-cell-powered vehicle, a sort of glorified golf-cart. Wezelby went separately in his own vehicle. Northrop held the remote as one of the junior staff drove at thirty miles per hour, marking the pace of the giant. In less than twenty minutes, they reached the rear fence and entrance into the back of the estate.

Northrop gave the signal, and the procession headed back. Adin kept getting distracted by the sense of being watched. Using the giant's perception, he felt several small animals being overridden in near proximity.

The Wellstone group were gratified to find that the field rat, as it scampered among bushes and trees, was easily able to monitor the giant. Doron let Neville try the joystick, then gave it to Neville's friend, Cyrell, the video-game ace. Both passed with flying colors. At this point, Neville, who had joined both Group One and Two on expeditions, would be at Northrop's for the gala affair. As Ian and Doron had noted, Neville was first in line to use the shoulder-launched rocket, having excelled in the simulation chamber.

An hour later, the giant was back in its cage.

In the Dakota House, Adin was rubbing his head, pressing his temples to minimize the inevitable headache. A few hours later he and the earl were back on secure-phone—at least, they believed it was secure.

"It went perfectly, well done!" Northrop congratulated Adin in good cheer. "Are you feeling all right? Still getting those headaches?"

"Yes, but they don't seem as bad. I think we can do the whole thing without a hitch. Remember, all staff should be ordered not to approach or go beyond the altar of the Druid garden, not under any circumstances. They are not to broach the throne area or try to look behind the curtain," he admonished.

Northrop replied, "They know this. I've also arranged for curtain area to be under a discreet guard. The staff will be warned that they will be shot at or dismissed immediately if they trespass. They believe that it is holding a gift for the Royal Family to be presented *in absentia* at the festivities."

Adin and the earl quickly signed off with much still to do.

By late afternoon a retired makeup artist—a member of the Underground—was visiting the Wellstone estate. He had worked the London theatre circuit, and now was on hand to disguise the hired "servants" from their group. Given the off chance of being identified by Cambridge faculty or other guests, this was a needed precaution. Ian gambled that the locals, caught up in the demands of the grand affair, and surrounded by many new faces, would hardly take notice.

Chapter 45

On Friday, the final day before the conflict, Ian distributed several of the anti-tank weapons to two former British military commandos, also members of the Underground. Gerald had brought them by and they were inside the barn.

One of the ex-commandos ran his hand over the American AT4 shoulder-launched weapon. "Yes, we've used these in field exercises in the past four years. They're highly effective and fairly accurate. In fact they're light enough to strap to your back."

His mate nodded, impressed.

Jon and Jeremy were introduced to the two men and shook their hands. "Looks like we'll be on the front lines together, pressing into the facility," Jon said.

One commando replied, "We plan to be on off-road motorcycles. You just give the word when you need us to do something. We will hover near you at the front or remain within earphone range."

As Gerald drove the ex-commandos off, he reminded Ian and the others, "Remember, after the big meeting tonight at Clive's, there will be a separate meeting at my house."

* * *

Ian gave the overview and final details in Gerald's lounge. He reminded them, "Remember, if conflict at the underground facility blows open before the event at Northrop's, Northrop's whole affair will shut down immediately. That will end our main objective. We cannot afford for that to happen. Do not start things at the underground facility until Northrop's event is well underway. Vikram will give the go-ahead. You are to wait near the facility till those of us at the earl's estate give Vikram the signal. Understood?" The group nodded.

"Vikram runs central control at the Wellstone estate. If any of us needs to speak with any others—assuming direct contact breaks off—we can communicate through him. We will have earphones, headphones, cell phones and other devices."

As the meeting broke up, Gerald insisted they have a brief prayer, which he led: "Lord, help us overcome this terrible thing that has entered our midst in New Forest and ruined so many lives, even killing innocent people. Help us be brave, Lord, and protect us. Amen."

Most of the Cambridge guests bowed their heads out of courtesy. It was a quaint country prayer. However, Jon felt strangely touched. And Doron, as he told Vikram that night, felt something resonating in his spirit.

Vikram smiled as they turned in, "Is Doron the great skeptic now opening to new possibilities?"

Doron earlier that day reminisced to Vikram some of the gifted mentors of his early teens whom he had never met beyond the Internet: George Koch of Oracle fame, a member of 4-Sigma, Prometheus and Triple Nine ultra-high-IQ societies, who went off and started a church after an overpowering encounter with God, and Koch's close friend, also highly gifted, who had gone to India a mystic and come back a changed man, also touched by God.

Off by himself, Jon e-mailed Jack right before turning in:

"Jack, tomorrow might be our last day on earth. Jeremy and I will be entering the facility, monsters and all. It will be full engagement. I'm scared. Doron also wanted me to tell you that Adin Mocatta will be at the Dakota House. Vikram, who's operating central control, will signal you when things are ready on your end. Timing is key. Hope we live another day. Love, Jon."

* * *

Gerald enjoyed playing the role of the wealthy, anonymous donor, having been given full details by Doron. He was meeting Jehovah Bob's manager in person for the first time. They sat in a corner of a country pub owned by an Underground member. Gerald gave the manager a local map marking the back gate entrance to Northrop's estate. "Everything has been set up," Gerald told the manager. "We will meet where the X is, on a local farm; then your caravan of cars will follow us through the gate. Couldn't be simpler."

273

The manager asked the wealthy donor, "So we'll be entering an actual Druid ceremony where Jehovah Bob can expose the pagan priests? (Gerald nodded.) Fantastic."

Then he said, "Jo-Bob, I mean Jehovah Bob, needs his supporters on hand. But we need to lose those who are not part of the faithful. So to do this, we sometimes use a diversion."

The manager admitted their secret strategy to ditch hostile hangers-on: "Jehovah Bob has a double he sometimes uses on large tours or when he is tired and needs time off." He winked at Gerald, the wealthy donor.

"In make-up, the cape, and all the other stuff, it's almost impossible to tell the two apart."

Gerald feigned being most impressed.

"What if we get Jehovah Bob's double to act as the decoy by leading those trying to tag on off in another direction," the manager proposed. "Then, once they're gone, we can come out of hiding and secretly follow your group to the back road of that estate."

"That's a very good idea," Gerald responded, sounding eager.

The manager stressed, "We've made a deal with a television group. We will need this great event recorded to play on the cable back in the States."

Gerald reassured him, "I'm sure we can manage it."

The manager winked. They shook hands and departed.

* * *

Jehovah Bob was all ears as his manager gave him the news. "I just talked to our supporter, who, by the way, wired an extra £100,000 into the account. All we need to do is get on board the biggest gravy train on Earth as they escort us through a hidden road on this estate. I'm talkin' serious costumes and decadence. Your luxury hotel is all lined up. And … you'll have someone real special awaiting you, and she won't be dressed, either. Sound good?"

Jehovah Bob was plum excited. He did a quick Elvis wiggle.

He pictured the prostitute awaiting the returning hero after his battle with the pagans, witches and Druids. Then, as his double made a grand entrance into a three-star hotel in another region—distracting the public—Jehovah Bob, out of view and in disguise, would be sneaking through the private entrance of a remote super-luxury hotel, to be greeted by a willing call girl. Truth be told, that was the real reason for the diversion tactics of the double. It freed up the TV evangelist for his late-night escapades. But he couldn't tell that to the faithful.

He could see it now. He'd stand there in his superhero outfit, all rocket ready, as she smiled at him adoringly. Not only that, but millions of dollars would be pouring into his coffers from this crusade. *Now how ahhh-sweetums can it get?*

Chapter 46

Saturday had arrived, and the appointed hour was fast approaching.

With the earl's Druid garden completely cordoned off, and no staff allowed within visible range, Adin walked the giant from the Fortress to the throne, followed by Northrop's electric cart, then Wezelby behind him, driving separately.

Wezelby hooked the giant's right ankle up to the anesthetic after it had seated itself. The large bottle and the translucent tubing were hidden on the back side of the throne. Wezelby had put the remote on the quiescent setting so that the giant would not stir after it sat down.

The earl then ordered Wezelby to return to the underground facility and remain ready should the Deep Earth Lab director need him.

Northrop had already told the diminutive Cambridge scientist, as painfully obsequious as ever, that it was the desire of Deep Earth Lab's directors to safely view their creation away from any possibility of public scrutiny.

Wezelby scooted off back to the Fortress in the electric vehicle, feeling flattered that he was entrusted with such a secret. In minutes he returned to the underground facility. The other two remaining giants seemed restless. Though Northrop had taken the remote for the giant and hidden it on the throne, Wezelby nervously put the dedicated remotes for the remaining giants in his pocket.

Meanwhile, Adin soon returned to normal consciousness now that the giant was seated and anesthetized. He wanted to minimize the broadbanding effort before the great event that evening. He looked at the clock and saw that it was 3 p.m. in Manhattan, 8 p.m. at Northrop's. This gave Adin at least three hours to spend before the big event.

Feeling pent-up energy, Adin decided to go on one of his occasional walks in Central Park West. The main gate, where John Lennon took the same walk, was just across the street. Adin left the Dakota House, crossed the street and entered Central Park West. Manhattan was in the mid-80s. Jack, in disguise, observed Adin from a safe distance.

Jack knew that he had to enter the Dakota House no earlier than 6 p.m. He was on standby to get word from Vikram. Jack had assembled just the right crew for the operation, dressed as repairmen in the appropriate vehicle and waiting a few streets away. Other agents were there in the park.

* * *

Members taken from Groups One and Two were busily at work in the front areas of Northrop's New Forest estate. They were appropriately attired as servants greeting the arriving guests, motioning them where to park when not acting as valets (and receiving huge tips in the process—"Why go to Cambridge living like a pauper when you can do this!", Neil remarked).

Their duties included sorting the guests by their color-coded guest cards—the earl's elaborate, endlessly obsessive protocol of ranking people by importance—and then escorting them to the various pre-assigned front garden areas where there was ample outdoor seating, drinks, and then dinner starting a little after 8:00. Well into the evening, their duties included carrying various drinks and snacks about the gardens. Their private cars, armed with explosives and various weapons, were parked to the side and against the fence in the side parking area allotted for staff.

Just before dinner was served, Vikram monitored the giant seated on the throne in the distant roped-off back section. He'd earlier watched the walk to the throne. He switched to the eyes of their implanted field rat. Neville's friend, the Cyber gang's ace game-player, was operating the joystick of the field rat. At the right time, when Doron or Ian gave the signal, the rat would gnaw the nylon tube to stop the flow of the anesthetic.

Ian and Doron gave their pass to one of the Wellstone members at the gate as Ian pulled up in the SmarTruck. "Please come in," he smiled, feigning not to recognize them. "Sir," he pointed, "perhaps you might want to park over there under the trees." Ian tipped him for appearance's sake and entered the gate.

Ian drove the SmarTruck to the distant side area designated for guests and parked the large armored van in an enclosure of trees almost out of view. It did not even draw so much as a glance—the advantage of the SmarTruck—as it perfectly resembled one of the high-end SUVs.

It was in a perfect location for Ian and Doron to put on their outfits where they could exit the van in the invisibility mode. Backup shoulder-launch missiles and other weapons were in the SmarTruck should they be unable to access the missiles hidden in the bushes in the back area.

Like Vikram, they could monitor everything from the vehicle. Doron quickly went through the monitors, then looked at Ian when they saw the giant sitting on the throne on one of their hidden cams.

* * *

It was 10:30 p.m. Vikram had initiated a secret protocol. He'd told nobody.

Vikram was still the record-holder of an Internet-generated phenomenon known as flash mobs. As the original news story reported, "Using mass e-mailing, the organizers bring together 'inexplicable mobs'—in which large crowds suddenly arrive in public places, then dissipate on cue." The whole game is synchronicity as real people suddenly arrive at a given location.

One of his flash mobs became so large when it gathered on the Stanford campus that it headlined the national evening news. Thousands of people appeared out of nowhere in a matter of minutes. They even came in from neighboring states.

Jon was the first to notice something unusual as he and Jeremy stood on the front lines, waiting to approach the facility on Vikram's cue. The crowd seemed to double in size every few minutes.

Jon, Jeremy and the two ex-commandos just slightly ahead of them kept looking around, becoming increasingly amazed at the crowd, signaling each other with a look that said, "Can you believe this!"

Jeremy turned to Jon and confessed, "Honestly, and I am not exaggerating, but this is beginning to remind me of the sort of crowd that shows up at Wembley Stadium when Manchester United takes on Arsenal for the regional soccer cup."

Jon guessed that thousands strong were gathered by 11:10 p.m. But, as only Vikram knew, they were not going to go away until well after midnight, the designated time of dissipation.

"This is heaven-sent," Jon remarked to Jeremy. "This huge mob will be perfect for the operation. I mean, we can really overwhelm the facility!"

Someone halfway back in the crowd held up a sign that read, "Go Jon and Jeremy!"

Jon smiled at Jeremy, then buzzed Vikram to ask if he knew what was going on. After a long, protracted pause, Vikram replied, "I think this will give you an edge on the front lines. It cannot escape the media. Reporters should be on hand very soon. And yes, it is known as a flash mob."

Vikram then asked over Jon's earpiece, "Okay, Jon, are you ready? Move forward slowly!"

Jon relayed the signal from Vikram to those from the New Forest Underground to begin the slow three-mile walk to the front gates of the underground facility.

Jon waved and the two ex-commandos started up slowly on their motorcycles, crisscrossing ahead of the front line. Jeremy noted that one driver was on a reconditioned Royal Enfield; the other had one of the new Triumph dirt bikes. Resembling the endless array of backpackers that came to New Forest in the summer months, the two ex-commandos had modified backpacks strapped to their backs.

"Innocuous-looking, aren't they?" Jeremy remarked to Jon as he nodded toward the backpacks.

"Yes, they're beautifully disguised," Jon responded.

They looked off and saw another of their Roundtable mates, whom they knew was carrying a heavy .50 caliber machine gun under a blanket in his convertible. The car had the top down and was pacing the crowd near the motorcycles. Their friend driving waved at them.

Another car nearby from the New Forest Underground had a jerry-rigged speaker on the roof. They signaled Jeremy as they pulled close by, moving with the crowd.

He brought out the remote microphone and addressed the crowd. "We need to stay quiet for half an hour at least. Then get ready for action like you've never seen it."

According to plan, those leading the front line were still disguised as an ecology protest march, and got little more than a yawn from the locals and the police. "That's how you get a massive crowd right to the gates with minimum alarm," they had agreed at the meeting the night before.

After weeks feeling caged up, Jon and Jeremy loved being outside with this huge mob.

Then another thing hit Jon as he looked back and noticed a number of torches lit. The growing mob approaching the facility were starting to resemble villagers approaching Castle Frankenstein.

"This has to be courtesy of Vikram's Central Casting," Jon commented to Jeremy.

Chapter 47

In his ongoing adrenaline rush as the hour approached, Adin felt the same butterflies in his stomach he used to feel when he was on the Yale crew just before a big race, as he did at Henley, when his Yale team not only beat out Harvard, but edged past Oxford in the final moments. That moment of crossing the finish line was etched forever in his mind, just like in the photograph on his office wall. But today, a certain aggression boiled underneath it all, almost a distended rage. Part of him wanted to go wild.

Adin was taking his usual walk through the relatively safe midsection of Manhattan's Central Park, timing things right up to the big event at New Forest.

He tried to ignore the endless procession of defective people passing him in the park, all resembling bruised, ugly root vegetables. He passed a family of turnips (perhaps Gypsies), a woman who resembled a rutabaga (a Russian immigrant, old and overweight) and countless other genetic riffraff, and longed for the day they would all be purged from the earth, *when Deep Earth Lab operates under the sanction of world government—and how close this has become—then we can rid the earth of these defective genes. It will be a time when some men will become gods.* Until then, he would have to bear the indignity of these encounters.

Adin had another thought. *This is what probably ended my first marriage.* As much as he tried to hide his disdain for ordinary riffraff, his wife had become aware of his elite views and began to detest him. Then when she learned of his philandering on trips to Europe and England, divorce was inevitable. Adin was a man of fine tastes in everything. And as his wife had begun to age—more quickly than normal, as far as he was concerned—so his interests shifted. She had been a stunning woman, but then came the small pockets of cellulite, the sagging breasts and the varicose veins. It was one more bitter root in his past.

Adin had learned to be good at forgetting.

Deep in thought as he rounded out his walk in Central Park, Adin was completely oblivious of several members of Jack's team following in the distance. The rest of the team was in the basement of the Dakota House, monitoring the Central Park team on secure-channel.

Adin stopped and calculated his timetable. He had time for an early dinner in a nearby upscale French bistro. After dinner, he would return to the Dakota House and be able to relax in a quiescent mode till the time of overshadowing was at hand.

Another thought entered his mind as he walked through the door of the small restaurant: *Northrop and I will soon have up to a billion euros to split—providing the investors at Northrop's are impressed tonight.* He stopped that thought right in its tracks as he said to the waiter, "Let's go with the petite fillet."

Adin returned to the Dakota House after the early dinner. He felt something in the air, but had learned to downplay his inner alarm-bells, now almost constantly going off when he was in one of his paranoid moods. He entered his apartment, closed the oak door and breathed a sigh of relief.

He decided to sit down and look out the window overlooking Central Park West. At 6:30 p.m. local time—11:30 p.m. in England—he would take the largest dose of neurochemical he'd ever taken.

* * *

Jehovah Bob hung out with his manager in the large SUV, chugging a second beer. They were parked deep within Northrop's private forest in an open area off the private road. A canopy of large trees almost completely covered them.

The local greeting party (the New Forest Underground) as well as some of Jehovah Bob's faithful were parked away from the televangelist's van. As was customary among the faithful who had the privilege of tagging along, God's warrior was given plenty of space before any event, above all, before conflicts of this magnitude. The faithful knew Jehovah Bob needed to be alone, for even now, he was in his van, praying and emptying his heart before God. "He's consecratin', be quiet," was the byword.

The televangelist tossed the beer bottle into the corner of the SUV and sat back with a blank look on his face. He turned to his manager, who had worked with rock bands for years asking, "You got the stacked one, right?" His present client, Jo-Bob, was no different in the end from the hedonistic musicians he had managed over the years in numerous punk and ultra-metal bands. "Yes, she'll be waiting," he nodded, trying to conceal his impatience.

He then admonished Jehovah Bob, who reached for another beer, "Honestly, Jo-Bob, keep it down to no more than four beers. We need you alert. After all, we're going to invade this guy's secret ceremony right on his property. It'll be in the middle of some Druid ritual. We need you sharp, really sharp. This is our one big chance for the best event footage we've ever gotten. And we may never have this kind of chance again."

The televangelist grunted, and quickly changed the subject. "Where's Bob Two (the double)?"

"He's hanging out in a limo on a side road while they check on a large protest near the town square. Might be good for a quick cameo."

* * *

It was the longest day of the year. In Britain, that meant New Forest would go dark a little after 11 p.m. By 9 p.m. there was plenty of light, and adding to it was a large, rising full moon.

Doron and Ian checked all the stations as they waited nervously in the SmarTruck. Vikram relayed to them dramatic footage of the gathering crowd getting ready to march toward the underground facility. It was being beamed to Vikram through their secondary set of digital cams that several members of Group One were now operating.

Doron gave Ian a positive hand-sign when they saw shots of Jon and Jeremy at the head of the crowd, especially when the ex-commandos slowly edged ahead on their motorcycles. Then Doron spotted one of the signs, courtesy of Vikram, and said to him, "You pulled a flash mob on us and didn't tell a soul."

"I knew we needed an extra touch," Vikram laughed triumphantly.

"Well done on the mob bit, Vikram," Ian remarked. "That is an amazing crowd. That is going to really help us. But we must contain them so things don't get out of hand. All actions must be determined by what happens here on this end. If something breaks too quickly at the underground facility, it will really mess things up here. Keep them in tow. We should be synchronized on both fronts."

"Of course," Vikram agreed.

Ian and Doron performed a very brief test of the TV uplink in the van, and their contact in L.A. gave the thumbs-up. "It's as clear as anything our own crews send. You guys must have quite an operation." Before he started probing—they were after all the hidden contact in Britain—Ian broke off.

"This van is worth its weight in gold," Doron remarked.

Doron and Ian left the SmarTruck at about 9:40 p.m. with their suits' invisibility mode on. Before they left, they programmed the laser cannon to extend a little after 11:00. It would be dark in the woods where it sat and would not look substantially different from a lot of high-tech things on vans.

They moved stealthily to the side gardens, with Neville scouting ahead for them in auditory contact via earpiece. Dressed as a servant and in very effective makeup, Neville pretended to be on an errand. For anyone looking closely, behind him was the faintest visual ripple of bushes and trees. It was like moving a slightly concave glass over a picture; a mild distortion could be seen but no more.

Neville thought to himself, *What an incredible invention the Yanks have come up with from their endless military engagements.* He wasn't sure it was all worth it, but these techno suits were amazing.

When they got to the back area where the forest began, Doron and Ian retrieved the wireless TV cameras that had been hidden. The cameras also had a high degree of invisibility and camouflage function.

Neville left them and went off to retrieve at least one of the French Eryx missiles hidden in a duffel bag deep in a large bush. It was hidden in the woods near Ian and Doron, who remained in wait mode. Neville would tear off his makeup the moment things heated up. He found it quite confining.

Vikram waited for word from Ian to open the gate of the underground facility. Doron reminded Ian, "A heavy mortar rocket far off or an anti-tank missile or a Semtex explosion would blow the entire plan."

"If it did happen, we would have to go into phase two. We'd get the field rat to chew the tube, and that would be it," Ian responded.

Vikram was also in countdown with Jon's brother, Jack. Doron had shared his theory of Mocatta's being a part of the equation, going into altered consciousness and overshadowing the giants. In the last 24 hours, enough had been said between Mocatta and Northrop to establish Doron's theory.

Vikram told Ian and Doron over their earphones, "Jack's ready to blast through Mocatta's door on our signal. At present, Jack is in the basement of the Dakota House. A new guard is on duty outside—one of Jack's men. The other was quietly escorted away by the FBI where he could not contact Mocatta. Mocatta is up in his apartment."

Neville was now positioned to give Doron and Ian all the backup they needed. He would be ready to take any of several French Eryx missiles anywhere and fire it on command.

Doron and Ian were in the shadows, recalling to one another where the gardening crew had planted the various charges of Semtex.

"It's a minefield," Doron whispered.

"But timing is key. The creature must be almost standing on the charges, or within five feet," Ian amended.

Ian then repeated to Doron what he'd said at Gerald's the night before, "If for any reason Vikram becomes unreachable—say a SWAT team hits the Wellstone estate or he has some unexpected equipment failure—we will go with your alternate plan."

Doron assured Ian, "The auto remote protocols can definitely be triggered from the SmarTruck. Don't worry."

Ian and Doron were beginning to sweat as the midnight hour approached.

* * *

As they marched slowly toward the facility, Vikram told Jon over his earphone, "The Weasel is under auto-command. He just opened the side door at the front gate. The guard booth is also now unlocked. When he gets the command, he will then open the front gate." Jon signaled the commando on the Triumph, who raced well ahead of the crowd, and took out the guard with a single shot to the forehead before the man could react. The commando gave Jon and Jeremy a signal. Others joined the commando at the guard booth, allowing him to return to the front line.

As 11:40 p.m. approached, an enormous crowd, stretching down the road as far as the eye could see, stood maybe 400 yards from the front gates of the underground facility.

"There's no guard to report what's going on," Jon confirmed to Vikram. "He's been taken out."

"Yes, I saw it from here. Bravo. We've been overriding their surveillance cams with a status-quo feed for the past few hours."

The Weasel was now in wait mode. He could not remember getting a call from Dr. Lederberg nor putting away his cell phone.

All local media among the crowd maintained strict silence, waiting for the go-ahead. That was the deal. Earlier in the evening they were briefed by a local in the Underground, "A premature radio or cell-phone report will compromise the entire operation, killing the real story, and you don't want that to happen, do you?"

They were also told, "If you report what's going on before we give you the go-ahead, some of our mates on the front line risking their lives will be killed. Before you can even finish a sentence, we will bloody kill you." They understood.

Indeed, each of them now had a member of the New Forest Underground walking behind them with a loaded gun in addition to escorts on either side. Such had been Agent Jack's message to Jon regarding media silence. "Here's the simple instruction: 'If you talk, I'm going to have to kill you.'" It worked.

This was one quiet crowd of ecological protesters, indeed, magnificently behaved!

Chapter 48

Northrop was feeling "deliciously exuberant" as he watched his grand gala event unfold like some perfectly choreographed Andrew Lloyd Webber extravaganza playing in the West End.

By 10 p.m., the esteemed lord and his inner circle of guests were in the grand dining hall, decorated to look like something from the heyday of the British Raj, with waiters wearing turbans and dressed in white Indian kurtas. They feasted on a spectacular array of grand culinary delights enhanced by wine, port, brandy and anything else they desired.

The second- and third-tier guests outside were in a celebratory mood themselves, feasting on cuisine almost as exquisite as that within the manor. Waiters pirouetted about the various garden dining areas, balancing large silver trays laden with poached salmon, lobster thermidor, filet of sole, ham, roast beef, wild boar, duck confit and steak filets cooked three different ways. The smell of cannabis, strong drink and tobacco wafted through the air.

After dinner, the earl remarked to one of his old friends as they wandered out on to the porch and sat down, a brilliant full moon filling the sky, "I couldn't have ordered a more impressive night sky for our great unveiling."

Northrop scanned the panorama of guests feasting and drinking in various gardens as raucous laughter filled the air. In the Druid gardens the various Druid, Wiccan and Neopagan celebrants were busily preparing for the rituals. Only two of the earl's Oxfordshire servants would be allowed access. All other temporary servants would be given leave while the regular servants cleaned up.

Northrop fingered the remote control, hidden safely in his pocket. He looked at his watch, keeping in mind when to turn off the giant's anesthetic. Wezelby, upon surrendering it earlier in the day, reminded the esteemed lord the means to get the remote to stun or kill the giant by various settings. But Northrop already knew that none of these dire options would be necessary.

He had been able to communicate with giant number two, "the ancient one," to growing degrees.

Northrop turned to his friend and observed, in their ongoing conversation, "The creature's semantic wiring for language is quite different from ours. It is unquestionably intelligent and has been undergoing a process of deep awakening."

"It's like being a royal heir and waking up in some third-world shanty fully disoriented," Northrop said, trying to elaborate on its mind-state to his close friend. "In truth, this glorious creature is like an amnesiac beginning to tap distant memories. You see, it really is a god. It just doesn't fully know it yet."

The friend nodded as he blew a swirling ring of smoke into the night sky. The smoke drifted upward toward the moon.

Northrop and Adin agreed that the unveiling would begin at 11:30 p.m., which would give Adin time to overshadow the giant as the effects of the anesthetic wore off. That time was now very near.

What Northrop hadn't bothered telling Adin Mocatta was that if this creature reached its full potential, it would no longer be Adin overshadowing the giant, but quite the opposite. But the former Rhodes Scholar, ever brimming with confidence, wouldn't have heard it even if Northrop had implored him. The earl hoped this didn't happen.

Northrop immediately hit the remote to cut off the anesthetic as Vikram saw it disconnect with a click.

"He just disconnected the anesthetic with his remote," Vikram relayed to Ian and Doron.

Cyrell, guiding the rat with the joystick, shrugged to Vikram and moved the animal some distance from the throne.

"Apart from giving us one of the views of what is going on, it may yet come in handy later," Vikram responded as he checked the various views of the stationary monitors on Northrop's estate.

Let things fall where they may, the earl thought as he left the manor toward the garden areas, followed by his inner circle of dinner guests.

He gathered the crowd with a loud announcement, then led them according to protocol. Those in the inner circle were directed to the very front with grand seats positioned on the lawn, close to the altar and bonfire.

The crowd entered the Druid garden behind Lord Northrop. He waved his arm, and they quickly spanned out to various areas demarcated by Persian carpets that had been spread on the dense lawn. Upon each carpet was an array of blankets and large silk pillows. Incense was strong in the air as woodwinds played a soft melody in the background. The Druid priests were already attending to the bonfire blazing into the sky. Northrop and his inner circle marched to the front.

During the time the guests claimed their seats on the numerous carpets dotting the lawn, a Wiccan ceremony was underway in the large front area. Witches, nude and masked, stood in a circle at the front. A Wiccan, who was masked as the horned god, stood in the center of the circle with two high priestesses before him. They held swords pointing to the blazing-white full moon. *Awesome*, Northrop thought.

The earl then noticed that the celebrants near the altar were lit by the full moon while the bonfire's flames radiated flickering hues of orange and red. Above them in the night sky, the last rays of twilight were quickly folding into night. A blood-red sunset had left crimson streaks above, soon to vanish as darkness fell.

As the rituals unfolded, a discernible force began to fill the air and mount in power. Doron felt it and so did Ian as they looked on from within the forest facing the front of the Druid garden. To their right, perhaps 50 yards away, stood the camouflage curtain over the giant's enclosure area backed by the dense forest.

Ian and Doron had begun moving in the shadows to take establishing shots of the Druid garden and the initial ceremonies for the full film edit at Drudge Network. Their camera feed was being sent live via satellite from the SmarTruck to Los Angeles.

Vikram quickly heard back from L.A. "The feed is coming through loud and clear. It is being delayed as agreed." Sitting in the control seat, Vikram immediately passed on the message to Doron and Ian through their earpieces. "You're on live, and they say it looks terrific."

Moments later, Neville, directed by Vikram through his remote headset, moved near his two invisible compatriots, standing further back in the shadows. The Eryx shoulder-launched anti-tank weapon had been successfully retrieved and was next to him behind a tree. Neville was ready to mount it in seconds.

Neil, according to plan, had gotten back to the SmarTruck and was ready to move on command.

The last remaining members of the Wellstone group and the New Forest Underground had been dismissed and paid. They pretended to leave.

Now, armed with various weapons, they were hidden behind various trees nearby, ready to act as backup on command. Their cars, still in the darkened parking area, would not be noticed among the many others there. A large number of servants would be cleaning up for hours to come.

* * *

Adin started seeing vividly through the giant's eyes, the semi-transparent curtain showing rituals in clear view. He could now hear the rituals loud and clear. He ran the usual routine of tests and verified that he was sitting on the massive throne. He gripped one of the chair's arms in a simple motor-response test. He felt it as if it had been with his own hand. He could also smell the incense acutely. There were other odors he could not make out.

Adin Mocatta's view of the festivities below him was that of an upper balcony seat looking down. None outside could see him towering above them in the darkened area, covered by the camouflage curtain, a virtual one-way mirror made from some unique fiber.

The giant's consciousness that Adin was riding and overshadowing shifted beneath him. The pagan rituals below were equally in view of the creature whose consciousness ran in a separate subordinate stream beneath Adin's. The rituals seemed to awaken something in the creature. Adin could feel it squirming beneath him. His mind locked down harder on it. The Nephilim resisted.

On the outside, before the altar, the celebrants carefully followed the program on cue. The key celebrants of the final rituals were occult adepts who knew, as did Lord Northrop, exactly what they were doing. He was thinking of the famed occultist of the early 20th century whose books, paintings and occult paraphernalia he had collected over the years, indeed, his hero. *Aleister Crowley would be deeply moved if he were here.*

Earl Northrop had set up the Great Invocation to exact specification. It was preceded with the Summoning Ritual of Dark Powers that Crowley had meticulously described in his writings. And, indeed, this dark ritual was not without effect—not on Adin, who felt nothing (and believed nothing)—but on the ancient one he was overshadowing, or struggling to overshadow.

The massive being—resurrected through twenty-first-century DNA technology—was waking up. Procreated in the distant past from fallen angels, this creature could smell the key ingredient of sacrifices—blood, human blood.

The creature sensed it coming from the skin of the tiny humans in the rituals, in the priests, in those looking on, and in those spanning out across the field. *Blood*, it thought, as it also began to feel the pull of the full moon.

Chapter 49

What the Wellstone group didn't know—with the exception of Doron and those chosen to implement his plan from the New Forest Underground—was that Northrop's gala affair was about to be invaded in the most inconceivable way, such that only an alien intelligence from some distant galaxy could have concocted a means by which such ontologically disparate beings could even cross paths. It was a one-in-a-quadrillion chance. But it was about to happen.

An uninvited guest and his grand entourage were starting to appear, not from the front of the manor, as all the legitimate guests, but by means of a private road in the rear garden area, a road that emerged from the forest that few even knew about.

The moment Doron saw moving outlines in the darkness behind the Druid garden, butterflies fluttered in his stomach.

* * *

Jehovah Bob slowly crept ahead as the private road let out in the side rear of the Druid garden. He looked on in utter amazement as he saw the flames of an actual Druid bonfire rise into the night sky. Near it were the weirdly dressed priests. He was getting his *gobble-gobble* prophet's voice of judgment all ready to roll out in its gravelly thunder.

His followers crept close behind him, bent over and hugging the hedge, in glorious expectation. "God's warrior" was about to show these Druid reprobates who was master. His manager, out of range of the followers, whispered, "This is better than anything Hollywood could have put together. Talk about something that will grab a TV audience. This is it, Jo-Bob, you are looking at a minimum of $50 million. That's what I'm sayin'—hell, *sixty* million and not a penny less!"

Jehovah Bob, feeling grand rewards ahead, stealthily led his throng toward the altar while sticking to the shadows. Surprise was his big weapon.

"The camera's rolling," the manager whispered as they crept ahead in the shadows. Following the faithful entourage was the British television producer, now doubling as newscaster. Behind him was his crew with Skye Network. He stopped and looked on in stunned amazement, then quickly signaled their own cameramen to start shooting. They fanned out in different directions, shooting live.

The producer/newscaster then buzzed the helicopter pilots on standby and told them to take pictures from the air and start approaching immediately.

The team's portable GPS unit indicated to the pilots exactly where they were located. If they needed lighting for optimal pictures, the searchlights on the news helicopters could light up the entire area almost as bright as day.

The moment the American evangelist was about to appear in the open, Gerald and his team quietly reversed directions back to their cars, quickly heading to the other front of battle.

* * *

Adin, in full broadband mode and under the largest neurochemical dose ever, was having difficulty overshadowing the creature. He had noticed it becoming more powerful each time. Of course, as he reminded himself, he was sitting safely in Manhattan and not near the massive creature he was overshadowing. Adin Mocatta was thousands of miles away from New Forest and couldn't be touched. If need be, he could just disconnect and walk away. He could call it a night and head off to his favorite nightspot, Manhattan's premier club for millionaire bachelors, ever filled with attractive women. But that would be admitting defeat.

In the middle of what was clearly a ritual leading to the Great Disclosure, the bonfire in full blaze and celebrants impressively attired, Adin saw a strangely clad figure suddenly appear and begin dancing in front of the altar. It reminded him of a sand fiddler crab, tauntingly dancing sideways, shifting side to side, then skipping ahead forward in a mock charge, then back—again and again. His arms were holding out his cape for theatrical effect. This interruption was clearly out of sync with the ritual.

Adin noticed Northrop's face frozen in shock and outrage. The earl began gripping his head with both hands, in a moment of shocked fury.

In a screaming fit, Northrop approached the dancing man whose hair resembled wings, fanning out from the side.

The man in the cape started taunting Northrop in a twanging accent, rebuking in a familiar American redneck King James English.

Circuit-blowing rage took over Adin's mind in a moment of recognition. On the other side of the thin curtain was *JEHOVAH BOB, IMPOSSIBLE, JEHOVAH BOB ... HERE ...*

He snapped, lost all control of the creature that he had been struggling to overshadow. He and the giant seemed to merge into one single mind of seething rage. Adin's desire to kill Jehovah Bob went off the chart. The revenge fantasy had returned in full. He/the giant began standing up, rising to near-treetop level.

* * *

As Jehovah Bob continued his taunting dance in front of the altar, Ian thought, *Doron, you set this up! You are an utter genius. It is something I would not have believed possible. I would have vetoed the very idea. Incredible. It's got to be the supreme coup. I am speechless.*

Vikram clicked in over their earphones, laughing, "You win the Academy Award here, Doron. This completely blows away my flash mobs. ... Oh ... wait, Drudge Network is sending a message. ... They say we can name our price for the live feed. Keep it coming. It will be all over the States when I give the go-ahead."

Doron and Ian were moving about with their cameras to get the best angle on Jehovah Bob's mocking, taunting dance, with his gutter drawl of prophetic rebukes.

From the shadows behind him emerged a group holding tiny vibrating "angels." They pointed them right at Northrop as they echoed accusations.

The earl was beyond all self restraint. Wide-eyed and raging, he ran up and started smashing the "angels" out of people's hands as he headed for Jehovah Bob.

This act emboldened Jehovah Bob and his entourage, knowing they would be portrayed as heroes on American TV.

The evangelist yelled at Northrop and those conducting the ceremony, "**Priests, pagans** and **perverts**!"

The priests rushed at the evangelist and his followers, joining Northrop in the fray. Jehovah Bob's camera crew was recording it all.

Ian noticed the head of the London Sadomasochism Society in his signature black leather mask (this one with red leather horns) and black leather outfit, with buttocks and genitals exposed, jump into the fray. He ran up to one of the shocked women and yanked a vibrating angel right out of her hand.

As she looked him up and down in shock, he peeled off the angel's clothing and ornaments, like shucking an ear of corn. He held it up for what it was—a large, vibrating dildo. He pointed it right in her face, then in Jehovah Bob's. He tried to cram it in the televangelist's mouth as Jehovah Bob nervously backed away, knowing he had been exposed. His followers were beginning to look doubly shocked.

To make his point, "S&M Man," as Doron called him, lined up the dildo next to his own organ. "See what it is!" Now the faithful were blushing and beginning to retreat in shame. Some of the women trotted off, sobbing. S&M Man was having a demonic epiphany, seeing the American followers of their charlatan crushed. "When you are beyond shame you can do anything" was the byword on S&M Man's Web site.

Some of the pagans reacted with uproarious laughter, then cheered their hero as he took a partial bow, turning back to the American redneck for further degradation.

But Jehovah Bob's sand-fiddler dance became even more defiant and taunting as his cameraman got it all.

Doron and Ian noticed the curtain ripple. They scrambled backwards, away from the front area, while making sure not to trip, with their cameras still pointing at the scene, now on wide-angle.

A terrifying creature appeared at tree-top level.

Like tearing a Kleenex from a box, it ripped the huge curtain down, then looked at the people below. Adin felt his rage increase. He/it smelled fear.

The one in the cape with rhinestones and winged hair was too preoccupied with his dance to see it. His back to the giant, he was darting in and out and taunting those near the altar.

The crowd fell silent, mouths dropping in sheer terror as they looked up.

The beast took one step forward. The ground shook. It towered over the crowd.

The winged-haired man far below looked up, then gagged. His legs froze. He could not move.

The creature, Adin/Nephilim, looked down, then made a low growl that filled the air like a bandsaw from hell. Far off, on the other front, Jon gave Jeremy a sidelong glance.

Adin felt a strange alchemy between his and the creature's consciousness. Rage was the fuel and common bond. Adin could feel himself surrendering.

Then the overshadowing suddenly shifted like a wrestling reversal, and Adin was now pinned under the crushing weight of an alien mind.

Dread beyond anything Adin had ever imagined filled him.

In less than a second he was back in Manhattan standing before a large open window. The giant was controlling him like a hand in a glove. He wasn't safely out of range.

Adin fought as he lifted the window open. His body was fully under the directive of another will. He looked on helplessly as his leg straddled the ledge of the window high up above the ground. Then the other leg. Both legs were now hanging over the ledge. He was sitting looking down, bent forward. Terror. He hated heights. He heard a loud sound on the other side of his door. *What was that?*

Suddenly Adin's arms pushed his body till it slid off the ledge. He was in free fall.

* * *

Jack and his men blew the door right off its hinges. A deafening explosion echoed through the hallway of Dakota House.

They ran in. In a rear wing, Jack saw an open window and an empty chair.

Jack heard a yell from one of his agents below and looked out the window.

Adin Mocatta was speared like an earthworm on a fish hook, twitching in agony. He had fallen directly on the tall wrought-iron fence made of tall spears guarding the rear entrance to Dakota House, not far from where John Lennon was shot.

Jack tore down the stairs and watched his former quarry twitch in a protracted and agonizing death, impaled on a spear passing through his body, as a growing crowd of onlookers quickly filled the street. *What an obscene way to die*, Jack thought.

In minutes Jack was back in Mocatta's apartment. He soon found the neurochemical and other incriminating items. They now had *carte blanche* from the FBI to hit anything they wanted.

Jack's attention briefly switched to events in England. He disappeared to another part of the apartment and hooked up with Vikram on secure cell.

"How's my brother, where is he?"

Vikram responded hurriedly, "Jon just entered the grounds of the underground facility, and two giants are out. I need to get back to them. Will keep you updated."

Vikram told Jack before signing off, "Turn on the TV. You'll see what's happening on this end better than anything I can tell you. Gotta go."

Jack and several of his men saw the live footage coming in over the Drudge Network on Mocatta's large hi-def screen.

It was utter chaos at Northrop's. They were seeing helicopter footage as well as what Doron and Ian had shot. It was a scene out of a horror movie, except this was real. Jack realized it was open season on Deep Earth Lab for him and his team. The beast was out, and now he was seeing it.

* * *

The great Nephilim, now rid of the irritating secondary human consciousness that it forced to jump out the window in its own strange world, picked up the ugly creature below that had been doing the taunting dance.

It put the little man in its mouth, bit off the lower half, then spit it out, holding the wriggling top trunk. The Nephilim smelled and tasted the blood … the blood … the blood. Any real sacrifice needed blood and death.

Between two fingers it held the still-living upper torso of the tiny man, its mouth open in agonized horror. The giant moved it closer for inspection.

Jehovah Bob screamed as the giant's hideous face examined his intestines hanging in midair. He squirmed helplessly.

The Nephilim then moved it over the bonfire and held it over the flames, slowly lowering it in. The screams of agony resounded across the Druid garden.

Jehovah Bob had, indeed, encountered more than he had ever bargained for, and it was all being broadcast live.

Now the crowd was scrambling and running frantically in every direction. They stumbled over one another, running into hedges, falling over and screaming.

The giant grabbed another visitor and this time bit its head off, chewing it as one might a raisin. The taste of blood was delicious. It bit the lower torso and chewed it, then threw the remains on the roof of the house. It grabbed handfuls of squirming people. Dumped some in its mouth, half-chewed them and spit them out. Other handfuls were thrown into the forest. These small creatures were offensive to the Nephilim.

It suddenly noticed that above it in the sky was something circling with a bright light beaming down, lighting up the whole area. It hated the light and the irritating rotor sound. It reached out to grab it and crush it, but the object went higher, tauntingly higher. The Nephilim pulled up a garden tree and threw it at the object. But it swerved out of the way and headed further out in the distance, out of reach. Buzzing, taunting, circling, the object shone a full light in its face, briefly blinding it. Rage.

The giant waved away the bright beams from its face while it headed out on the field of grass, crushing the scampering crowd below, their lives in the hands of chaos. It stepped on some and grabbed handfuls of others. It chewed them and tasted more blood.

A second bright light appeared in the sky, then a third. The three noisy objects in the sky with bright lights circled near it.

* * *

Jehovah Bob's gruesome, mangling and agonizing death in the flames of the bonfire had been captured clearly on Doron's and Ian's separate cameras, as they filmed from the shadows, like assassins on a mission.

After the televangelist's hideous death, they filmed Northrop pleading with his dark god as he was lowered into the bonfire. "I am the Ipsissimus and mauster of the gate; I brought you back." Then came a final wail of agony.

Doron and Ian rapidly caught on camera scores of others being killed in a virtual slaughter. Both were aware that soon the monster would be in range of the planted Semtex explosives.

"I can't wait to kill it," Doron told Ian nearby.

"It's getting close," Ian replied in a low voice.

Bodies were devoured or thrown incredible distances.

Vikram blipped in. "Let me know when you're ready for me to trigger the explosives should you have any problems on your end."

"We're watching for range," Ian responded. "We've got our remotes ready. Just remain on standby if we need you."

Doron and Ian held their Semtex remotes in their free hands supporting the TV cameras.

* * *

All channels on British television were suddenly interrupted, now carrying the live feed. Astounding footage was coming through of some gigantic creature killing people on the estate of a British lord. It had been verified. Footage of Jehovah Bob, then others, being killed by the immense giant had just filled the screen.

The chief producer at the London headquarters of Skye News broke in and warned, "What you are seeing is not some prank like the *War of the Worlds* broadcast by Orson Welles. This is happening live in the south of England in New Forest. But turn off your sets if you are not prepared to see deaths of the most gruesome sort. … We will switch you to our local producer and newscaster on the scene."

The producer/newscaster appeared as he yelled over his wireless mike while running along a base of trees, "I swear it looks like they have summoned either Satan himself or one of his demons."

Suddenly—before they could edit it out—the newscaster was shown in real time being snatched from the ground and eaten alive. The hideous creature picked him up at the base of the trees. The man wailed in terror over the microphone while being lifted in the immense hands. The Skye cameraman, frozen, recorded the scene.

The late-night audience in England watched as the lower half of the newscaster's body was bitten off. His upper torso was held as it poured out blood while various organs were dangling beneath the torso, still alive.

The man squirmed in agony as he hung from the creature's thumb and forefinger—an abominable sight. He would get his long-sought reward; unfortunately, it would be posthumously—handed to a widow in an impersonal conference to numb applause.

Shocked and speechless at the live telecast, the vice-chairman of the network—who had been watching *Masterpiece Theatre* till this blipped in—immediately phoned the Minister of Defense. Skye News replayed the shocking footage for hours, each time adding editorial segments as things developed in New Forest. (Skye News, monitoring Drudge Network's live telecast, forged an exclusive agreement between the two networks.)

The Minister of Defense issued an emergency decree. Fighter jets and attack helicopters were scrambled to New Forest, armed with laser-guided missiles and a host of weapons. An armored division had been ordered to leave within the hour. All local police were to act as backup to the military in what was now a national emergency.

Next, a helicopter circling near the enraged creature was on camera. The creature kept trying to swipe at it. The bold pilot approached but just beyond reach. Unexpectedly, as one would use a stick behind the back, the great beast uprooted a tree and swung it at the helicopter.

It plummeted out of the sky, fire and smoke following it to the ground, then a loud explosion.

The Skye News ground crew ran to their truck on the back road. In seconds they were driving at full tilt, racing off the estate. The two remaining helicopters were told to film until they were ordered to leave. They were not to taunt the creature, but get the best shots they could.

At present the massive giant was standing near the manor house, crushing a large hedge and small tree as it gazed at the roof. Bodies were strewn about the lawn.

* * *

Ian saw Neville, no longer in disguise, tracking the creature from behind holding the Eryx anti-tank missile. Neville crept out into the open, the missile mounted on his shoulder. A helicopter was filming the whole thing.

Ian and Doron moved closer to Neville and hit their respective switches. The Semtex exploded like thunder.

The creature screamed in agonized rage, looking about as it fell to one knee, leaning slightly against the manor.

From the view of one helicopter, half its leg had been blown off. It bellowed in rage as the air shook.

From the other helicopter, zooming in from the front, a small figure behind the giant came into focus, kneeling on the turf. A loaded missile-launcher was positioned on the kneeling man's shoulder. Meanwhile, the other helicopter got the full-perspective shot. Britain was looking on in stunned amazement.

The young man shot the creature from behind with a missile. With a thunderous flash it hit the monster's chest area. Wounded, it leaned the upper half of its body against the house. The young man reloaded. The giant sank down on its good knee, then began to crawl toward the young man, dragging the obliterated leg.

Two strange greenish ripples of light were caught on camera, moving across the lawn toward the man with the shoulder launched missile.

The ripples materialized into two men, standing next to the man kneeling with the missile. "Beamed there like bloody *Star Trek*," one pilot commented to the other. "We got it live," the second replied.

Ian yelled to Neville, "We're behind you. It's almost in range for us again."

From the helicopter's vantage point, the two men who had materialized seemed to be speaking to the man with the missile.

The two men who had materialized, holding remotes, now triggered them.

A second charge of Semtex exploded with massive force, blowing the giant's arm off at the elbow where it had pressed near a hedge. It roared, shaking the forest trees—a dual sound of an especially hideous nature.

The young man kneeling—now in a close-up frontal view with the two men still holding remotes beside him—took aim and fired. With a roar and a huge flash the giant's massive head was severed from its neck. The creature dropped to the ground and died.

Neville stood up and shouted to Doron and Ian, "We've done it!"

The three men embraced, choked with emotion.

The frontal close-up taken from above of Neville kneeling and firing a shoulder-launched missile as Ian and Doron stood dramatically to his side, each holding Semtex remotes—with a massive creature in the foreground—was all over the front pages of Britain's morning papers, then various papers across the world.

Captured from a helicopter, in a split second, was an act of heroism and courage that would resound across Britain and the world in ways unforeseen.

Ian's dad, half a world away, seeing the front page picture in color, with the headline, "Modern Knights Slay Beast," at a newsstand in Adelaide, would choke back tears of pride as he plunked down the change, unable to talk, and walked off to be alone. When he recovered his voice, he booked a flight back to Britain.

The two Skye News helicopters lingered briefly to film the dead and the maimed strewn across Northrop's estate before heading off in the direction of the underground facility. They passed directly over the giant throne, then over Northrop's rear fence connecting to the underground facility.

The final live news segment at Northrop's, taken from the helicopters, was of the three running to the SmarTruck, where Neil awaited them, soon speeding out the gate, the laser cannon fully extended. The helicopter filming the three heroes was told, "Head for the Burley town square."

The other surviving helicopter got near Burley, then was redirected. "Head for Stonehenge and get there quickly."

Chapter 50

Jon and Jeremy heard the creature roar in the distance when it tore down the curtain and came out of hiding. "Must be Northrop's heating up," Jeremy guessed.

"That should free us up on this end very soon," Jon answered.

The front line had started flooding through the main gate as an endless river of people rapidly moved along the road toward the Fortress.

Jon and Jeremy waved to the crowd to span out beyond the confines of the road. Torches and flashlights could be seen stretching off in the distance.

The two ex-commandos were still riding parallel to the front line on the grass as the throng headed in the direction of the Fortress, a bright full moon moving with them, lighting up the walk, fifteen minutes at a fast pace.

Vikram clicked in and told Jon and Jeremy, "Media silence is now lifted. Pass the word. The Weasel has been opening every door in the facility, including the underground door at the Fortress. The two remaining giants are riding the lift up to ground level. They look a little drugged."

Vikram searched the facility again and saw that the remaining scientist in the Fortress other than the Weasel was lying dead. Vikram theorized he had been hit from behind with a hammer or blunt instrument.

Fifteen minutes later, loud explosions could be heard in the distance.

Jon felt something as they rounded the bend toward the Fortress, now in view.

A shadowy figure in the distance was moving around at treetop height, silhouetted against the greenish lights outside the Fortress. Jon and Jeremy didn't miss it.

Another explosion thundered some distance away. "Sounds like Northrop's place is really going ballistic," Jeremy noted.

"Get ready if the creature comes any closer," Jon whispered as they both held grenades, ready to pull the pins and throw.

Jon noticed one of the motorcycles weaving in and out of the trees near the massive form in the shadows. *Be careful.*

The giant suddenly appeared from out of the trees with a single stride—the road between its legs. It towered above the crowd. It was 80 yards away from Jon and Jeremy.

With a bloody half-eaten body still hanging from its mouth, the immense creature resembled Goya's painting of Cronus devouring one of his sons.

It held the body between two fingers like a living appetizer, then threw it off in the distance. The once-bold crowd ran screaming in different directions.

Jon and Jeremy backed into the shadows, all set to throw their grenades. They could hear the motorcycle nearby.

Moments later the giant inexplicably disappeared back into the trees, not to be seen again.

Wonder what might have caught its attention? Jon wondered after a few minutes passed, and they put away their grenades.

As they continued looking for the giant, the Fortress coming closer into view as they moved ahead, Jon prodded Jeremy, "Remember at the pub discussing the occult frenzy during the time of the Nephilim?"

"Yes, I do. I never forgot that."

"Well, Stonehenge could be acting as a magnet right now," Jon continued. "A million plus, the big global event." Jeremy nodded.

Jon, in touch with the ex-commando in view patched in, said, "Try to track it if you can, but stay at a safe distance. Join us with the launcher if it comes this way again."

"Roger. Will try, but can't see it at the moment. It moved too quickly for me to set up a moment ago. Almost had it in my sights."

Vikram cut in on Jon and Jeremy, "I'm pretty sure the two giants headed out in opposite directions at the top of the lift."

"Well, the creature we just saw seems to have disappeared. Any new reports?" Jon asked.

"I'll check local radio for reports. Gotta go." Vikram cut out to intercept the regional police being addressed by the Ministry of Defense on secure channel: "Wait for military backup. Helicopters are now en route to Burley. Tornado GR5s will be covering the entire region. Ground forces are being dispatched."

More explosions were heard in the distance coming from the direction of Northrop's. Jeremy commented to Jon, "It sounds terrible, like a war going on. Hope Ian, Doron and the others survive."

Vikram cut into their headsets regarding the Northrop battlefront. "Doron, Ian, and Neville are alive. They just killed the beast moments ago. I am worried that some of the others didn't make it, but I am not sure. Military support is also on the way, including jetfighters."

"Thanks for the news; it helps us," he replied. He then asked Vikram, "Any word from Jack yet?"

"He just told me that Mocatta's dead. Jack's fine. He asked about you."

Jon and Jeremy were close to the Fortress, seeing the crowd surrounding it. Evidently this crowd was well beyond the giant when it appeared at the halfway point. Various newsmen were trying to enter.

Several minutes later, Vikram cut in, "It's completely over at Northrop's. Doron, Ian, Neville and Neil are heading your way in the SmarTruck. They asked where the two giants are and whether you had seen either since the one disappeared. I told them they'd vanished."

Jeremy and Jon took turns speaking, "We're definitely concerned that they could wreak havoc somewhere else. Our bet is that Stonehenge could be acting as a magnet. Can you patch us into the SmarTruck?"

"Will do." Vikram signed off.

Over the SmarTruck speakerphone, Jon broke in, "Bravo on what you managed to pull off at Northrop's. It sounded like Dunkirk from here."

Ian and the rest responded, "Thanks, we're all a bit dazed but grateful to be alive."

Neville added, "Practice on the weapons simulator was not wasted by any means. The missile fired as I thought. It really worked."

Jon told them the bad news. "Keep in mind that our two giants have apparently disappeared and Vikram is trying to find them."

"Yes, we know. That's why we are collecting the two of you now."

Ian said, "Activate your GPS units. We'll be there in a few minutes. See if you can round up the blokes on motorcycles. If so, send at least one of them to the Burley town square. Need at least one shoulder-launched missile there as soon as possible. There's a big crowd."

"Confirmed. See you soon," both Jon and Jeremy responded.

In the distance Jon could see one of the ex-commandos with the missile launcher on his shoulder, standing behind a tree. But no target could be seen.

Jon relayed the message to him over the earphone. The ex-commando signaled Jon and sped toward the gate on his motorcycle.

Jeremy and Jon noticed a helicopter, evidently coming from the direction of Northrop's estate. It had its searchlights on, with near-daylight brightness flooding the trees.

While Jon and Jeremy were waiting in the shadows, Vikram checked in about something else—the remote protocols. "So there will be no chance of government cover-ups or media spins or any other impeding agenda after the whole thing has been broadcast," he said, "perhaps this would be a good time to unleash the protocols. I am calling to get the official vote. Ian, Doron, Neville and Neil have just voted 'yea' from the SmarTruck. Give us your vote."

"It's unanimous," Jon and Jeremy replied. "Go with it."

Vikram hit the Enter key on his computer, unleashing the remote protocols as he told Jon and Jeremy, "We've seen too many official investigations hide evidence. Now they can't."

* * *

Wave after wave of the protocols sped across communications channels in a multiphase assault.

In one wave, every Deep Earth Lab member recorded in the black book, and, consequently, confirmed in the psychiatrist's database as having been programmed, was now being called in Dr. Lederberg's voice. This protocol restored all memories that had been blanked out by the psychiatrist.

The subjects were commanded to remember all prior sessions that they had been told to forget, including the suicide programming.

They were next told to remember all information about Deep Earth Lab that had been blotted from memory.

They were then each commanded to compose and send voice-recorded confessionals with signed text backups to specific locations including a list of government heads, Skye News and Drudge Network, several law firms, independent agencies, the FBI (directed to Jon's brother Jack Hunt) as well as a friend of Ian's father who was high up in MI5. The digital phone calls would repeat until each one was confirmed.

Simultaneously, the Internet global protocol was launched. Doron and Vikram had created a two-phase worm virus that went out to a vast proportion of the world's population. It would enter computers that had already been set up with "back doors" through a previously sent worm virus.

A benign virus, it would temporarily take over more than a billion computers, releasing them when the routine was fulfilled. It first took each computer to the webcast of present events unfolding, now looped in perpetual replay. This included telecasts from Drudge Network and Skye News.

After these were seen and acknowledged by the viewer, it next went to a webcast containing the background information that both Round-table groups had put together. A moving header described Deep Earth Lab's horrors using a well-edited summation from both of the DVDs:

It began with a simulated Internet access into Deep Earth Lab's High Gate cyber-entry, including the query, the password, the DNA-sequencing screen and added points that Jeremy had provided.

There was the high-definition segment of the drive by the "Island" and the shocking footage of the child-giant jumping on the scientist in the white lab coat.

Then came segments of the Palo Alto psychiatrist ordering the pro-grammed deaths of a number of key subjects.

The unveiling at Bohemian Grove of the dog-man.

The "Diary of Dread" of Jon's former roommate, with all the back-ground footage of the Miata lying at the bottom of Devil's Slide.

Finally, the remote protocols ended with the recorded bios of each of them at the Wellstone estate.

Within 24 hours, the remote protocols had captured over a billion viewers, who, by default, were now witnesses. Major media began using segments in ongoing broadcasts. Any cover-ups were now impossible.

* * *

Gerald phoned Vikram on his cell. "Okay, got the info you wanted. I just heard from a fellow I know who lives on the outer edges of New Forest. He tells me he just now saw a massive giant walk on the edge of his property, sticking to the dark forested areas and fields while avoiding

RETURN OF THE GIANTS

lights. But the moonlight was enough. Just the sight of it paralyzed him in terror.

"What concerns me is that if I am correct this thing is heading straight out of New Forest, as the bird flies, directly on course for Stonehenge. As you and I know, Stonehenge tonight has perhaps a million people. I reckon all hell will break out. You blokes guessed this might happen. Well, now we know it has."

Vikram responded, "Get the local media to send out an alert that at least one of the giants seems to be heading to Stonehenge, mentioning the enormous crowd there. It could reach the Minister of Defense beyond any of our attempts to get through to him on the phone. I am sure jets are headed that way in any event."

Gerald responded, "Great idea. I'll get right on."

"Doron can help us get to Skye News," Vikram added. "You know they lost a helicopter at Northrop's, don't you?"

"Yes, I heard. Horrible," Gerald responded.

Vikram relayed what he'd just heard from Gerald to the SmarTruck as they were entering the facility. Doron gave Vikram the direct numbers to get to Skye News.

Then Doron told Vikram, knowing the others could overhear it, "Since jets and attack helicopters are being sent into the region, Stonehenge is probably less than ten minutes away for a jet. But to get there in the SmarTruck would take at least 50 minutes on an empty road with no traffic. The road will be crammed with people. We've checked, and there's traffic choking all approaches to Stonehenge."

He then added, "I just remembered a cryptic statement from Northrop: 'They are drawn by the full moon and the blood, the moon and the blood as the moon draws the tides, as the smell of blood draws creatures of the night.'"

Ian and Neville looked pensive.

"Well, Stonehenge is astrologically based, and the moon is a primary force in its positioning," Ian offered.

Doron added, "The full moon at the summer solstice at Stonehenge would be the most powerful magnet conceivable to draw these creatures, especially when you consider the record-breaking crowds." He asked rhetorically, "Can you think of a greater presence of human blood than a vast, open crowd? ... If the moon locks into Stonehenge as a kind of beacon, then we may have something irresistible to these creatures. We have the moon and the blood, and both are focused at Stonehenge!"

He suddenly recalled to the others his apprehension about his mother being there.

Ian and Neville reminded Doron of her *possible* trip. "It has never been confirmed."

Doron resolved this issue days back and reminded himself: *I am not responsible for her. People have tried to warn her for years about different things, and she simply does not heed warnings; she almost has contempt for sound advice. She is an adult, responsible for her own choices. I cannot rescue her this time.*

From the SmarTruck, Jeremy and Jon came into view, waving from the side of the road.

When the two boarded, Vikram checked in over the speakers, "Okay, a quick update. There have been corroborating sightings of the giant heading to Stonehenge. Also, I did get through to Skye News. They have dispatched one helicopter in the direction of Stonehenge. I believe it's the one that just passed over where you are. I told Skye News that the helicopter can try to distract the giant with the floodlights, perhaps drawing it away from the crowd, where there is bound to be a mass slaughter. Skye News had originally warned the Minister of Defense during the chaos at Northrop's. They just told me they would get to him immediately about Stonehenge. Meanwhile, I believe the other giant that Jon and Jeremy saw could still be lurking in the Burley area, probably heading to the town square where there is a crowd."

Ian sped for the gate while Neville continued checking the radio for recent sightings.

Suddenly there was a radio update:

"We've just gotten reports of one of these creatures heading in the direction of Stonehenge. There are also unconfirmed reports of another giant in the forest near Burley. The crowds seem as curious as they are afraid. It is an odd human characteristic that when people should be running from danger, they are drawn to it. We can only hope the creature does not come to the Burley town square. Take courage. The RAF has been alerted."

Ian reminded the others, "Well, mates, we've still got the laser cannon and the two remaining shoulder-launched missiles."

"Hopefully, at least one of the commandos still has a missile left," Jon added. "One of them should be in the town square by now. I sent him on ten minutes ago. And Jeremy and I have our grenades."

Neville assured, "All it takes is a good hit. We can do it, mates."

Ian jammed the gas pedal to the floor as the van barreled out the gate of the underground facility, skidding onto the approach road and almost running over several body parts lying on the road.

Chapter 51

Stonehenge was ablaze as Druids and Neopagans amassed at the summer solstice ceremony, well surpassing the anticipated half-million mark. Glowing fires stretched out across the landscape of endless fields as Druid priests circled the great central bonfire within the ancient pillars of Stonehenge. A blazing full moon shone down on the celebrants like a spotlight.

This was the most glorious sight Doron's mom, Linda Swift, had ever beheld—enhanced, of course, by powerful Hawaiian sinsemilla, among other things, that she and her Wiccan lady friends had been sharing from the time they left London together in the van.

Close to the action, and away from her English companions, Linda stretched out a blanket and lay atop a broad boulder to watch the ritual summonings up close. Truly she was "at home," as she occasionally used to say. Under the majestic moon, she felt a rare peak experience coming on.

Midnight was upon them—bringing the full conjunction of the summer solstice—as the grand invocation within the ancient pillars reached its climax. Wiccans, Neopagans and Druids joined forces in a dramatic final ritual, surrounding the great bonfire as they chanted. Magic was truly in the air.

Linda looked on as she started to feel the presence of the gods (she hadn't connected with any men yet, but had already gotten admiring looks).

She suddenly heard a distant thunderous rumble. Maybe they were explosions, an untimely intrusion from the age of technology. *Oh, to bring back the harmony and intensity of the ancient world that understood the mysteries of nature*, she thought.

She lay back, studying the night sky while trying to ignore the jet. Then she noticed that the moon seemed to be literally sitting on the head of a vast creature standing above them like a god. She realized, of course, that she was having a glorious mystical view of another dimension—what some might crudely call a hallucination. Surely, she was peering into the realm of the gods. *Good old THC*, she smiled to herself. Tetrahydrocannabinol was the powerful alkaloid in marijuana that always jump-started the other psychedelics and inevitably opened the doors to other dimensions for her.

Now the corona of the moon shone from behind the head of this massive celestial being. As she studied the light shifting from the moon behind the head of this heavenly being, her mind played with the light patterns. A halo of glowing static electricity appeared, now dancing in multicolored hues, then changing into an aura of divinity again. What a supreme vision. Surely this was the ancient god in his primal form.

Those at Stonehenge had, indeed, summoned a great god, she thought. It stood silently, unmoving, as the bonfire below radiated light that rippled and flickered across its massive body.

A long-time connoisseur of psychedelics and visionary experiences, Linda was surprised at how starkly real this creature appeared, the noble god, standing above them. It seemed to be as solid as the pillars of Stonehenge. She felt as if she could walk over and touch it.

And evidently, someone else felt the same way. Someone in a hooded robe was clumsily trying to climb up on its huge foot, falling over each time in the process. *He's way too stoned*, she thought to herself. *Gotta know when to put down that pipe.*

As she lay there with her eyes glazed, Linda found it odd when a second moon appeared in the sky. It was moving! This bright light was moving behind the head of the massive god while the stationary moon, the one that was there before, continued to sit on the giant's head like a crown. Then the second moon directed light over the pillars like a searchlight. Then she heard the sound of powerful rotors.

Under the added light, the huge god reached down and picked up the robed fellow, trying to mount its foot. The moon no longer backlit its head. As the creature moved, the moonlight revealed more of its body. She noticed that the god put the robed man in its mouth, then chomped him in half. She heard an agonized wail. Wow, what a vision! She would have to tell her friends.

The giant's hand released the horrified wailing man over the great bonfire of the ancient temple—*the first human sacrifice.*

Then she began hearing other screams. The Wiccans and Druids performing the invocation ritual began scattering into the blackened fields.

The god held another body, now headless, and threw it in the distance. Wet drops hit her in the face like rain. She wiped them from her cheek and saw red on her hand as the second moon shone a bright light in her area.

Now an approaching thundering sound could be heard in the distance.

* * *

Ian drove the SmarTruck via the back route to the Burley town square.

They entered the downtown park just as a giant emerged through the trees on the far side of the square, its back to the woods.

The crowd scattered in terror. Those closest to the giant were stumbling over one another as they tried to flee. Those further back began waving torches to distract the creature as they backed away from it.

It was in a feeding frenzy, oblivious of those gathering behind it. It grabbed handfuls of people, chomping down on some, throwing others into the distance. It roared. One man behind it ran up and threw a bucket of gasoline on its legs, then ran back. The creature turned and grabbed him, and threw him off into the distance.

Neville and Doron—who, with Ian 40 minutes ago, had already killed the first giant at Lord Northrop's—exited the SmarTruck. Neville quickly set up the Eryx missile on his shoulder, aiming it at the giant as Doron assisted him.

Further off, midway in the park, one of the ex-commandos came into view, trying to get his range with the shoulder-launched weapon. He then drove into the trees behind the giant and shot, the explosion barely missing the creature. The commando and his motorcycle were swatted like an insect. The commando and his motorcycle were held up then thrown in the distance.

There was no telling where the second ex-commando was at the moment. Perhaps the explosion they had heard a few minutes earlier had been his missile, evidently missing its target as well.

Ian, who had only briefly tested the laser cannon, was looking through its viewfinder. The light indicated that it was still charging its capacitors.

Jon and Jeremy grabbed their grenades from their bag and headed outside. The creature was too far away for them to hit with an ordinary throw.

Jon challenged Jeremy, "Ready for the run of your life?"

Jeremy nodded.

The laser cannon's ready button came on while Ian was attempting to center the crosshairs in the middle of the giant's head. The creature moved, and Ian tried again.

The giant was holding a screaming man out in front, de-limbing him above the crowd. The crowd screamed as they were spattered with his blood.

Ian shot the laser cannon just as the giant moved, grazing him. At the same time, several men behind the giant ran forward and threw lit torches at its feet, igniting the gasoline from the rear of the creature.

Neville shot the missile as the creature moved from the flames. It just barely grazed it, exploding in the trees behind it. The Nephilim roared and began stalking in the direction of Neville and the SmarTruck. Ian was waiting for the capacitors to recharge.

The crowd moved away from it and toward the sides of the park.

It picked up more people and flung them in the distance. Several landed on the rooftop of the downtown café on Main Street. Others just missed the SmarTruck. The flames incensed the giant's rage as it struck at the fire on its lower legs.

The helicopter, which had been above them, dramatized the whole scene as the searchlight beamed on the giant. Jon and the rest of them instantly realized that the whole event was live on national television, just as it had been at Northrop's earlier.

Neville missed again when the searchlight dazzled him in the eyes, suddenly beaming on him. Doron coached, "Okay, last missile. Plenty of time." Neville, in full concentration, steadied it on his shoulder for a final try as the creature approached.

Jeremy and Jon sprinted forward, holding the grenades and ready to pull the pins.

Ian was in the countdown mode as the laser cannon was recharging.

The giant continued stalking forward. It grabbed a car, parked along the side of the square and hurled it at the SmarTruck, just missing. It picked up another car.

* * *

Stonehenge was in chaos. It seemed that the helicopter was attempting to draw the massive creature away from the crowd near the pillars. The light on the giant became brighter as the helicopter flooded its face tauntingly, flying around its head like an irritating insect but still out of range of its arms. Skye News reminded the pilot about how they lost their first helicopter earlier that night when the giant swatted it out of the air with a tree.

Linda, still lying stoned on the nearby rock, realized how tangible and realistic the hallucination was when part of a severed human arm landed on top of her. She picked it up and finally got the point. This wasn't a hallucination.

The roar of the massive creature echoed across the region like a sound from the bowels of hell.

It grabbed those running from the area of the bonfire, hurling them far out into the greater crowds. Another handful was dropped into the flames. Others were chewed in half, partially eaten, then tossed great distances.

Doron's mom suddenly realized that maybe she needed to move from the area. Unknown to her, she was perilously close to Doron's worst vision of her, somehow winding up in the giant's mouth in her final moment of self-destructive dramatization.

Much more stoned than she had realized, she swayed and lurched in her gossamer gown as she got up and stumbled off in the dark, away from the pillars. Each time she looked over her shoulder, the creature, now fully lit by the helicopter—its face like one of those angry Tibetan deities on the old tankas in Nepal—seemed to track her. As she stumbled on feebly, it approached. Finally she fell on her back with a *whump*, looking up.

The sound of an RAF jet, a Tornado 5 armed with Brimstone armor-piercing missiles, took a low dive, making a thunderous roar. The creature bellowed at it and swatted in its direction. The helicopter kept trying to taunt it.

RETURN OF THE GIANTS

Linda crawled backward while the huge being was distracted. She looked up and heard the jet approaching again. Now she kneeled in the meadow almost prayerfully, hearing the thunder from the technology she so disdained.

The vast assembly of pilgrims at Stonehenge looked up into the night sky. They tracked the RAF jet approaching the giant, this time almost at head level. All of a sudden, a Brimstone missile flashed out like a lighting bolt as the jet banked off to the side. The missile sped toward the giant, exploding with savage force on the ground behind it.

At that moment, the giant was moving beyond the altar and toward the field of pilgrims. It grabbed a handful and threw them at the helicopter as the jet was heard in the distance. One body glanced the rotors and the helicopter began to sway. The giant pursued it. It swatted at the helicopter and missed.

The thunderous sound of the Tornado jet was approaching again.

The helicopter moved away as was ordered by Skye News, rising higher beyond the giant's reach.

The creature began stomping on the pilgrims. It reminded Linda of demonstrations in Napa Valley of the ancient method of making wine. But these weren't grapes. She looked and saw one of her friends, who had come with her from London, completely flattened to a pulp. The horror of the moment began to sink in.

She ran weakly, then stumbled. It seemed to be looking at her. It moved in her direction. She could see a hand reaching toward her from the night sky. It spat the pulp of a body in her direction. The giant's hand came closer as the thundering of the jet got louder. Linda fell to the ground as the hand missed her by only a foot. Now she lay on her back, flattened out on the field, looking up. The hand was reaching closer and would have her in seconds. Linda whimpered.

The hand grabbed her. She felt as small and helpless as a humming bird held tightly by some big man. Now she was ten feet off the ground, doubtless heading into the creature's mouth.

A second flash issued from the approaching jet.

The giant's head blew apart. The massive creature, caught by a missile as it was stooping forward, began to sway and topple sideways, pilgrims running and scrambling away from it.

Bits of the creature's head landed far out into the distant fields, the dismembered giant raining down on the land of Lilliputians—tiny men and women who had been invoking ancient forces, clueless as to what might be summoned.

A second missile hit the thorax as the creature toppled, blowing it apart.

Linda hit the ground with brute force and rolled out of an open hand connected to a severed forearm. Death couldn't have come closer. She was fortunate to be close to the ground.

Stunned, speechless and stoned, Linda and her Wiccan friends—minus the one who had been turned to jelly—stumbled away from Stonehenge weeping. They searched for the van parked on the road but couldn't find it, the stuff of nightmares. The owner, her hand shuddering, fumbled with the remote. They saw the headlights blink in the distance and ran to the van.

They somehow reached a road and sped off, swerving like drunks with several near-collisions. It was, indeed, the solstice from hell—"Stoned-henge," as Linda called it as they drove toward London in silent dread.

* * *

Vikram clicked over to Ian in the SmarTruck, still waiting for the laser cannon to recharge, the second news chopper above them. "Both fronts are on the news, look your best. The giant at Stonehenge was just hit by the Tornado's Brimstone missile."

Ian responded, "We're trying to take this one out as well. I'm ready to fire. Over and out."

Several things happened in perfect sequence.

Jeremy and Jon ran forward, pulled the pins and threw their grenades at the giant's feet under the brilliant light of the Skye News helicopter. The grenades blew up, stunning the beast. It wailed in rage.

Neville's second shot took off a shoulder and an arm. It bellowed in agony and rage as it swayed.

Inside the SmarTruck, Ian fired the laser cannon in a slicing motion. The crowd looked on in awed silence. The laser beam cut across its neck. The giant's massive head slowly slipped forward along the cut, then fell to the ground as the body began to topple in slow motion. It reminded Jon of a tree coming down.

The massive creature soon lay lifeless.

Jon looked on deeply moved as the locals cheered at the heroes who'd come in the nick of time.

The news helicopter showed a vast crowd surrounding the SmarTruck. They hoisted Neville, Jon, Jeremy and Ian on their shoulders.

When they were put down, Jon looked at Jeremy and Ian. "There's still unfinished business at the Fortress."

Ian responded, "We must make sure that there won't be any cover-up, not now, not ever." He drove off the multipurpose assault vehicle, with the crowd cheering as they left in a scene worthy of *Mad Max*.

When they reached the Fortress, one of the Skye News reporters was in the process of interviewing a most cooperative subject, a Cambridge scientist named Wezelby, who had gotten a second phone call that night.

Wezelby was "singing like a canary," as Doron and Vikram predicted.

An editorial in *The Times* summed it all up in the following Sunday's paper:

Those young men who had first come to New Forest under the cloak of darkness, had, in a single night, vanquished the formidable giants of Deep Earth Lab—not just with brilliant strategy and technology, but with self-sacrifice, dedication and courage. England needs to remember this lesson. Why have such men of virtue all but vanished? Or have they? Is there yet hope for us?

Chapter 52

Doron's mom was driven straight to Heathrow Airport from Stonehenge. She had never been more terrified in her life and could not wait to leave England. They had driven in shocked silence through the early morning hours from Stonehenge to the airport. She begged and pleaded with them at the airport counter and was finally given a seat several days before her scheduled return.

As the flight to San Francisco reached cruising altitude, the cabin crew handed out newspapers while serving coffees. She lay the early morning edition of the *Telegraph* in her lap. After she finished her coffee, she turned the paper over. Linda was suddenly hit by the shock of recognition as her breath froze in her lungs.

Headlining the front page of England's premier newspaper was a large color photo. Caught in an immortal pose were three young men—soldiers in battle. Standing next to a man kneeling down and holding a missile launcher on his shoulder was her son, Doron, facing this massive beast while holding a remote explosive detonator in his hand. Doron looked like a movie star, his blond hair standing out as he wore some kind of military outfit. All three of the handsome heroes were frozen in a classic pose with determined looks on their faces.

The headline proclaimed, "Courageous Young Men Conquer Giants."

Doron's mom sat in stunned silence, then folded the paper, tears streaming down her face. That was her son, Doron, not just a genius born with great capacity, but with something that DNA can't confer—character—and those laudable traits of self-sacrifice and heroism. Doron was a hero.

She wanted to stand up and tell everyone on the plane—this disheveled, silly, haggard-looking woman who had become a cartoon in her own eyes. How could she have given birth to so noble and brilliant a son? Nevertheless, she stood up, showed the picture with tears streaming down her face. "I don't deserve it, but that's my son, Doron."

There were shouts of praise and applause.

Suddenly she longed to turn the jet around and head back to hug Doron, but where? She knew she could never find him. Indeed, as she wept to herself, she knew that she had never really been able to find him, not mentally, rarely geographically, and never when she wanted to.

* * *

At the Wellstone estate Jon woke up late, having slept in while Ian's chefs toiled to create a world-class breakfast. Nothing was spared. They acted as though they were serving the royal family. They had already read the morning paper and fully appreciated the heroic mission that these bold men had undertaken.

After breakfast, Ian opened the front door to gaze at the garden and stood there speechless. He waved to Jon.

Ian and Jon stood outside amazed. Along the walkway and drive, stretching far out, were flower arrangements. The large bouquet leaning against the front door had a gilded card. Ian read it to Jon, then the others:

> "We are unspeakably honored that you have used our house. You have been true heroes and will always be heroes in our eyes. We would be honored to have you use this house, and we insist you use it, any time you want from here to eternity—In God's Sovereign Grace, The Wellstone Family.

> P.S.—Thank you for taking down that dark facility that housed so many monstrous things."

All of them were standing outside amazed and touched by what they saw. Jon commented to Ian, "The Wellstones must have spent thousands of pounds for these floral arrangements lining the drive."

It was only now dawning on Jon and the others that the battle was truly over.

Suddenly, they couldn't wait to get back to Cambridge.

* * *

When the convoy reached Ian's manor in Cambridgeshire, Ian nervously parked the SmarTruck outside. He knew he could not hide a thing from his father. The Land Rover and other vehicles were parked along the driveway behind it. He was nervous and hoped he would not get too severe a scolding. After all, he'd taken his father's prized vehicles. But worse than that, he had completely raided the weapons room, sacrosanct to his father.

Standing in the front door above the stairs, with an inscrutably sober expression, was Ian's father, Viscount Edwin Greville Marbury. Here was a man who, true to British aristocracy, had been emotionally reserved Ian's whole life. Starting at age seven, all Ian would ever get was a strong handshake or a pat on the shoulder, rarely more.

As Ian walked up the stairs, he saw tears in his father's eyes and running down his cheeks. Before he could say a word, his dad locked him in a deep embrace and stood frozen for long moments, choked with emotion and trying to speak. Finally, as the others looked on, Ian's dad said, "Ian, I can't possibly tell you how proud I am of you. You have bested the greatest knights in this family's long history. You are a true hero, and I can only say that I am honored to have you as a son." Ian, choked up, never dreamed he would ever hear those words.

Ian's father wiped his face and looked down at the others and said, "Thank you for joining my son in this terrible battle. All of you are heroes. Might I have the honor of your company for a special dinner to celebrate what all of you have done? I know of a few Cabinet members and others who would love nothing more than to join us for dinner."

* * *

That afternoon, the group—minus the two who didn't make it—fulfilled Ian's longing to have a victory toast at the Anchor Pub on the Silver Street Bridge. "Drinks are on me," Ian shouted as they got back into in their cars.

They walked in, and the owner silently led them to Ian's favorite table. "It's on the house. We're honored to have you back," the pub owner said as they took their seats around their regular table beneath Ian's favorite poster, the RAF pilot giving the thumbs-up.

As they offered victory toasts, a crowd of locals quietly gathered in the room, standing in respectful silence, looking on in awe. Ian and Jeremy noticed several Cambridge dons of note standing with the gathering crowd.

The owner of the pub came from behind the bar, carrying a large painting-shaped object covered with paper. "I've been waiting for you to come before I put it up." He hung it up next to Ian's favorite poster of the RAF pilot. Then the pub owner pulled away the paper.

On the top, in large gold letters, were the words, "Take Courage." This first-edition poster was a frontal close-up of one man kneeling and firing a shoulder-launched missile as two men stood dramatically to his side, each holding explosive detonators. It was Ian, Neville and Doron with their names inscribed at the bottom of the poster.

It moved Ian to tears as he was pictured fighting for England on a poster that now hung next to his favorite poster. It was almost too much—that and the rare hug from his father. He drank his beer, fighting more tears. Doron and Neville soon teared up as well as they slapped Ian on the back and gave him a hug.

Then from out of the crowd a soft female voice began repeatedly calling, "Vikram … Vikram … Vikram."

He turned and noticed a familiar face smiling in the back of the crowd. It was his adorable cousin Nirmalli, clearly choked with emotion. She then pointed to someone just behind her. The face moved into view. The shock of recognition hit Vikram as a torrent of emotions overwhelmed him.

It was Sharmilla, shaking as she walked forward. Vikram rose slowly from his seat in shock. As he met her halfway, she lay her forehead on his chest. He pulled her in and hugged her as they stood in silence, temporarily oblivious of what anyone thought.

Vikram walked her outside so they could be alone. He held her shoulders and took a long look into her eyes. As he stood facing her in the alley, he kissed her on the forehead, then gently held her head in his hands. They hugged again, neither needing to say a word. Vikram knew he was holding his future wife, this girl he had longed for from the moment he left India. He realized he had never been happier in his life.

Chapter 53

Jon emerged from Trinity College to go on a final, soul-searching walk with one day left in Cambridge. Jeremy had been summoned to the lab for a surprise ceremony in his honor. Wezelby, after replays of his confession in the media, had been dismissed. A quiet revolution was going on at the Cambridge department of molecular biology.

Jon loved Cambridge, so richly layered in history, which he would sorely miss almost as much as his close network of friends who with him had survived a larger-than-life event. Now Jon had to deal with the fact that he would never be the same. His perspectives and values had shifted.

Jon wandered Trinity Street to the corner and went up Saint Andrew Street to the church. He quietly entered the empty sanctuary to sit alone, reflect and maybe even pray. For a while he just leaned back with both arms stretched along the back of the pew as he studied the stained-glass windows and high ceiling. He felt at home. He then leaned forward, lowered his head and began praying silently to a God whom he hardly knew. As his prayer came to an end, a hand gently pressed on his shoulder. A familiar voice continued praying in a low voice, entreating God's grace and protection on Jon and his future choices. After all the things Jon had been through, he now, more palpably than ever, felt a new kind of hope. The hand gave his shoulder a reassuring squeeze.

Jon looked up as Reverend Mark Ashby smiled down and said, "Since we last talked, I had a sense God was going to use you, Jon, but I never quite imagined how. Your questions now completely make sense. You and the others have been true heroes, and I have loved reading about it. It does seem that the creatures you battled were those very giants we discussed—the Nephilim. Jon, I am very glad to see you alive and honored you came by." His earnestness was transparent.

Jon replied, "Your wise words about the giants were the only thing that made sense to me by the end, Reverend Ashby…"

"Call me Mark, please."

Jon continued, "I can see why God wiped them out. I'm still trying to get a handle on the sheer evil I felt in their presence. I'm only sorry that it took this kind of thing to wake me up. But better now than never. It will take some time to process it all."

Reverend Ashby invited Jon to a private chapel room for a deep and earnest prayer together. Jon felt hit with a force that almost drove him to tears. As he shook Reverend Ashby's hand on the way out, the reverend looked him earnestly in the eye and said, "Promise to look me up the minute you return to Cambridge. My wife and I want to have you over for dinner. I have greatly enjoyed knowing you, Jon. What you did out there was truly courageous. Please give the others my best."

As Jon walked away, an odd thought entered his mind out of nowhere; one day he would be getting married in this church and Mark Ashby would be performing the wedding. In truth, Jon had been fighting acknowledging the chemistry he'd felt for one girl he had met with Jeremy. He had been drawn to her, but had too much on his mind. Maybe things would be different now.

As Jon walked back to Trinity College to meet Jeremy for lunch, something drew him into the gardens behind Saint John's College, where Vikram had his original epiphany while watching the geese.

In the distance, under a tree, Jon saw Vikram and Sharmilla facing the river as the ducks and geese swam by. Sharmilla was leaning into his arms, looking on as Vikram hugged her from behind. Jon quietly left, exceedingly glad for Vikram, whom he loved like a brother.

As he continued walking Trinity Street, Jon reflected how breathtakingly beautiful and feminine Sharmilla was and what a fit she and Vikram were. They really did look like two Indian movie stars together, as Jon had seen them earlier going arm-and-arm and hand-in-hand. Jon walked away, reflecting upon what a lifetime reward they would be to each other.

Vikram told Jon later that, apart from the brief trip to India, he planned to stay in Cambridge for the summer. The marriage between him and Sharmilla was already in the works. If that wasn't reward enough, Vikram got a telegram from India that morning, hailing him as a hero and inviting him to meet the Prime Minister of India. Vikram's father and uncles were beside themselves with pride.

* * *

The grand dinner that evening put on by Ian's father, Lord Marbury, included some surprises beyond the spectacular food.

One British Cabinet member stood up at the dinner table to give a toast. "It seems that two young men here whose lineage already fills Burke's *Peerage*, namely Ian Marbury and Neville Goodwin, have been recommended for the Order of the British Empire. Also recommended are two other English heroes, Jeremy Saint John and Neil Boyd." Their mouths dropped to loud applause and more toasts.

"And ... our American cousins here are to be given a special commendation," the minister concluded with a broad smile. Applause again filled the room.

Ian, Neville, Jeremy and Neil were stunned as they left for after dinner brandy.

The owner of the world's premier interactive computer-game company walked up to Doron, Ian, Neil, Neville and Vikram, standing together in a corner of the lounge. He introduced himself to "the world's greatest hackers," as *The Times* called them, and asked, "Gentlemen, I wonder if you would be interested in putting together an interactive computer game, tentatively called 'The Giants of New Forest'? I think worldwide sales would give your lives a bit of a boost."

They were speechless again, and accepted the offer without a pause. Doron realized his money problems had just ended. Royalties for such games of late had gone through the roof. Inevitably, each of them would emerge as multimillionaires.

Soon after, Ian's dad spoke up in front of the drawing room fireplace to get everyone's attention. "This just came in." He held up a new poster.

It was the picture taken from the Skye News helicopter over the Burley town square, of Jon and Jeremy, with grenades in their hands, charging the giant. Jon hit Jeremy in the ribs. Jeremy smiled proudly.

Lord Marbury announced in an ironic tone as he held up the poster, "Apart from the two obvious heroes here, if you look hard you can see Ian in the SmarTruck, aiming the laser cannon." The poster was destined to become almost as popular as the first one of the famed three slaying the beast at Northrop's, where Ian was much more prominent.

In a corner of the drawing room Jon was standing alone at an open window to get some space and fresh air.

A refined-looking man came over to Jon and said, "I hope I am not intruding, but I understand that some of your friends have already agreed to create a computer game with a very successful company. Now, don't you think there should be a book? I happen to own a publishing group, here and in the States. Jon, would you be interested in writing a book about this powerful event in which you have played such a pivotal role? After all, didn't it all start with a roommate of yours at Stanford who died in a very suspicious way?"

Jon realized it would be the perfect way for him to process and finalize the whole adventure. He replied, "Thanks for this offer. I'm a little stunned. Apart from some unforeseen event, my tentative answer is yes. I just hope I'm up to the task."

They had a gentleman's handshake as the publisher said, "And bring aboard anyone you wish. You might decide it's better to co-author the work. My company will send you an advance as soon as we get the signed contract. I will send you the contract immediately."

Jon decided to remain silent if he was queried about the interchange. He was aware of the lucrative computer-game deal shared among his friends, who were prodigiously gifted in computers, but there was one close friend of his who had been left out, a fellow of modest means who had graciously played host to Jon, sparing nothing and expecting nothing in return. Jon wanted to give this dear friend a surprise, but he wanted to time it right.

When they returned to Trinity College after the elegant dinner, a package addressed to Jon and Jeremy was waiting at the door. It was a gift of premium Havana cigars, rare scotch, crackers and Beluga caviar from Jon's dad. A private note to Jon, brimming with pride and affection, was typical of the long, close relationship he and his father shared.

Jon's sister then called from Manhattan and wept over the phone. The Drudge Network scene of her brother charging the giant in the Burley town square had reduced her to tears. She was still weeping on and off. Jon promised to see her in Manhattan very soon.

Then Jack called and arranged to meet Jon at the San Francisco Airport the next day. Deep Earth Lab was under full investigation in the Bay Area. "Dinner is on the FBI, any place you want. Let's go for a four star in the city, whaddya say?"

* * *

Early the next morning Jeremy announced, "Jon, I insist on the honor of driving you to Heathrow Airport. I will not take no for an answer. Forget about the train. It's a very straightforward drive, and after what've we've been through, you need to go in style." Jon was not about to argue.

They threw Jon's bags in the back of Jeremy's Austin-Healey and had a triumphal drive out of Cambridge in the vibrant summer air.

As they approached Heathrow, Jon reflected on the fact that they had become best friends, almost in the way Doron and Vikram had become like younger brothers to him. Great loyalty had been forged. Among those who had assembled at the Wellstone estate, there was nothing that any of them wouldn't do for the others.

Jeremy parked in the short-term lot and insisted on walking with Jon to the gate. At the entrance of the security checks, Jon turned to Jeremy and made the challenge, "Yesterday I was given an offer by a prominent publisher to co-author a book on the entire drama we've been through. Would you consider joining in it with me? I think the rewards will be considerable."

Stunned, Jeremy responded, "I would love nothing more."

Jeremy gave Jon a hug at the departure gate of Heathrow Airport, then stood watching as the tall, handsome American walked through the checkpoints, soon disappearing into the large departure area.

Jeremy had been privately ashamed that he had been a bit envious of the others after they got the offer to do the game. Now he was beside himself with gratitude and joy as he stood at the gate. He knew Jon would be back before too long. Jeremy gave a final wave.

As he drove back to Cambridge, Jeremy decided to go to the Sunday evening service at the church of Saint Andrew the Great. Jeremy realized that his closed-door universe had been pried wide open by a drama that no one could have dreamed up in a thousand years. Jeremy, too, had begun to feel his atheism perishing in the foxhole of battle.

* * *

Jon boarded the plane with a high-powered, vintage Dean Koontz thriller he'd gotten at the airport bookstall, hoping this would give him direction in how to write his own real-life thriller.

On the flight to San Francisco, feeling the toll of accumulated exhaustion, Jon realized the deadly conflict had emotionally peeled him like an onion. He wanted time to rest and heal before he started writing.

Jon emerged from the San Francisco International Terminal to await Jack's arrival.

While he stood outside by the curb, Jon looked up at a hazy blue sky that had just appeared after a brief rain shower. Emblazoned across the sky in the direction of the Pacific Ocean was a bright, vibrant rainbow.

What a greeting, Jon thought. Then he suddenly remembered the sign given to Noah after the Great Flood, which had wiped out the Nephilim—*a rainbow*.

Near the bottom of the rainbow Jon noticed Jack's car approaching, a hand waving out the window.

* * *

Appearing in bookstores around the world within the year was a dramatic account of the final battle in New Forest and the events leading up to it. It was a truly heroic epic authored by Jon Hunt and Jeremy Saint John and dedicated to Jon's former roommate, Spenser, who had paid with his life at Devil's Slide. The book, titled *Return of the Giants*, began taking the world by storm from the moment it was released.

The End